GRETCHEN

By

Brian K. Little

Brian K. Little

COPYRIGHT

Copyright 2021 by Brian K. Little

Editor: Karen Russo
Proofreader: Chuck Greenwood
Cover art: Jay Fife
Back cover art: Brian Little
Color illustrations: Mick Corcoran

Exceptions:

True characters: Jacob Conkle, builder of Conkle's Mill; Edward H. Gill, engineer for Sandy and Beaver Canal construction, 1837; Queen Alliquippa, Seneca leader, early 1700's

True locations: OHIO: Beaver Creek State Park, Clarkson, Conkle's Mill, East Liverpool, Hambleton's Mill, KayBee Roller Rink, New Lisbon, Salem, Sandy and Beaver Canal lock and dam system, Scotty's Bar, Sprucevale Pottery, Sprucevale Village; PENNSYLVANIA: Aliquippa, Midland, Pittsburgh: EUROPE: Cardiff, Wales; Paris, France

True events: Cold Run Reservoir Dam break, Sandy and Beaver Canal construction

ISBN- 9798505018842

Gretchen

DEDICATION

Dad,

Dan,

and

Bart

Wish you were here to share in this journey!

ACKNOWLEDGEMENTS

With sincere gratitude I would like to thank the following:

My mother, brother, and sister

Kerrianne Boulton, overseas consultant
JoAnn Bobby-Gilbert, proofreader
April Busset, ghost hunter consultant
Victoria Conto, back cover model
Wendy and Mick Corcoran, technical consultants and artist
Jay Fife, front cover artist
Hay Gorby, back cover model
Chuck Greenwood, proofreader
Jennifer Harris, inspiration
Stuart Little, Welsh consultant
Karen Russo, editor
Ismael Sidi, technical consultant
John Smith, inspiration

Family and friends for their encouragement and support

Life's ups and downs for helping me find my Walden

Reviews

"Brian Little uses his storytelling craft to weave folklore and fiction with history for a fascinating tale of intrigue and romance." ***Anne Pearson, Central Pennsylvania***

"While editing this book for the author, I became so engrossed in the fast-paced storyline, I found myself forgetting to edit. I was just flipping page after page to see what happened next and had to go back to edit it afterward. This story entwines not only an obviously well-researched history of the Sprucevale area and construction of the Sandy-Beaver Canal, but several well-known local legends - ghost stories, if you will - into a unique and interesting novel. The plot twist at the end is completely unexpected. A good read for not only Columbiana County residents familiar with the legend of Gretchen's Lock, but anyone who loves a good ghost story." ***Jo Ann Bobby-Gilbert, Associated Press award-winning news reporter***

"I cannot believe Brian is a first-time author with no formal writing training. His ability to keep the reader in suspense and turning the pages throughout '*Gretchen*' is incredible. He leaves you wanting more. The character development is just right, and the story transitions are seamless. The well-researched history is blended in such a way the reader is unaware he is learning about the local history. The unexpected twists in the final chapters are very emotional. I highly recommend reading it." ***Jeff Bennett***

"Thank you for giving me the opportunity to read your amazing book before being published. I am beyond honored by that. I do have to say this story line was amazing. And it gives us readers a whole new aspect of the legends. Growing up in the area you hear all kinds of different stories. But... this one... This one right here makes you feel like you're living it. The plot and year that it takes you to makes it all quite real." **Patty Beaver**

"The vivid descriptions pull you in as if you are part of the story. The twists throughout make it a true page turner to the very end. You won't want to put the book down. You will want to reread again to capture all of the detail this book has to offer." **Heather Morris**

"Twists and turns from the past to the present and in between! Fans, both young and old, of the legend of Gretchen and those who would like to learn more of the local legend of Gretchen's Lock will love these old and modern-day mysteries and love stories. The characters become people we care and worry about, and their stories stay with us long after we close the book. Read it to see what I mean." **Denise Marcelt**

"'*Gretchen*' has as many twists and turns as the trails in eastern Ohio that the author takes you on. Join his characters as you journey from Ohio's early canal days in the 19th century up through the latter part of the 20th century in a multitude of interwoven lives."

"Just when the reader thinks they have the plot, the victims, and the transgressors figured out, Brian Little adroitly whisks you off in a different direction. You will think, 'Wow, I didn't see that coming.'"

"The beauty of '*Gretchen*' is that by the time you are finished reading the book, you will have strong feelings about each of the main characters. There are characters that you root for, and characters that you despise. The author has a big winner in '*Gretchen*.'"   ***Chuck Greenwood, Ohio Valley News***

"The story-telling talent of this new author is quite a joy to experience. When he asked if I could do some grammar editing, I thought it would be a 'one and done' reading. Not so, as I read through every chapter as he provided it, I became so involved in the history and legends, I had to re-read to make corrections. The author's insistence on accuracy, details, and the exact right words required several visits until it was just right. His version could easily become the new 'Gretchen and Esther of Sprucevale' legend. I am certainly emotionally attached to '*my* girls.'"   ***Karen Russo, editor***

"Whoa, never thought history, romance, and the paranormal could be so gripping and entertaining, a real page turner!"
Asked to be kept anonymous

"A story about true friendship, tragedy and vigilante justice. Great read!" **Candace Sipes**

"Hauntingly addictive. You won't want to put it down and you won't want it to end." **Amanda Michewicz**

"Brian does a great job taking you through so many twists and turns in his book! You're in for a great read that you won't want to put down!" **Susan David**

Chapter 1

Eastern Ohio, North America 1837

"**T**hese are beautiful," the young teen said as she bent over to get a closer look at the new flowers that had blossomed recently. "Father will love these for the dinner table tonight," she whispered to herself. Gretchen picked the flowers and arranged them in one of her small hands. Satisfied with her fist full of nature's magic, and the pungent fragrance swirling about her in the breeze, a brief smile spread across her face, but it was soon replaced with guilt. "I miss Mother so much," she said, as her eyes teared up. For a brief moment, she wondered, *Was it wrong to experience a bit of happiness this soon?*

It had only been a few months since she and her father had arrived in Sprucevale from Ireland. Once, she had anticipated this new adventure in her family's life, Gretchen, now, could only hope that she would love her new home here. She could still remember her mother's excitement upon hearing that her father had been hired to oversee the construction of a new canal system in the wilderness of a fairly new state called Ohio. They all knew it was an incredible opportunity for him to move up in his company, but the fairy tale was short-lived when her mother became extremely ill on the voyage. The bewildered daughter had prayed to God to heal her mother, but sadly her prayers went unanswered. Gretchen remembered never leaving her side, holding her hand until the end. She disallowed having the last memory of her mother being the burial at sea. In her mind she kept her mother's image alive, refusing to forget her endearing face, her contagious smile, her soft gentle voice, and the security of her mother's embrace. The excitement she felt at the beginning of the long voyage turned into the heartbreak of moving into a new dwelling without her. Her grief had smothered her spirit, leaving her hopeless. It was an ominous cloud over her young life, especially when she thought the sorrow would never ease.

When she arrived, she was swept up in the beauty of the nature surrounding her. The thick, strong trees seemed to touch the clouds, and the meandering stream tumbled over countless rocks as it wove its way through lush vegetation that clung to the banks. The new, colorful wildflowers carpeted the ground and wooded hills providing a serene environment fit for the unique species of animals whose characteristics filled her with wonder. This enchanting new world was nestled deep within a steep valley that seemed like a fortress of protection for what was now left of her family.

Again, Gretchen was haunted with guilt. "Mother, I know you're in heaven watching over us, but I so wish you were here right now with me. We miss you so much. I want to be with you."

"Who are you talking to?" A startled Gretchen whirled around and saw a thin, raven-haired beauty staring at her. "You know people are going to start talking and think you're stranger than you already are. Then again, are you talking to the flowers?" Laughing out loud, the other teen abruptly stopped and looked seriously at Gretchen. "I swear I don't know why you are my best friend," the girl said, as she turned around and began walking away. "Are you coming?" she asked. Gretchen gathered up the last of the flowers and followed her friend.

Esther Hale, daughter of the local pastor, was one of the few girls close to her age in the area. As her *supposed* friend walked with a confident stride, Gretchen thought, *Best friend? Now that's a joke! All she does is put me down and treat me like a servant.*

Even though Esther was older, she had become a companion to Gretchen, someone she could talk to about things only a mother usually discussed with her daughter.

Interrupting the rustling of leaves as they walked, Gretchen asked, "KittyKat, have the new workers arrived yet?" KittyKat was the nickname Gretchen had for Esther, for Esther always had a way of sneaking around, and with her raven hair, and deep rich brown eyes, it always reminded Gretchen of a cat she used to have in Ireland. Esther liked the moniker.

"Meow," Esther replied, while pawing the air, causing Gretchen to smile. "Not yet, but I hope there are at least some boys our age who don't stink like whiskey and manure or have fat bellies." Gretchen chuckled at Esther's statement. "Maybe we can find you a boy, someone who likes little girls, especially since you're not a true woman like me yet." Esther enjoyed destroying Gretchen's pride every chance she could.

Why do I let her talk to me that way? Gretchen thought. *She may be beautiful on the outside, but sometimes she is such an ugly person with a dark soul on the inside.*

11

As they walked, Gretchen heard only half of Esther's self-indulgent talk about how beautiful she was, and how every man in the area wanted her hand in marriage. Gretchen's thoughts ventured back to the beauty of the area. *I think I could live here forever, and maybe I could be happy someday. I wouldn't need a husband, just the beauty of nature.* Gretchen became so lost in her thoughts, she didn't realize that Esther had stopped. It was too late to avoid running into her companion's back.

"You stupid little bitch," Esther scolded, as she smacked Gretchen on the side of her head. Esther raised her arm again to strike Gretchen but stopped when she heard the sound of wooden wheels coming down the path. Gretchen's pain was quickly replaced with excitement when she saw the wagons filled with new workers.

As the caravan stopped, the workers jumped out. The two girls saw mostly older and middle-aged men walking around, stretching their limbs. Suddenly, Gretchen saw a younger boy who couldn't have been more than a few years older than she. He was tall, with blonde hair, and from what she could tell, he had the most beautiful, sparkling blue eyes she'd ever seen.

To her surprise, he looked directly at her and smiled. Gretchen felt a rush of warmth flush her cheeks, causing her to turn away and cover her face. *Stupid! Stupid! Stupid!* Gretchen thought to herself. She took a deep breath and regained her composure before turning her head and watching the new workers still stretching and walking about. Unable to resist, she found her attention being drawn back to the boy with the alluring blue eyes.

"Look at him, Gretchen!" Esther remarked. "Is he not one of the most handsome young men you have ever seen?" Esther checked over her own appearance before she boasted, "Trust me, flower girl, by the end of summer, he will be mine!" Esther had a sickening grin on her face. "Look at him, Gretchen! He can't stop staring at me, can he?"

Gretchen had noticed, however, that he was really looking in *her* direction and smiling. *Oh no,* she thought, *I hope I don't have on a dirty dress. Does my hair look unkempt, too? Something must be wrong since he keeps staring at me!* Gretchen quickly checked her dress as her hands ran along the sides of her head to feel her hair, hoping it wasn't too frizzy from the afternoon humidity. She panicked when she noticed the young man, along with an older gentleman, heading directly towards their location. As they approached, Esther stepped in front of Gretchen, hoping to block her younger friend from the view of the handsome young man.

"I'm Esther . . . Esther Hale. And who might you be?"

"John Bowman, Miss. From Inverness, the Scottish settlement not too far from here," the older man replied. "Can either of you beautiful lassies point out where I might find a Mister Edward H. Gill?"

"He is my father!" Gretchen interrupted, before Esther could reply. "I can show you where he is."

Mr. Bowman smiled at Gretchen, while Esther's glare burned with rage. "That is mighty kind of you, young lady."

"I'm Gretchen Gill," she replied, "But you can call me Gretchen."

"And as I said, I'm Esther Hale, Mr. Bowman," she said, pushing Gretchen aside to step in front of her, trying her best to make sure Gretchen wasn't seen. "And is this your son, Mr. Bowman?" Esther asked.

"Why, yes, Miss Hale," Mr. Bowman replied.

"Yes, ma'am. I'm Johnny Bowman," the young man said. Esther extended her hand, palm-down, for a formal introduction, but to her amazement, he didn't notice her gesture at all. She waited for his touch with her outstretched hand, but instead, he simply nodded. As Gretchen and the Bowmans left toward the location of her father, Esther's hand dropped toward the ground, along with her pride.

While walking, Gretchen did her best to hide her flushed cheeks, even though she looked occasionally into the eyes of her new companion as often as she dared. She found herself becoming lost in the breathtaking blue.

"He must like other boys, or even farm animals," Esther whispered under her breath as they walked farther away from her. "Why else would he be interested in Gretchen? After all, the girl is built like a small boy. She has no curves, no bosom, and she's smothered in freckles. And that awful reddish blonde hair, that alone would turn any decent boy away." Satisfied with her assessment of the younger girl, Esther turned and strutted away, making sure she walked by the new arrivals, thinking she would be gifting them with a glimpse of her beauty.

"Miss Gill, how do you like America so far?" Mr. Bowman asked. Gretchen was startled by the question that had interrupted her admiration of Johnny.

Gretchen

"I love it, sir," Gretchen replied. She began to say more, but she stopped when her father stepped out of a tent.

Chapter 2

"**F**ather, this is…," Gretchen proudly started to speak to her father but was interrupted by Mr. Bowman.

"Mr. Gill, I am John Bowman. It's a pleasure to meet you." He extended his hand to Gretchen's father. "And this strapping lad is my son, Johnny." The young man extended his hand as well.

"Pleased to meet you, Sir," Johnny greeted.

As the engineer exchanged pleasantries with the two new men, Gretchen couldn't help but admire her father: such a proud and strong man. Standing over six feet tall, neatly combed red hair, chiseled jawline, and a perfect gentleman's posture were features that commanded respect in the eyes of his peers. Through everything that had happened to him this year: leaving Ireland, losing Mother, and being strong for both of them, he was still able to oversee the canal being built. He had not broken, maybe bent a little, but not broken. Her heart beat proudly, and she stood up a little straighter at the sight of her father as a small admiring grin crossed her face. Gretchen also felt the sadness in her heart, along with the burden in her soul of the secret she'd hid from the eyes of the watching world.

At night, when the work was finished for the day, the proud, strong man disappeared, and the true sadness of their lives returned to reshape their beautiful, but sometimes melancholy world. After her mother had died, Gretchen's father was like an immovable stone anchoring the largest boat in the mightiest storm. He was there every time she broke down when the pain was too much. Her father was unshakeable until the day that Gretchen was making her mother's beef stew, and he entered the room to the aroma of its cooking.

"*Mo Cuishle!*" he said. "That smells wonderful!" Silence filled the small cabin, as the once unbeatable warrior, in her eyes, bled for the first time. She could see the tears starting to rise in his eyes: the pain, the loss, and at that moment, she realized he was just a man.

Soon after that day, Gretchen's father partook in drinking rum to help him sleep at night, but lately it had gotten worse. He drank until he passed out. The proud supervisor who all the workers saw every day on the job site and looked up to with respect and admiration, was a broken man who cried himself to sleep at night.

"Why, God? Why? Why did you have to take her?" Those grief-stricken cries became words of warning in Gretchen's ears that her father had succumbed to the tears of the corn once more. Gretchen had also asked herself that same question many times, but she felt herself becoming the lady of the house and knew she had to be strong for her father. Her mother had been a strong woman and Gretchen wanted to follow her lead. Every night, as her father slipped into an alcohol-induced sleep, Gretchen made sure she covered him with a blanket before kissing his forehead. She prayed for any signs that her father's dark journey through sadness would be erased by morning. Regardless, every morning, Gretchen still saw nothing but her father who appeared as her shining knight. No words were ever brought up about the previous evening's events or actions. Just a nod and a loving smile were shared between the two.

Gretchen's thoughts would go back to her mother, as she looked deep into herself to feel her mother's loving embrace. She would find the strength in her mother's love, which still lingered after the few, difficult months that had passed since her death.

"Gretchen! Have you seen Esther?" her father asked, with a sternness in his voice that made her realize she had been lost in her deep thoughts again.

"Earlier, Father, when Mr. Bowman and his son arrived," Gretchen replied, with her head and eyes lowered.

"Her father is looking for her, so why don't you run along and see if you can find her," he ordered. Without waiting for a reply, he continued talking with the father and son. Gretchen turned and walked away, but with a slight tilt of her head she sneaked another look at the boy with blue eyes at the exact moment he was sneaking a peek of her as well. Smiles crept across both of their faces as Gretchen giggled before sprinting away.

"Now where could Esther be?" Gretchen asked out loud, as she stopped to survey her surroundings. As she looked left, then right, then left again, while touching her chin with a questioning look on her face, she thought, *If I were Esther, where would I be?* Gretchen pondered for a moment, then a devilish grin spread across her face, followed by a giggle. "Where the men are, of course!" Gretchen said with a nod as she made her way down the dirt road that led to the canal system. The sounds of hammering against stones, and men talking loudly, could be heard long before she reached the work area.

She arrived where a new section of wall was being built to channel the water's flow. Workers carefully fitted freshly hand-cut stones into their assigned locations. She had spent hours on the hill along the canal system watching the men perform a beautiful dance to the rhythmic beat of the hammer and chisels, with all the workers knowing each others' dance steps.

As Gretchen peered for signs of an alleycat in heat, a voice called out from above.

"Afternoon, Miss Gretchen!" one of the workers yelled from up on the wall, followed by another as she walked along the base of the construction.

Gleaming, with a friendly smile on her face, Gretchen took the time to say hello to each worker she saw, while her eyes scanned side to side looking for Esther. From below, she saw the arrival of the Bowmans walking along the top of the canal, following her father's lead as he pointed out objects in the work area. She couldn't make out what they were saying, but she wasn't really trying. She found herself just staring at the handsome young man.

Noticing her, the young Bowman waved to her and shared a friendly smile. Gretchen felt her heart skip a beat as warmth grew in her cheeks. This time she did not try to hide it, but instead wore it with pride.

She watched as her father and the Bowmans turned and walked away from where she was. After a brief moment Gretchen shifted her attention back to finding Esther. "She's not anywhere around here. I wonder if she's…?" she said softly as a different location came to mind.

With new resolve, she decided to go look in Esther's special place. About a half hour's walk up the stream rested a huge rock, completely out of place in the middle of the creek. No one knew when or how it got there. Her friend had shared its location with her when she and her father first arrived in the valley. Esther liked to tell her a story about a giant, who was afraid of stepping on fish, because they were all slimy. So, one day, he picked up a huge boulder gently placing it in the slow-moving stream so he could avoid the water and the fish. Even though Gretchen didn't believe it, she did enjoy the way Esther would come alive telling the tale. Then, there was KittyKat's favorite subject. She always loved to just sit there and talk about boys and tell Gretchen woman stuff. Lately her favorite topic was that she was a woman and boasting all about her own refinement.

One time she had followed Esther and a local boy there and had witnessed more than she wanted to, but of course, she never told her she had seen them. With an alleycat being an alleycat, Esther made sure Gretchen knew all about what happened and explained all about star gazing from one's back. Gretchen listened to her tale in wide-eyed disbelief.

"He put what? Where?" Gretchen could still remember Esther explaining that to her, and the idea still shocked her to this day.

The trail to the huge stone had always been a little out of the way from the canal site. It was almost up to the new mill built on Jacob Conkle's farmland in the Echo Dell valley. Gretchen and Esther had spent many hours at Conkle's Mill watching the men add the finishing touches. But with the repairs of Hambleton's Mill completed, there wasn't any reason to travel that far from Sprucevale, unless it was to spend time on the rock. The journey to the boulder was so beautiful Gretchen was glad she had an excuse to travel it. Stately giant trees lined the pathway like soldiers standing at attention. With their branches reaching high into the sky, they created a canopy of shade from the sun as she traversed the winding route. Coming upon a clearing along the trail she noticed a lone figure sitting on the stream bank.

"Esther?" Gretchen asked, squinting to focus her eyes on her friend, as she cautiously approached. The young girl slowly went up to Esther who had not noticed her arrival. Gretchen examined her as she sat alone, not saying anything, completely unmoving, just staring off into the distance. "KittyKat?" Gretchen asked again, "Is there something wrong?" Her question was again met with silence. Carefully she sat down next to her friend. Esther stared straight ahead and made no acknowledgment of the new presence. The concerned girl observed the unresponsive older teen more carefully, looking for any sign of what may be causing her friend's strange behavior. The raven-haired girl's eyes seemed to be empty and her breathing slow and soft. Following the length of Esther's body, she looked for a reason for the girl's strange trance, when suddenly Gretchen noticed Esther had her dress pulled halfway up, with her hands resting on her bare legs. Trails of crimson ran down the outer sides of her tightly pressed thighs.

"Esther, what happened? Are you alright?" Gretchen asked with alarm in her voice, but her friend remained silent. *Something looks wrong,* she noted, looking more carefully and watching Esther's fingers. As she opened her hands to stretch them, in one quick motion Esther dug her fingernails down into her skin and curled her fingers. Pieces of removed flesh hung from her fingernails as her fingers recoiled like the talons on a bird of prey.

Blood emerged from the freshly sliced pale skin. Gretchen was silent and in complete shock at the actions she had just witnessed. Transfixed, unable to move or look away, her thoughts ran wild on how to help her friend, when suddenly the atmosphere felt different. Warm breath tickled her neck, and Gretchen turned quickly, only to find the older girl inches away from her face. Anger and hatred burned in Esther's eyes with her face contorted in a growl. With teeth clenched so tight that not even air could pass through them, Esther uttered one single word, "BITCH."

In complete astonishment, Gretchen fell back away from Esther. Lying on the ground, the traumatized girl scrambled away from the horror of her friend's unexplainable conduct. Panic quickly replaced fear as the flight instinct took over.

"What are you doing, Gretchen? Did you trip yourself again?" Esther asked in a calm loving voice. Completely ignoring the events of a few seconds ago, she stood up and strolled to the stream to wash the fresh blood from her hands, then returned to offer a helping hand to Gretchen.

Still confused about what had transpired and struggling to stand, Gretchen was unable to hold her bladder and felt warmth followed by wetness running down her leg. The shock and horror of what had just happened faded away as shame and embarrassment crept into her face. Bringing her hands to her mouth, incapable of hiding her shame, she turned and ran down the path towards home. Her mind tried to comprehend Esther's strange behavior. *Maybe she was playing a game with me and trying to scare me, but why hurt herself like that?* The look in Esther's eyes had been loathing disdain and rage. Gretchen had many times thought her friend had a dark soul, but for the first time Gretchen discerned the real Esther.

Chapter 3

A few days passed before Gretchen felt comfortable enough to leave home. She knew her father would be curious about her odd behavior. Resorting to a lie, Gretchen told her father that she wasn't feeling well. When her father would ask of her ailment, she would simply reply, "Uh, Father, Umm, woman stuff," and look down to her pelvic area which would promptly end the inquisition.

Her response would be met with, "Huh, Ohhh," and raised eyebrows, followed with a smile. Then he quickly headed off to supervise the canal work while Gretchen faked not feeling well. Esther would stop by the work site, like clockwork every day, expressing her concern and her missing her best friend to Mr. Gill.

Maybe Esther had just played a game that day and I'm just overreacting. That had to be it, Gretchen thought. *Esther is, after all, a little narcissistic with a touch of vanity, but she is my friend and is kind of a big sister to me. Through all her self-loving nonsense, she's always been there for me and calls me her best friend.* Gretchen smiled with confidence. *Yes, she is my best friend, too, and best friends should always forgive and always be there for each other.*

With a new resolve in her heart, Gretchen decided to leave the cabin and greet the beautiful spring day. After a few steps out of the door she stopped, closed her eyes, and leaned her head back to feel the sun's rays shower her with warmth. A smile replaced the look of concern and confusion that had been haunting her for the last few days. Gretchen asked herself, "Now where is my favorite alleycat?" as she started to run to Esther's. A few days later the two best friends were as close as could be again, laughing, talking about boys, and enjoying everything the spring had to offer near Esther's special place.

"Gretchen, what is it with you and flowers?" Esther asked while watching the younger girl picking the newly blooming yellow buds.

"To give to people I care for and maybe help bring some joy and radiance into their hearts," Gretchen replied while handing a bouquet to her. "For my best friend in the whole world."

"Gretchen, you forgot something." With a stumped look on her face, she stared at Esther.
"We are the only two young women of age in this encampment. So, unless we want to be in the constant presence of the young whiffets, we are each other's only friends," Esther laughingly replied to Gretchen. Both girls started laughing hysterically, neither one of them noticing the young man with blue eyes standing behind them.

"What's so funny?" Johnny asked, causing both girls to let out a startled scream at the sound of his voice.

"Damn you, Johnny Bowman! You scared the devil out of me!" Esther yelled while throwing a nearby stick at the young man.

"I doubt that is possible. Your father gave up trying years ago," Gretchen laughingly said as she remembered many evening conversations since arriving in the Americas. Pastor Hale would sit with her father over tankards of spirits, as he would talk about his daughter's sinful nature, and about "that girl" being the death of him. Esther and Johnny joined in the round of laughter.

After regaining his composure, Johnny murmured, "This place is beautiful." He surveyed nature's masterpiece of many colors and textures. Looking back at the two girls, he asked, "So what are you two doing out here?" The girls shared a glance and a smile with each other.

"Wouldn't you like to know, Mr. Bowman?" Esther replied while strutting up to Gretchen. She extended a hand for Gretchen to join her, "Shall we, my love? Let's make our way back to the palace and leave this peasant boy to his duties."

"Yes, my dear. Please lead the way," Gretchen replied with a curtsy, in a mocking aristocratic voice.

The bewildered man stood there as the two young women skipped away, laughing and giggling. Johnny smiled, then shook his head from side to side.

* * *

Saturday night, Johnny found himself singing joyful songs and sharing ale with his fellow canal workers around a fire after a hard week of work that put them ahead of schedule.

"Drink up, men!" someone called out among the workers. Johnny grabbed his stein and took a big drink, then wiped his chin clean from the spilt drink. End of the week intoxication had become the tradition during the pleasant spring evenings in the workers' camp. Trying to keep up with the seasoned drinkers, Johnny found himself consuming too much, too fast. Standing, he looked for a good place to relieve the building pressure in his bladder. Staggering up to the first tree he could find, *Come on, Hurry up,* he thought as he fumbled with the front of his pants, hoping to succeed before muscle control gave way. "Ahhh," Johnny said in wonderful euphoria, as he tilted his head back in relief. With his eyes closed, the young man didn't notice that, in the shadow of the night, Esther was stalking him, waiting for the right moment, like a wolf waiting for the perfect moment to strike its prey.

"I got something for you." Esther sprang towards him from out of the shadows. While still in midstream, the young man turned to face the unwelcome visitor. In shock, Johnny tried to avert his aim from her direction, but his slow drunken reflexes made him unable to avoid having the urine splash onto Esther's dress. Panicked, Johnny started apologizing, but Esther just smiled and handed him the yellow bouquet that Gretchen had given her earlier.

"I picked these for you," Esther said as she held them out as a sign of her endearment.

Johnny hastily closed up his pants and took the blooms from Esther's hand.

With hands together and kicking her one foot, "I only give flowers to people I like," she flirted, while bowing her head with a coy smile on her face. "If you would like, I have a special place we can go to, and I can show you how much I like you," Esther invited while nervously rocking foot to foot.

"Esther," Johnny said while still staring at the flowers, "I saw Gretchen hand you these posies. They were meant for you."

Esther stared in shock, trying to find the words to cover her actions. "Uh... I... No. These are different ones; I threw those away..."

Johnny handed the fraudulent gift back to Esther and walked away shaking his head. "Good night, Miss Hale," was all he said.

Tears started to form in Esther's eyes as her heart sank. Turning, she ran away, disappearing into the night, leaving no sign of her presence ever being there, except for the scattered small yellow flowers which the darkness of the night quickly devoured.

Gretchen lay in bed reading a book which had come in on the last wagon shipment. The strangely titled book by a lady named Mary Shelley had caught Gretchen's eye. *Frankenstein* seemed such an odd name for a book, and it piqued her curiosity. *Father is still with the men at the fire. It's good for him to be around other men and not spending his evening at the cabin reliving the past,* Gretchen thought. Lately, she found herself afraid some of the mannerisms that she learned from her mother might send her father into dark despair.

Reading by candlelight with her blanket pulled up tight to her chest, Gretchen looked up from the pages to see the dancing ghosts created by the flickering from the small wax torch. Anxiety from the written words in the novel, mixed with the ambience of the room, set her small heart racing. In spite of the tension-filled atmosphere she found the book impossible to put down. *"Nothing is so powerful to the human mind as a great and sudden change."* She read out loud.

Falling deeper into the seductive language of the gripping story, Gretchen was unprepared for the sudden, unexpected sound of a bang from outside the cabin. In a panicked frenzy, her eyes searched for the source of the sound. A startled Gretchen leapt to her feet as she heard a second loud bang on the dwelling's wall.

"Hello, who's out there?" she yelled in a distraught tone. Holding her breath, she strained to listen for a reply.

"Gretchen, help me, please," came a faint sobbing voice from outside of her bedroom wall. BANG! Again, something was hitting the side of the cabin. Scurrying, Gretchen grabbed her reading candle and rushed outside.

In the darkness of the night a shadowy image stood against the rough log cabin wall. Gretchen approached the figure slowly with the candle in her outstretched hand, while clenching the book close to her chest to aid in self-defense.

"Who's there?" she asked in a shaky voice, as she ventured closer to the night shadow.

The silhouette said nothing in response. Gretchen watched in dismay as the dark shape leaned its head back and smashed its forehead into the side of the dwelling. Running up to the form, with no regard for her own safety, Gretchen grabbed the mass, and shouted, "No!"

The candlelight revealed Esther standing there with a blank stare in her eyes, the same stare Gretchen had observed last week, and something else Gretchen could not quite make out.

"KittyKat? Are you alright?" the worried girl asked.

"Gretchen, you're my best friend, right?" Esther asked in confusion, but Gretchen was unable to speak. Esther's beautiful face was now hidden by a veil of crimson flowing down to her chin with drops of blood spotting her dress.

Chapter 4

Sitting by the fireplace in the cabin, Gretchen, with loving hands, washed away the blood which had started to dry on Esther's face. "Esther, I'm always here for you," she told her silent patient. "Whatever is going on, I might be able to help." She continued to wash away the dried blood, then tucked a loose strand of Esther's hair behind her ear and lifted her chin up to see her eyes better. Staring directly at Gretchen with a tilt of her head and uncertainty in her eyes, the older girl studied her as if she were someone she had never met before. "You're my best friend and I need you in my life," Gretchen reassured her while rinsing out the crimson-soaked cloth in the basin. "We can get through this, whatever is ailing you." Esther's eyes followed every move that her young nurse made.

"Do you think I'm pretty?" Esther asked in a soft, cracking voice.

"Thou art the most *bean álainn* I've ever seen, even with thine scarlet veil covering thine perfect face. All the other felines in all of thine kingdom, pale against thy beauty," Gretchen replied while dabbing the cloth on the gash just above the beginning of her forehead hairline. "God must have thought he was making an angel when he created you, my lady," she told her as she inspected the cut on Esther's head. "I'm going to have to sew this wound. Are you comfortable with me doing that?" Gretchen asked while still looking closer at the opening. Esther reached for Gretchen's hand and pulled it to her chest next to her heart.

"I know I've been a bad person to you sometimes, Gretchen. Please forgive me."

Gretchen placed a finger to Esther's lips. "Shhh, KittyKat," Gretchen replied, bringing a small smile to Esther's face. "Now hold this on your head. Don't move! I have to fetch the needle and some thread." She sprang up from her seat, leaving her patient holding a damp cloth to her injured area, and headed directly to a desk sitting in the corner of the cabin. She dug through the drawer, moving various items while Esther watched her every action.

I understand now. How could I have not seen it before? Gretchen is the most pure of heart person I have ever known, freckles and all, Esther thought to herself. *From this day forth she will know how much she means to me.* Esther smiled at Gretchen as she returned with her sewing implements. She looked around, then decided to move Esther to the floor in front of the fireplace, as Gretchen sat in a chair behind her. "Now, this is going to hurt," she comforted Esther in a motherly voice. "Ready KittyKat?" Esther replied with a small smile and one half-hearted paw movement.

Hesitating, the unsure Gretchen thought, *Mother taught me to sew, but this is a human and not cloth.* Trying to decide exactly where to begin, Gretchen retrieved the memory of the one time back in Ireland, Father had cut himself badly and she helped Mother sew his injury. She readied herself and studied the gash meticulously. After she combed Esther's hair to the side,

32

Gretchen carefully pushed the needle through one side of the wound and exited on the other, then with steady hands tied it off. Esther flinched a little. "Oh, I'm sorry. I'm trying not to hurt you," she exclaimed in a panicked voice. With fresh tears streaming down her cheeks, Esther leaned back against Gretchen's legs and wrapped her arms around her calf, hugging the young seamstress's leg.

"Just a few more," Gretchen said in a slow reassuring voice. Esther, not flinching or saying a word, just held on to her with the grip of a person afraid she might fall to her death if she loosened her hold. "Last one." Gretchen knotted the final stitch and leaned down to bite off the excess thread.

"All finished," she said with pride of a job well done. No words were exchanged between the young women as they sat there in silence. Reaching down to touch Esther's chin and tilting her head up, "How's my little KittyKat now?" Gretchen questioned. The corners of Esther's mouth started to show signs of a smile as new tears streamed down her cheek.

"Do you love me?" Esther asked, while staring directly into her friend's eyes.

"Of course, I love you, KittyKat. You're my best friend." Answering in a strong confident voice, Gretchen reached down and hugged her. She wiped the tears away from the older girl. A loving smile spread across her face as she reached up and gently touched Gretchen's cheek, seeing her friend's beauty for the first time.

"I love you too, my strange Flower Picker," Esther conveyed proudly. Gretchen watched Esther's eyes light up with happiness as a hint of the candlelight flickered in the reflection of her pupils.

"I don't know what's wrong, Esther. Would you like to talk about it?"

Rising from the floor, she responded, "I'll see you tomorrow, Gretchen." She turned away and headed for the door. She paused for a second to turn back around and smile once more with new tears of happiness in her eyes. *"Gretchen," the name never sounded so sweet on my lips.* Esther said it again, this time reaching up to touch her lips to feel the words of her endearment ride upon her voice. With a new joy in her heart, she headed on her way home.

Gretchen smiled at the thought of seeing her friend happy and being herself again. *Maybe all she needed was a knock on her head?* She laughed at her thoughts. *"Shame on you, Gretchen Elizabeth Gill for thinking such thoughts."* She found herself still smiling a little as she cleaned up the bloody cloth. Carrying the basin outside to empty the contents on the ground she felt the warmth of the night. *I can feel the moisture in the air getting worse*, she thought. *Tomorrow in church is going to be dank and miserable.*

Her father would be heading to a small town just south of Sprucevale and would be gone most of Sunday. She had gotten a lot of her chores done earlier, leaving just a few things for after church, then the afternoon would be hers.

Heat lightning flashing in the night sky captured her attention. *It's going to be a rainy summer and that means mosquitos according to Esther,* she reminded herself while shaking her head at the dreadful thought of the pesty insects. *I need to mention it to Father, maybe he can find something in town to help. Esther said the fires did little to help last year.* Gretchen made a mental note to tell her father tomorrow before he left.

Now, what was I doing before ...? Frankenstein, the name visited in Gretchen's mind from nowhere. Astonishment, followed by excitement, appeared in Gretchen's face as she ran back into the cabin to continue her dark journey into the beautiful, twisted world of Mary Shelley.

Chapter 5

Earlier Sunday morning Gretchen had waved goodbye to her father as he and his companions began their trek to town. "Make sure to look for something for the mosquitos," Gretchen had told her father as he was mounting his horse.

"Yes, my daughter," he replied while trying to hide the small smile that crept across his lips. She knew that his heart was always wrapped around her fingers. She was a selfless person, always giving more of herself than asking in return. Mr. Gill made sure that when his precious flower wanted something, he normally gave in to her requests.

She watched as the silhouettes disappeared among the rich shadows of the forest tree line. Smiling, Gretchen thought of all the exploring and fun she and Esther could do after church today. *I'm going to start her day out with a smile, and I'll be able to check on her after last night.* Gretchen felt her chest swell with pride thinking about how she was able to supply her comfort and security while nursing Esther's wound. *I feel like we became closer friends after last night and something special happened between us. I could see it in her face.* She thought of last evening and the smile and joy in Esther's face. Gretchen made her way across the freshly tilled land, where small dandelions projected from the earth on the edges. She stopped to admire their beauty, then started carefully picking a bouquet. Arranging the stems in her hand, Gretchen gently bit her lower lip with the intense expression of a painter trying to find the perfect shade of color. Rotating her hand containing the yellow art, Gretchen smiled then continued on with her trip to the Hale home.

Esther lay in her bed. The early morning's sunlight started to fill her room with warmth, helping to wash away the cold darkness that made its home in her room every night. Esther's mind was a whirlwind of thoughts. *How could I have not seen it before?* Esther stretched her arms above her head and yawned while making her hands into fists. *All those boys, playing the flirting game with men, while giving into their desires and my own. True love was right in front of me this whole time. Gretchen, beautiful Gretchen.* Speaking her name in her own head was enough to bring Esther a happiness that made her heart pound faster with the thought of seeing her today. The pain from the self-inflicted wound from last night was eclipsed by the joy in her heart this morning.

Out of the corner of her eye, she noticed a strange shadow dancing up and down across her bedroom wall. She carefully studied the movement to discover the source of the entertainment. Turning to her bedroom window she caught small movements of yellow objects. She smiled with happiness as her eyes glimpsed reddish hair bouncing up and down just below the hand holding the yellow flowers. Esther jumped up and ran to the window to see a beautiful ray of sunshine, not from the sky, but from below her sill. Through the opening, Gretchen felt the bliss coming from Esther, who waved and gestured with one finger and disappeared from view. Esther, brimming with happiness, rushed from the cabin to greet her, barefoot and still in her nightgown.

Gretchen started to speak but was cut off by a thunderous voice.

"Get thee back in this house immediately and put dress thyself!" the voice of Pastor Hale rang through the house walls.

"Morning, Gretchen!" Esther said as both girls giggled at her father's frantic voice.

"I wanted to check on you this morning and bring you these flowers," Gretchen said as she handed her the bouquet. Esther's heart skipped a beat for a second as she accepted the priceless treasure presented to her. "Let me see your wound in the light."

Esther happily obliged her request and lowered her head for inspection.

"I worried about you after you left last night. I had to come check on you. Are you alright, KittyKat?" Reveling in the moment of jubilation, Esther found herself unable to form words. "Are you feeling better?" Gretchen asked again. Esther simply answered with a nod and a smile. "Good," Gretchen replied. "After church we have the whole day to ourselves," at which Esther nodded in excitement.

"Yes, we do," Esther finally replied in a small shy voice, without breaking eye contact.

"Alright, I've got a few chores to do before church, shouldn't take long. So, I'll be there in time, if you want to wait for me outside and we can sit together." Gretchen reached and squeezed her friend's hand then started her trek home.

"I love you, Gretchen," Esther shouted out.

"I love you, too, KittyKat," smiling, she skipped away. "You're my best friend!" Gretchen yelled out as she quickened her pace.

"I'm your only friend, Gretchen, you don't need anyone else. You're mine," Esther said in a soft voice, as the girl disappeared from view. Esther returned to her room, and thoughts of delight filled her mind. *I need something special for Gretchen, something for her, her alone, to always know I'm there with her.* Esther reached up, grabbing a section of her raven hair and twirled it in her finger, *Just for you, my love.* Esther wound her hair up into a tightly twisted string and ripped hard downwards on it. She felt the hair start to give way to the violent action. Sharp pain screamed through her head, but she stood with unmovable resolve and yanked a few more times with a newfound strength until the hank of hair and skin came free.

The feeling of pain was soon replaced with pride in her accomplishment. Esther swiftly started to braid the hair that she had removed from her own head into a bracelet. "Now Gretchen you will always have something of me with you," Esther proudly boasted to a crowd of none. Small amounts of blood started to pool where hair used to be. She reached up to examine the newly formed injury. Her fingertips, with a strange shade of crimson in the morning light, returned to her view. Esther studied her digits before placing them in her mouth to clean away the evidence of her actions. *If pain is the price for Gretchen's love, then it's a price I am willing to pay.*

Chapter 6

Standing outside of her father's church, Esther waited patiently for the first sight of Gretchen. Completely focused like a cat waiting for a mouse to move, she didn't notice Johnny Bowman approach from her side.

"Esther, I was hoping to catch you before services started. I wanted to say that I'm so sorry for the way I acted last night towards you. I was drinking and your gesture was from the heart, and I should have acted like a gentlem ..." Esther interrupted Johnny before he could finish his apology.

"It's just fine, Johnny. You have nothing to say you're sorry for." Esther continued, "I wasn't thinking right, and after a long night of self-discovery I'm the one that needs to say I'm sorry to you." Confused by the conversation, Johnny listened. He took in every word, trying to find a reason for her admission of wrongdoing.

"I acted like a hedge-creeper, and I see that now."

Johnny smiled at Esther. "It's completely forgotten," he told her. "I was going to ask that maybe I could join you and Gretchen today, and maybe have you show me around this beautiful area?" he asked her as she continued her search.

"Yes, sounds fun," Esther replied without really paying attention to what the question was. Her eyes lit up at the sight of a young woman with beautiful copper hair. "Gretchen!" Esther yelled while waving high in the air to the approaching girl to help Gretchen find her among the small gathering of five people who were exchanging the gossip of the week.

"Alright, I'll see you both later today," Johnny told Esther as she started to move towards Gretchen.

"Oh, yes..., right..., Nice talking to you, umm… Johnny," Esther said as she turned her attention completely towards Gretchen and rushed to the young girl. Smiling ear to ear, Esther greeted Gretchen, "I started to worry you weren't going to make it."

"You think I was going to miss a chance for us to sit next to each other? I love my father but sitting next to him in church isn't the greatest pleasure in the world," Gretchen replied. Esther reached down and took her hand.

"Well, today you are mine," Esther told Gretchen while leading her toward the church. Gretchen looked at the bonnet on Esther's head. Satisfied that it was covering her wound from unwanted attention, she turned her focus on the people outside of the church. The girls smiled and exchanged formal "Good mornings" to everyone as they climbed up the few steps.

Esther and Gretchen walked into the church and quickly sat on the benches near the doors. Both teens giggled as they slid across the rough planks while bumping into each other. Gretchen watched Reverend Hale as he walked to the front of the church and readied himself by opening his Book of Prayer. Without speaking a word, he projected such an authoritative aura. She studied him, wondering how a small, soft spoken, older man could captivate everyone and leave everyone feeling the love of God in their hearts every Sunday.

Esther bumped her shoulder into Gretchen's to get her attention. "I have something for you," she whispered. She nudged Gretchen's leg to hand her the bracelet she had made earlier that morning.

Gretchen reached down and took the gift. A smile graced her face, "Esther, I love it, put it on for me." Gretchen's excitement drew looks of disdain from a few of the congregation. Embarrassed by her loudness, she mouthed, "I'm sorry" back to Esther's father. Unwavered, he returned his attention to the rest of the congregation.

The girls giggled softly as Esther tied the bracelet to Gretchen's wrist. Gleaming with admiration, she looked at it and reached down to take the other girl's hand and held it. *Esther is such a wonderful friend. I completely misjudged her.* Gretchen thought as she looked at her and squeezed her hand in a thanking gesture. She returned her attention to Pastor Hale while still holding her best friend's hand in friendship.

Gretchen truly does love me, and no one will ever come between us, not ever. Esther thought to herself while watching Gretchen, whose face was still flushed with happiness at the gift. She returned to watching her father but unhearing, as she basked in the love she felt while holding her true love's hand.

Later that day at Esther's rock, both girls sat immersing themselves in the summer sun. "Did you hear that they are going to start breaking ground on Lock 41?" Gretchen asked.

"Isn't that your favorite place to find your flowers?"

"Yes, but with them raising the water level the ground will flourish and new growth will be everywhere with Gaia smiling down from Olympus." Gretchen closed her eyes to imagine the beauty.

"I'm so glad you like your bracelet," Esther said, changing the subject back to her gift.

Gretchen opened her eyes and proudly showed her bracelet off. "It's mine and you can never have it back. I still can't believe you cut your hair off to make me this," Gretchen replied while admiring Esther's priceless gift. She lay back on the stone and closed her eyes. "It's hard to believe that this spot on this rock can be so comfortable to lie on," Gretchen proclaimed. "I could fall asleep here."

Esther giggled in an ornery voice and answered, "That spot is good for other things, too. Trust me, I know." Gretchen sprang up from the spot wide-eyed and screaming. Esther fell back laughing as Gretchen wiped off the back of her dress like it was covered with some unseen creature.

"Esther Marie Hannah Hale, I can't believe you knowingly let me sit there," Gretchen scolded in a stern voice. A small smile slowly appeared on her face. "I should have expected that from my KittyKat. I still can't believe you let someone take your purity. What would thine father think?" Gretchen said mockingly as she moved over to sit closer to her friend.

"Gretchen, I want to enjoy life and all these rules are made by men and the church to control women. Well, it's my body and if I want to, then I can. That includes not using thine, thee, thou, and all the other religious rhetoric when my father is not around," Esther said while placing her hand on Gretchen's.

"That's very liberal of you, Miss Hale, and coming from the pastor's daughter, shocking, but very refreshing."

43

Esther and Gretchen both looked for the owner of the voice that had just broken their moment of girl talk. Two figures emerged from the trail, Johnny Bowman and a young man climbed up on Esther's rock.

"Next thing you'll be saying is that women should have the right to vote," Johnny's companion boasted.

"Esther, Gretchen, may I introduce to you my childhood friend, Jake Birchham?" Johnny asked. Gretchen looked at the young man. *He's a very handsome man with black-as-coal hair parted on the side, skinny face, thin lips and dark brown eyes,* Gretchen thought to herself. She smiled at Jake but his attention was completely on Esther.

"And why shouldn't women be allowed to vote?" Esther asked the young man. "Why shouldn't women have a voice in matters that also affect them?" she pressed on. "One day a woman may even be the president." Johnny started to laugh then looked to Jake for affirmation, but Jake held his gaze on Esther and smiled.

"I completely agree," Jake replied to the subject of his interest.

Esther sat in amazement that this young man would agree with her. Over the last few years, she'd had arguments with her father about a woman being a man's equal. Her father would always justify his stance by spouting church doctrine to her. Esther still remembered the horrified look on his face when she told him that maybe she would just take over his church and change the doctrine one day. Now, this stranger's understanding of women's suffrage was a breath of fresh air to her. This was certainly a welcome addition to the girls' afternoon of the usual mindless chatter.

"There is nothing a man can do with his mind that a woman can't," Jake told Esther as he approached and sat next to her. Johnny slowly took a seat next to Gretchen.

"Ummm, I wouldn't…," Gretchen started to say as Johnny sat down in Esther's special spot. Both girls covered their mouths and started boisterous cackling. Laughing so hard, Esther fell backwards. Quickly Jake reached for her, preventing her from falling off the rock into the water.

"Whoa there, beautiful. I got you," Jake said while pulling Esther back up to a secure spot.

"Well, thank you, Mr. Birchham," Esther said while looking directly into his brown eyes. *Something in those dark eyes scares me,* Esther thought to herself. *Those eyes…*

"Please, Esther, call me Jake. Mr. Birchham is my father," he informed her.

Regaining her composure. she asked, "So what brings you to Sprucevale, Jake?"

"Well, work, and someone had to watch over Johnny as he is away from his clan," Jake boasted.

"Jake, come on, I'm the one always saving you from getting into mischief," Johnny fired back. "Like that one time with crazy old farmer Mattern and his cattle," Johnny started to laugh while telling the tale.

"That's not fair. It was raining and I thought they would like a nice warm house to stay dry in. Who would have known that cows can walk up stairs but always avoid walking down?" Jake said.

While both men laughed, Gretchen watched, then joined in the laughter. She found herself skeptical about Johnny's friend. *Something about him. He said he was here for work, but his hands show no signs of ever seeing a hard day's labor. Something about this man is not to be trusted.* Gretchen thought but continued to join in the merriment.

"For a stone, this spot is really comfortable," Johnny said while leaning back with his hands behind his head. Gretchen covered her mouth and laughed along with Esther who spit through her hand. "What?" Johnny asked. His question was met with more laughter from the two young women.

"What kind of work are you looking for, Jake?" Gretchen asked, trying to chase the thought of Johnny's comment about the rock from her mind. "I've noticed by the looks of your hands, you're not one that has put many calluses on them?" Gretchen queried. Jake stared directly at her with cold lifeless eyes, which sent an icy chill down the younger girl's back. *Did I just ask something that I shouldn't have?* she thought to herself. Jake's face softened and a friendly smile quickly returned.

"Well, I'm good with math and bookwork accounting, so while Johnny is good with a hammer and chisel, my hammer is a pen." Jake smiled with his reply and turned his gaze back to Esther. *Something in the way he stares at Esther isn't right. He's Johnny's friend and Johnny is a good man. I doubt he would associate with the wrong type of people.* Gretchen decided she was just being overly protective for her friend.

Later that evening, after an afternoon spent questioning Jake's intentions and character, she was happy to see her father walking into the cabin. Relieved that he had safely returned, she ran to him.

"How was your trip, Papa?" Gretchen asked while giving him a hug.

"The trip was uneventful, but we met with the company investors. They are wanting construction to be expedited." He walked to the coat rack and hung up his jacket. Gretchen watched as he pulled something from his pocket. "I love you, my Flower." Mr. Gill stood, holding his hands behind his back. Gretchen stood for a moment trying to contain her excitement, knowing he had something for her, then quickly she rushed back to her father. Mr. Gill stood like a giant man compared to Gretchen. As she moved left then right to see what her father was hiding, Mr. Gill successfully defended every action she tried to make. Laughing, her father finally said, "All right, all right, close your eyes, and reach out." Gretchen tightly closed her eyes and bounced up and down in anticipation. She felt her father place a small box in her palms. "You may open them now," Gretchen's father instructed. The obedient daughter's gaze fell upon a small red velvet box. "Go ahead."

Gretchen was all thumbs as she started to open it. Finally, she slowed enough to lift the lid. Tears filled her eyes as she looked at her father's precious gift. It was a beautiful locket necklace adorned with a gold framed cameo with a lady's portrait in the center. Gretchen stood there, tears streaming down her cheeks.

"Now your mother will be with you always," Mr. Gill told the young girl with fresh tears in his own eyes.

"Please, Father, would you put it on me?" She turned around with her back to him as she lifted her shoulder length hair. Smiling proudly, Mr. Gill clasped the ends of the delicate chain together around his daughter's neck.

"There you go, my *mhuirnin*," Mr. Gill said as he kissed the top of Gretchen's head. She ran to the mirror to inspect the image of herself wearing the necklace. He approached and stood behind, admiring his daughter's beauty. "Your mother would be so proud of the beautiful young woman that you're becoming," Mr. Gill boasted.

"I wish she were here, Father," Gretchen responded.

"As do I, Flower. As do I."

Chapter 7

Gretchen awoke to the stumbling sound of her father getting prepared for Monday morning's work. She climbed out of bed, yawning and rubbing her eyes. Gretchen asked her father, "Is the groundbreaking on Lock 41 starting today?"

"Yes, my Morning Glory. Today we break ground," her father replied. "Should we be expecting you and the young Miss Hale to honor us with your presence?"

"Someone has to supervise and make sure the work is done correctly," she responded, standing tall and cocky with eyes still asleep. Her father walked over to her and kissed the top of her head. Smiling and waving to her, Mr. Gill headed outside.

"Make sure your chores are done first," Gretchen heard her father call out while he made his way in the direction of the work site.

She quickly dressed and finished up her chores, making more time for herself and Esther. *I can't wait to show Esther my necklace that Father got me.* She looked down as she raised the pendant to her view, then looked at her wrist with Esther's bracelet on it. She felt the rush of happiness and for the first time the guilty feelings didn't follow. Gleaming with joy, she hurried to Esther's cabin.

From the side of the cabin, a dark figure stepped out from the shadows and watched the young woman leave. "Not a bad body, a little young, but she might be fun," he said with one corner of his mouth curled up in a snide grin. Glancing around, he turned and made his way into Mr. Gill's cabin.

Esther heard the knock on the door as she was getting dressed. From outside she heard a voice that brought a smile to her face.

"Where's my KittyKat?" the voice rang out. Esther rushed to the door to see Gretchen standing there with an extended arm of wildflowers that she had picked on the way. Gretchen asked, "You ready for our big day? Work on Lock 41 starts this morning!" Esther took the flowers from her hand, slowly raised them to her nose and smelled their fragrance.

"They are beautiful, thank you, Gretchen," she replied. "You better believe I'm ready." She smiled and thought about how lovely it would be to spend the day with Gretchen, plus the working men were also a bonus. An ornery grin crept across her face. Gretchen pushed her shoulder.

"Esther, did the alleycat just show up?" she jokingly asked.

Biting her lower lip, she coyly replied, "Maybe," causing Gretchen's cheeks to warm up again. "You know you can watch again if you like. I wouldn't mind," Esther deviously remarked. Gretchen's eyes grew wide, and she gasped while covering her mouth.

"How did you know I saw you and that boy at the rock?" she inquired through a muffled hand.

"I knew you saw me and... what ... was his name?" she stopped, trying to recall which young boy it was. After a short pause, she continued, "After that, I remembered you couldn't look me in the eye for a whole week. You never asked who the young man was, so I figured that you were watching us and that's why you didn't ask the boy's name," Esther replied.

Gretchen stood there with a complete loss of words. Esther simply smiled and took her hand when Gretchen's new pendant caught her eye. "Oh, what is that?" she queried as she pointed to the necklace.

"Father brought this home last night for me, so now I have something from everyone important in my life," Gretchen replied. Raising up the bracelet that Esther had made of her own hair, Gretchen asked, "How's your head?" She lowered her head to be inspected. "I really did a good job. If you don't part your hair, no one will ever be able to tell. It might not even leave a scar." Esther smiled and pulled Gretchen in for a hug.

"You're the best," Esther told Gretchen, as they exchanged smiles. "Let's grab a blanket so we can relax and watch the men work today," she said as she took Gretchen's hand and walked back into the cabin. With a blanket in hand, the young women hiked to the location of the construction of the new lock for the day's entertainment. As they arrived, the morning sun had just started poking its head through the tall trees, filling the valley with rays of golden streaks. Gretchen noticed the ground had been broken and large amounts of soil had already been hauled off. The girls took hold of each end of the blanket to lay it out. Gretchen surveyed the area and saw her father with some other men. He looked like a musical conductor the way he swayed his arms. The men beside him watched his every direction as the workers below moved in rhythm. While other people heard the noise of men yelling and the horses and the hammering,

Gretchen could see and almost hear the music. If she closed her eyes and listened, a great composition was being performed.

"Gretchen, come join me," Esther said, disrupting her thoughts away from the great score being played. She smiled then took a seat next to her friend. "I didn't think they would ever make this much progress in such a short period of time," Esther told her as she looked around admiring with wonderment of what men could do. "Before your father took over, the previous engineer would show up to give orders to the foreman. Then he headed back to his cabin to spend time drinking and entertaining whatever local woman needed a few coins. Nothing ever got done."

Gretchen felt pride in her chest for the compliments about her father. "What happened to him?" she inquired. She had heard her father mention him, but nothing was ever really said.

"Last I heard, he was running a wagon for hire. So, I guess if he is his own boss, no one will care what he does on his time, as long as the cargo makes it to its destination." Both girls turned their attention back to the work site.

Esther reached over and touched her friend's hand in a gentle caress. Looking down, Gretchen affectionately squeezed Esther's hand as a warm welcoming smile crossed her face. Feeling the warmth start to rise in her cheeks, Esther started to speak when a voice interjected.

"Gretchen, Esther, there you two are," Johnny Bowman called out while waving overhead to them. The young women watched as he started to climb up the small hill to invade their observation point. "I've been looking for you two. They asked me to take the wagon up to Conkle's Mill for supplies. Would you two like to make the journey with me?" Johnny asked.

"Conkle's Mill? Why not Hambleton's Mill?" Gretchen asked.

"They are installing a new millstone and having issues with the alignment, so they are having someone coming from Pittsburgh to help. But he won't be here for three more days," Johnny answered. "Would you ladies care to grace me with your company on today's adventure?" Johnny asked while bowing like an English nobleman.

"If Lady Esther wants to go, we would gladly accompany you on your journey," Gretchen replied. "Shall we, my lady?" Gretchen asked while looking at her. Esther grinned, jumped up and grabbed the blanket with one hand and Gretchen's hand with her other. The young women ran down the hill while Johnny took to pursuing them to the wagon.

In the shadow of the cabins a lone figure watched the three teens as they departed on their mission. He noticed the sitting order of the group. The unseen stalker's eyes burned with rage and jealousy as the wagon disappeared down the path. *She will be mine,* he told himself, as he turned and made his way into another cabin.

Gretchen loved riding in the wagon, even though the view of the horse wasn't the best. Being up high in the air gave her a new perspective of the area. Soon the canal locks system would be completed and the height of the water could be controlled. The stream would rise, allowing the boat to be pulled along the waterway by beasts of burden and large amounts of cargo could be transported swiftly. Pride rose in her chest again. *This feat is going to be made possible because of my father.* Suddenly Gretchen's daydreaming was broken by the sound of Esther's question.

"So, what makes you so special that you get to go to the mill, instead of using a shovel to move dirt, Mr. Johnny Bowman?" Esther asked with a wicked grin on her face.

"Well, I'm a stone cutter and it wouldn't be a good idea to have something bad happen to me, then I wouldn't be able to use the tools of my trade," he replied to the young ladies. Esther bumped into Gretchen to get her attention. As Esther made hand motions of a royal queen having her hand pampered, Gretchen tried not to laugh but Esther's performance sent her laughter over the edge. Johnny looked at the cackling girls and just shook his head while continuing to hold the reins of the horse. A smile came to life on his face as he took a quick glance at the two. They whispered in each other's ears with giggling replies to the questions that Johnny couldn't make out.

"Alright, alright," Esther stated as she pulled away from Gretchen.

"Mr. Bowman, is there someone special at home waiting for you? And four-legged females count, too."

"Esther!" Gretchen hit her in the arm for asking such a question. She simply smiled and laughed a little.

"It's alright, Gretchen. And yes. There is someone at home, with two legs, waiting for me," Johnny rebuked.

"Your mother doesn't count," Esther snidely replied.

54

"Florence Wade is her name," Johnny informed Esther. Suddenly Gretchen's heart sank a little from hearing the news. "Our parents arranged the marriage a few years ago. She is from a good family and her parents are going to give us some land, so it works out good for all involved," Johnny replied half-heartedly, which Gretchen could hear in his voice.

Gretchen went silent, wrapped her arms and slipped inside herself, as Johnny continued telling Esther about his future spouse. *Why did I think he would be interested in me?* Gretchen thought to herself. *He was just being nice and I took it completely wrong.* As the wagon rounded the bend of the trail the silhouette of Conkle's Mill appeared ahead.

"We made good time, almost noon," Johnny boasted.

Esther nudged Gretchen, "What's wrong, Gretchen?"

She made a half-hearted smile. "Just thinking," came her reply.

Realizing something was actually wrong, Esther reached down and took her hand. "I'm here for you and I will always protect you," she said while trying to comfort her.

Gretchen simply smiled and asked, "Best friends?"

Esther replied with a loving look, "Best friends," and kissed her on the cheek.

Chapter 8

The mill sat on the west side of the creek. The girls had made this trip before, but on foot, back during its construction. Gretchen found the area very relaxing; she liked how it was more open and flatter than most of the valley. Water from the stream was diverted into a pond near the mill. A wooden wall dam in one corner of the small lake was made to let the water flow down a trench. It cascaded over the paddlewheel to turn and make the millstones work. Gretchen closed her eyes and listened to the water moving the wheel in the rhythmic sound of the mill's heartbeat.

"Do you two want to come in with me?" Johnny asked with an inviting smile as he jumped down off the wagon.

"Thank you for the invitation but stretching my legs and looking around is what I need at the moment," Gretchen replied. "You can go if you want, Esther." Climbing down from the wagon, she started to walk away without waiting for an answer.

"Come to the mill when you're done; we shouldn't be long," Johnny called out. With her head down, Gretchen walked toward the pond. *Every time I get my hopes up, all I do is get disappointed and hurt. Why can't I be pretty like Esther? Why do I have to be so ugly, so unlovable?* Gretchen thought, as sadness filled her heart. Tears started to pool in the young lass's eyes as the reflection of not having anyone to love overwhelmed her. The heartbroken girl wrapped her arms around herself for comfort, as she walked around the back of the mill.

Gretchen's eyes were greeted with the sparkling of the pond. Freshly grazed grass outlined the reservoir. Small wake trails left behind from the wild mallards violated the smoothness of the surface. Their graceful movement helped Gretchen take her mind off her sad heart. The honking of a young goose pulled her attention to the far side of the mill basin where she saw a large rodent slide off the bank into the water. Gretchen thought, *Could that have been a beaver?*

"Well, hello there, young lady. Aren't you a pretty one?" Startled, Gretchen snapped around to find the author of the voice. A large-bellied, unkempt man in his 40's, sat on a crate, peeling an apple with a small knife. Taking a bite of the fruit, he smiled at Gretchen. "Been coming here for a while and I don't think I've had the pleasure of meeting you," the man crooned. Gretchen, at first, didn't fully listen to him; the black and missing teeth in the man's mouth were distracting her attention. "Do you have a name, bonnie?" the man asked.

"Ah, um, it's Gretchen," she answered in a very small cautious voice.

"Gretchen, hmm, that's a pretty name for a pretty young lass. Would you like a taste of this apple?" The man offered her a slice of apple that he had just bitten a piece of. "Taste for a taste" he grinned, displaying his wide variety of mostly unnatural teeth colors. Gretchen felt her stomach lurch at the thought of the apple that had been in his mouth.

"Um, no thank you, sir ...." Before Gretchen could finish her response she heard a familiar voice.

"Stay away from her, you piece of shite!" Esther rushed up to Gretchen, pulling her into her arms. Holding Gretchen, Esther turned and glared at the man with the eyes of a protective mother.

"Esther Hale, look at you. Last time I saw you, you weren't much more than a skinny weed. Now look at you. Very nice pillows you have growing there," the man exclaimed while licking his lips and wiping apple juice from his matted beard.

Still confused, Gretchen looked at her protector and asked, "What's wrong, Esther? Do you know this man?"

"Remember the engineer I told you about, who was your father's predecessor?" Esther asked. Gretchen thought for a second and nodded. "This is him," she disdainfully told her while keeping a watchful eye on him.

"Soooo, you're Gill's daughter," the man stated while sitting up straighter with new interest. "Your father is a real piece of work, costing me my employment. He could have kept me on but got me fired because I wouldn't kiss his arse. Well, now seeing young Miss Gretchen here, I can think of all kinds of ways he can make up for it. Your father owes me and I'm sure that little crimson thatched cottage of yours can be payment enough," the man angrily retorted. Without warning, Esther lunged at the man so fast Gretchen didn't realize she had left her side. In one swift motion, she knocked the man off his crate and snatched the small knife from his grip.

In disbelief, Gretchen rushed up to her. "Esther!" she cried out in a panicked voice as Johnny darted around the corner. Astonished, Johnny discovered Esther lying on top of an older man and in her hand, she held a knife to his throat. A small dot of red appeared under the pressure of its sharp edge.

"Please don't, I'm sorry, please, please I... I beg of you, I was just joking," the man pleaded in a distressed high-pitched voice. Looking at Esther, Johnny found nothing but pure rage in her eyes. Taken aback for a second, he shook the image from his mind. He grabbed Esther and tried to pull her off the helpless bloke, only to find her resolve would not be interrupted.

"Esther, come on, get off of him!" Johnny pleaded over and over.

"Please, Esther, Stop. You are scaring me. I beg you, please get off him. I don't want anything bad to happen to you. I need you with me," Gretchen cried. Her words slowly started to process in Esther's brain. Relaxing, she backed off the man while a grin appeared across her face.

"If you EVER talk to Gretchen that way again, I'm going to make a tobacco pouch out of your stones!" Esther warned the man. She stood up and slid the knife into her dress pocket. The man hastily scurried to his feet and rushed around toward the front of the mill. Gretchen approached Esther to give her a calming, thankful hug.

Johnny walked to join the girls when the smell of excrement suddenly filled the air. He fought hard, but the laughter escaped his mouth followed by Esther's. Gretchen looked at the two of them in confusion and then the new odor arrived to perk her senses. Her eyebrows raised, a smile slowly crossed her face and then a laugh broke through her lips. Johnny bent over trying to hold his belly but the addition of Gretchen's laughter sent him over the edge.

"Please, please stop, stop or I'm going to piss myself!" Esther spouted as she crossed her legs and held her lower belly. Blinded by laughter from Esther's impending problem, Johnny stumbled back and disappeared behind the crates. "Oh, No!" Esther, turned and stiff-legged, shuffled to the outhouse.

The ride back to Sprucevale was filled with small talk between Esther and Johnny. Gretchen used the time to reflect on the day's events, trying to make sense of all that had transpired. Johnny being in an arranged marriage was shocking news, but Esther's action had taken center stage in her mind. *Yes, Esther had almost cut a man's throat, but she did it to defend me.* Gretchen turned to look at her friend, who was absorbed in banter with Johnny. She had noticed Esther took the knife and concealed it in her dress; now she watched her hand fondle the hidden object concealed in her pocket as if it were a new toy and she wanted to memorize every inch of it. *Esther has changed toward me in the last week, from being mean to me, to now being my protector. I wonder what has changed.* These thoughts plagued her mind.

"Gretchen, did you hear me?" Esther's voice snapped Gretchen back to the present.

"I'm sorry. I was daydreaming. What did you say?" Gretchen replied, then waited for her to say something about her being weird. Esther just smiled and pulled her in close and tightly hugged her.

Gretchen

"Gretchen, you are just too cute. That's why you're the best," Esther proudly announced to the world. "I was saying that I think I'm going with my father tomorrow. He is going to New Lisbon. I may be gone for a few days. Are you going to be alright without me around?" Esther asked and waited for a reply. Gretchen sat unresponsive while she looked at Esther. *Her eyes, something in her eyes had changed. Her brown eyes seemed softer toward me, more loving and caring,* Gretchen thought to herself.

"I'm not sure if I'm going to be able to survive if I don't have KittyKat around to be my knight in shining armor if something happens to me," Gretchen replied with her loving smile accompanying her answer.

"I should have a slow day tomorrow, so I'll watch over her if that's acceptable to you, Lady Esther," Johnny said to the young ladies in his best Sir Knight voice. Gretchen blushed a little as Esther laughed.

"Sir Johnny, I leave the lovely Gretchen in your care until I make my glorious return," Esther informed the child-man. "But remember, if anything happens to her…," she pulled the knife from her dress and flashed it in the air. "I still need that tobacco pouch!"

Johnny and Esther resumed their conversation again as Gretchen leaned on Esther. She rested her head against her friend's bosom, twirling a lock of Esther's raven hair. She closed her eyes to enjoy the sounds of nature on the return trip. Her personal KittyKat wrapped her arm around her and rubbed Gretchen's temple in a comforting action.

61

Chapter 9

"**G**retchen, wake up, sleepyhead." Gretchen's eyes fluttered as she escaped the dream realm to find herself lying across Esther's lap. "Welcome back, sleeping beauty," Esther teased as she brushed the hair out of Gretchen's face. Startled, the half-awake girl sat up realizing she had drooled while she slept. She looked down on Esther's dress to notice a small wet spot. Embarrassed, she quickly wiped her chin and corner of her mouth.

"I'm so sorry, Esther, I didn't mean to," Gretchen apologized. But Esther stopped her and smiled. Reaching up with her hand she helped wipe the corner of Gretchen's mouth with her thumb. Looking into Esther's eyes, *There it is again, the sparkle, the tenderness,* she told herself. Gretchen felt her heart jump with joy knowing that Esther truly did care for her. Being her best friend was real and was more than just spoken words.

"Welcome back, you three," Jake stepped around the front of the wagon. "Sooo, any big adventures to tell?" he asked.

"Well, we found out if you eat apples and add Esther, it cures constipation," Johnny told Jake. Snickering, the three friends broke out into hearty laughter that left Jake confused. Not wanting to feel left out, he smiled and went along with their happiness.

"Gretchen, your father wanted me to tell you that you should get home and start dinner, if I saw you," Jake conveyed to Gretchen.

"Well, I'd better be making my way back then," Gretchen told the group. Walking up to Esther and hugging her, "Be safe and get back soon. It wouldn't be the same around here without you filling my day with excitement." Esther closed her eyes and let the hug envelop her as she leaned down to the smaller girl and inhaled her scent. Feeling every inch of Gretchen's body, she memorized the way she felt in her arms.

"*Slán Abhaile*," Gretchen told her friends as she turned and began trotting back to her father's cabin.

"I'd better go report to the foreman. Have a safe trip, Esther," Johnny told her as he left for his mission.

Jake stood next to Esther with his elbow crooked and his hand on his waist, "May I have the honor of escorting you home, Miss Hale?" Jake asked.

"Yes, you may, Mr. Birchham," came her reply as she laced her arm through Jake's. "So, what job did you find?" she asked.

"Well, I was able to find work in supplies and in ledger keeping, so it's a perfect fit for me."

"That's good that you found something you are good at and have an interest in."

"Have you lived here long, Esther?" Jake asked.

She thought for a minute, then replied, "Well, my mother and father came from a small village, Lucerne, north of here. They moved down here when I was very young, when my father took over the church. It's been just me and him. So, this area is pretty much my whole life except for a few small trips my father and I make."

"Your mother, did she pass away?" Jake asked. She tensed for a second then looked out in the distance while she searched for the correct answer. She nibbled on her lip and breathed deeply, then exhaled.

"Father has always just said, 'your mother is gone and that's all you need to know.' I've heard rumors while I was growing up that she ran off with another man and a few said with another woman. So, if that was what happened, either way, she left her child. So, the answer to your question is, I'm going to say that my mother is dead." Esther's eyes clouded up a little.

Jake stopped and turned Esther to face him, cupping her cheek in his hand. "You don't have to be sad anymore. I can be here for you and can give you the life you deserve."

Jake's words gobsmacked Esther, leaving her speechless. He looked her in the eyes and leaned to her face. His kiss at first shocked Esther from a response, but then she closed her eyes and started to feel the moment of his tender soft lips against hers. Pulling her in close, his arms encircled her waist, closing the distance between them.

"Please... stop," Esther told Jake as she withdrew from their embrace. "I'm sorry, I can't. You are very attractive and any woman would love to be in your arms, but I can't," Esther advised the young man.

"Why? I can make you happy. I can give you a future, security, everything a woman would want in a man. I give you my heart, Esther, it's yours," Jake professed to her.

"Therein lies the problem," Esther began, averting her eyes from the young man's vision.

"What problem?" Jake pleaded. "What is it?" Bewildered, he asked again, this time picking up Esther's chin to look her in the eyes.

"I can't give you my heart because it belongs to someone else. I've pledged it to them in this life and beyond," Esther explained to the young man. Jake stood there speechless, as his eyes glazed over. She leaned in and kissed his cheek. "I'm sorry," she said, apologizing to her suitor, and turned to head home alone.

Jake stood there motionless. Sadness slowly slipped into his heart as his pride was destroyed.*It is always about Johnny. Everyone loves Johnny.* With his head hanging low, he returned to his cabin.

Esther made her way swiftly back to their dwelling where she greeted her father with a kiss on the cheek. "How early are we leaving in the morning?"

"Before sunrise, so thou needest to get everything ready tonight," her father replied.

"I shall, Father," came her response as she headed into her room. Esther spotted the flowers that Gretchen had presented to her that morning. Holding them tightly in her hand she lay on the bed and admired them. She pulled them to her bosom, closed her eyes and relived the moment of feeling Gretchen in her arms. "I love you so much, Gretchen, that it hurts me knowing we will have to be apart for a few days. But when I get back, I will get on my knees and proudly profess my love for you and show you what you mean to me," Esther whispered to the blossoms. Her heart sped up with growing anticipation of the excitement of when she would feel Gretchen's lips for the first time. She played the vision out over and over in her mind.

Chapter 10

Thunder rolled through the Sprucevale valley shaking the ground. Gretchen shot up from her bed alarmed by the unexpected sound. "Oh no, Esther!" she said as she looked for any sign of the sunrise. *How long have I slept? Is it near morning?* With the dark storm coming, there was no way for her to tell.

Gretchen had hoped for rain to help cool the area, but she didn't want it to hinder Esther's journey. The first sign of a breeze entered the cabin which brought joy to her but also fear. She had heard storms in America could be very unpredictable, by the way they popped up and then disappeared. She closed her eyes and prayed, "Please, Heavenly Father, protect Esther and Mr. Hale on their travels."

Getting out of bed to look at the night sky, Gretchen wondered how far away the storm was when she saw flashes of lightning to the south. To figure the distance of the storm she began to count on her fingers, "One, two, three..." she stopped at nine as she heard a low but growing rumble. Gretchen started to leave the window when a bright flash of lightning exploded in the night sky, exposing a dark mass running around the corner of the neighboring cabin. Gretchen stared at the spot where the form was, waiting for the distant lightning to illuminate the area again so she could grasp a better view. Her thoughts quickly turned to the nasty man at the mill earlier that day, sending a cold chill racing up her back. The thought of what he had implied he wanted from her was the subject of nightmares. Gretchen calmed herself and let out the breath she didn't realize she had been holding and continued to watch. *He was too fat and old to move that fast,* Gretchen thought to herself. A small chuckle escaped her mouth and the safety of her room and cabin pushed the worrisome thought from her head. *It was probably an animal or the night playing tricks on my mind,* she told herself. Turning back toward her bed, she quickly climbed back in and pulled the covers over her head for security. The night was hot and humid, and under the covers would just make it unbearable to sleep, but she felt safe and needed safety more than comfort tonight.

The distant lightning lit up the night sky as the shadow stared into Gretchen's room. Smiling at the thought of his plan and the part that Gretchen was soon to play, the man turned and headed away from the window back into the forest.

Morning light crept into Gretchen's room as the young girl dressed for the day's activities.

"Gretchen, are you awake?" came the call from her father as he slowly opened the blanket that led to her room.

"Yes, Father."

"Good, I'm heading up to the Lock 41 site, so make sure to get your chores done, and don't wander far out into the woods today because I'm fairly sure there will be some more storms later," Mr. Gill instructed his daughter.

"Yes, Papa," came her reply as she walked up to him and kissed his cheek. Mr. Gill smiled, as he lifted her chin to look at her face.

"You are the spitting image of your mother. She would be so proud of the beautiful young lady you're becoming, as am I proud to call you my daughter," Mr. Gill told her with an admiring look on his face. Gretchen felt her cheeks start to warm but instead of turning away she stood proudly.

"I love you, Father," Gretchen told him in a heartwarming voice. A tear started to form in her father's eye.

"I love you, too, my Flower. But you still have to do your chores," he said, as she jumped up and threw her arms around him in a hug.

Gretchen spent most of the morning cleaning the cabin and washing clothes. Hanging the damp clothes, her thoughts went to Esther, *Wonder if they made it to New Lisbon yet?* She missed her friend already and hoped she would return soon. *She makes everything more interesting. I could go visit her special place and enjoy the sun or maybe I should go to my secret place.* Pondering her options, Gretchen decided the latter would be perfect.

Gretchen quickly finished up her chores, then headed out for some special time with the valley she loved. Walking the trail that led to Lock 41, Gretchen made a right that led to an incline along the path near the water. Halfway up the steep hill, she spotted an old friend, the first friend she had made when she and her father arrived in Sprucevale. "Hello, Mr. Oak, did you miss me?" Gretchen walked up to a single oak tree towering in the middle of a group of small hemlocks. This tree always seemed out of place, up on the hillside, high above the valley with only evergreens in its company. A stranger in a strange place, just like her, so the tree became something special to Gretchen.

"I'm so jealous of you. Every morning when you wake up you get to see this beauty before anyone does," Gretchen murmured to the tree as she knocked on the trunk and then ran her hands over the bark. Lovingly, she placed her cheek on the tree and looked out over the valley to share the breathtaking view of nature with her friend.

"I'll stop back when I come back down," Gretchen told the statuesque giant as she continued up the hill. Almost to the top, she spotted her personal walkway that dropped down over the cliff face of the hill. A narrow winding nature trail that made its way under the top of the slope, it ended at the mouth of a small cave. Gretchen had found this natural cave when she first started exploring and since then it was her own secret place, one she didn't share even with Esther.

Gretchen sat on a rock surveying the valley. To her right she could see the work that had been done on Lock 41 and she could almost see her cabin from up here. Low-line trees protected her from unwanted attention or wandering eyes. This was her second home, a secluded place of reflection for her. She closed her eyes and let the sunlight bathe her as she enjoyed its warmth kissing her face.

"Now this is a view!" Startled, Gretchen snapped to attention at the sound of the voice that had desecrated her sanctuary. Johnny walked up and sat down next to her. Confused with feelings of both anger and happiness, Gretchen tried to force a happy face. Johnny was the one person she would share this special place with, but, on her terms, not his.

"What are you doing here? Do you even have a job here?" Gretchen asked sternly.

"Well, I saw you walking up the hillside and I did tell Esther, I would watch over you while she was gone," Johnny told her as he scratched his head. "And after yesterday, Esther is not someone I wish to trifle with." With a friendly smile, Johnny tried to placate Gretchen from the surprise of his unexpected visit.

"Sorry about my defensiveness. I didn't expect anyone to be following me, and I'll ask again, why aren't you working?" she queried.

"Well, they are expecting high water soon from the storm last night, so we are kind of on wait and see, so I thought I'd spend some time with you. If that is acceptable?" Johnny asked while tilting his head to one side and flashing a childish smile. Gretchen's anger melted away when she saw the smile and those beautiful eyes. Even though he was promised to someone he still made her heart skip a beat.

"Well, since you're already here, I guess your company is welcomed..., this time!" Gretchen smiled coyly back at Johnny.

As the morning passed, Gretchen took time to explain to Johnny how she found this spot. He listened intently to her confession of her heart's love for this valley. Johnny couldn't help but notice the way her eyes lit up when she talked and the excitement in her voice.

She doesn't realize how beautiful she is, the softness of her skin, her shining reddish hair is radiant in the sunlight, Johnny thought and decided, *it is now or never.*

"Gretchen," Johnny interrupted. She looked at Johnny to see what his question might be when his lips met hers.

A high pitched muffled "eep," escaped Gretchen's lips as they kissed. She stared at him wide-eyed in shock. When her mind finally understood what was happening, she relaxed and closed her eyes and melted into the kiss. Johnny reached up and placed his hand on the side of her neck to pull her closer. Unsure what to do, Gretchen followed Johnny's lead. Desiring to feel the warmth of his body, she allowed Johnny to pull her in closer. Unbridled passion built between them as they embraced.

Gretchen's mind started racing. *I'm kissing Johnny, my first kiss, what do I do? Do I keep holding my breath? Do I stop him when I need to breathe?* Gretchen suddenly realized that all she had to do was breathe through her nose. A small chuckle made its way to her mouth.

"Was that all right?" Johnny asked while pulling back from Gretchen.

"Yes, God Yes, everything is perfect," came her reply. Johnny smiled and pulled her to his lips. Gretchen wrapped her arms around his neck. A building hunger in her soul took control of her being as time seemed to stop.

Johnny pulled slowly away from Gretchen's lips and rested his forehead against hers. "I've been dreaming at night of kissing you, Gretchen," Johnny confessed. "I know this is wrong with me having a betrothed, but I find my thoughts of you overwhelming my heart. Please don't bid me ill will." Johnny closed his eyes and breathed deeply. Gretchen leaned in and kissed his lips again and smiled.

"I understand, this marriage can't be what you want, and God knows you're on my mind, too. But I thank you for being my first kiss. I will always treasure it, but we can never do this again," came Gretchen's reply. Johnny nodded in agreement.

"Never again. We will still be fast friends and we will remember this moment, and it will be a treasure in my heart as well," Johnny sadly responded. Biting her lip, Gretchen suddenly smiled and launched herself onto Johnny for another kiss. Wrapping her arms around his neck and knocking him over backwards onto the ground, Gretchen kissed him passionately. Their lips slightly parted to share a deeper kiss. A few small kisses followed, and Gretchen helped herself off of Johnny.

"Alright, starting now we will be friends," Gretchen said while wiping away a small amount of dribble from her chin.

Johnny sat up smiling, "Gretchen, you are so special. People will remember you forever!"

"Thank you, Johnny." Blushing, Gretchen stood and offered her hand to help him up. "We should maybe head back down now. You go first and I will wait a bit, then head down so people won't get the wrong idea," she told him. With a mixture of sadness and joy, she watched as he started down the hill. Once he was out of sight, Gretchen decided to head to Lock 41 and see her father.

After telling her forest friend of her first kiss and saying goodbye, she headed to the bottom of the hill. She made a right and felt herself float up the path along the stream. Gretchen was shocked by the sight of the creek. *I wonder when the high water will arrive?* she thought. Lack of rainfall had lowered the level. Areas that were usually smooth flowing water with the sunlight sparkling reflections were now rippling from the stones protruding to the surface for the first time since she came to the valley.

Gretchen was astonished by the view when she reached Lock 41. So much work had been completed. Almost all the ground had been dug out and masonry workers were busy adding stones to the walls.

Wait, if the stone cutters are working, why isn't Johnny here? Gretchen scanned the area looking for her father. "Miss Gretchen," an older black man called out to her as he walked up to her. "If you're looking for Mr. Gill, I'm afraid he's not here. He got called back down to the workers' cabins. People are saying something's happened."

"Thank you," Gretchen replied to the kindly gentleman. Rushing back to the village, her mind raced with thoughts of endless possibilities. *It had to be something bad for them to call Father.* Clearing the last of the wooded area she arrived in the small settlement. She was struck by increased fear by the absence of the workers and their families from the bustling of their daily lives. Distraught, she quickened her pace as she ran past the empty homes, looking left and right but seeing no one. Along the trail near Hambleton's Mill, she observed a large group of people. Rushing up to the gathering, Gretchen, started shoving and pushing through the throng, desperately searching for her father.

Spotting his red hair, she forced her way through the crowd to join him at his side. With his attention drawn toward the center of the gathering he didn't notice her arrival. Gretchen reached up and touched his arm and asked, "Father, what's wrong? He looked down at her with a sad look in his face and then returned his attention back toward the direction of the mill. Following his line of sight, Gretchen gasped when she saw the local constable loading a shackled Johnny into a wagon.

Chapter 11

"**J**ohnny!" Gretchen cried out. Leaving her father's side, she tried to run to him as the mass of people blocked her way. In a panic she searched for an unobstructed path. Unsuccessful, Gretchen watched the wagon start to pull away with Johnny in the back. Angry workers shouted obscenities at the arrested man as the cart started to ascend the trail heading north. Gretchen silently stood as the wagon and its prisoner traveled farther up the trail. Johnny sat with his head down like a defeated man. "Oh Johnny, what did you do?" Gretchen asked under her breath.

Turning, she found her father a few yards away talking to the job foreman. The young girl rushed up to him. "Father, what's going on? Why did they arrest Johnny?"

"Gretchen, go home and we will talk tonight," her father replied.

"Father, just tell me," she pleaded.

"Damn it, child! I said home, NOW!" her father commanded.

With tears in her eyes, Gretchen spun and ran home to the cabin. In all her 14 years, her father had never talked to her that way and the pain in her heart was crushing. *Even at his worst at night he had never yelled at me.* Her mind replayed everything that had just transpired. Heartbroken, she dashed into the cabin and flung herself onto her bed. Gretchen curled up and hugged her pillow.

Sounds from the sobbing girl filled the cabin. Outside her window, a lone figure stood like a statue and listened to

Gretchen's pain. A smile of pleasure appeared on his face as he turned and swaggered away.

Later that evening Gretchen's father returned home and entered her room. Sitting on the edge of her bed he laid a hand on her shoulder. "Gretchen, my Flower. I'm so sorry I raised my voice to you, but the time was not right for me to explain everything." She lay there, unmoving with tears still in her eyes. "I know you and Esther are friends with the young Mr. Bowman, but he got caught doing something very bad, and I'm just glad you didn't get pulled into it."

Gretchen shot up from her bed, "Father, what did he do?" Gretchen begged for answers. "Please tell me!"

He reached and took her hand in his. "Mr. Bowman has been stealing from the company. Last night he broke into a cabin and stole items, and this morning he didn't show up for his shift. His co-workers went to his cabin to check on him and that's when the items were found." She stared at the floor as her father continued, "The authorities figured that he was trying to move them out this morning before anyone suspected his wrongdoing. Evidently he didn't realize the rain went south last night so he would be needed today for work." He squeezed her hand in reassurance.

"What's going to happen to him?"

"Well, his family does have money so they should be able to afford a good legal consultant. So maybe a few years of incarceration, but it's something not to worry yourself about," her father told her. Mr. Gill stood, patted her head and left her room. "I'll give you some privacy if you need it. I love you,

Gretchen, and I'm sorry about losing my temper. I'm going for a walk. Will you be alright?"

"Yes, Papa, and I love you, too." She sat on her bed and thought about everything that Johnny had told her this morning and most disappointing was about how he lied to her about not working today. "Esther, please come home soon. I need you," Gretchen pleaded out to the empty cabin.

Thunder echoed again in the valley waking Gretchen from her slumber. Lying in bed she turned her attention to the window to see the flashing lightning, as the rain danced on the roof of the cabin with a rhythmic sound. Replaying the earlier events, she tried to find a reason for Johnny to be stealing. Sleep started to creep up on her again when a flash of distant lightning revealed a man's figure standing outside her window. Gretchen screamed and jumped out of bed and ran to the corner of her small room. Her father was abruptly awakened by the panicked sounds of his daughter. Still feeling the effects of the alcohol he had drunk earlier that evening, he stumbled out of his bed to make his way into her room.

"Gretchen, what's wrong?" he asked.

"Someone's outside my window!" Gretchen frantically wailed. Grabbing his pistol and a lantern, he rushed out the door. Concerned for his safety, Gretchen followed her father outside. Mr. Gill circled the cabin exterior searching for the trespasser. He went to the back side of the cabin with his gun drawn. With no sign of a voyeur, Mr. Gill lowered his lantern to inspect the ground only to find half-eaten apple slices near her window. Returning to the front of the cabin he encountered a small stationery figure. He raised his lantern to reveal a shivering wet Gretchen.

"There's no one there, my little one," he reassured his daughter. "The only thing I found was apple slices that someone must have dropped earlier." Gretchen's knees buckled upon hearing the last part of what her father said.

"Apple slices?" she asked with a wide-eyed look.

"Yes, half-eaten apple slices. Why?" he questioned. She brought her hand to her mouth and rushed back inside. "Gretchen, what's wrong?" Mr. Gill called out as he followed her retreat. She sat on her father's bed with panic in her eyes. Mr. Gill sat next to her and pulled her close. "It's alright, Flower, I'm here. What's wrong?" he asked again. A clearly shaken Gretchen explained in a whimpering voice about what had happened at Conkle's Mill the other day. Not saying a word, he held her tightly as she cried herself to sleep in his arms. He gently laid her in his bed and stood up and went to his desk. Tomorrow he planned to add more patrols in the evenings and be on the watch for this possible defiler. Mr. Gill rubbed his head, *Something strange is going on around here and I am going to find out,* he thought.

Gretchen awakened in the morning to find herself alone in the cabin. When she was up and moving, she discovered a note on her father's desk awaiting her.

Dear Gretchen,

I wanted to let you sleep and get some rest. I am headed up to Lock 41 early this morning to discuss adding patrols at night and to make sure that man doesn't come anywhere near you, my flower.

Leave your chores for tomorrow, enjoy your day and read and relax. Do not travel about unattended.

It rained all night and the creek will be rising, so please be aware of the water.

Love you, precious Daughter

Gretchen smiled and held the letter to her chest. In all of her 14 years of life she had never gotten a letter from her father and now this simple piece of paper held the love of a father for his daughter. Gretchen carefully folded the paper and took it to her room. After her first few steps she could sense something did not feel right down below. Gretchen lifted her dress to find out that her journey to womanhood had begun. In shock she cried out, "Esther, please come home soon. I need you now more than ever!"

Almost every day for the whole week the rain came which slowed the work on the canal and finally the wet conditions brought progress to a standstill. Gretchen spent most of the time reading books and lying in bed fighting with unfamiliar cramps that she would have to deal with monthly now that she had become a woman.

Gretchen's father had added more patrols which made her feel safe for the first time since she had seen the mysterious shadow. Finally, one morning she awoke to the joyous vision of sunlight shining through her window. Gretchen leapt from her bed to welcome that long and forgotten friend. Her face lit up with jubilation as she could see a beautiful light blue cloudless sky. She quickly dressed and ran outside. Gretchen's ears were met with the sounds of a loud raging river replacing the sounds of the normally calmly flowing watercourse. Taking her shoes off and picking up her dress, she waded through the puddles of water left by the week-long deluge. Stopping and staring at her reflection in the standing water, Gretchen's thoughts went to Esther. *With the rain finally ended she should be on her way home soon.* That happy notion brought a big smile to her face.

"Gretchen?" A voice came from behind her and she turned to see Jake standing near her cabin.

"I wanted to stop by and check on you and make sure you're alright after what happened with Johnny and all that," Jake told her as he placed a concerned hand on her shoulder.

"I'm fine. I was shocked at first. I really thought I knew him but after thinking about it, I actually only knew him for a month. I know everyone has their secrets and his secrets are for him to tell. I'm sure he had reasons for doing what he did, but that's something he has to answer to God about. What about you? He was your childhood friend. How are you coping?" Gretchen asked the young man.

"Honestly, Gretchen, I'm not surprised, he is …, was... a friend, but I've always felt there was something about him that couldn't be trusted. Did he tell you that he stole my betrothed from me? I was to marry Florence, but he went to her family and convinced them that she should marry him." Jake lowered his head and turned away from her.

"Oh, I had no idea." Gretchen placed a hand on his shoulder in consolation.

"He took so much from me, and he was my brother, not by blood, but still my brother, so I forgave him. That's what brothers do," Jake told Gretchen while still facing away from her view, as he spun his tale of woe to her.

"You're a stronger and better man than he, Jake," she reassured him.

"Gretchen, I'm going to go now. I just wanted to stop by and check in on you and also to let you know there are good people still left in the world and we are not all like Johnny." Jake turned and gave her a quick awkward hug and walked away from her. She stood there. No words were said, but none were needed. Jake held his head down as he walked away. *Knight to king's three,* he thought.

Gretchen watched Jake disappear around the corner of another cabin. Even though she didn't trust him, her heart felt sad for him. She went back into the cabin to start her morning chores. With the ending of the rain and her cramps being gone for this month, Gretchen smiled and thought, *Today's going to be the start of a new, excitingly unpredictable passage into my womanhood.*

Chapter 12

The next morning Gretchen awoke to her father's voice.

"Gretchen, I'm leaving. Don't forget your chores. By the way, I will be home late tonight. Make sure the firewood is stacked and the ashes emptied from the fireplace."

"Yes, Papa. I'll come by and see you this afternoon when I'm finished," she told him as he headed off to the work site. She felt so alive. Springing out of bed, she thought, *Today is going to be beautiful, sun's out, humidity's down, and Esther will be home soon!* She dressed and started her chores with a smile adorning her face while she worked. With her work completed, the carefree girl hurried out the cabin door and headed to Lock 41.

Watching Gretchen travel down the path, the night voyeur turned back towards her cabin. Satisfied that no eyes were upon him, he quickly entered the Gill's homestead then reemerged 20 minutes later. "Now all I have to do is wait," he told himself as he attached a note to the door.

The trip to Lock 41 was magical to Gretchen today. New plants had sprung to life after all the rain and budding flowers would soon be painting the valley with their pallets of colors. She had spent an hour visiting her father and watching the men work. She heard a few of them talking about Johnny, but they changed the subject when they saw her.

She decided to head back to the cabin to wait for Esther's arrival. Excitement filled her heart. It had been almost two weeks now since she had seen her friend. So much had happened and she knew that Esther would want every detail. Gretchen skipped around the corner of her cabin to be greeted by a note attached to the door. She took it down and looked around, confused. *It's addressed to me, that's very odd. Shouldn't it be for Father? Wonder if it's from Esther?* With her mind swirling with confusion, she opened the letter written on canal letterhead.

> *Dearest Gretchen,*
>
> *Please meet me downstream at the location I drew out at the bottom of this letter. I am innocent. I did not do what I'm being accused of. I wish I could see you there, but I must be careful, whoever put those things in my cabin is still in Sprucevale.*
>
> *I only know that I can trust you, I need your help to clear my name. Don't tell anyone, as of right now, everyone is a suspect.*
>
> *Forever yours my love*
> *Johnny*

Gretchen's heart skipped a beat. She knew deep down inside that Johnny was innocent and now she had no doubt. She carefully studied the map drawn out on the bottom. She folded the paper and ran to the creek following the directions on the map. "He wrote 'forever yours my love,'" Gretchen repeated to herself as her heart pounded faster. *Love, he loves me.* She rationalized, *the wedding must have been called off because of the accusations, so that means we can be together. Nothing can be in the way for us now and I can let myself fall completely for him!*

84

Navigating along the creek, Gretchen finally found the clearing that was marked on the map.

"Johnny, I'm here," Gretchen called out. She turned and looked all around, but there was no sign of him anywhere. "Johnny?" she called out again, but this time the sound of sloshing footsteps approaching could be heard. A figure stepped out from behind a tree. Elated, Gretchen started to run up, but stopped quickly after realizing the man was not Johnny.

"Afternoon, Miss Gill, I'm glad you found my letter," he greeted the young woman.

Gretchen stopped dead in her tracks. "Where's Johnny?" she asked angrily.

"Well, most likely he's still locked up trying to figure out who set him up. I'm sure you're asking the same thing. So let me help you. I did," he boasted.

"Why would you do something like that, you're supposed to be his friend, Jake?" Confused, Gretchen angrily asked while trying to read his expression.

"Friend! Far from it. I was his. He was never mine. That bastard got everything. He always got the prettiest girl, the best jobs. Growing up, all I heard was how great Johnny was. Well, thanks to me, he's going to be known forever as a thief, and now I'm going to get everything I deserve. The job, the woman, it's all mine. When I go home, people will brag about me," Jake replied with a triumphant smirk across his face.

"You can't do that. I will tell my father and he will stop you. I always knew there was something wrong with you, and if you touch me, I'll scream, and the patrol will hear me! So, you better just tell the truth and turn yourself in and maybe they will give you mercy," Gretchen defiantly advised him.

"Gretchen, Gretchen, Gretchen, no one will hear you. We are downstream from everyone, and thanks to the extra rain we have just had, the rapids here will easily drown out any shouting you decide you need to do," Jake smugly boasted, knowing the trap had been sprung.

Fear suddenly crept into her mind. *Oh no. He's right, no one will hear me because of the noise from the creek and no one is patrolling this area because there is no work being done downstream yet.* Gretchen started to back away from Jake.

"So, Gretchen, are you ready for a little talk?" Jake walked up to a tree and leaned back against it. "Things are going to change around here from now on. First off, you will tell no one of what I told you. See, remember I told you that I'm good with coins? Well, I adjusted the company books and took some extra money and secretly hid it in your father's cabin. Not to worry, no one will ever know it's missing unless I happen to point it out and they find Mr. Gill in possession of a large number of coins hidden in his cabin. As I see it, Johnny most likely will get a couple of years for small trinkets and tools. Imagine what they would do to your father, a well-respected engineer, for stealing a small fortune." Gretchen swallowed hard and fearful tears started to rise to her eyes as she remained unmoving and silent.

"Second, you are going to end your friendship with Esther. No longer will you talk or spend time with her. She is mine and you are not welcome in her life. Nod if you understand, little girl." Gretchen gave a small nod with tears streaming down her cheeks. "I don't care how you do it, but when she comes back, you will end your friendship with her," Jake told her with authority in his voice.

Gretchen's mind was racing trying to comprehend. *How did everything end up this way? I have no choice but to agree with what he wants. I can't lose Father, too. Esther would understand that I have to protect Father.*

"Oh, one more thing," Jake added as she looked at him with pain and confusion in her eyes.

"Remove your clothes!"

Chapter 13

Gretchen stared blankly at Jake.

"You heard me, take off your clothes." Jake sternly ordered her to comply.

Without thinking she replied with an angry, "No!" Jake pushed off the tree and started to approach Gretchen.

"Gretchen, let me explain this to you. We can do this one of two ways." Jake produced a knife. "I can just cut your throat and dump your body in the water and be done with you. No more Gretchen and of course, they will never know it was me, because thanks to Johnny telling me about what happened at the mill and a few carefully placed apple slices outside your window. Well, you know, who they are going to think killed poor little Gretchen. And trust me, for a while that was my plan, because you have vexed me one too many times. But after the first time I watched you bathe from outside your window and saw the treasures you possess; I've decided to give you a second option. So, I'm going to give you a few minutes to decide," Jake advised her.

It was him outside of my window! Dear God, this man is pure evil, and if I don't do this..., please someone help me! Gretchen fell to her knees. "Please, Jake, don't do this, please! I beg of you," she cried out, but Jake just stood there enjoying her tears and anguish.

"Well, Gretchen, what's it going to be? Do I turn Gretchen into fish food or..." Jake stopped mid-sentence as Gretchen stood up and started to undo the buttons on her dress. "Very good, my little unplucked flower, me and you are going to have such good times. Oh, I forgot to mention, this will not be a one-time thing, you will be at my beck and call for my earthly desires," he informed her.

Gretchen removed her dress and stood there in her petticoat. She stared directly into his eyes in defiance. *If I'm to give into this man's desire and be used this way, I WILL NOT GIVE HIM THE PLEASURE OF ANY MORE OF MY TEARS,* Gretchen thought to herself. Jake walked around her, first touching her hair to bring it to his nose, then came around to face her.

"Such pride, it's almost a shame to break this little filly," Jake told himself, but found himself taken aback when he looked into her eyes. In all of his life he had never seen what pure hatred looked like, but now he saw it staring directly at him. Jake instinctively pulled his knife up for protection. Quickly he regained his composure and noticed the pendant that adorned Gretchen's neck, "Well, what do we have here?" Jake curiously asked.

Gretchen reached up and grabbed her father's gift in her hand and clutched it close to her chest. "You demanded my body for your sick twisted game, and I agreed for fear of forfeiting my life, so take what pleasure you want with my body. I will not stop you, but if you try to possess this pendant, I will fight you with all I have and never submit." Gretchen's words struck fear into Jake. *Never had anyone stood up to him like that before.* Jake backed away a few steps as his mind tried to comprehend what was happening here. The power and strength of Gretchen's words were not something he thought would happen. *Where was the crying little girl he had fantasized about?*

Gretchen saw the doubt in his eyes and watched as the knife dropped from his hand as he backed away. Quickly retrieving the knife from the ground, knowing that she had created an opening, she pushed on. Standing her ground, she reached down to gather up her dress and started to back away from Jake, who was now battling confusion in his mind.

She turned and started to run when she heard a thud and felt a sharp pain on the back of her head, dropping her to the ground. With bewilderment about what had happened, Gretchen rolled over to make sense of what had just occurred. Looking up she realized Jake was now on top of her. He reached down to grab her necklace and the instinct to live and protect the gift took over as she reached up with her hands and dug her fingernails deep into Jake's flesh, forcing him to reel back in pain. Jake covered his cheeks for a second, then withdrew his hand to see it covered with crimson.

"You bitch!" Jake cried out as he swung down with all his might. The impact caused Gretchen to see dots of white. She lay there in a daze, the taste of blood in her mouth. Reaching up to defend herself, another blow came down upon her, followed by another and yet another. Gretchen fought to see her attacker's next move, but she found her vision was not right. She saw red but then blackness quickly came. She struggled to regain consciousness, but another blow soon followed, preventing any attempt to move.

She felt a burning sensation from around her neck. *"No,"* she screamed inside her head but was unable to make her body obey. Strange sounds of clothes ripping and other unknown motions with him laying upon her perplexed her. She felt herself slipping back to the black abyss again.

"Gretchen, are you still with me?" Jake asked as he kicked his unconscious victim. "If you can hear me, I can't wait for our next time."

Jake's words found their way into Gretchen's subconscious, stirring her awake. Trying to roll over to her side, she tried to spit out the blood only to find her mouth would not cooperate correctly. She pushed the blood out of her mouth with her tongue. *Why aren't my side teeth in a straight line?* She lay there with her tongue exploring the now crooked jawline. Gretchen struggled to move, only to find her body not completely responding the way it should. Attempting to lift her head to look around, she found everything was blurry with dark spots in her vision. She made her way onto her stomach and started crawling to the water. Gretchen found herself back in darkness. *I just need to rest for a bit, and I'll be fine.* Her body went limp as her head fell to the ground.

The evening sun was starting to hang low when a coach bearing two passengers arrived at the Hale's cabin. Esther stepped out of her father's carriage. "Your KittyKat is home, everyone!" Esther announced to the valley.

"Esther, please, is that any way a lady is expected to act?" Mr. Hale reprimanded his daughter.

"Sorry, Father, I'll get our belongings into the house."
Quickly, she unloaded the carriage and kissed her father's
cheek.

She grabbed a small package and hastened to Gretchen's.
Esther's excitement built as she neared the Gill cabin, clutching
firmly onto the gift she had gotten for Gretchen, *I can't wait to
give her this book of poems I got for her.* Her eager thoughts
were soon replaced with fear as she could see the look of
concern in Mr. Gill's face when she ran into the open door of
the crowded cabin. "Mr. Gill? What's wrong? Where's
Gretchen?"

Chapter 14

Gretchen finally stirred as the sun started to sink lower on the horizon. Lying face down in the dirt, she felt the tightness and swelling from her facial injuries along with a burning numbness pulsing through her jaw. "Help me," Gretchen attempted to cry out, but a sharp shooting pain flashed through her jaw as she clenched her teeth in misery. *Why did this happen to me?* Waiting for the agony to pass, her tongue repeatedly returned to the gaps in her teeth. Fresh bloody drool flowed from her mouth onto the ground. *Please someone, help me. I don't want to die here.*

The young teen reached out with her arms and struggled to pull herself closer to the water inch by inch. Pausing to judge the distance to the creek she slowly brought her hand to her face and tried to rub her eyes to clear her vision. White hot pain burned through her cheek; tears instantly formed but she fought through it. Gathering her strength, she slowed her breathing to help calm herself. *Think Gretchen, think. When Father gets home he will know something's wrong because he knows I'm always there to greet him.*

Resting, Gretchen assessed her injuries. Her left eye was swollen shut and her vision in her right eye was clear but blurry at times. *So tired. I just want to lay here and go to sleep.* She fought the urge. *Stay calm,* she told herself again. Breathing slowly and remaining completely still, she felt the first bite of a mosquito on her lower back. The unclad girl was now aware most of her clothing was ripped and tattered, leaving the exposed skin for insects to feed on her. Losing the battle to stay awake, Gretchen laid her face on the ground again and fell unconscious once more.

Like lightning bugs at night, lights from lanterns flickered creating spots in the deep black woods around Sprucevale. A chorus of, "GRETCHEN!" echoed through the valley. Every worker joined in the search for the missing young woman whose smile brought happiness to all the laborers who knew her from the work site.

Esther, unable to sit and wait with the other women of the settlement, decided to follow her intuition and journey downstream from Sprucevale. Fearing that Gretchen may have fallen into the high swift water and washed down the creek, Esther searched the shoreline for any signs of her love.

"Any luck?" Esther turned to find Jake standing behind her holding a bloody cloth to his cheek.

"Nothing yet. What happened to you? Why are you bleeding?"

"Ummm, I don't know these woods well, even in the daylight. Sooooo, I lost my footing and fell into a briar bush, and I'm all scratched up, but I'll be fine. I'm more worried about Gretchen. Maybe we should head back upstream, maybe we missed her," Jake suggested as he motioned for her to follow him.

"Look where you want, I'm going this way," Esther informed him as she turned and continued downstream towards the sound of fast-moving water.

Gretchen lay unmoving as she stared at the darkness of the night. The combination of the full moon and her unclear vision created dancing shadows in her limited field of vision. *At least I'm not alone now with my mind creating dark witnesses of my death.*

Welcoming the enveloping release, Gretchen slowly started to rest her eyes for the last time as a strange dim light broke through the darkness of the woods. Shimmering in the distance, reflections flickered in Gretchen's eye. *Is it an angel coming to take me to be with my mother?* Gretchen thought as the light became more brilliant. *God, I'm ready. Please come and take away this pain. Mother, I'm coming to be in your arms again.*

Gretchen heard a voice and a beautiful angel with black hair emerged from the light.

"GRETCHEN!" Esther screamed. "Oh my God, Gretchen. Everyone, she's over here!" Esther rushed forward and quickly rolled the half-naked girl into her lap. Tenderly cradling her, she looked down and recoiled from the sight of Gretchen's battered face. Her left eye was completely swollen shut and her nose now pointed to the right. Esther's tears streamed down her cheeks. With trembling fingers, she reached to touch Gretchen's swollen jawline now covered with mud and dried gore. Gretchen opened her eye and tried to speak, but no words followed as she coughed up a mouth full of clotted and fresh blood.

"SOMEBODY HELP HER!" Esther screamed louder as she rocked Gretchen in her arms. "Please, somebody help her," she sobbed. Holding a lantern, Jake turned and gloated, then joined in yelling for help. Moving closer to marvel at his achievement he was surprised to have his light reveal the paper addressed to Gretchen lying on the ground. Jake stepped closer to Esther and quickly picked up the evidence while Esther's attention was on Gretchen. *I am truly blessed.* Jake thought. *I completely forgot about the note. If Esther would have listened to me and headed back upstream someone else might have found it. I have a guardian angel looking out for me.* Jake turned away to hide his grin.

Esther pulled off her full skirt to cover Gretchen's nudity. "Gretchen, stay with me, please, stay with me," Esther implored. One by one the workers hurried to the place of her pleading and screaming.

Gretchen stared at her angel who was holding her. *How beautiful this angel is*, she thought as strange voices started to surround her. Feeling the angels lift her off the ground, she pleaded to them in her head, M*other, I want to be with my mother.* Ascending into the air she turned her head to the right to see the devil inches from her face. *No, no, Devil be gone! Why am I seeing* the *devil, not my mother?* Gretchen stared as the devil transformed into a smiling Jake, the very man that had done atrocities to her. Gretchen fought and thrashed but quickly blacked out again in the arms of her personal angels.

Anxious workers and their families, who had gathered outside the Gill cabin to await news of the missing girl, moved aside as Mr. Gill directed the group of men carrying his daughter to his bed. More and more continued to arrive as they heard that Gretchen had been found.

"Where in the hell is the doctor?" Mr. Gill shouted out to the crowd of people.

A distraught Esther shoved her way through the bystanders. Blood stains covered the front of her petticoat as she knelt on the floor and held Gretchen's hand. Fresh tears fell from Esther's eyes as she held the hand of her unconscious love. "You're home now. It will be alright."

"Esther, did she say who did this? Did she say anything?" Mr. Gill asked his daughter's rescuer.

"No sir, she tried, I think she tried to say something but started coughing from the blood in her mouth," she responded, sobbing.

"Everyone move back," came a voice from the door of the cabin. A small older man strode through the gathering of people. "Damn it, I said move!" The company doctor quickly examined Gretchen's shattered face and reached for his bag. "I need someone to ride to East Liverpool and tell Dr. Jackson that we have a young woman here in dire need and someone to ride to New Lisbon and tell Dr. Green the same thing." Every man in the cabin volunteered to go, but quickly the job fell to a few men that ran to their nearby horses and left at lightning speed.

"Mr. Gill, I need to be honest with you. Your daughter is in very bad shape and I've seen men not survive this type of head trauma. But it must be something to do with that damn Irish blood in you and her," he advised without taking his attention away from his patient. "All I'm going to be able to do is give her some tears of the poppy to help with the pain."

Mr. Gill nodded, as Gretchen moaned with small cries of anguish as the doctor administered the medication. He walked around the bed to where Esther was sitting on the floor. "Miss Hale, why don't you go freshen up, she's going to be sleeping for a while."

"No, I can't leave her. This is my fault. I left and I wasn't here to protect her. I will not leave her side ever again!" she emphatically replied.

"Esther, just take a few minutes," Mr. Gill said calmly. "I'll be right here; she will be alright. The medicine will cause her to sleep for hours, and rest is what she needs right now. When one of the two doctors arrives you can be here with her." His voice soothed her a lot and Esther agreed and went outside to gather her thoughts. The concerned workers who had been outside waiting for news gave Esther a wide berth for her to walk and be alone.

Looking skyward, "Whoever did this will pay, I swear to you, God, I will kill them myself!" Esther vowed with fists clenched in rage.

Chapter 15

Gretchen drifted off to sleep and found herself falling through a kaleidoscope of images as one came into focus in front of her. It was a beautiful meadow of flowers on a small incline under a radiant spring sky. Gretchen walked through the knee-high blooms mixed with field grass. With outstretched hands she let the tips of her fingers brush the natural spray of blossoms.

"It's so beautiful," the young girl said. As she shielded her eyes to survey the moorland in the hazy distance, she saw a figure. Walking forward, she could see a woman with blonde hair bent over. *Is she picking flowers?* Gretchen thought as she watched the lady stand up and give a welcoming wave to her. The friendly pretty woman was wearing a red shawl and an amber dress with a linen apron that billowed with the slight breeze of the day. Squinting, she seemed to recall this vision in her eyes, *that looks like,*

'MOTHER!" The word erupted from her soul. The young girl ran like the wind to the woman. Gretchen saw her long curly blonde hair that helped highlight her striking slate blue eyes. "MOTHER!" she cried out again as she closed into her mother's hugs. Gretchen buried her face into her mother's gardening apron as she held fast to her. "Mother, I've missed you so," she sobbed as she felt the lady stroke her hair.

"Shhh, my bonny lass, everything will be just fine," Mrs. Gill told her daughter. Gretchen looked up to see her mother who was smiling at her.

"I've missed you so much, Mother. Can we just stay here and never leave?" Gretchen asked.

"Not yet, Gretchen, it is not your time. But when you come back I will be here at this very spot waiting for you," her mother told her.

Gretchen held both arms around her mother's waist. "I love you, Mother," Gretchen said with tears in her eyes.

White hot pain pulled Gretchen from the dream and her mother's loving arms, as the newly arrived Dr. Jackson examined her jaw. "Everyone, clear out of this room! I need to complete my examination on this poor child," the doctor commanded the onlookers. Then he looked toward Gretchen's father. "I'm sorry, Mr. Gill, for her privacy, I need to ask you to step out, too. This is not going to be pleasant with this kind of trauma. So please, Mr. Gill." Gretchen's father agreed to the doctor's argument and closed the cabin door on his way out. Outside, Mr. Gill found a quiet but frantic Esther shifting from foot to foot. Walking up to the young girl, he put his arm around her and drew her in close. She laid her head against his side and started sobbing again.

"Please tell me she's going to be alright?" she sobbingly asked Mr. Gill.

"Honestly, I don't know, but my little girl is tough and if anyone can pull through this, she would be the one. She's a fighter, just like her mother," he told the weeping girl, then pulled her close for a comforting hug.

Mr. Gill thought to himself, *I can't break down like I have before. Gretchen needs me to be strong for her.* He then looked down at his daughter's dear companion. *Gretchen is so lucky to have such a caring and good friend.* Esther raised her eyes to see Mr. Gill looking at her with a slight smile on his face and a tear starting to flow down his cheek. She collapsed back into his chest and began to weep once more.

About an hour later the doctor opened the door to the cabin and called to Mr. Gill. Esther rushed up to the door as he was almost inside.

"Can I please go sit by her side?" Esther asked. Mr. Gill looked to the doctor for a reply, at which the doctor nodded. She rushed to the side of her dear companion who was lost in sleep again. Taking Gretchen's hand into her own, she lowered her cheek to rest against the union of hands. The muffled voices of the doctor and Mr. Gill broke through the silence, making their way to Esther's ears.

"Mr. Gill, I'm going to be straight with you." The doctor waited for his consideration. "She is very lucky to be alive. She's in very bad shape. This is going to be a long road to recovery." Pausing to affirm his attention, he continued. "Beside a broken nose, which is the least of our worries, her jaw is broken, and there is possibly a broken orbital socket. I must be honest with you, she will possibly lose her left eye. It is full of blood, and if we are able to save it, she will most likely be blind on that side. She received major head trauma, so swelling of the brain is also a possibility. She is covered in mosquito bites. So, swamp fever is something of a concern now. Mr. Gill, there is something else." The doctor lowered his voice.

Esther got up and moved closer to hear the hushed voices. "We may have to worry about pregnancy. There are signs of an assault on your daughter. I'm sorry to have to tell you that," the doctor finished. Mr. Gill grasped for his chair as his strength left his legs. He lowered his head as he started to cry silently to himself.

"What needs to be done, Doctor?" Mr. Gill asked while staring at the floor.

"We are going to have to wire your daughter's jaw closed to help set the jawbone. Removal of a few teeth will be required so the poor girl can get nutrition. I can give her morphine for the pain, but you may want to not be here when we do the procedure." Gretchen's father looked up at the doctor while processing what had just been told to him.

"No, I'm going to be here for her. She needs me here," Mr. Gill informed the doctor.

"I understand. I'll send my assistant to gather everything that will be needed from the carriage, and we will start," the doctor explained. Esther quickly returned to Gretchen's side as Mr. Gill and the physician re-entered the room.

"Esther, can you wait outside?" Mr. Gill asked her as they made their way around Gretchen.

"Can I please stay? She needs us, both of us," she pleaded.

"We may need her to help hold down your daughter," came the response from the doctor as he laid out the instruments that he would be needing.

The doctor looked at the young unconscious patient. "I'm sorry, Miss Gill, but the morphine is only going to help a little," he apologized as he began his work. Screams from the cabin echoed all throughout the valley, stirring nightmarish images for the workers sitting outside of the Gills' cabin. Most sat there quietly with their heads down while wiping tears away. Others prayed for Gretchen to pass out from the pain and give her some mercy from the torture she must be going through.

Jake sat next to a tree reveling in his beautiful tragedy that he alone had created. With his head hung low to help mask the cruel smile that covered his face, he thought, *I did this. Me, I've taken everything that she loves away from her, and she has no one left but me. There is no way anyone could survive the hell that Gretchen is going through. Doubt she makes it through the night. You did good, Jake Birchham, you have done really well. Looks like checkmate.* Jake sat up and leaned back on the tree. He put his hands behind his neck and closed his eyes to enjoy his victory.

The morning sun stretched its rays of light into the somber Sprucevale valley as it tried to wash away the gloom of the previous night. Many men still hung around the cabin hoping for good news on the fate of their sunshine of the valley, their beloved Gretchen.

Pastor Hale made his way into the cabin to find the doctor finishing his wrapping of Gretchen's head. Esther sat in a chair next to the patient and Mr. Gill stood next to her.

"Pastor Hale, good to see you again. I just wish it were under better circumstances," Dr. Jackson said, while extending a hand.

"How is she?" Pastor Hale asked the doctor.

"Well, we got the jaw set and stitched closed and she had a lot of contusions that needed a few stitches. Gretchen is one strong, young woman. Most men would have passed out from the pain, but unfortunately, she stayed conscious through it all, poor child. But she truly is a fighter," the doctor told the pastor as he was packing up his medical bag. "Now she's in God's hands to help heal physically. Mentally, that remains to be seen. This is hard for anyone, but for a 14-year-old child, this is going to be hell for her to live with," the doctor told the gentlemen in the cabin. He turned and walked into the next room, then sat down for the first time since he had arrived last night and closed his eyes.

"Mr. Gill, do they have a suspect?" the pastor asked.

Clenching his fist, the man, whose daughter had just walked through hellfire twice, answered, "Yes, the former engineer." Esther sat quietly next to her Gretchen. Her mind plotted her actions against the beast that did this to her love.

Chapter 16

After a long night of not leaving Gretchen's side, Esther was convinced by her father to return to their home. As he accompanied her, the pastor offered words of assurance. "Esther, our heavenly Father will serve rightful justice to the sinful malefactor and his acts of evil. This is all in God's hands!" he exclaimed while placing a hand of comfort on her arm. Heartbroken, Esther pulled away from his reach. *I don't need a pastor. Don't act like you care. You knew about what happened to my love, and you couldn't even take time from your sleep to check on her well-being last night. This is for ME to do, no one else, not even God! I will go out tonight and find him and make him pay,* she thought with an accelerating burning rage.

Once back at their cabin she withdrew immediately to her room. She worked out a plan of vengeance. Then she sat and waited for nightfall. Tears rolled down her cheeks as she remembered the heart-wrenching events from last night. She had tried to assist and give Gretchen strength, but all she had been able to do was cry and feel useless in Gretchen's time of need. The sounds of her love screaming out in pain would never leave her ears. Esther was comforted by the knowledge she was sleeping now. The doctor told them she would most likely be out for a day after the trauma. Esther looked out of her window and saw that the sun was starting to set. *As soon as Father is asleep. I'm going to find him; I know his route. He is a creature of habit.* Esther pulled out his knife and decided it was time to return it to its rightful owner.

That night near the stream a few miles away, an overweight older man sat watching the fire and reminiscing about the strange blonde child, almost white-haired girl who showed up the other night. *Oh, what a night, and she didn't even want money,* he thought to himself and chuckled. Staring into the crackling flames he heard a strange noise which came from the woods where shadows recoiled.

"Who's there? Come out!" he shouted into the darkness with a pistol in hand. A slender form in a white chemise emerged from the shadows of the darkness. "Stop right there! Who are you and what the hell do you want?" he yelled. Squinting at the lustrous figure he made out that it was the pastor's daughter standing before him. "Esther, stay right there. I don't want no problems with you. I'm sorry about what happened at the mill. It was all just in fun," he nervously explained to her. Esther moved slowly up to him.

"I came to say I'm sorry, myself. I overreacted and I was jealous of Gretchen because you didn't have that kind of interest in me that day," she told him as she started to undo her straps. "I remembered when you would flirt with me when you were the engineer. I was too young to know what you wanted, and now that I'm older, I want you to do all those things to me that you talked about when I walked by," Esther told him as her attire fell from her body. Light from the fire danced across her nude shape as she seductively approached him. Stumbling back a few feet, he regained his composure and smiled as he placed the pistol down, then sauntered up to meet her and admire her physique. Esther reached up and touched his face. He pulled her in close and started groping her body. She whispered in his ear, "Did you have fun with that girl last night?"

Thoughts of the white-haired girl at his camp last night popped into his head. "Oh yeah, she was a wild one, a real screamer." He tried to kiss Esther's mouth when a sharp pain erupted from his back. Recoiling, he reached with both hands to find the purpose of the pain. Esther jumped onto him and continued to thrust the knife into the man. She stabbed madly at his neck as blood sprayed out into the air. When he fell to the ground, Esther jumped on top of him and thrust the knife over and over again into the man's chest. Panting and sweating, she stood up and wiped her face with her blood-smeared hand. The effect was like an artist's brush painting broad strokes of bloody gore across her cheeks and mouth. The man lay there motionless except for his chest that would rise and bloody air bubbles would appear with a strange sound of breathing. Esther tilted her head to the left and stood there fascinated by the sight, until finally, there was no more movement. Gracefully she walked to the creek and carefully waded out into the moonlit water to bathe herself. She kneeled in the stream to cleanse her soul of her sin by taking cupped hands of water and letting it gently cascade upon herself. A sense of calmness and accomplishment spread into Esther's heart as she purified her body in the moonlight. Returning to the corpse, Esther looked down and said, "I hope you rot in hell!" She dressed, then began her euphoric walk home knowing she had avenged Gretchen.

Esther arrived home just before sunrise and quietly entered the house to get a few hours of sleep. Thoughts of the justice she had served swam through her head. *For Gretchen, I would do anything. When I wake up I will take the book I bought and read it to her.* She decided that it was going to be her job to take care of her angel. *No man will ever come between me and my Gretchen.* Esther drifted off to sleep as the sun broke over the horizon.

Gretchen slowly opened her one eye and looked around the room to see her father sleeping in the chair next to the bed. Her head hurt so much, but it was nothing compared to the pain the doctor had put her through. She had tried to be strong and brave. Gretchen reached for her father's hand to stir him awake. Panic struck at the sight of her bare wrist, *My God! Esther's bracelet. It's gone. Esther will be so hurt with my carelessness!* she thought to herself.

"Good morning, my Flower," her father said with a comforting smile, pulling Gretchen back from her panic only to see the pain in his eyes. He gently squeezed her hand, "How are you feeling?" She tried to reply before she remembered the night of horrors she had had and instead just gave a small nod. "The doctor said you're going to have headaches and pain from your jaw. He left some poppy tears here for me to give you if you need some." Gretchen nodded and gave his hand a quick squeeze. "Do you think you're well enough for me to leave for a short bit? I have to meet with the village officials. I won't be long." Gretchen squeezed his hand harder as her body went rigid. Her father observed terror in her eye.

"Don't be afraid, little one," he quickly reassured her. "There is a trusted company employee standing watch."

After being reassured of her safety and nodding "yes," a disheartened and apprehensive Gretchen closed her eyes and listened to her father leave.

"Hello, my dear flower." Startled, Gretchen opened her eye to a voice but not that of her father. "Oh, my dear Gretchen, you're tougher than I thought. So good to know that you are going to recover," Jake tormented her. "It was so convenient of the company to ask me to be your guard today, so we could have some uninterrupted time together." Fear gripped Gretchen to where she could not move. He walked up to her and placed his hand on her knee and moved up her leg. "Oh, poor dear Gretchen, the innocent darling of Sprucevale, what decent man would want a used, ugly child like you now?" Jake moved his hand all the way up to her pelvic area. "However, since I picked this flower, it's mine to have whenever I want. So, you get better soon, I have already asked for some night guard duty. I plan many night visits."

A tear escaped down Gretchen's cheek as she defiantly moved her leg away from his touch. He violently grabbed her thigh and with an ugly smile on his face he told her, "Stop it! You are not the innocent doe, who when cornered, violently fights for her life. You are nothing but my personal tail and any man who is willing to pay me for it. But as ugly as you are going to be, you will probably have to pay them to get a man's attention at the bawdy house." Gretchen glared in anger as she weighed the truth of his lies. "I want to remind you of our agreement because it would be a shame if something happened to your father. Well, time for me to change my face and get back to guard duty, but I am looking forward to many nights of satisfying you."

Turning to walk out the cabin he heard rustling from the direction of her bed. As Jake turned back to see what Gretchen was doing, he was stunned to see she was sitting up and glaring at him with foul disdain. She pointed to him and held up her hand with her thumb and pointer finger indicating two inches and then pointed to his manhood. He couldn't see her mouth for the wrapping, but he knew she was smiling. Anger built as he clenched his fist and stomped towards her bed.

"Gretchen?" Esther called out as she walked into the cabin to see Jake standing next to her. "Oh, hello, Jake." She greeted him with a mystified look on her face. Aghast at Esther's intrusion, Jake quickly stepped back from the bedside.

"Ummm, Hello, Esther. I heard her stir and I was worried, so I stepped in to check on her," he stammered. "Well, I'd better get going. Get well soon, Gretchen. We all miss you," Jake declared as he rushed out to the cabin's porch.

"Oh, my sweet Gretchen, I am so happy to see you are awake," Esther exclaimed as she hurried to sit next to her. Emoting sadness rather than joy, Gretchen reached to hold her friend's hand. "My poor Gretchen, what's wrong? Are you in much pain?" Esther looked down as she felt Gretchen's grip tighten on her hand.

"Oh my, you lost the bracelet. Don't fret, it will be fine. I can make another for you." Gretchen shook her head "No." Esther said, "I know you are concerned about the effects of your injuries, but you will always be a beautiful angel to me. Your recovery is more important to me than anything." Gretchen pulled Esther's hand close to her chest. "If something happened to you I don't know what I would do," Esther cried with tears streaming down her face. "I love you, Gretchen," she told her. Gretchen continued to firmly grip her hand. Esther stood up and gently kissed the bandages that covered Gretchen's mouth, then watched as Gretchen drifted off to sleep.

Gretchen awoke a few hours later and relief showed in her eye as she discovered Esther sitting beside her still holding her hand.

"I brought you a gift from Hanna's General Store in New Lisbon." she said as she pulled out a package and started to untie the bundle. She could tell by her body movement that Gretchen was excited to see what she had gotten her. She took the book out of its coarse brown paper wrap and showed it to her. "It's a book of poems by," Esther turned the book back to her and read, "Edger Allan Poe."

Gretchen's sad eye lit up and she clapped her hands. "You know of him?" Esther asked.
The injured girl nodded her head quickly. "Well, I'm going to read this whole book to you, starting right now." She began to read the first poem, "*A Dream Within a Dream. /Take this kiss upon the brow! /And, in parting from you now, /Thus much…*"
Upon overhearing Mr. Gill talking to the local constable, Esther stopped reading and told Gretchen, "I'll be right back." She tiptoed to near the open cabin door to eavesdrop.

"Well, all we know is, he was scheduled to be in Clarkson yesterday, but he never showed up. We had people there waiting, so he may be on the run. But we will find him," the constable told him. Gretchen's father thanked the man and started back to the cabin as Esther quickly returned to the bedside and resumed reading to her. Mr. Gill walked in to check on Gretchen as he found Esther reading. With a wave and a smile, he turned to leave the two young ladies to enjoy each other's company.

Esther continued to read aloud:

I stand amid the roar
Of a surf-tormented shore,
And I hold within my hand
Grains of the golden sand--
How few! yet how they creep
Through my fingers to the deep,
While I weep--while I weep!
O God! can I not grasp
Them with a tighter clasp?

Gretchen folded her hands and closed her eyes as she listened to her friend's soothing voice.

Chapter 17

A few days had passed when Esther heard her father talking outside of the Gills' cabin.

"Yes, he's been dead for a couple of days. They are thinking possibly a bear attack," Pastor Hale told Gretchen's father. "He'd been torn apart, and many scavengers have been feeding on the body," he continued. "I have to discuss something with you on a sensitive matter," Pastor Hale stated. "Please, let me explain everything before you reply."

Gretchen's father nodded in acknowledgement.

"Sprucevale is a very small hamlet. With the canal running directly through the village, this area will benefit from its commerce. We, the leaders of the community, will be looking into attracting people and businesses to come to our little settlement. We would like to offer our condolences for what happened to your daughter. It was a terrible act of violence. Since justice has been dealt out by God, we hope you understand, we will not keep a record of this tragic event. And we would like your corroboration in this matter and will gladly compensate you for any inconvenience." Pastor Hale extended a hand to Mr. Gill as he waited for an answer.

"This is something, last week, I would have had to say, 'let me think about it,' but after the news you have just presented to me, I want this to be over and have my daughter recover. So, I will agree, but let me inform you and the other council members that I don't want anyone coming down and asking Gretchen for a statement about the events when she's finally able to speak in a few months. Do we have an understanding?" Mr. Gill firmly stated.

With a cock of his head, "Thou hast made a wise decision." Pastor Hale smiled in agreement and the men shook hands.

Esther returned to sit by Gretchen's side. Her patient softly moaned as she watched her sleep. *She's still in a lot of pain but her spirits are improving each day. And soon we will be able to spend the days walking through the woods and being in love,* Esther thought. As she imagined her red haired bonnie and herself holding hands walking along the creek, her heart skipped a beat.

Later that evening as the sun was setting, Esther was walking home when a familiar voice called out her name.

"How's Gretchen doing?" Jake asked, running up to her.

"She is doing better. The doctor is coming by tomorrow to change her wraps, so we will know more then," Esther replied with a hint of sadness in her voice.

"What's wrong, Esther? You don't seem yourself. Is there something I can help you with?"

"It's something I don't know how to say, and I'm not sure how to…" she drifted off, unable to find the right words.

"Just say it. We can straighten the words up after you release what is bothering you," Jake encouraged, while placing a comforting hand on her shoulder.

Esther took a deep breath and walked a few steps before suddenly pivoting, and announcing out loud, "I'm in love with Gretchen!"

"Oh, but you are both .... I didn't expect that," he stuttered as he was taken aback. *Damn it. No! She's meant to be mine. I am the one she is to love, me, no one else, me! This ruins everything,* Jake thought while his mind wrestled with the unexpected news.

"And I want to spend the rest of my life with her," Esther finally confided in him.

"How does Gretchen feel about this? And what about your father? Is he going to approve?" he questioned her.

"I'm not sure, but I think she feels the same way. And, as for my father, I know Gretchen and I are both women, but as an adult, I shall not need his approval for a Boston wedding," Esther stated strongly. "I'm just not sure how to approach Gretchen with this. I'm afraid she might reject my love."

"Esther, I think you should tell her," he said, all the while, thinking to himself, *Come on Jake, think, what can I say? I need a plan. How can I stop this revolting union?* "When you were gone, all she did was talk about you. I think you should take a chance," he said as he plotted his next move in his game. "If you want, I can go with you for support," Jake suggested.

Esther walked a few paces from Jake as she considered his offer. *He's right. I need to do this. I know she loves me, and once everyone sees how happy we are, I know our union will be blessed. I'm going to do it. Tomorrow!*

"Thank you for being such a selfless person. I am so glad I trusted you with my secret." She smiled and hugged him. Deciding that tomorrow would be the day that she professed her true feelings to Gretchen, she ran home with new vigor from Jake's moral strength.

The next day Esther and Jake serenely walked together to see Gretchen.

Jake asked her, "You are awfully quiet today. Are you feeling apprehensive? Are you thinking of changing your mind?"

Esther shook her head, "No."

"So, how many times last night did you rehearse what you would say today?"

Esther nervously smiled and jokingly responded, "More times than you have fleas on your head."

Jake laughed. "You are strong, Esther. I know you can do this," he said, encouragingly.

"Thank you for being a shoulder in my time of need."

"I will always be here for you, Esther. But if you don't mind, I'll wait outside. I'm not big into doctors and stuff like that makes my stomach turn," Jake told her.

She took a deep breath and continued into the cabin to find Dr. Jackson had removed Gretchen's bandages. Esther watched as the doctor examined her injuries. The left side of her face still resembled a painter's much-used palette of splotched colors under her eyes, left cheek, and along her jaw line.

Thank you, Dr. Frankenstein for removing my wraps, as she reached up to feel her battered face. *I wonder if I look like his Creature now,* Gretchen thought.

"Still a little tender?" Dr. Jackson asked the injured girl. She replied with a small nod. "Well, you're going to have that, but I think we can leave most of the bandages off."

Thank God, I don't have to put up with those hot itching things, Gretchen happily thought.

"But I want to keep your left eye patched for now, to keep the sunlight out and help the healing," he told Gretchen with his head tilted as he looked closely at her wounds. "Are you able to eat through the extracted teeth or do we need to remove a few more?"

Gretchen nodded. She excitedly waved "hello" to Esther as she caught sight of her best friend smiling in the back of the room.

"Well, my dear, I would have to say you are healing nicely. In four weeks we will see about removing the stitches and see how the jaw is healing. I bet you can't wait for a real meal," he chuckled, as he gently patted her leg and began to gather his instruments.

"Let me walk you to the door, Doctor," Mr. Gill stated as he led the way. Esther watched the two men leave as she heard a patting sound. Gretchen motioned for her to join her on the bed.

"How's everyone's favorite young lady?" Esther quickly turned, stood up, and greeted her father who was walking through the door. The pastor moved to stand next to Gretchen and graciously smiled down at her. "I wanted to stop by and offer a prayer and see if thou needest anything and offer Esther's service to do thine chores while thou art healing."

"Father! Thou dost not have to offer my services, as I plan to be her lady in waiting!" Esther retorted. Shocked, her father nervously laughed while opening his prayer book to read a passage.

After a short prayer, Pastor Hale announced, "I pray thee gets better soon. Don't exhaust my dear Esther as she has home chores she forgot this morning."

Esther nodded and rolled her eyes behind his back as he left the cabin. With that KittyKat gleam in her eyes, she returned to sit next to her friend. Gretchen acknowledged her adoring behavior in their own private language with a cat paw motion.

Giggling, she reached to stroke Gretchen's red hair. "We really need to wash you up and brush your hair," she said while softly touching her friend's cheek. Gretchen grasped Esther's hand as her eyes expressed an unspoken, "Thank you."

"Why don't I ask your father if I may clean you up. Would you like that?"

Gretchen nodded, "Yes."

"I will go ask," she said as she joyfully skipped out of the room.

Jake stood outside of the cabin listening through the open window as an evil grin spread across his face. *Everything is almost ready. Soon all of my planning is going to pay off. I was surprised to find out Esther was after Gretchen and not Johnny. Guess he really was innocent.* Jake laughed to himself as he thought he must truly be blessed with fate on his side.

Esther re-entered the room. "Are you ready to be my Gretchen again?" Her query was met with Gretchen's muffled happy sounds. Esther returned to her side with the pitcher, washbasin, and a fresh linen. She gently dabbed the moist washcloth onto the girl's bruised face. "I wonder if there is the beautiful girl I know under all this mess?" she murmured as she rinsed out the bloody fabric.

She carefully washed her face, removing the crusted brown dried blood. "I like taking care of you, Gretchen. You know that, don't you?"

Gretchen nodded as she reached up to squeeze Esther's arm.

She wiped the cloth along Gretchen's lips and looked her in the eye. "I love you," she said. "I'm sorry this happened to you, and I know it's my fault for not being here for you, but that will never happen again because I will protect you. I will never leave your side. You will be my life." Esther placed the cloth in the wash basin as she saw a tear in Gretchen's eye and a small smile on her face. Resting her hand on her cheek, Esther asked, "May I take care of you, Gretchen, forever?"

Gretchen reached up to touch the hand on her cheek and nodded, thinking, *Friends are always there for each other.*

She swept her thumb across Gretchen's lips. Looking deep into her eye, Esther drew herself in closer. "I love you, my precious Gretchen," she told her as her lips met Gretchen's.

"What the hell do you think you are doing? Get back away from my daughter!"

Esther turned to see Mr. Gill and her father standing in the doorway. Out of sight, Jake hid behind the door filled with self-satisfaction, smirking and proud of what he had just accomplished.

Chapter 18

"What? No, wait. You don't understand," she pleaded as he violently dragged her away from his daughter. As Esther struggled to escape his hold, Mr. Gill was successful in impeding her attempt to return to her love. She screamed, "I love her, and she loves me!"

"How dare you defile my little girl like that with your acts of perversion?" Mr. Gill screeched at Esther. She attempted to explain but was interrupted as Pastor Hale grabbed his daughter's arm and dragged her out the door.

"Damn it, Esther. What the hell are you thinking? Calm down and stifle thy mouth!" her father admonished her as she tried to escape his grip. Two nearby canal workers, upon hearing the ruckus, ran to help the pastor load the hysterical young woman into the Hale's carriage. Jake climbed in to restrain the flailing girl in his lap. Her father took the reins and quickly drove the horses away with inhuman screams echoing through the valley.

Mr. Gill sat next to Gretchen as she shook her head frantically at him. She tried to talk as her concerned parent gave her tears of the poppy to calm her. Gretchen slowly settled. Soon her eyes grew heavy and she drifted off to sleep. Mr. Gill sat there trying to figure out how something like this could have happened. *Thank God that Mr. Birchham came and told us that Gretchen needed us or we may have never known about Esther pining for my little flower.* He stood and leaned over to kiss his sleeping daughter's forehead. *That's strange, she feels warm. Must have been from the reprehensible actions of that tribade,* he thought to himself as he went to sit on the cabin porch. His thoughts were interrupted by the nuisance buzzing of a mosquito.

Jake helped the pastor get the hysterical Esther into the house, then took his leave. Angry voices escaped through the cabin walls as Jake stood outside. He leaned back to enjoy the loud impassioned debate which was the desired product of his actions.

"I will not accept this type of behavior in my house! I did not raise you to become the whore of Babylon!"

"Father, you don't understand! I love Gretchen and she loves me!" Esther insisted.

"I WILL NOT HAVE TALK OF LEWD BEHAVIOR WITH ANOTHER WOMAN IN MY HOUSE!" he commanded while slamming his fist onto a table. "It is sinful enough that thine own mother brought disgrace to our family by taking up with that white-haired harlot! My daughter will not be part of a Boston marriage as long as she wants to be my daughter."

"And that's the reason my own mother can't see me. Because she found a better lover with another woman and not you." Esther's statement was met with her father's backhand across her cheek. A warm burning sensation of pain shot through her face as her father pushed her into her room.

"Pray and beg for God's forgiveness. A woman shall not lie with a woman as she does a man!" He slammed the door shut.

Esther lay on the floor, heartbroken. "Please God, I can't lose her." Tears streamed down her face as she screamed and repeatedly pounded her fist into the floor.

Jake listened to the sounds of Esther's heart breaking and turned to walk away with his own heart beating with excitement that everything was working out perfectly.

Days passed as Esther lay in bed. A rhythmic tapping at her window did not register in her sad mind. Numb from the pain of her broken heart she felt nothing else, not even the dried crusted blood on her clenched hands crossed on her chest. Unblinking eyes stared into space as the insistent knocking on the window finally pulled her attention away from the ceiling. "Gretchen!" she cried out. With her heart racing, Esther sprang from her bed and reached the window. Esther's heart sank as she saw Jake standing where her heart was hoping to find her Gretchen with a handful of flowers and a beaming face. He stood outside of her window with a helpful expression. Esther turned and fell to the floor. New tears streamed down her cheeks.

"Esther, please, don't cry. I've come to help."

Wiping away her tears, "How can you help me?" Esther hopelessly replied while staring blankly straight ahead. "I've lost her forever."

"Well, I was thinking that maybe you could write her letters of endearment and I could deliver them to her everyday, so she knows your love for her is unwavering. She could write back." Esther's eyes brightened as she wiped the tears from her face and sprang up to the window. "You would do that for us?" Esther asked. Jake nodded.

"She's 14 and you're 16, right?" he asked. Esther nodded."

"Next year under law she could leave with you. You two could run away together," he informed her as her heart found new life.

"Oh, Jake, you have made me so happy. I can't believe you're willing to help us. You are truly an angel."

"Why don't you write me something and I'll take it to her today. I'll make sure her father doesn't discover anything about this," Jake assured her.

Esther's face lit up as she rushed away to start writing her confession to the young girl. She collected her stationery and quill and sitting at the writing desk, wiping away tears of happiness, she began her declaration of love.

My Dearest Gretchen,
Just a few words for you, my love. You are my whole world. You are the sunshine in the morning, you are the stars at night. I'm sorry that we can't be together right now, but I will wait on you forever. You are the owner of my heart and soul. Please get better soon because nothing can keep us apart. Even if I die tomorrow, I will search the afterlife for your hand. You give my life meaning. Jake has agreed to help us, my love. So, we can trust him and help bring our separate hearts into one heartbeat forever. I will be awaiting your reply with passion in my heart for you, my love, my forever.

Your immortal beloved,
Esther

She sealed the letter and with shaking hands passed it through the window to Jake.

"I will take this to her in the afternoon, as soon as her father leaves to check the work progress," Jake replied as he put Esther's hopes and dreams in his pocket.

Esther watched from her window as her confidant carried her heart to her love. She turned away after Jake had left her view. With new optimism she jumped on her bed with excitement. *Gretchen, my love, my beautiful Gretchen,* she thought in her head. Looking down, Esther noticed the fresh cuts of release on her legs as her dress rose with her jubilation. She tilted her head and studied them; fresh dried blood partially covered older scars. She reached under the bed for her sharp shiny friend. *The directions of the cuts are not uniform. We need to fix that,* she thought. Esther created new cuts and studied them like a sculptor. Blood streamed down the sides of her leg as she admired her new artwork.

Jake spent the rest of the week between his work and playing his part in his master plan. Receiving a note daily from Esther, he would tell her that he had handed it to Gretchen, but she was unable to correspond back because of the ever-watching eye of her father. Esther's notes became more frantic, professing her love, but Jake would always make up some excuse for why Gretchen couldn't write back. *Everything was working out perfectly,* he thought. As Jake completed the monthly inventory ledgers the door to his office opened.

"Mr. Birchham, could I have a moment of your time?" Mr. Gill asked. "I'm sorry you had to witness that terrible incident last week."

He nodded. "It was an unfortunate event for everyone involved."

"In my concern for my daughter, I may have overreacted in the moment. Thinking more clearly, I have faith in my daughter's decisions in life."

Jake nodded.

"The last few days, Gretchen has not been doing well. We think she may have swamp fever," Mr. Gill spoke as his voice broke a little. "The doctor stopped by yesterday and thinks Gretchen should be able to pull through." Mr. Gill stopped to regain his composure before speaking again. "Gretchen wants Esther by her side if the worst comes," the shaken father told Jake as he wiped the tears from his cheeks. "She wrote a letter for Esther. I would give it to her father, but with his deep devotion to God and religious principles, I am not sure he would deliver it. I know she is your friend, and I would be grateful if you could pass it on to her."

"I will make sure she gets this. I know she has been very worried about Gretchen but can't come to face her from the embarrassment she caused everyone," Jake told Mr. Gill as he received the letter. "But I will talk to Esther and encourage her to go to see her dearest friend."

"Thank you," Mr. Gill replied.

After finishing the daily log, Jake returned to his cabin. He pulled a locked case from underneath his bed. A small wooden box contained all of Esther's written hopes and dreams and the pendant he had taken as a memento of his night with Gretchen. Jake closed his eyes and leaned his head back, gripping the pendant in his hand, a rush of memories flooded his mind as he relived his conquest. Employees' voices from outside his cabin heading home from work, interrupted his reverie. He quickly wrapped the keepsake and put the unopened letter from Gretchen in the wooden chest and replaced it back under his bed.

Frustrated from weeks of unanswered letters, Esther paced in front of her cabin waiting on Jake's return. For the last three weeks she had written daily to Gretchen. Each time he would say she read it but was unable to reply because of her father's presence. Somewhere deep inside Esther, a small voice started to make itself heard, "*Jake is not being truthful to you. He's not your friend,*" Esther tried to push those thoughts away, but they grew with every passing day. It all started a few weeks ago when, strangely, Jake had befriended her father, much to her surprise. "*He's supposed to be your friend, not your father's,*" the small voice admonished. She could not figure out how they had become so close and why they spent so many hours together. "*Remember, Eve thought it was an innocent serpent,*" the small voice apprised her.

"Where is he?" Esther asked in exasperation as she sat on the porch. Shielding her eyes, she looked up at the bright noon sun. "Why is he taking so long?" Looking down the trail she saw two shimmering silhouettes coming towards her. Esther's heart skipped a beat as she recognized Jake. But her excitement was short-lived as she was able to make out that her father was walking with him. Jake stepped back as Mr. Hale walked up to Esther and hugged her tightly. "Father, did something happen? What's wrong?" she asked in puzzlement from her father's embrace.

"Dearest Esther, I'm sorry to inform thee. Gretchen passed away last night, so it's time for thee to be strong and pray to God for forgiveness."

Chapter 19

"**W**HAT?" Esther screamed as she pushed back from her father's clutch.

"Esther, she's gone. She had swamp fever and she succumbed to it sometime during the night," he coldly told her as she frantically tried to free herself.

"NO, NO, NO, that can't be. You're lying. You would say anything to keep us apart," Esther wailed at her father.

"It's true, Esther. He's not lying. Gretchen's gone," Jake told Esther while trying to comfort her.

Breaking loose, she fell to the ground and started pounding her head with her hands balled up in fists. "She can't be gone!" she cried out as tears streamed down her face. After repeatedly pounding her head in self-destruction, she suddenly stopped and stood up holding her head in her hands. She primmed her dress and straightened her hair.

In this moment of clarity, she announced, "I have to see her, I have to." She turned to leave the two men to see Gretchen for herself.

"They're lying to you. It is not true. They would say anything to keep you away from her," the small voice reaffirmed her suspicions. "I'm coming to free you, Gretchen!" Esther promised as she ran toward the cabin.

Esther hid near the neighboring building as she observed Dr. Jackson consoling Mr. Gill on the porch. The doctor put his arm around him and walked him away from the cabin. Esther waited for the right moment to go inside to see Gretchen. Once inside, Esther placed the locking board up against the door. She turned towards the room she knew Gretchen would be in. She tried to move but stood there frozen. *Please be alive,* she thought. *This can't be the end of our beginning.* Esther took a deep breath and walked into the room. A blanket covered a small body lying on the bed. "Gretchen, I'm here," Esther cheerfully spoke as she approached the bed. Tears streamed down her face as she pulled the blanket down. "Gretchen," she stroked Gretchen's hair, "Just sleeping, that's all. You'll wake up soon. You will be so happy to see me." Esther sat on the bed and held Gretchen to her bosom. "Please, my love, wake up. It's KittyKat. Please just wake up, you can't go without me." Esther cradled Gretchen's body close and rocked back and forth with her. She heard banging on the door as voices called out her name. Esther kissed Gretchen's lips while shutting out the voices of the men trying to get through the cabin door. *She is so cold. I must keep her warm.* Esther climbed into bed next to her, pulling the blankets up to cover both of them.

"Soon you will wake up and be right as rain. We can go sit on my rock, watch the workers finish Lock 41, hold hands and walk the stream. Gretchen, we have so much to do together now. You just have to wake up. Please, my love, just wake up." Esther's tears fell from her face onto Gretchen's hair as she laid her head against her. "I love you, Gretchen," Esther tearfully told her as she stroked her cheek.

Hearing a loud crash with the door giving way to the weight of the men from the outside, Esther held tightly to her endlessly sleeping love as the men grabbed at her.

"No, don't touch me!" Esther screamed as they pulled her away from Gretchen's body. She held strong, refusing to let go, even as Gretchen's body was pulled to the floor with her. Esther screamed as the men pounded on her arms, finally breaking her grip.

"Please get her out of here," a horrified Mr. Gill yelled at the men as they fought to get the distraught young woman out of the cabin. Once outside, other workers helped with the flailing girl. A gathering of people stood outside as a restrained, defeated Esther was escorted off the porch by the men and Dr. Jackson.

"She will be alright. There is a place in New Lisbon that can help," Dr. Jackson assured Pastor Hale upon seeing him approach. "She is suffering from hysteria, I've seen it many times before," the physician told the pastor as the workers loaded her into his carriage. "There are many new treatments that will help her cope with the loss that she's feeling now," he reassured her father. Esther screamed and thrashed about as some of the workers bound her in the doctor's transport.

Pastor Hale stood in shock as they pulled away with Esther still screaming Gretchen's name. *Why, Esther, did thou have to bring shame to thy family? Thy mother did enough damage,* Pastor Hale thought. Slowly he walked up to Mr. Gill who was being consoled by Jake as well as leaders of the community.

"Mr. Gill, we would like to offer our condolences. Your daughter was special to everyone here and we will help you anyway we can," one of the leaders spoke. Mr. Gill stood in silence just looking out to the stream. He had no more tears to cry.

"Before I came to America, I had a beautiful wife and daughter. Now, in less than a year, I have lost everything." He did not move or look at anyone as he walked a few feet then turned."Gretchen loved the area where Lock 41 is being built. So, you want to help. Lock 41 shall be called Gretchen's Lock in honor of my daughter. I am not asking. I am telling you. I want to give her a place to rest in the lock until my contract is complete. Then I'm taking her home. I want to be done with this God-forsaken place." Not waiting for a response, he turned and walked back into the cabin to be with his daughter.

The word of God should help in his time of need, thought Pastor Hale as he started to walk to the cabin.

Stopping him, Jake placed his hand on his shoulder and suggested, "It's best to just give him some time with his daughter."

"You're right, and after the shame Esther has brought to our two families, I doubt he will ever speak to me again," the pastor said, lowering his head. Both men said nothing as they walked away from the cabin and headed to the pastor's house.

* * *

The sun shone down on the valley the day of Gretchen's burial. Mr. Gill stood strong as they laid Gretchen into her crypt on the west side of the lock. Every man had worked extra shifts to make sure she had a place to repose. Gretchen's Lock had been completed well before schedule, built with the love every man had for the little ray of sunshine who would greet them every morning with a smile and a wave. The grieving father watched as each man paid his last respects to Gretchen by laying a flower on her casket.

"Miss Gretchen was a beautiful young lady. I'm so glad I had the honor to know her," a worker told Mr. Gill as he shook his hand. Mr. Gill had no words to say, no tears left to shed. First his wife; now his daughter; he was tired, he just wanted to go home.

As the sun started to set, the grieving father found himself alone standing at his daughter's grave. Looking out in the woods, he could now see why Gretchen loved this area so very much. She had told him many times about the music of nature. Mr. Gill closed his eyes and listened to the sounds of the soothing flow of the stream cascading over the rocks. Opening his eyes, he could see the trees waltzing in the wind to the melody of the songbirds and, yes, inhaling deeply, the scent of the flowers, all brought a certain peace. Out of the corner of his eye he caught a fleeting glimpse of rusty colored hair quickly disappearing into the woods.

"Gretchen?" Mr. Gill said, looking towards the tree line. *Did I really just see her?* He shook his head; *I'm just seeing things.* Mr. Gill turned and started back to the cabin. *A few more months for everything to be completed and I will be able to take my Gretchen back home,* he thought. Several images swam through his head, including the excitement of Gretchen and his wife on the last day before they came to the Americas, the joy of seeing Gretchen's smiling face as she brought in flowers to place on the table, the way she strengthened him in his time of need. Mr. Gill walked into his cabin. Not looking down as he closed the door behind him, he missed the single yellow flower lying in front of the cabin door.

Chapter 20

The afternoon sun shone down on a lonesome carriage as it pulled up to the Hale residence. Esther stepped out of the coach that had brought her home to the fanfare of one. A year had passed since Gretchen's tragic death. Things had changed since her incident. The canal was finished to the Ohio River and Mr. Gill had taken Gretchen home with him, leaving only memories of the once radiant flower. Even with the sun shining down on the peaceful valley, to Esther, it seemed not as bright as it was a year ago.

"Esther, you're home," Jake's voice rang out as he walked up to her. "I'm so happy to see you again," Jake smiled. "Your father wasn't able to get away from a church meeting, so I wanted to be here for you." Jake offered a hug to her, but Esther just walked past him.

"I would like to be alone," Esther informed him as she headed to the canal. She had to find the memories, before they would be lost forever. Picking flowers along the path, Esther made her way to the place where she and her beloved had once shared a blanket, which was now called Gretchen's Lock.

"I miss you so much. No matter what they did to me, I would never let go of you in my heart," Esther said softly. She stood next to the sunken earth which for a short time had held Gretchen's casket in its cold embrace. Esther refused to cry but stood strong and silent. She would show no weakness ever again. She had endured the abuse and beatings that came when she cried at the hospital. She learned to bury her emotions and to behave how the doctors wanted her to. Now she was free from that prison and she would never go back. Inside she wept for her lost love, but never would she show that emotion to the world again.

Esther stood there remembering the day she and Gretchen sat on the blanket watching the workers begin work on Lock 41. A strange feeling of being watched crept up on Esther. "Hello, is someone there?" she called out. She quickly scouted the area for signs of spying eyes but heard only the sounds of the water and birds. Esther placed a bouquet of blue flowers on the ground and turned to head back home, but the feeling of being watched was burned into the back of her mind.

Walking into the Hale home, she observed her father reading documents at the table. Hearing her footsteps, he looked up and greeted her, "Esther, my child, welcome home." Pastor Hale stood and walked up to hug her. She stood emotionless, arms pressed to her sides, as her father pulled her in tight. "I am so glad to see thee." Esther's expression showed no sign of change, she just stared away from her father.

"I am glad to be back home, Father. Now that I am fixed and free of sin, things will be just fine," Esther told her father in a very monotone voice. "May I be excused to go to my room?"

"Why, yes, my dear, please, thou must be tired from thy journey. Go rest, and I will come get thee when dinner is ready in a few hours," he replied as he kissed Esther's cheek. She walked into her room and lay on her bed. A single tear escaped down her face as she turned towards the wall and closed her eyes. Outside, a single flower on the windowpane fell to the ground as a gust of wind knocked it from its resting place.

After a few months, Esther slowly adjusted to the routine of village life, never showing more than a submissive attitude to Jake or her father. Even though Jake came by every day to spend time with her she kept him at arm's length. She never let him see her true face, even when he attempted to comfort her.

"Esther, we all miss her," Jake told her as they walked together in front of the Hale's cabin.

"Thank you for being here for me, Jake. Please understand, even though I am trying, even with your help, it is still so hard for me to let go. I go to see her every day. I know she's not there, but I feel like she is still here. Sometimes I even …," Esther trailed off, not finishing her statement as Jake turned and faced her. He took both of her hands in his.

"I'm here for you, Esther. I'm not going to leave you. You have my heart," Jake declared.

"Father told me this morning he has something important to talk to me about tonight, so I hope you understand. I must take my leave of you to go spend some time with Gretchen before then." She gave him a quick hug and walked away.

"Hello, my love, I miss you so much," Esther said as she arrived at the lock with flowers in her hand. As she began to sit on the ground the feeling of being watched returned again. *Who is watching me?* Esther thought to herself. She scanned the area, but as always, no one could be found.

"It's a beautiful day, today, Gretchen. We should be sitting on my rock, just enjoying the sun on our faces and talking. Why did you have to leave me? Does God hate me that much?" Tears started running down Esther's cheeks. She started to wipe the tears away when a sound jolted her attention across the creek. Esther stared unceasingly at the area, *I know that sound came from over there, and I swear I saw a flash of reddish hair disappear behind that tree,* she thought to herself. Esther kept watching but then shook her head, *"You can't let people know you're seeing things. You can't go back there again,"* the small voice reminded her. Thoughts of the last year's living nightmare at the hands of the doctors flooded her mind. Esther stood trembling as she tried to push the thoughts away. "I'll see you tomorrow, Gretchen," she promised her love as she kneeled down to kiss the earth. Reluctantly, she began the journey home for the undesired meeting with her father. From behind a tree a small shadowy figure watched and reached out with a hand as Esther withdrew.

"Father, I am home," Esther announced as she walked into her family dwelling.

"We are in the dining room, Esther, please come and join us," her father's voice rang out.

Join US? Esther found the comment puzzling. *Why had he said join 'us' and not join 'me'?* Esther walked into the dining room to find Jake and her father conversing with each other.

"Esther, my child, please have a seat," her father told her. "Jake and I were just talking about the future of Sprucevale." Esther sat next to Jake as her father continued, "With work finished on the canal and that new investor from Cleveland bringing in that Old World money, this area will be bigger than

Pittsburgh if things go as planned." Pastor Hale smiled and raised his glass of whiskey towards Jake, then drank it.

"Esther, I have some matters we need to discuss." She sat there quietly listening to her father. "First, I have some exciting news." She sat up a little to pay more attention to him. "I received word they will be building a new church in Salem. It has been offered to me." He paused then continued. "I have decided to take it, so I shall be leaving at the end of the month."

Esther stood up and hugged her father. "I'm so happy for thee, Father. Shall I be joining thee there?"

"Esther, I shall be leaving this house to thee as a wedding gift."

"What? Wedding gift? What are you talking about?" Esther asked in puzzlement.

"Thou art getting married. Jake hath asked for thy hand in marriage and I have given my blessings," Esther's father proclaimed.

"No, I will not marry Jake!" Esther screamed back at her father.

"Thou shalt marry Jake and bring honor back to our family name!" Pastor Hale yelled. Silence filled the room as both father and daughter glared at each other. Clearing his throat and calming his voice, "Esther, I only want what's best for thee. Jake is earning a good living and he will be able to provide for thee. He is becoming a pillar of the community. With my departure, I will not be here to watch over thee and take care of thee. I love thee, Esther. Thou art my world and I am trusting Jake to take care of thee." Pastor Hale spoke while attempting to pull Esther into a hug.

"What! Thou lovest me?" Esther fired back at her father while pushing away from his embrace. "Thou canst stand there and sayest thou lovest me, after what I went through? I went through hell at that place. Every night I cried myself to sleep, just to wake up and face the morning in a steam room locked in a box! Where were thee, Father? Answer me! Let me help thee. Thou were not there. Then, if I was lucky, the workers wouldn't abuse me, but thou would not know about that because thou were not there. Every week I had to go through a hysteria massage in front of the physicians' colleagues and students, and now, thou carest about me! If thou only knew the shite I went through because thou lovest me so much," Esther screamed at her father as she turned around and ran out of the cabin.

Pastor Hale started to follow her when Jake stopped him. "Let me talk to her. Right now is the time for calmer heads." Pastor Hale nodded to him. Outside, Jake found Esther standing next to a tree just staring out into the woods. "Esther, are you alright?" He placed a hand on her arm.

Recoiling from his touch, Esther explained, "He just doesn't understand what I went through. I'm trying to be better, but everywhere I look, all I can think about is her. Now he tells me this. No offense to you, but I don't love you. I can never love you. I have no heart to give. How could you want that in your life, let alone a loveless marriage?" Esther asked Jake as her eyes fell to the ground.

"I miss her, too, Esther. I know that you don't love me, but maybe in time you will grow to love me. I still want you as my wife and I have enough love in my heart for both of us. Esther, let me take care of you. You will have my support and if you never love me, at least I can always be there for you as your friend." Jake pulled Esther into his arms and felt her walls crumble as she started to cry.

"Let it all out. I'm here for you and I will be strong for you always," he whispered into her ear.

"I will marry you," Esther sighed softly through her sobs. *Father has left me no choice in the matter. Jake understands my heart. He will be, foremost, my friend and always be there for me.*

Jake smiled as he held her close, but his attention was uneasy. *Why do I feel prying eyes upon me?* Jake thought to himself. Ever since Esther had returned he had felt the chills of an attentive gaze on him whenever he was near a wooded area. The feeling was something he could not shake off.

Chapter 21

"**H**ello, Gretchen," Esther greeted the empty resting area where her friend, her love, once lay. Esther adjusted her dress as she sat down and placed wildflowers on the newly growing grass next to the grave. "I'm sorry, I haven't been here in a while, but a lot of things have happened, and I want to tell you all about it." Esther lowered her head and closed her eyes as the sun peaked out from behind some dark clouds, shedding warmth on her face.

"Father left yesterday to be the pastor of a new church. He left our place to me as a wedding gift, can you believe that?" Esther paused like she was waiting for an answer. "Can you believe that your KittyKat is getting married? Yes, me, but it's not something that I want. It's Father who pushed me into it." Esther continued to recount the events that had taken place a few weeks ago. "Jake is a handsome man, gentle, kind, a hard worker, and I know he loves me. Even though I only consider him a friend, I'm sure that in time, I may grow to love him." As Esther finished her update to Gretchen, a cold chill suddenly enveloped her skin causing her to cross her arms for warmth.

"That's strange, the sun's still out and yet it suddenly got really cold," Esther said as she stood up while rubbing her arms together for heat. As she paced around the disturbed ground of Gretchen's former place of entombment, a movement caught her attention. *Something moved over behind that tree*, Esther told herself as she watched the area for signs of someone. *Why do I feel like someone is spying on me every time I come down here?* Esther started to look around for the source of the feeling, like a cat waiting on a mouse to appear. Ever since she had returned home, the impression of someone observing her while she visited Gretchen's Lock had become normal. Sometimes it was a warm feeling like the watchful eye of a parent, except for today. Today was different. It felt like pure evil was eating away at her soul. While keeping sight on the area where the movement had been, Esther quickly headed back to her home. She had spent many a day considering herself safe and peaceful as she walked through these woods alone. But today, she ran. She ran as fast as she could to create distance between her and the ominous evil that she felt.

Jake watched Esther run down the path from behind the tree where he had been shadowing her. *Stupid fool. She almost saw me. I have to start being more cautious.* Pushing his way through the low-lying shrubs, Jake began to follow her, waiting to ensure his movements did not alert Esther. He became suddenly aware of a strong burning sensation on his right forearm. "What the hell?" Jake quickly pulled up the sleeve of his shirt to expose the area of the burning feeling. Four small red parallel lines appeared on his forearm, "Did one of the branches scratch me?" He stood there in puzzlement. *I must have gone through some kind of ivy to get a reaction like that.* As he stood there examining the red lines a feeling of being stalked made the hair on the back of his neck rise. "Who's there?" Jake called out, looking around and waiting for a reply that never came.

Frustrated with not knowing who was watching him and the persistent burning on his arm, Jake swiftly made his way back to the Sprucevale settlement.

As soon as Jake arrived at the hamlet he was halted in his tracks. Upon hearing a long ago forgotten sound, he stopped. *What? That's Esther's laughter,* Jake said to himself. He stood in disbelief as Esther showed signs of happiness while she talked to two young men. *She hasn't laughed since last year. I am the one who should be bringing her joy!* Jake thought as anger at his impotence filled his heart. Her girlish giggle burned into his soul as he saw her enjoying the men's company. She touched the one's arm and smiled and threw her head back laughing with him. *This will not be allowed! Esther is mine! How dare she talk to another man, let alone share happiness with him!* Ducking behind a wagon to avoid being spotted, he watched Esther's moment of merriment. Clenching his fists, thoughts of teaching Esther a lesson seethed in his head. He would have to train her like the dog he had when he was younger. *That dog wouldn't listen, so beating the dog into submission was the final solution to teach it to behave. He didn't learn too many tricks but at the end of his life he did learn to play dead.* Jake smiled to himself as he remembered the power he felt when he beat the dog with a spade until it no longer moved. He would train Esther to be the perfect dog after they were married. She would have nowhere to go, no one to turn to, as her life of service to her master would begin.

Esther turned and waved goodbye to the young men and headed away. Jake waited until he knew that she was out of sight before approaching them.

"Hey, you two, what do you think you're doing talking to my betrothed?"

The two young males looked at Jake and then at each other. "What? You mean Esther?" one of the men asked Jake.

"Yes, Esther. You have no reason or right to talk to her and if I ever see you even looking her way, I will deliver a sound thrashing to the both of you." Jake stood there, fists at his side as the men looked at each other and started laughing.

"After you," the one young man said while bowing to the other and extending his arm out to his side.

Jake felt himself hit the ground followed by the taste of blood in his mouth. He tried to get his bearings as the young man lowered down to him and delivered another blow to his face, followed by another. A strange thought entered his mind as the man continued to hit him. *I wonder if this is what it felt like for Gretchen, the night I beat her into submission?* As quickly as it started, the beating stopped. Jake lay on the ground trying to make sense of his surroundings as he heard the young man tell him, "Lay there and bleed like the worthless gash you are!" Both men laughed as they walked away from him.

Anger boiled in Jake's blood as he tried to right himself. *This is Esther's fault. Why did she have to be such a lady of easy virtue?* Jake stood up, dusted himself off, then headed for Esther's place. But a strange voice came from his left side. He turned to look but no one was there. *I must have been hit too many times because I could have sworn I heard the sounds of a girl laughing.*

Esther sat in her father's rocking chair remembering the strange evil feeling of a presence near her earlier today. *I've felt like I was being watched before, but it was never the feeling of something villainous. Is someone following me?* These questions were left unanswered when she heard a sudden knock on the door. She was startled from the chair. "Who's there?" she called out. Getting no response, she started to open it a little when Jake's weight pushed it wide open as he fell unconscious to the cabin floor.

Jake wasn't sure how long he was out, but when he awoke the blood on his face was washed away and Esther was sitting next to him. He tried to sit up, but Esther, with a friendly hand, stopped him before he could move.

"What happened, Jake? Did you get robbed?"

"No," Jake replied. "I got into a fight with two men for their behavior was not very becoming of a gentleman."

Esther fought hard, but a smile slowly began to form on her face. Jake felt pride growing in his chest that he had made Esther proud of him, but that pride was short-lived as Esther's smile broke into laughter.

"Oh my, please forgive me. I'm sure you fought bravely for a smaller man that is as well-kept as yourself." Esther grinned as she reached down and touched his cheek. Fury started to build in Jake's soul as he swung up and slapped Esther across the face, knocking her backwards.

"I was defending your honor! You walk around Sprucevale acting like a dog in heat. You're to be my wife and you're making me look like the fool of Sprucevale!" Jake sat up and stared at Esther as she cowered on the floor.

Realizing his mistake, he rushed to her side, and declared, "Esther, I love you. I'm doing this all for you. I told you and I promised your father I would take care of you so when you go out, you're not to talk to anyone, do you understand?"

Esther nodded as tears flowed down her cheek. *Why do I have to be that way? I was wrong to laugh about him trying to fight. He was defending my honor.* "I'm sorry, Jake, you're right. I won't talk to anyone. It was wrong of me to be flirting with other men. I promise I'll try and do better." Esther rose to her knees next to Jake and hugged him and started crying into his chest.

He held her while stroking her hair. While holding onto her, an evil grin grew across his face. *Good doggy,* he thought. He was so proud of how this was working out. He now had Esther exactly where he wanted her. She was only for him. The sensation of fire scorching across his face caused Jake to recoil from her. Covering his left cheek, he screamed.

Frightened, Esther panicked. "Jake. What's wrong? What did I do?"

"My face. It's on fire!" he cried in agony.

Quickly she retrieved the wet cloth she had used earlier and handed it to him. "What's wrong?" Esther asked Jake as he covered the area that burned like red hot embers.

"I don't know. I was hugging you and crying with you when my face felt like it was on fire. It happened earlier today when I was…" He stopped himself before he let his spying on her slip out.

"Let me see," Esther told Jake as he removed the cloth. "There is a red mark on your cheek. It is not welted, but it is red," Esther told him out loud, but to herself she thought, *It's red, but strangely, it's shaped like a small handprint, like someone smacked him. I can even make out where the fingers landed.*

Chapter 22

Hours passed before the burning sensation on Jake's cheek had finally subsided. He decided it was time to head home from Esther's. Today's events had left him dumbfounded. He still felt the pain of the beating he had taken earlier but it had its worth. He now had Esther completely where he wanted her. She was starting to show signs of submission. She had nowhere to run and no one to turn to. He should have been happier, but twice today he had experienced something his mind could not comprehend. *It had to be some kind of ivy I got into. I must have touched it when I was looking at my arm and then at some point rubbed it on my cheek,* Jake thought as he neared his place.

Once inside, Jake took time looking in a mirror at his bruised face and surprisingly the red mark had all but disappeared. "That was odd," he said as he turned to pour a shot of whiskey. Jake guzzled the alcohol in hopes it would give him a good night's sleep. Lying in bed, thoughts of the future played in his mind. Soon he and Esther would be married. With the money he had taken, he would be able to buy some land and wait for the area to build up and sell it for a huge profit. He had befriended a few of the wealthier families in the area so his life of struggling would be over and with his submissive wife by his side the world would be his. He slowly drifted off to sleep.

"Oh my God, Fire! My skin's burning!" Jake shot up from his sleep and started tearing off his clothes. Reaching for the basin near his bed, he quickly covered his skin with the wash water to stop the searing pain his body was going through.

He halted when laughter erupted from nowhere in his cabin. *The sounds of a blithesome girl, How could that be? There's no one in my cabin but me, but the sounds came from in this room.* He hastily lit a candle to find the owner of the sound. Fighting back the pain he was feeling, Jake stopped still and listened, craning his ear and holding his breath. His eyes searched frantically.

"I must be hearing things," he proclaimed as he walked up to the mirror to inspect his body. Streaks of red covered his chest like a large cat's claws would leave, but no welts, just red lines. *Is that a handprint?* Jake moved closer to the mirror to look at the reflection of a strange mark on his neck.

"BASTARD!" A disembodied female voice rang out, cutting deep into his ear. Frightened, Jake stumbled backwards and fell into the chamber pot sitting on the floor. Bodily waste, which he had forgotten to empty the night before, flew into the air covering the helpless man. Female laughter erupted inside the cabin as he slid in the waste while trying to find his footing. Crawling out of the room, Jake experienced the feeling of red-hot pokers burning into his buttocks. He scrambled to his feet and ran naked and screaming out of the cabin.

The cabin door slammed shut, unassisted, after Jake made his exit. Standing outside, he could see the light from the candle illuminating the interior. He calmed his breathing while keeping a careful watch on the windows. A shadow moved inside and came to rest facing his position. He could tell it was a smaller person. *Who was in there? Why couldn't I see them?* Fear turned Jake's blood cold as the shadow dissipated from his view.

Am I seeing things? he frantically thought to himself. He stood there watching, then took a small step towards the cabin, having decided it was all in his imagination. Or was it a bad dream? "Just breathe. It's not real," he reaffirmed himself.

"JAKE!" the voice called out. Suddenly a burning feeling came to his cheek, the same place that last year, Gretchen had scratched him. "MY FLOWER!" bellowed in his ear. Jake stumbled and fell again. But this time he took off before he was able to stand. He tripped and now on all fours, Jake launched himself upright and ran faster than ever before. As the sound of a laughing female voice grew more distant in his ear, he sprinted to Esther's cabin.

She was almost asleep when she heard a loud banging.

"Esther! Help me! Please, let me in." *Why is Jake outside my door at this time of night?* That thought bounced around her head as she finally opened her door. Naked, Jake was lying against the outside of the house, his eyes wide with fear. His skin, for him, was more pale than usual. Esther reached down for him as he turned to grasp her in a tight hug like a child waking from a bad dream.

"Jake, what happened? Why are you naked?" Esther asked, but no audible answer came from his mouth. With much effort, she helped him to his feet and guided him to a chair next to the fireplace. Esther retrieved a blanket for him. He had not stopped shaking since she found him outside. She poured a glass of whiskey from the bottle her father had left and handed it to him.

"What happened? Where are your clothes? You're soaked in sweat and ...," Esther detected a strong stench ascending from Jake. Remaining silent about the smell, she wondered how that odor got there. He took the glass in his shaking hands and drank it down. His eyes stared at the flames erupting from the warming fire.

"Esther, I don't...There was...something...in my cabin...with me. I heard a voice...but no one was there. I think I'm going...mad." Jake raised both hands to his face and let out a whimper. Esther studied him for a few minutes as his words danced around in her thoughts.

"AND THEY SAY YOU'RE THE CRAZY ONE!" the small voice mocked her.

Hush! Esther told herself. "Jake, look at me. You were in a fight and got hit in the head who knows how many times. You could be seeing things because of that." Esther reached down and took his hand and continued, "When I was getting treated for my problem this last year, my doctor told me that being impacted in the head could cause a person to see things that were not there, so maybe that's what happened to you." Esther squeezed his hand for reassurance. "I will make up the bed in the guest room as you get cleaned up. I will lay out some clothes my father left behind. You can stay here tonight." She poured him another glass then made her way to the spare room.

In the morning she found him sitting by the fireplace. The Jake that Esther had agreed to marry was back to his happy loving self as he greeted her with a smile.

"Thank you, Esther, for helping me last night. I thought about what you said about getting hit in the head. I think you're right." Jake smiled at her. "Today is the last day of my day shift on the gate at the lock, so after today I'll be able to start spending more time with you."

Esther smiled and gave him a friendly hug. They had not been able to spend much time together and it would be nice to learn more about him since she would be married to him soon. Standing outside of her cabin, Jake kissed the back of her hand, then made his way to the lock. She started to think about what could possibly have happened last night. After she had taken care of a few things she would go to Jake's cabin to investigate for herself. *Something must have happened to him. I've never seen a man so scared in my life*, Esther thought to herself. She turned and headed back inside.

Much of the day had passed when Esther finally made her way to Jake's cabin. When she walked in she was dismayed to see it in complete disarray.

"What happened here last night?" Esther questioned while looking around. "Oh, God! Where is that awful odor coming from?" she asked aloud while pinching her nose shut. Moving to the windows, she pushed open the shutters, then proceeded to the bedroom. "This place really needs some fresh air," she said. As she opened the window and saw the fall leaves changing color, Esther thought to herself, *Maybe I should change, too.* She turned from the window to be greeted with the source of the terrible smell. *The damn fool must have been drunk last night and couldn't hit the chamber pot,* she thought. Feeling the need to make up for yesterday, she began searching for cleaning materials. "I really disappointed my fiancé yesterday with my alleycat actions …" Esther stopped dead in her movement. Gretchen had always called her that when she flirted with the young men.

"Oh, Gretchen, I miss you so much, my love." Esther let out a sad sigh, then resumed her task. She brought in fresh water and got down on her knees to start scrubbing when a small chest underneath Jake's bed caught her attention. Pulling out the small box from its hiding place she studied the wooden chest closely.

"Hmmm, wonder what Jake's hiding from you?" the small voice rang in the back of her head.

After jiggling the lock and shaking the box a few times to no avail, she decided that she should put it back and maybe it would be best to let sleeping dogs lie. *This is Jake's personal thing and I am being meddlesome.* Esther thought as she turned back to cleaning the floor. Rinsing the rag, a small click caught her attention. She turned quickly to find that the source of the sound was the box under the bed. She pulled it back out and to her amazement, the lock on the chest was unclasped.

She opened the case to find unopened letters, accounting books, a personal logbook, and a rolled piece of fabric. She opened the log to find that Jake had been keeping a journal of his life since coming to Sprucevale. Thumbing through the pages, she found an entry about how he set Johnny up and made it look like he was the one stealing. *"How could he do that to his friend? What kind of monster are you going to marry?"* the small voice asked. While replacing the journal and other books into the chest she turned her attention to the neatly folded parchments. "Wait, aren't these the letters I wrote to Gretchen that Jake said he had delivered?" The puzzled girl fanned through the neatly stacked letters when a letter with the name, *Esther*, caught her eyes. Suddenly, the sound of voices from outside the cabin alarmed her. Not wanting Jake to know she was looking through his personal belongings, she quickly gathered all the letters and the strange cloth packet and wrapped them in her apron. Replacing the unlocked chest under his bed, she headed rapidly out of the cabin. In her haste, she forgot to close the door. With confusing thoughts rolling in her mind, Esther walked with urgence to get home. Behind her, Jake's cabin door slowly closed as rain clouds started to approach from the south west.

Chapter 23

Esther sat at her table staring at the letter in front of her. Hesitating, with trembling hands, she picked it up and just held the letter addressed to her. She was filled with excitement and fear as she slowly unfolded the parchment.

"*Why did Jake have this when it was meant for you?*" asked the small voice. Tears streamed down her cheeks at the first sight of Gretchen's handwriting.

> *Dear Esther,*
> *I don't know where to begin, so I will just say what's in my heart. I miss you so much and I need you beside me. Dr. Jackson told me that I came down with swamp fever. Please don't worry. I will be fine and as soon as I'm better we will be sitting together on your rock, laughing and spending time together.*
> *I have something very important to tell you. This has to stay between me and you. DON'T TRUST JAKE. Please, I beg of you not to say anything to him, but please, please, please stay away from him.*
> *I know you must be full of questions, and I will explain everything to you in person. Just don't let him get close to you. He is not what you think he is. I wrote and explained to my father about our friendship, and explained everything between us, and he has agreed to let you be by my side.*

Esther, you are my best friend and I love you, too. I don't know if we love each other the same way right now, but no matter what, I need you to be here.

I'll be waiting for you, so please hurry.

Love, Gretchen
Ps. Miss you, my KittyKat

Esther held the letter to her heart as she laid her head on the table and cried. Outside the rain started to come down, and distant thunder rumbled, causing the shaken young woman to sit up. She began to inspect the letters she had sent to Gretchen. None were opened but all sealed like the day she sent them. "Why Jake? Why didn't you deliver them? You told me that you personally handed them to her!" she shouted out loud. Picking up the small cloth packet and holding it in her hands, she could feel an object enveloped in the fabric. With shaking fingers, Esther manipulated the cloth to discover the opening as Gretchen's pendant fell to the table. Staring in disbelief, Esther let out a blood curdling scream. "NOOOO!!!!" erupted, filling the empty house.

The rain continued through the night. Esther sat on her bed just staring at the walls of her room. Her mind was flooded with questions that only Jake could answer. Rage slowly drifted into her soul, but she would confront him tomorrow. Tonight, she rehearsed the questions in her head. Reaching under her bed to her hiding place, she grabbed her shiny sharp friend which would comfort her. But tonight, she didn't cut herself. Tonight, she grasped it for mental security. It held the answers to unasked questions.

The following day in the late afternoon, Esther made her way to Jake's cabin. The rain-soaked ground created pools of water that Esther ignored and walked right through. Never averting them, she kept her eyes locked ahead of her like a predator hunting prey. Arriving at his cabin, she knocked on the door.

"Esther, my love, it's so nice to see you. But you shouldn't have come, you'll be caught in the rain if the storm picks up again," Jake greeted her as he tried to pull her in for a loving hug. Jake hugged her but felt no return to the embrace.

"Esther, is everything alright? What's wrong?"

"Explain." With eyes burning into his soul, she held out the letter from Gretchen.

"What's that?" Jake replied while trying to keep a blank expression.

"EXPLAIN!" She screamed inches from his face.

His mind raced, *Oh my God. That's the letter from Gretchen! How did Esther find it? Calm yourself. Think. Did I leave the chest open? How much does she know?* Jake took the paper while proclaiming he had no knowledge of what the letter was.

"Well, maybe you could explain these instead." Esther threw the letters she had written to Gretchen into Jake's face. Raising his hands for protection, he stumbled back a little from the angry vixen.

"Please calm down. It's not what you think. Gretchen's father returned these to me after she passed away. I was going to return them to you. But after you came back, I didn't want to upset you since I thought you needed time to adjust."

Esther weighed his reasoning for having the letters. *Could he be telling the truth?* Esther thought about how plausible his answer was as a small voice countered, *They were still sealed, Remember what Gretchen said, 'Don't trust Jake.'*

"Jake, I really want to believe you, but your answer does not account for one thing." Jake stood stock still as she opened her hand.

"It was you, wasn't it?" Esther held out the pendant. "The night Gretchen was assaulted her pendant was taken by her attacker." Jake grabbed the pendant from her hand. Esther smacked him across the face. "You bastard!" she screamed at him. Esther was ready to hit him again when a blow to her face knocked her to the floor.

"I did it for us," Jake yelled at her. He drew back to strike her again, but when he reeled back the burning feeling returned to his neck. He could feel it this time, two invisible hands squeezing around his throat. Fighting through the pain, Jake screamed, "Get off me!" while swinging wildly in the air at his unseen assailant. Feeling a moment of release, he reached down, grabbed Esther, and dragged her bodily from the cabin. With great force, he threw her face first into the mud.

Coming up on all fours, reaching down deep, Esther, in a fit of rage, launched herself upon Jake. "YOU KILLED GRETCHEN!" she screamed.

Jake threw her aside. "You belong to me and you better start learning your place," he told her as he began repeatedly openhandedly smacking her in the head. Esther fought as her screaming turned to sobbing. In a moment of clarity, he stopped and pulled Esther to stand in front of him, realizing that someone might spot them. He brushed her hair aside and wiped the blood from her lips.

"Listen, you are going to be my wife. You should be grateful for everything I have done for you. I'm going to go to work and you are going to go home like a perfect wife. I will be by in the morning. You will start learning your place as a soon-to-be-married woman. That is, unless you want to end up like Gretchen," Jake told her with both hands rubbing up and down her arms. Satisfied that he had gotten through to her, he turned, with the pendant in hand, and headed off toward the canal. Low rumbling sounds could be heard in the distance as thunder made its presence known.

"The rain will be here soon. So, you better get home now, my love," Jake called back to her.

Walking to the canal, Jake ran through the events that had just transpired. *How had Esther found the letters? How did she unlock the chest?* But the one thing that really unnerved him was the feeling of the small hands on his throat. The burning feeling had faded, but the memory of the tightening hands was still there. Tomorrow he would talk to Esther. He would explain everything and guilt her into seeing that this was all her fault. One way or another she would be his wife. *When I'm done with her tomorrow, she will be on her knees offering the world to me.* Jake smiled at the thought. Tonight, he would prepare for everything that needed to be said tomorrow.

Esther stood outside of Jake's cabin with tears falling from her eyes and blood running from her lips. She was lost and had no one to run to. Her father was too far away to ask for help. Plus, she was sure he would explain to her about a wife's submissive role in a marriage. Esther was completely alone. Her eyes fell as she just wanted to give up when a warm feeling came across her chest, like the loving embrace of a friend or lover. *"She's here with us now, we are not alone anymore,"* said the small voice. Closing her eyes and tilting her head back, she crossed her arms over the invisible touch. Peace swept over her. She needed to make things right and she knew what she had to do.

Lightning lit up the night sky as the rain continued to fall. Jake was not looking forward to going outside with the weather like this. Images of today's events randomly repeated in his head. He had planned everything out perfectly; every angle was covered. *I wonder if someone saw something and told Esther,* he thought. *No, it couldn't have been. I was too smart about it.*

When he was younger he heard someone say, "Knowledge is power." He spent most of his time reading everything he could find. He always felt he was more intelligent than most. *My plan was perfect,* bounced around in his head again. But she had shown up with the letters and his trophy. *How did she get in the box without him knowing?* Before Esther had confronted him about it, he had checked everything, even the lock was intact.

"Jake, it's almost time to do a check on the gates," an older gentleman stated as he interrupted Jake's thoughts. He wasn't even sure of the man's name. He had seen him around for a while but never really talked to him. All he knew was that he worked the night shift, and he was to learn the lock gate keeper's routine from him.

"Right on it," Jake answered as he stood up to put on his heavy wool jacket to help keep some of the downpour off him. Before he headed out he lit the night lantern to take with him.

"Watch your footing, wouldn't want you falling into the water," advised the experienced gentleman to his young protege.

The path leading up to the locks was spotted with puddles of water. Usually on the day shift, Jake would just do a walk-through to make sure everything was secure, but since it was night and with the rain coming down steadily, he would have to keep careful watch on the rising level. With the heavy downpour earlier today, flooding could be an issue, and Jake's job tonight was to also measure the water height. If it rose too fast he would have to open the flood gates more to help slow the destructive force of nature. He finally made it up to the first water level indicator. The stream was rising, but not too fast. Jake stood there listening to the raging, fast moving force for a minute with his hands in his pockets. His thoughts returned to what had happened earlier with Esther. *How did she find the chest and the pendant?* He could feel his trophy from the night of the conquest. Pulling it out to look one more time at it, he knew he had to get rid of it just in case Esther found someone to believe her tale about him. Jake drew his arm back and threw the pendant into the rising creek. BOOM. The lightning crashed hard close to Jake. Startled, he jumped a little as he felt the static electricity in the air.

"Forget this! Let it flood!" Jake exclaimed. As he turned to head back to the small shed to get out of the rain, a figure stood in front of him. Jake recoiled in fear at the sight, a woman in a rain-soaked dress with wet hair covering her face, arms to her side, stood motionless in front of him. Jake steadied himself and raised the lantern to view the female form.

"Esther?" Jake gasped at the sight of the woman standing in the glow of the beacon.

Chapter 24

Hair clung tightly to her face as shadows from the light danced across her. Jake could see that her absent eyes were staring directly at him. Her clothes were drenched with the rain, making them sag with the weight of the water drawing all the loose material down.

"Esther, what in God's name are you doing out here?" Jake said as he rushed to her.

Lowering her head, she answered. "I'm sorry." A soft, almost inaudible sentence came from Esther's mouth. He strained to hear her words as the raging waters nearly drowned out her whisper.

Pulling her close, "It's alright, my love. I'm here now," Jake told her in a comforting voice. CRACK! Lightning and thunder hit at the same time. *This storm's really picking up. Standing this close to the water is not a good place for me to be,* he selfishly thought.

"I'm so sorry," Esther sobbed into Jake's chest. He felt her wrap her arms around him. Jake made a comforting sound to her. All his planning to manipulate her in the morning rushed from his mind. She was broken and completely his now.

"Come on, Esther, let's get you out of this rain, love," Jake told her as he tried to pull out of the hug. But she held tightly to him like a scared child.

"Please forgive me?" Esther said in a childish voice as she looked up at him. "Please forgive me, for not being there, Gretchen."

"Huh, Gretchen?" Shocked, he looked down at her. "Esther, why are you talking to …" Jake stopped when he felt the sharp blade plunge into his lower back. Air left his body as the knife entered his torso. He felt white-hot pain as warm dampness gushed from the wound. Jake fell to the ground. In his youth he had witnessed many fights. With this much wetness, he was sure she had stabbed him in the kidney area. He struggled to his knees as Esther came behind him and cradled his chin in her hand. Using the knife, she brushed his hair back.

"Esther, why?" he struggled to ask.

"Shhh, it's all right," she cooed.

"Esther. Please, don't do this. I love you. Help me and I... I will forgive you," he begged her as his blood flowed to the ground. Leaning his head back to look into her eyes, Jake saw the primal animal she had become. Tilting her head to the side she looked down into the fallen man's face with her teeth clenched and her lips curled in a snarl.

"Meow!" Esther growled. She pulled the knife in a swift motion across the front of his neck, creating another opening for his windpipe.

Jake quickly placed both of his hands on his neck as blood erupted out of his mouth. His cries for help were nothing but gurgling sounds escaping from the opening in his throat. Trying to stand, Jake staggered when an unseen force pushed him into the turbulent stream. Jake's body recoiled from the shock of the cold water as air left his lungs. He kicked with all of his might and he fought against the disorientation caused by the swift moving current. He had always been the strongest swimmer among his friends, even Johnny. With the speed of the swift current, he calmly used the flow of the stream to his advantage, with the knowledge that the cold water would slow the bleeding. This would allow him a little more time to get to the creek bank. With his chin tucked, his head finally broke through the surface of the water. He took a deep breath of life-saving air only to have water rush into his windpipe. While pressing one hand to his throat, he was startled by the impact of something ramming him. Jake reached behind to find the rough texture of a log bumping into him again. Pulling it to him, he clung to the buoyant object for dear life and began to frog-kick to attain the stream bank.

With the storm's fury increasing, Jake turned to locate his attacker with the help of the brightness of the frequent lightning. Squinting through the downpour, Jake saw not one, but two figures standing on the gate wall. He stared in disbelief, as he involuntarily gasped, *No it can't be.* His brain screamed, *She's dead!* as the red-haired girl rested her head on his beloved's arm. His brain raced to comprehend exactly what he was seeing.

A new pain pulled his thoughts back to his predicament. He felt the first of many impacts on his legs as sleeping giants made their presence known. During his first summer here, Jake had secretly spied on Esther and Gretchen playing along the rocky shoreline. Now submerged in high water, the play area had become his abuser. Another flash of lightning revealed a low hanging limb over the water as the fierce stream carried him closer to the stream banks. *Reach, Jake, Reach, You can do this,* he coaxed himself. With newfound strength he extended his hands up to the lifeline. *Yes!* He celebrated in his mind as he grasped the limb with both hands. Straining to hold the branch, he started to pull himself. *That bitch, I am going to teach her a lesson when I get out of this. Thou dost not know how blessed I am.* Hand-over-hand, he inched his way toward safety. *Just a few more feet and I've got it,* he hoped. Seeing a fork in the branch, he maneuvered his arm around the obstacle when a sudden burning feeling seared the back of his hand. Wincing, he felt the force of the water twist his body as he was dangling by one arm. *Do your best, you dead bitch, a little bit of burning is not going to stop me. I can get through this. I am going to live,* he boasted to himself. Straining against the cold death grip of the water, he regained a weak hold on the branch.

"Just give up, my flower. It's easy. Just let go and die," a female voice whispered in his ear.

"No!" Jake uttered a muffled, blood filled gurgle while he held tightly to the branch, refusing to give up.

The mocking female laughed next to his ear as he felt increasing weight upon his shoulders. He tried to bark out, "Get off me!" but the blood gagged the words before they could exit his mouth. The burning sensation on his wrists grew with intensity as he looked to his wrist to see the impression of two small invisible hands scorching his skin. With skin ablaze, Jake let go of the branch as he lost his resolve to live. The man's final scream was drowned as the cold river water rushed into his gaping mouth. Shadows in the night watched as his extended hands slowly receded into the water as the swift moving current engulfed its newly found prize.

Emotionless, Esther stood at the canal, her closed hand extended out over the water. *"Just let it go,"* the small voice said. Opening her hand, she dropped her knife into the water's turbulence and then turned to head for home feeling that she had lost everything. The rain had slowed as she began her journey alone. A small lonesome figure watched from a distance.

Justice was done but now there was nothing but emptiness in her heart. *How could I have been tricked by that evil man?* She had trusted him. *Men have taken everything I loved away from me!* The thought raged inside of Esther's mind. *I will just go home and lock myself away from the world.* Esther slowly made her way to her cabin, she opened the door and walked to her bed. She flung herself down, still in her wet clothes. Staring at the ceiling, she thought, *Nothing else matters anymore.* Slowly her eyes closed as sleep overtook her body. A whirlwind of images flashed in her dream state coming to rest on a scene of herself and Gretchen walking through the woods. With the scent of flowers filling the air, the sunlight chased away all the shadows of despair. Gretchen bent over and carefully picked a flower.

"This is for you, my beautiful KittyKat," Gretchen told her as she handed it to her. Esther looked at the smiling face of the young lady and then to the blossom.

"It's beautiful, like you, Gretchen," Esther said with a smile and tears forming in her eyes.

"It's all right, my bonnie. It needed to be done," the young golden red-haired girl assured her.

"But I am dirty, I have sinned, I killed men. How can I be worthy of your love?" she sobbed, falling to her knees. She looked down at her hands, deep crimson covered them. The flower in her hand was now replaced with the knife that she had disposed of in the rising creek water. Blood dripped from the blade and covered the flowers on which she now knelt.

"Thank you, all will be forgiven. But for now, 'An eye for an eye and a tooth for a tooth.'" Gretchen told her as she bent down and gently kissed the top of Esther's head. "I love you."

Esther abruptly awoke from her dream. She tried to figure out which world she was in at this moment, the real world or the dream world. Tears filled her eyes again as the truth of her surroundings presented a world without Gretchen and without love. She closed her eyes tightly, trying to hold on to the dream that had brought Gretchen back to her. She could still smell the flowers, but the image of the small redhead girl was fading away.

Why do I still smell flowers? Esther thought to herself. She opened her eyes and sat up. All signs of yesterday's rain and cloudy day were now replaced with rays of sunshine. "Gretchen!" Esther cried out as she looked around the room. Freshly picked flowers covered her bed. She picked up one to examine the blossom. Confusion filled her head as she began to get out of bed when her feet felt more of them dotting her bedroom floor. Waves of emotion struck her at the same time. Esther stumbled out of her room to find the cabin floor covered in forget-me-not flowers. Weeping, she fell to the floor and gathered a bouquet and held it to her bosom, crying out, "Gretchen!"

* * *

A few weeks later, a well-dressed man stood outside of the local meeting hall to greet the carriage that had just arrived. He and the passenger exchanged pleasantries and started to make their way inside

"My apologies for running late, something unexpected came up." The late-comer smiled while gesturing back. The other looked back to see his meaning and noticed a young white-haired girl waiting in the carriage for the passenger's return.

"Just doing your founding father's duty?" the man asked, grinning as he opened the door to the meeting place. Six men sat around the table watching as the two entered the room. They were greeted by an older gentleman sitting at the head of the table of the board of directors. Next to him sat the town recorder.

"Nice of you to finally join us. We were wondering if you were ever going to make it." The men took their seats and didn't reply to the comment.

"Shall I continue?" the older gentleman asked. Not waiting for an answer, he started again.

"Mr. Birchham's bloated body was found five miles downstream, near Fredericktown. The constable searched his cabin the day after he disappeared and discovered quite a few interesting items. Evidently, Mr. Birchham was not what he appeared to be. It seems he kept detailed books of all his actions." Puzzlement was shared by the men at the table. The older gentleman continued, "Let's just say, without going into too much detail, we recovered quite a bit of money from his place, along with many of the stolen items for which a fellow worker was jailed. He paused for a minute. "We also found in his writings that he was the one responsible for the assault on the Gill child." He stopped and walked to the window thinking, *The evil bastard bragged about it in his journal along with all his other crimes. He wrote of his pride in setting up his best friend.*

"Looks like justice has been handed out," one of the gentlemen at the table spoke.

"I suggest the board put this behind us and move on," the chairman said, as he turned back to the men sitting at the table. "With the canal open and running, the last thing this company and this settlement needs is word of this horrible incident getting out. We don't want to frighten our potential investors. Mr. Birchham's death is being listed as death by lightning, hence, an act of God."

"More like an act of Miss Hale," the recorder smirked, while continuing to write the minutes of the meeting.

"What about the Hale woman? She was to marry him," one of the board members asked.

"Well, we believe she's the one that dealt out the judgment on Mr. Birchham," the chairman answered.

Curious eyes looked towards him as one of the men asked, "What makes you believe that?"

"When the constable and I went to her place after Mr. Birchham's disappearance she admitted to avenging the attack on Mr. Gill's daughter and now she is claiming that the girl has returned from the afterlife. She went on and on about her true love coming home," the older gentleman stated.

"Should we call the doctors for her? Maybe she needs help again," one of the men asked.

"The poor girl's been through enough," the older man said. "We will keep a watchful eye on her and let her be."

"Will she be a danger to others?" a concerned gentleman asked.

"No. She's quite docile now. We supplied her with opium. She has insisted she has no desire to leave her home. When we visited, we found her totally disheveled. There were freshly picked flowers everywhere in her house."

"What about the pastor? Has anyone notified him?" a voice asked.

"From our latest correspondence with him, it appears he has shunned his daughter," responded the recorder.

As the meeting concluded, the men all agreed with keeping the true events of the tragedy erased from the minutes and keeping the meeting amongst themselves. They all shook hands with the older gentleman as they left, but one stopped to talk to the chairman.

"Sir, I do have one puzzling question about the whole thing," the man asked the senior.

"It's November. Where did she find the fresh flowers?" he asked. The older gentleman just smiled and looked at the other man's carriage, nodding upon seeing the young lady waiting for him.

"You best not be worrying about those flowers. Concern yourself with that flower." The older gentleman gestured toward the carriage and patted the man's back as they adjourned.

* * *

The first snow came late this year as Esther stared out her window. This would be the first Christmas in Sprucevale she would spend without her father. She was still waiting for at least one correspondence to the many letters she had sent to him. She hoped he would visit her but evidently the heavy rains and weather had made the trip from Salem to Sprucevale too dangerous. She would just sit here and wait for Gretchen to return. Esther had a few visitors stop by to check on her well-being and asked her to spend time with their families, but she dared not leave. "I have to be here when my true love comes for me," she would tell them. They would leave her supplies, but she would just set them on the table and return to her spot by the window.

The snow started to pick up and night was approaching. *I hope Gretchen will be well with the snowfall,* she thought as she rubbed her eyes. She had trouble sleeping since the dream she had. *If only I was awake the night she brought the flowers, we could have left together.* Esther yawned and stretched her arms above her head.

"Maybe I'll just take a short nap," she said while taking a sip of poppy tears. "I can leave the door open a little so Gretchen knows she can just come in." Pleased with her idea, Esther cracked the door open and went to lie on her bed for a short sleep.

She awoke to the blustery freezing wind hitting her face. She was so cold. The door to the cabin had blown wide open. Windswept snow was swirling around on the floor. Esther tried to get up but the numbing temperature had taken her strength away. She lay there trying to call for help, needing to move, but her body would not accept the command.

"Anyone, please, help me," Esther called out in a weak voice. A small blurry figure with an outstretched hand appeared at the door. Her heart skipped a beat as she realized who the figure was. She reached out from her bed.

"My love. . .," her voice trailed off as her arm fell and her eyes closed, never to reopen.

Chapter 25
East Liverpool, Ohio
1981

A 14-year-old boy stepped up in front of his classmates, looking to his teacher for the okay to start his report. The Ohio history class was made up of 25 students and most were friends of the young Chris Bowman. Living in a small town had afforded him the opportunity to be in the same classes with them from the first grade until now. He had a small group of very close companions, but all that meant was they would rib him more if he messed up on this report. He remembered back to the time he was reading out loud in science class and said something else instead of the word organism. This was a mistake about which his friends took every opportunity to remind him.

The teacher, Mr. Washington, stood in the corner and gave Chris a nod. Mr. Washington was everyone's favorite teacher. He was a tall slender man in his mid-40's with short blonde hair. Depending on what mood he was in, he would be clean shaven or trying to grow a beard. *This month he must have given up on the beard,* Chris thought as he steadied himself to start his report. Looking up, he saw his friends staring at him, just waiting for him to falter with any words.

Chris laid his report on the stand. The podium was old with spots of chipping black paint which revealed many other colors underneath. Chris wondered if this thing was old enough that his parents might have used it when they went to school here many, many, many years ago in the 50's.

"Anytime now, Mr. Organism," the voice of a classmate rang out followed by a few giggles. Mr. Washington turned to glare in the direction of the comment causing the students to quiet down some. He turned back to wait with the rest of the students to hear Chris's report.

"The Legend of Gretchen's Lock," Chris read out loud."Just north of here is an area we know as Gretchen's Lock.
It was part of the Sandy Beaver Canal system.
It was started in 1828 and was finally finished in 1848.
In 1837, E.H. Gill was hired as the chief engineer to oversee construction of the lock system from New Lisbon, Ohio, to the Ohio River.
He was from Ireland and brought his wife and child with him on the voyage here.
His wife became ill on the trip and died.
They buried her at sea.
Mr. Gill's daughter's name was Gretchen.
She was a 10-year-old girl.
She contracted malaria and died.
Her father had her entombed in a section of the canal called Lock 41.
Her last dying wish was, she wanted to be buried with her mother.

So, upon completion of the canal, Mr. Gill had his daughter unearthed and returned with him to Ireland to be buried at his family's cemetery plot.
But the ship ran into a storm and was lost at sea.
Through the years many people have reported seeing a young girl walking the lock system at night, and many have said they can hear her crying out, 'bury me with my mother.'"

Chris cleared his throat and proclaimed "So, she is buried with her mother since they are both buried in the Atlantic Ocean."

"In 1838, Esther Hale was to be married but was left at the altar by her husband-to-be.
The jilted bride would wander the settlement area in her bridal gown.
One day in December someone noticed the door to her cabin was open.
They went to check on her.
She had died during the night's snowstorm.
She had lost a lot of weight like she hadn't eaten for a month.
She was still wearing her wedding dress when they found her body.
Legend says she haunts the local bridge as she waits for the return of her true love.
Her image can be seen late at night on the bridge that crosses the waterway.
If you're a man and she touches you, she will take your soul.

Chris picked up his report and returned to his desk. Mocking applause from his friends erupted as he sat down.

"Way to go, Chris, not bad, but I like your sex reports better," commented a girl behind him as she placed her hands on his shoulders.

"Thanks a lot, Jenn, for ALL your support," Chris retorted. Jennifer Harrison was the only girl in his tight band of friends. She had very pretty, blonde hair which she always changed depending on what hairstyle was in fashion this week. She had those deep hazel eyes that made you want to talk to her. She was very friendly to everyone and loved to pick on Chris. As a friend, no one could ask for anyone better. She was tough and very protective of their group of companions. If anyone said anything bad about them, Jennifer was the first to jump to their defense. She was also the most talented of the group. Singing, piano, guitar, anything musical, Jenn could do it.

"What are friends for?" she replied, as they both looked at Mr. Washington. The teacher made his way to the front of the class. He lowered his head and shook it in disappointment, then rested his nose on steepled hands before looking directly at Chris.

"Mr. Bowman, could you please explain something to me?" He stopped for a second, but then continued, not waiting for his response. "How is it that in Mr. Little's biology class you did a tree frog report long enough that some people might consider it a novel? I asked you to do a report on Gretchen's Lock and it's barely a page. What is that all about?" Mr. Washington finished his questions and waited for his reply. Of all the students the

177

instructor had had over the years, Chris Bowman, without a doubt, was something special. This kid was smart, scary smart. Mr. Washington remembered hearing about him as he came up through the grades. Teachers talked about how not to get into a debate with him because his mind didn't work like normal students. He knew things other kids his age had no idea about. Chris Bowman was every teacher's dream student, so when he turned in a half-hearted report for class, Mr. Washington was more than disappointed. He was almost angry that this star pupil didn't do his best. *That report was so bland for his talent. I bet he wrote that before class started, probably while I was taking attendance*, he thought.

"It's a fairy tale. It's not real. There is no scientific proof of ghosts," Chris replied in what seemed to be a challenging voice.

"What about all those people through the years that have seen a little girl walking in the woods and what about the sawmill?" one of the classmates asked. Chris turned and started to reply, but the student continued without giving him a chance for a rebuttal. "My uncle was working as a lumberjack in the 40's. He told me about how things were always disappearing and machinery mysteriously would stop working. But when they left Gretchen's Lock the equipment was fine again."

Another voice piped up as the first boy finished his remarks. "I heard on the last day the mill was open, workers were cutting a piece of wood and screams of a young girl filled the air." In awe, the students all turned to look at him as he continued.

"At first, they thought the combination of a dull saw blade and hard wood caused the awful sound but once the saw came to rest, the screaming could still be heard. Everyone heard it. With all the weird things that were happening there, the men walked off the job. None of the workers returned, leaving the portable sawmill there."

Shaking his head, Chris turned and glared at the boy.

"Carbon monoxide poisoning," Chris remarked to the boy. "The exhaust from the engine running the saw blade caused them to hear and see things," he retorted, then looked around for any other classmates who needed to be educated.

"C-O-2?" the inquisitive pupil asked.

"No, C-O. Carbon monoxide, not C-O-2," Chris informed the student of his mistake.

"Valid point, Mr. Bowman, but would you mind if you let me be the teacher?" Mr. Washington said while looking sternly at Chris. "If history has taught us one important lesson, it is that *allll* legends and stories start with a speck of truth," Mr. Washington interjected. His voice pulled the now chatting students back to his class as he regained control.

"But ghosts? Really, Mr. Washington?" Chris asked.

"My house has a ghost," spoke out one student, followed by others all claiming to have a ghost in their house or knowing of someone who has a haunted house.

"Ok. Calm down everyone. Let's not lose focus," Mr. Washington spoke out again. Drawing the young minds back to the assignments was more important than their current discussion.

"Ok, now, who's next with their report?" he asked, looking around the class as a lone hand raised up in the back. "Yes," he called out to the student, "Would you like to go next, or do you have a question?"

"Ummm, I have a question, Teacher," the pupil said. "Then what is C-O-2?" he asked as laughter erupted from the students.

"Well, that would be plant food, luv!" A new, strange female voice with a weird accent intruded into the class.

Chris turned toward the classroom door to find the owner of the comment. His eyes came to rest on a young girl with light auburn hair with hazel eyes lighting up her pale face. She looked to be taller than he, but his eyes dropped quickly and blood rushed to his cheeks in embarrassment, when he noticed she was looking at him with a grin adorning her face. Jennifer tapped on the back of his shoulder and asked, "Who's that?"

"May I help you, miss?" Mr. Washington asked the young lady as he walked over to her. She handed him a note. He took it and read it with a smile. "Well, it looks like we have a new student," he announced to the class whose attention was transfixed on the newcomer.

"Would you care to introduce yourself?" Mr. Washington invited.

"Hi, my name is Alexis Plant, but you can call me Lexi. This is my first time across the pond to the States."

"Where are you from?" Jennifer quickly asked.

"I'm from Cardiff, Wales. I just moved here with my family. My father is heading operations in the new plant they are building here," she told the class.

"Well, in that case, let me be one of the first to welcome you to Ohio history. Please take any open seat you want," Mr.

Washington told her. As she looked around for a seat, Jennifer motioned her over to an empty desk next to her.

"You know why Jenn does that? She doesn't want any pretty girl going after you," a boy next to Chris said.

"Lance, you're nuts. Jenn is just a friend. We have known each other since kindergarten," he responded. Chris had known Lance Jones forever. They grew up on the same street and had always been friends. In their friends' circle, Lance was the chubby one that everyone liked. He was unique with sandy blonde hair and a pale complexion that made his cheeks redder than normal when he was happy. Lance was shorter than Chris, but when it came to a friend who was always there, he was a giant. The new girl sat next to Jenn and began talking before she was seated, but Chris was not going to give up on this debate he was having with the teacher.

"Maybe the only speck of truth in the Gretchen's legend is the canal itself," Chris called out.
Mr. Washington shook his head, refusing to go back to the discussion with the youth.

"Mr. Bowman, isn't your summer going to be spent with your parents doing an archaeological dig down at the locks?" the teacher baited him.

Chris nodded. His parents were both involved with the local parks and being archaeologists, and with their expertise they were heading an archeological dig over the summer. This meant Chris would be spending his vacation there among the rocks and ruins of old foundations that could be found throughout the Sprucevale area.

"Well, maybe since you will be down there all summer you can do your own research and find the truth about the legend of Gretchen's Lock," Mr. Washington sarcastically suggested. Chris started to reply when the class bell rang. Frustrated, he gathered his books then started to stand when Mr. Washington spoke out.

"Remember, everyone, we have only two weeks left before your summer vacation starts, so no more homework for the last two weeks." Looking around to see the smiling faces of the students he added one more thing, "Remember class, don't search for your Walden, but build your own."

Chapter 26

Chris watched out the window on the bus ride home. The thought of the torture he would have to endure this summer was a point of depression he was feeling right now. He had hoped his parents would let him take some extra classes, but they wanted to do this as a family. *All summer, every day, loading and unloading the car, carrying the equipment through the woods, and looking at rocks! God must hate me,* he thought to himself, but his self-absorbed thoughts were soon interrupted by Lance.

"So, you want to do something tonight since it's Friday? Chess? Or I just got a new board game that has castles and dragons that I've been wanting to play," Lance suggested.

Shaking his head, Chris replied, "I wish. Mom and Dad planned on starting at the crack of dawn tomorrow, so I'll have to be in bed early."

"Man, that's gotta suck," Lance said as Chris's attention returned back out the window of the bus. He stayed silent the rest of the ride home as Lance continued to talk about girls and new sci- fi movies coming out soon. Chris nodded and agreed with most of what he said.

"Chris?" Lance said while shaking Chris's arm.

"Um," came his response as he tried to figure out what was being asked.

"It's our stop. See you Monday. Have fun looking at rocks," Lance said as Chris grabbed his backpack to stand.

"You suck! See you Monday," Chris said with a smile as they got off the bus.

The next morning he stared out from the back seat of his parents' car. The trip to Gretchen's Lock was only about a 15-minute ride. It was too early in the morning for him to enjoy the scenery. *Most kids my age would be sleeping in and enjoying the weekend, but not me. No, my parents came up with this great idea for family bonding,* he thought as he watched blurry objects pass by.

"Are you excited, dear? A family out in nature, spending time together, you will be able to treasure this experience the rest of your life." Chris's mom rhetorically stated from the front passenger seat. He turned away from the window and stared at his mom. Mrs. Bowman smiled at her son. Chris was still getting used to his mother's new haircut. She always had long curvy brown hair that fit her slender build, but this last spring she decided that the 'mom look' was not for her anymore. She wanted to have a professional look, so her hair now was short. "Really short," Chris had said many times to describe her hair cut to his friends.

"Come on son, you know you can't wait to get your hands dirty," Chris's dad chimed in. Even though Chris's parents were the same age and high school sweethearts, his dad's salt and pepper hair made him look much older than his age of 42. They were almost twins in size, both slender and almost the same height of 5 '7." Chris always wondered if he was adopted because he was already the tallest in his family. He was not happy about the dig he felt he was forced to join. He would do this for them because they were very loving parents, always pushing him to be better in his life.

"Can't wait, Dad," Chris said with a pained smile. They loved this kind of work, so he would not do anything to spoil this adventure they had planned. The state grant and sponsorship of this project was a perfect opportunity for them to be paid much more than their college salaries. Chris returned to looking out the window when the skating rink appeared. *Wonder who all went last night?* Chris thought. Kay Bee Roller Arena had been a staple of entertainment in the community. His own mom and dad went there as teenagers. On the weekends most of the local kids would go there. Chris's friends would all form a group and sit together in the seats that surrounded the skating floor. Only a few of his companions knew how to skate, but they would always hang out as a group of special friends.

"Well, so much for going there anytime soon," Chris spoke out loud.

"What did you say? Sorry, I couldn't hear you with the window down," Chris's mother replied.

"Oh, nothing, just thinking out loud," Chris exclaimed back to his mother. A few miles later the Bowmans' car descended down a long, steep, curving hill that turned to the left as they reached the bottom. Then they drove across a metal bridge crossing over Beaver Creek, the stream that was used as part of the Sandy and Beaver Canal system. *Esther's bridge. Wonder if you will come and take my soul; I am sure that will be better than digging in the dirt all summer!* Chris thought to himself. A faint smile crossed his lips. *Ghosts, that is so funny, like Santa*

Claus. Chris chuckled a little, then a thought jumped in his head. *Wonder if Santa had to worry about Esther when he came to this area.* He continued to smile as the car made another left, then turned into the park. Chris could see on the right side of the road where Hambletons Mill stood. Unused for many years, it now stood as a landmark of the past. The park was big, a little over 2,700 acres, mostly made up of trees, with two central park areas, Gretchen's and Echo Dell. Chris found the public picnic space of Echo Dell more open but preferred the trails of the Sprucevale area. The winding paths next to the famous Beaver Creek, with its crumbled ruins of the lock system every half mile, made it a new adventure with every visit. The road was paved and the grass on each side of it was freshly mowed. A few trees, here and there, added to its beauty. As they drove farther into the park, an old empty brick two story house stood abandoned. Behind that house he could see a hill covered with weeds and small saplings standing a few feet tall.

"Jake's Lock on the left side," Mr. Bowman called out. That lock wasn't as famous as Gretchen's. *The story goes that Jake was a lock keeper, who on a stormy night was struck by lightning and died.* Chris always thought the legend was completely boring. *If you go outside in a thunderstorm, near water, and at that time there wouldn't have been many trees. Naturally lightning would have found the shortest way to the ground,* Chris thought and rolled his eyes. The Bowman family pulled into the parking lot and was quickly surrounded by people who had volunteered to help with the dig.

"We're here! Don't forget your book bag and don't wander off too far," Chris's mother told him. Today the Bowmans would lay out a plan and then survey the area, placing little flags to mark out where they would eventually dig for artifacts. Today he could just be a kid and explore. Chris had brought some books to read. His plan was to find a nice spot away from everyone, sit by the waterway and enjoy the privacy. Standing back, he watched his parents. His father laid a topographical map on the car hood. Like a musical conductor, he pointed to the map, then directed groups of people to their assignments. Chris studied the people as a familiar face was spotted in the group.

"Great, Mr. Washington volunteered. Just what I needed. What else is going to go wrong?" Chris said in a low murmur as he brought his hand to his brow to avoid being spotted by his teacher. He quickly made his way to the end of the parking lot to begin his adventure to the famous Gretchen's Lock. A small dirt path meandering to the east side of the slow-moving creek awaited him. Chris had found the hike was a great way to get lost in his thoughts. Daydreaming as he was walking, he felt his foot slide in something squishy. *Stupid horseback riders on the hiking trails, not only do I have watch for mud, but all of these stinking horse patties*! Chris's mind raced back to last year when he and his father walked these same trails when they came upon an old heavy-set rider feeding his horse apples. His father told him about being on the horse trails and not walking trails, but the old-timer said nothing, just kept cutting apples with a small knife and feeding them to his horse. *It was probably him and his creature.* Chris thought as he rounded the first bend of the trail. After a half-mile, the trail started to angle away from the stream which was now replaced by trees.

Wonder if any of my friends are awake yet, like me, he thought, while wishing he were still sleeping like they were. *At least I have some shade,* he consoled himself while looking up. The intertwining tree branches overhead created a nice cool canopy for him to walk. As he approached a white blaze on a tree indicating a small trail splitting off, Chris followed that narrow unkempt path off the main course. Doing his part to help keep it open and cleaning his shoes off at the same time, he stomped on the saplings that tried to reclaim man's footprint in nature. Walking about 45 yards, he reached his destination.

A small hill appeared in front of him as the trail went to the left of the mound. He followed the trail as it came to the opening of the lock. From the outside it was nothing but another mound in the forest. It extended about 30 yards with immature trees and bushes dotting the hill. But when he came around, the opening was cut right down the center with a wall of stone holding back the earth on either side. Chris stood inside of the channel marveling at the beautifully interlocking cut stones stacked on top of each other. He looked up admiring the workmanship that went into the construction of this lock. The structure stood about 20 feet tall. The young adventurer wondered how hard it must have been to make everything level and straight. Running his fingers along the walls, feeling the cut of the stones and the coldness they held, he was in awe.

"Wonder why there's no water running through them?" he said softly. Turning around and walking out of the channel between the walls, he turned right to see the stream at least 15 yards away from the lock. He remembered reading about a flood that wiped out most of the canal system. *Could the flood have changed the water path this much?* Chris thought to himself. That was something he would ask his parents tonight. He stood there wondering when the feeling of being watched caused the hair on the back of his neck to stand up. Chris quickly turned and peered out into the woods. Standing like a statue with his eyes glancing back and forth, he shook the feeling off as just an overactive imagination.

Investigating along the west side of the wall, he found a small path that would allow him to walk along the top of the lock. The path was wide enough for one person and was a small climb of about ten feet. Small trees and briar bushes reached up to snatch onto his clothes but jerking his body back and forth as he climbed helped free him from their grasp. From the top he could see the water to his left and the wall edge on his right. Small amounts of grass grew in areas with ivy intruding from the side. Chris studied the walls and thought again of how men without cranes and bulldozers built this. Admiration filled his chest for men long forgotten who had labored to construct this work of art. Walking along the top, Chris was surprised to find a spot in the earth that was sunken down, a rectangular shape about a foot lower than the surrounding grass. Curiously, Chris inspected the sunken ground, wondering if this area was the starting point of Gretchen being entombed in the lock.

"People and their fairy tales," Chris said as he shook his head. He guessed that most likely that the earth had settled around the block that made up the lock and it just happened to form this shape.

"When in doubt, science will provide the answer if you know where to look," Chris proudly stated. He noticed a few small flowers to the side of the divot in the ground. Walking over, he picked a few and walked back to the depression.

"Well, 'make-believe Gretchen's grave.' Here you go. May you rest in peace," Chris said as he laid the few flowers on the area. From behind him a sound of rustling leaves caught his attention. He pivoted to look but saw nothing but trees. *This is getting boring and my mind is playing tricks on me. It's time to head back closer to the base of my parents' operations,* he decided.

Chris hiked back to the parking lot to find everyone had dispersed. Voices of volunteers could be heard in the woods, but a few worked the grounds around the open grass area of the park. Chris decided to find somewhere nice along the water and maybe read some of the books he had brought with him. Jake's Lock was nothing special. Mostly it was trees and brush covering up the mound of dirt and fallen stone. Being hidden underneath foliage, the former glory of architecture was long gone. The overgrowth of weeds made it perfect for him to hide behind as he sat along the banks of the water.

Chapter 27

Chris loved to read, and science was his favorite subject, but today he needed something to help stimulate his expanding mind. Fishing around in his backpack he pulled out the latest comic he had picked up last night for the ride with his parents. Comics and sci-fi were his weaknesses. It was the place he could get away from the struggles of being the perfect student. He loved to let his mind wander as he read the colorful pages. He and his friends spent many hours discussing what would be the greatest superpower to have. The conversation soon would take a back seat to which female sidekick they would want. Most of his friends always liked the ones with big breasts and hardly any clothes. Chris liked those too, but the female sidekicks that would get into the middle of a fight and were almost gray characters were his favorite. That may have been the reason he always liked Jenn. She was ready to mix it up at the drop of a hat.

After finishing his comic, he looked around taking in the peaceful surroundings to appreciate the tranquility of this place, and for the first time, in spite of his many visits, he saw the Gretchen's Lock area for what it was. It was amazingly beautiful, with the trees standing proud with their branches extending over the water and jagged large rocks breaking through the ground to create gaps in the trees. The sounds of the stream running by made him feel as though he was being sung to sleep by a loving mother. Chris closed his eyes and let his head fall back to feel the sun's warmth on his face. If it weren't for the dismay of having to dig through dirt to look at rocks this would be a great way to spend a summer, just sitting by the water and reading books.

Why does it feel like someone is watching me? Chris thought as he slowly opened his eyes to the feeling of being stared at. It wasn't the feeling of danger, but more of someone's curiosity. Chris looked around but no one was near, except for a small squirrel running along the ground to scramble up a tree. Chris watched the squirrel but then turned back to gaze across the creek to see what he thought was movement behind a tree.

"Hello?" he called out. "Someone there?" He waited for a reply and carefully watched the spot of the movement, but nothing, and no one was there. Chris dismissed it as the shadows and his mind playing an optical illusion. He stood up and stretched his skinny body, running his fingers through his blonde hair to comb it back. Walking along the creek, he picked up a rock and tried to skip it across the water. The creek had many areas of deeper, calmer pools that created perfect conditions for rock skipping. Walking a little way down the stream to find some better-suited flat rocks to throw, a strange shaped rock caught his eyes. It was very flat and oval shaped. Holding it in his hand, and pulling back his arm, he was ready to release it when a piece broke away revealing a green and gold color design on the edge. He stopped and brought the stone closer for a better view. Bits of hardened clay fell from the edges as he scraped it with his thumb nail. Walking over to the stream he continued to clean the now visible item in the water.

"It looks like a pendant," Chris said out loud. "Is it gold?" he asked himself. He closely examined the item. *It's beautiful,* he thought as a female figure was revealed in the center of the trinket. He turned it over to examine the back, trying to find an inscription on the piece. *Years of being outdoors had worn away any writing that may have been inscribed on it.* His mind wondered who the owner could have been. *Maybe it fell from one of the flat boats that used to carry cargo and goods along the canal when it was running.* Chris could envision the boats being guided along the waterway, helped by a beast of burden pulling on ropes from the shoreline. Images of an unsecured crate falling from the boat and then disappearing within the damned up deeper water at that time flashed in front of him. Chris liked that idea better than the possibilities of some tragedy being responsible for the pendant coming to rest in the water.

The sun's angle was now starting to create long shadows on the ground from the trees. He knew the time was getting close to head back for the day. His mom and dad would be waiting for him. Chris stuffed the pendant into his pocket and headed back.

The parking lot came into view as he rounded the corner of Jake's Lock. He could hear his parents thanking everyone for their help as they stood in the center of the volunteers. Chris made his way to the group encircling his parents, taking great care to make sure that he would be in their line of sight. He was happy to see his parents' smile in recognition while still talking to the people. He could feel the pendant in his pocket as he shifted from one leg to the other. Carefully concealing himself from Mr. Washington, his eyes came to rest on a young girl staring directly at him. She looked to be about his age with reddish hair, pale face, and a thin body. With unmoving eyes she looked directly at him. Her look was not angry, but he felt uncomfortable as she watched him. Chris moved behind a few people to help block her view. He leaned back a little to see if she was still watching only to find she was no longer there. He returned to listen to his parents. Shielding his squinting eyes from the setting sun he noticed her again. Long shadows covered her face as her radiant hair moved softly in the breeze. Though her face showed no emotions, he could sense the curiosity in her eyes.

"Ok, everyone, thank you and see you next weekend," Mr. Bowman told the crowd.

The comment about next week caught Chris's attention, pulling his interest from the girl. "Next weekend?" Chris asked as he made his way to his parents.

"Yes, next weekend. The forecast is for rain tomorrow, so we will be taking Sunday off," Mrs. Bowman said. Chris felt the excitement building inside. With no work Sunday, he would be able to go skating tonight. A smile crossed his face with that idea as he walked back to his parents' car. Before climbing into the back seat, he turned to look for the young girl, but she was gone. *She must have already left with her parents,* he rationalized.

Chris watched out the window as his parents drove on the one-way road leading out of the park, all the while feeling the pendant in his hands. Turning it over and exploring every centimeter of the item with his touch, Chris thought again,

Wonder if this was something important to the person, some family heirloom, maybe a gift to someone's wife, or most likely from a father to a daughter.

"Did you have fun today?" his mother asked as she turned to face him.

"Yes, I did, and I found something," Chris proclaimed as he handed it to his mother to see.

She carefully looked it over and let out a "Hmmm, that's interesting. Looks to be early colonial, definitely 1700's or 1800's," she replied, then continued, "Where did you find it?" she asked as Mr. Bowman looked over to sneak a peek of the item of his family's interest.

"Along the edge of the creek down below Jake's Lock," Chris answered.

"Well, that would be something lost from canal boat travel. If you would have found it near the grass in the park, I would say then it was flood debris from a washed-out cabin," Mr. Bowman stated. "In the spring of 1853, Cold Run Reservoir near Lisbon broke, flooding the canal waterway. The grassy area of the park was once a thriving location of houses and businesses. The flood destroyed the majority of the settlement. It was so destructive it moved the path of the creek to where it runs presently. Most of the locks are not even near the water now. That's why if you found it near the lock I would venture to say it fell off a boat." Chris's dad told him as his mom handed the pendant back to Chris.

"Am I allowed to keep this?" Chris asked while tucking the find into his pocket.

"Well," his dad paused for a second, then continued, "We will have to document it and check it out better when we get home. But, I don't see a problem with that."

Chris smiled as he turned to watch out the window of the moving car. The haunting stare of the red-haired girl jumped into his mind. *Wonder why I didn't know her? Did she have on a school shirt?* he questioned himself. Suddenly he realized he didn't know what she was wearing. All he could remember was her face and the red hair. The thought troubled him a little, as he was very detail-oriented. He was proud of that fact about himself. For some reason the girl almost felt like a dream. He remembered most of it, though that small important detail evaded him. Chris closed his eyes, trying to find the missing details of the intriguing young girl.

Chapter 28

As Chris's mother pulled up to the roller skating rink, he could see there was going to be a crowd here tonight. The winter and earlier spring months always made roller skating one of the few options for the locals. During summer months, most teens would be vacationing out of state with their families or going to one of the two drive-ins, but this was May, so skating was the prime hangout for teenagers. Chris wasn't a very good skater, so most of the time he would just sit in the seats and talk with his friends, but tonight, he felt like maybe skating a little. The line was short in front of the rental skate window. As he stood impatiently behind two girls who couldn't decide which color skates they wanted, a familiar voice yelled in his ear as hands covered his eyes from behind.

"Guess who, nerd?" Chris quickly turned around to find the owner of the voice. Jenn stood there smiling, the orneriness in her grin made Chris defensive. Reaching back, he checked for a "kick-me" sign that he wouldn't put past her to do. Satisfied that he wasn't a walking billboard, he looked back at Jenn who had a partner in tow, the new girl from Wales.

"Hi, Jenn, and …" he thought for a minute. "Ummm, Lexi?" Chris said nervously, smiling at the two girls, hoping he was right with her name.

"Hi luv," Lexi said in return, with a smile of her own. Not trying to be too obvious, Chris looked at her seriously for the first time. Her shoulder length auburn hair was now pulled back into a ponytail, dark copper eye shadow made her already beautiful hazel irises stand out making it almost impossible not to stare into them. His first thought about her height was correct, she stood about an inch taller than he. She wore torn blue jeans with a flannel shirt wrapped around her middle, accentuating her thin waist. Following the contours of her body, he noted the words on her black tee shirt.

"Classical music is the godfather of heavy metal," Chris read out loud. Confused, he stared up at Lexi.

"She has a very unique taste in music," Jenn replied first.

Grinning, Lexi nodded in agreement. "Beethoven was the first headbanger."

"Headbanger?" Chris questioned.

"Don't ask, unless you have a few hours. So, you're skating tonight?" Jenn asked.

Chris smiled and turned to get his skates. "Sure am, so don't be watching my butt."

"It's hard not to with all the dirt you will have on it from falling," Jenn said with a laugh. "Everybody is over on the other side," she told him as she and Lexi turned to skate away.
Chris slung the skates over his shoulder and began to walk. Looking at the rink layout he had many times pretended to be a Roman citizen at the Colosseum watching the gladiatorial games from the single row of seats. Avoiding the clusters of cackling teens, he pressed his body against the handrail which separated the skating area from the seats. *I am Spartacus!* Chris smiled to himself as he made his way to find his friends in the throng.

"Hey, Chris, over here!" he heard above the rock music being played over the speakers. He could see Lance's hand raised above his head in a group of people, some sitting, others standing.

"Man, I'm so glad you made it," he told Chris as he joined his friends.

"So, how was the first day of playing in the dirt?" a voice asked Chris. He turned to see the tallest member of his classmates. Standing almost six feet, Bart Miller was the wildest one of them. A true daredevil, which, with his brown hair and good looks, made him also the ladies' man of the group. Chris had known Bart only for a few years, since his family moved to the area from Cleveland, but they quickly grew close.

"Well, it wasn't anything exciting, but I did find something cool." Chris reached in his pocket to produce the treasured pendant he had found.

"Let me see, too," Jenn said, coming up with Lexi in hand. Handing over his find to the two girls, Chris stepped back to allow them all to see. Pride filled his heart as he looked around at them. How lucky he felt to have people like this in his life, everyone different, but all equal in his eyes. He watched as each one of his friends studied his trophy. After seeing the new girl take her turn, he approached her.

"So, what do you think of America?" Chris asked Lexi as she turned back to talk to him.

"You Yanks are funny," she replied with her Welsh accent. "You talk strange, but other than that I like it so far."

Chris laughed upon hearing that Americans talk funny. Pointing at her shirt he asked about the meaning of it before remembering Jenn's warning.

"Well, most metal music has roots in classical You can find lots of the same structure and timing signatures in both styles, unlike most pop or top 40, which rely on a standard 4/4 time," she told him with a smile.

"I'm not really into music," Chris replied to her, "I'd rather spend my time learning about how the world works. So, I find that music is a distraction and it's not really my thing."

Lexi shook her head, "Jenn was right about you."

"What did Jenn say about me?" he inquired.

"She said that you're some kind of genius. You don't have time for girls or the fun stuff that you can do with them, which is a shame with a cutie like you," she teased, while lightly brushing her fingers up his arm. Chris felt the blood instantly rush to his cheeks. As he turned his head to hide his blushing, Lexi smiled at his reaction.

"Here, I wanted you to have this," Lexi said while handing him a folded paper.

Chris took it from her hand and, unsure what it was, looked to her with puzzlement and confusion in his face.

"It's my number, *gwirion*. Call me if you want," Lexi started to explain as Jenn unexpectedly grabbed her hand and led her to the skating floor.

Hollering back at Chris, Jenn giggled, "Get your own, nerd. She's mine."

Chris looked back to Lance who was now looking at the pendant. "So? Cool?" Chris asked.

"Very," Lance replied to him as he handed the item back. Chris studied his face. Lance's facial expression told him that something was eating away at him.

"Lance, I know you're wanting to say something, so go ahead," Chris told him.

"Umm, do you like Lexi?" he asked. Chris already knew where this was going. His friend was a great guy, but he didn't have very much luck with females. Lance was very shy, and as long as Chris had known him, he had always been a little chubby causing him to be very self- conscious. He would never ask girls out, but instead would crush on them from the sidelines.

"No, Lance, I like Lexi as just a friend. And before you ask, she gave me her number, but that's a call I'll never make. I have too much going on in my life to even think about girls. To me they're all like Jenn, just one of the guys," Chris stated, then placed his hand on his friend's shoulder.

He finally placed the pendant back into his pocket when the sound of a slow song broke through the air, causing Chris to make a break for the bathroom before Jenn could find him.

"Nope, not going to happen," the familiar female voice called out as Chris felt a hand grab his shirt, pulling him out to the floor. Jenn had caught him before he was able to find a hiding place. He wasn't the most talented skater, but between Lance and him, he was better, and Jenn would always grab him for the ladies' choice. She took his hand in hers as they started to skate around the rink to a song Chris didn't mind too much. It was a slow blues rock song about dreams. It was a mainstay of the rink. Every weekend they always played that song, so Chris guessed it must have been really popular or maybe the DJ really liked it. Hand in hand they slowly skated.

"Chris, I wanted to ask you something," Jenn said to him.

He turned to look at her and nodded. For all of Jennifer's teasing, she really was a great person. Chris waited for her question as they rolled along.

"What do you think of Lexi?" she asked.

"She seems nice, a little forward, but that may be from her being a foreigner," Chris said, then added, "She gave me her number, which really caught me off guard."

"Well, I like her and she's really cool. Did you know she sings opera? Can you believe it? I mean, who sings opera at 14 in the 80's?" Jenn said with admiration in her voice. Chris could tell that Jennifer would be her best friend. Jenn was a good singer in her own right and played keyboard. She was always writing songs. He could see that this was a match made in heaven. "Lexi asked about you and she thinks you're cute," Jenn said in a very serious voice.

Chris took a deep breath, then replied, "She's nice, but honestly, Jenn, I'm not interested in dating anyone. I have a future to study for and that would be a complete distraction for me."

Jenn rolled her eyes as she skated a little forward and turned around to skate backwards with him, grabbing both of his hands.

"I understand and I told her as much, but maybe you could think about it some," she told him.

Chris started to reply, but his focus was drawn to a young red-haired girl, standing with a group of people, staring directly at him. *That can't be...* he started to think when the sound of small rolling balls grabbed his attention. Curiously looking down, Chris watched as little silver ball bearings rushed by him. The quick stop happened before he had time to ready himself. He was launched forward into Jenn's chest, knocking her onto her back as Chris fell upon her.

"Jenn! Are you ok?" He quickly tried to take his weight off her. His question was answered by Jenn giggling and rubbing the back of her head.

"What happened?" she asked him while smiling and laughing.

He pointed down to his skates, "Rentals!" Jenn knew right then what had happened. Many nights they would sit and wait for people who rented skates to have the ball bearings in the wheel go out. They had made a joke of it. She wondered sometimes if the guy that rented the skates did it on purpose. One time, Chris had stated that the employees probably made bets on whose skates would fail first.

Chris made his way to stand up. With a helping hand he pulled Jenn to her feet. Laughter from his friends could be heard from across the rink floor.

Lexi skated up to them, "Are you guys alright?" she asked in a fearful voice.

"Yes, might have a headache tomorrow, not sure about him." Jenn smiled at her then looked at Chris, whose concern rested elsewhere. His head was moving back and forth as he peered back into the group of people standing near the seats. Jenn punched his arm. "Hello, Earth to Chris," she said as he turned his attention back to the two girls. He started to speak when Bart skated up to them.

"Jenn, may I have this skate, my lady?" he asked while bowing at the waist. She smiled and took his hand, leaving.

"*Et tu, Brute?*" Chris said while looking down at his broken skate, then hobbled his way back to his seat with help from Lexi.

"What were you looking at?" Lexi questioned him as they sat down in the open seats next to Lance. Chris took a deep breath, "Oh, I thought I saw some red-haired girl who was at the park today, just now when Jenn and I were skating. For some unknown reason she gives me a weird feeling."

Lance started laughing at him. Shocked by his response, Chris looked in his direction.

"Well, you're a dude. Weird strange feelings come with that," Lance said. Chris looked at his friend with raised eyebrows and his palms turned up waiting for an explanation.

Lexi stood up, smiling at him. "Call me tomorrow, luv, I'll be happy to explain. TTFN," she said then turned with a wink.

"TTFN?" Chris asked, looking at Lance who shrugged his shoulders.

A voice yelled out while going by, "Ta Ta For Now." Lexi waved while skating by.

Chapter 29

Chris walked through the woods to find himself standing at Lock 41. A young red-haired girl waved to him from the mound near the wall, gesturing for him to join her. The young girl twirled around, arms spread wide, her head tilted back as the bright sun lit up her face. Her red hair flowed in the air, tresses dancing in the sunlight giving it the appearance of streaming flames at the tips. As he approached her, she greeted him with a smile. She lowered herself to the blanket that had been laid out on the short grass.

"Come, sit, and join me," she said. Her smile was so friendly. Chris moved to sit across from her on the blanket. Her attention was not directed at him at first. She looked off into the woods, searching with her eyes. "I love it here. I've never felt more at home," she said while turning to look at him. Chris smiled when she met his gaze.

"I love your blue eyes," the girl told him as excitement filled her face. "Can I look at them?" she asked. Chris felt the embarrassment. Many girls had told him in the past about how they were so beautiful. It was a family trait passed down through the years, no matter who they married, the children from the union always had blue eyes. Chris nodded, then leaned forward. The girl's face moved closer to him. Suddenly he felt something change around him, the air became stale and unmoving. The sunlight dimmed, giving the surrounding area a strange grayscale effect. The air smelled of death. His stomach wretched as he looked at the girl to see if she was aware of the odor. Chris could see the flesh of her face sag and start to fall away, as her body started to decompose in front of his eyes. He screamed but nothing came out. The once young girl was now nothing but bones. Her once lively dress was now tattered, dirty like an old rag. Lifeless hair now adorned her head. Chris recoiled at the sight of bony arms extended for him. Pieces of old flesh still clung to her arms as other pieces fell away as she reached. With a sudden movement she plunged her fingers into the boy's eye socket. He felt the pain, white light flashed, then confusion for a second as he was looking at the ground and her at the same time. Then he felt a strange pressure, like having a tooth pulled. The pain came quickly. Tendons and muscles stretched, then broke or ripped away from their internal anchors, making a broken rubber band sound inside his head. Chris cried out as he brought his hands to his left eye, blood ran down his cheek, an empty space could be felt under his hands. In shock and disbelief, he looked up to see her holding his removed eyeball in her skeleton hand.

"Pretty!" the figure said lifting it closer to her wretched face to examine it more thoroughly.

"AHHHH!" Chris shot up from his bed in a gasp, sweat droplets dotted his face. As he panted to gain composure, his heart felt as if it could burst out of his chest any minute now if he didn't calm down. His mother had always warned him that watching the late-night horror show from Pittsburgh would give him bad dreams. Maybe she was right, but he needed to slow his breathing down and shake off the images in his mind. Sitting up on the edge of the bed he tried to remember the dream but not the whole dream, just the girl's face. *Was it the same girl from today at the park?* Still the image of the girl started to blur in his mind no matter how hard he tried to hold it.

The weekend came and went too fast for Chris. The nightmare from Saturday night ate at him the next day and continued on into Monday at school. He understood how the mind processed the day's events and that dreams were part of that, but this nightmare stuck with him. *Why that girl? Why that setting? Was there a hidden meaning behind everything?* he thought. Studying dreams was one of Chris's guilty pleasures that he would never share with his friends. To them, he was all about science and fact. Studying dreams was something people would make fun of him for. And God forbid, if they ever found out, they would never let him live it down.

The one thing that still bothered him the most was what he found Sunday morning. His left eye now was bloodshot, with two areas that looked to be almost bruised. The scientist in him figured that when he woke from his dream that he must have somehow bruised it in his panic. Pondering these questions had gotten him reprimanded for daydreaming in each of his morning classes. Placing his books in his locker, he realized his mind had more important things on which to focus.

"Yoo, Chris," someone called from behind him as he walked away from his locker. Stopping, Chris turned to find Lance and Rick Golden waving at him as they approached.

"Hey, Chris, I was telling Rick about that thing you found down at Gretchen's. Did you bring it?" Lance asked.

"No, sorry, I left it at home," he replied.

"That sucks," Rick said in disappointment. Chris looked at the odd couple. Unlike Lance, Rick Jones was almost six feet tall, with a muscular athletic build. He was a star football player and wrestler and Chris proudly called him his friend. Their friendship started a couple of years ago when Chris's group was being bullied and Rick came to their defense. His popularity among all of the students kept him busy, but he always found time for Chris and his companions.

Running a hand through his curly blond hair, he said to Chris. "Maybe bring it tomorrow, I've always liked seeing old jewelry. Maybe my mom could clean it up for you." Rick's family owned a local jewelry store, and his mom was an artist and magician when it came to repairing or cleaning up and restoring old jewelry. Chris nodded as the three teens headed to lunch.

* * *

Chris woke up early Saturday morning, preparing himself for a long weekend down at the dig site. The week had flown by for him. He had given the pendant to Rick, to have his mother take a look at it. Surprisingly, Mrs. Golden had cleaned it up very well and mounted it on an adult- sized leather bracelet for him to grow into. The biggest shock came when Rick's mother realized that her family originally made and sold it. While she was cleaning it, she had found a jeweler's mark that matched her family's business identification. Golden's Jewelry had been in East Liverpool since the 1800's. Rick's family had been there when the town was known as Fawcettstown, named after Thomas Fawcett, making his family one of the oldest in the area. The possibility of his ancestor creating this piece of jewelry was extremely high. Strapping the bracelet through his belt loop, Chris walked out to see his family already packing up the car.

His father turned to him. With a smile and using his most ridiculous voice, he called out, "Gooooood mornnnnnning, camper!"

Chris just smiled and wondered how adults could be so cheerful in the morning. He could never see himself becoming that way. But, this morning, he was not cheerful per se, but excited. Today, he hoped he would talk to the red-haired girl, the one who had haunted his thoughts ever since first meeting her gaze. He shook his head in disbelief as the realization gobsmacked him; he was actually thinking about girls. Oh, how Jenn and Lance would ride him about this. "Come on, Chris, get your head back in the game," he told himself in a soft voice.

"Hey, Chris, can you help grab a few things?" his mom asked as she carried a plastic tote box to the car. Chris nodded, then helped load the car knowing that within 20 minutes he would be unloading it again.

As they pulled into the Gretchen's Lock park area, Chris intensely looked for his target. Unorganized groups of people were spread throughout the parking lot. Exiting the car, Chris looked around to observe diverse age groups of people talking among themselves. A familiar voice cut through the din of various conversations, making Chris turn to look at the group to his left. Smiling faces welcomed him as he walked up to Jenn, Lexi, and Lance.

"You think we were going to let you suffer this all summer by yourself?" Lance greeted him, then continued, "Jenn and I discussed this and we wanted to come and help. Not saying we will be down here every weekend, but today, we are here for you."

Chris came closer and hugged his friends, when Jenn spoke up, "Um, question. We are not going to get dirty, are we? I just bought these shorts at Hill's Department store, and I'm not getting them filthy!"

Mr. Bowman heard the question and walked up and replied to the girl, "You'll get as dirty as you want. That depends on what you want to do."

Jenn smiled, looking at Chris's dad, "You're the best, Mr. Bowman. Lexi and I make great water girls and go-getters for people," Jenn said as she put an arm around Lexi, pulling her close. Both girls turned on the charm with their innocent angelic smiles.

Laughing, Mr. Bowman turned and pulled his son aside. "I'll make a deal with you," he said looking at Chris. "If you and your friends work hard this morning, I'll let you guys have the afternoon off for hanging out. Deal?" he asked, waiting for his son's answer. Chris brought up his hand with an extended pointer finger, gesturing "one second", then turned to discuss the option with his friends. Breaking from a small group huddle, they all turned, then agreed to the deal. Mr. Bowman handed buckets to the teens and pointed to the area they would be working. Chris stopped. *There's that feeling again,* he said to himself as the feeling of being observed crept up the back of his neck. Pivoting around, he thought he caught a glimpse of red hair ducking behind a tree along the edge of the park.

"Earth to Mr. Bowman, do you care to join us, or are you planning on standing there and taking a holiday?" Lexi called out in her Welsh accent.

"Holiday?" Chris asked with a puzzled look on his face.

"A vacation, you crazy wanker," Lexi said as she took his hand, letting out a loud breath in frustration at the boy for not understanding the meaning of simple English language.

Chris followed his friends, still allowing Lexi to hold his hand. The feeling of her warmth and the comfort that could be found in a simple gesture like this surprised him. It was nice but fear hit him fast. His thoughts went to Lance and the crush he had on Lexi. Faking a stumble, he freed his hand, hoping Lance didn't notice how long their hands had been entwined. Lexi turned to check on his welfare as her eyes moved beyond Chris.

"Looks like you have a secret admirer," Lexi informed him. Turning back, Chris was able to see his crimson-haired voyeur in the distance. He had decided earlier this morning that today was the day he would try to make contact with her.

Smiling, Chris waved to the girl, then mouthed a single word, "Hello." The girl stood there for a second and Chris could have sworn, even from this distance, he could see her cheeks glow red as she expressed a gasp on her face, then disappeared behind the tree again.

"Someone has a crush on you, my young prince," Lexi said laughing. "Well, I would like to inform her, the line starts... behind me." Her words took a few minutes to sink into Chris's brain. Turning to confront her on her meaning, his question remained unanswered as she ran to be next to Jenn and Lance. Suddenly, a strange thought came to his mind: *Am I becoming a young man? Or maybe it has something to do with this area that I am finally starting to see with my heart and not just my eyes? Or could it have been a heat stroke with the hot sun shining down on me?* Looking at the attractive girls in front of him, with thoughts of the whimsical-hearted girl hiding in the tree lines, something was definitely different. He didn't know when it happened, but this area had somehow changed him.

"Endless forms of beauty could be found here," he said with a small grin on his face.

Chapter 30

The boys worked hard most of the morning carrying buckets of dirt to a sifter as the two girls sat on a fallen tree in the shade. So far, they had just been watching, rather than helping.

"Are you girls ok there? I wouldn't want you to overdo it or break a nail," Lance called out to them as he struggled carrying buckets of dirt in each hand.

"Oh, luv, we are doing great, and the view is the best thing," Lexi called out as she winked at Lance. Blood rushed to his cheeks as shyness took over. Quickly he picked up his pace to hide his embarrassment as the two girls giggled. Chris, following Lance, stopped and gave the two vixens a stern look of disapproval.

Jenn bowed her head, stuck out her lower lip and replied, "Sorry, Daddy. We will behave." The two girls returned to whispering in each other's ears. Chris shook his head in disbelief then hid his smile from them. Teasing Lance bothered him a little. Although he knew it was all in fun, sometimes Lance took things the wrong way. As he passed him on his way back, Chris noticed him walking fast and if he wasn't mistaken, he now had his stomach sucked in and chest stuck out. "Go get 'em, tiger," he said, smiling at Lance as he went back past the girls. Chris made his way to the dirt sifting area. A group of people stood beside an elevated table with a wire screen mesh as a top. Chris handed his bucket to one of the workers and watched as the man dumped the contents into the sifter and with a shake of the table smaller dirt fell through the screen revealing larger objects and stones. "We got wood," one of the table workers called out with excitement. Chris smirked to himself and thought, *Of course you got wood, we are in a forest.*

Returning to fill his buckets he caught a glimpse of his admirer hiding behind a tree just down the path. Steadily he made his way to the spot. This time he would say "Hi" to her, then maybe bring to an end this *I - see - you* game that they have been playing. He made his way to the large maple tree standing alone among small bushes. "Hi, I'm Chris," he said as he rounded the tree. To his surprise the girl was not there. He circled the tree in confusion. *Where did she go? I kept my eyes on that tree all the way to it. If she had left I would have seen her,* he thought. The sound of a stick breaking to his left got his attention. Looking quickly, he only saw the tips of her crimson hair disappear behind a tree about 70 feet away from him. "I give up, you win" Chris said out loud then returned to walking back to the dig site.

Lunch time couldn't arrive soon enough for Chris and Lance. Sitting on the bank of the water Lance spoke first, "My arms hurt so much I can barely lift them." Chris, rubbing his own arms, commented that his felt like rubber.

"I can't believe you're going to be spending your whole summer here," Lance said to his friend.

"I know, but it's for my mom and dad, so I'll just bite my lip and fight through the pain of the work and the boredom," Chris replied looking down in defeat as they talked. "I can't believe Lexi and Jenn sat and watched us work, today," he said while noticing something hidden among the stones and dirt his feet had kicked up from the loose ground along the stream's edge. He looked puzzled then excitement grew as he reached down and picked up an Indian arrowhead.

"That is too cool!" Lance exclaimed, looking at the piece of carved stone in his friend's hands. "For someone that didn't want to be down here, you sure keep finding things."

Chris replied, "I know. Two times down here and I've found something each day."

"What did you find?" A female voice came from behind them followed by giggling.
Jenn and Lexi came and sat next to the boys. Lexi sat closer to Lance as Jenn leaned against Chris. He showed the two girls his latest treasure.

"What is that, luv?" Lexi asked as she held out her hand to look at it.

"Well, Lexi, that is an arrowhead from an Indian's arrow, most likely from the Mingo tribe," Chris said while handing it to her.

"Wouldn't it be awesome if it came from one of Queen Alliquippa's tribes?" Lance excitedly asked.

"Whoa, one bloody second," Lexi said. "You mean this is from a Red Indian?" Chris and Lance looked at each other trying to figure out what she meant. "Red Indian, you know. Lone Ranger and Tonto," as she made a gesture patting her hand over her mouth like an Indian call. Chris smiled and nodded.

Jenn pulled Lexi to her in a side hug and said, "Isn't she the cutest thing?" The teens broke out in laughter as Lexi started to show signs of embarrassment.

"Don't make fun of me. You bloody Yanks can't understand proper English!" Lexi spouted as she folded her arms across her chest, then turned her head away from them as she blew out air in disgust.

"Come on, guys. Leave her alone." Lance quickly came to her defense. She turned, then mouthed "thank you" to him.

"Who's Queen Alliquippa? Do you mean the city up the river in Pennsylvania?" Jenn asked the boys. The boys looked at each other with a surprised expression, then at Jenn.

"Weren't you listening in class?" Chris asked.

"No, she's too busy trying to get all buddy-buddy with the new Spanish teacher so she can pass his class," Lance told him.

Jenn glared at them, but Chris continued, "Queen Alliquippa was the leader of a band of Mingo Seneca Indians that lived near Pittsburgh."

"Plus, George Washington met with her during the French and Indian War, and that's who the city of Aliquippa is named after," Lance added.

Both girls looked at each other and started to laugh, "You two are such nerds, cute, but, still nerds," Jenn said.

Lexi quickly chimed in, "But you are *our* nerds." Lexi leaned over and kissed Lance on the cheek.

"Why don't we go exploring since we have the rest of the day. Lexi has got to see the famous Gretchen's Lock," Jenn said as she got up and extended a hand to Chris to help him up. Chris rose to his feet with a nod in agreement.

"Sounds like a good plan," he replied while pushing the arrowhead into his pocket. Jenn took Lexi's hand and led the way as the boys followed. Across the creek from where the teens had been sitting, a young red-haired girl stepped out from behind a large tree to watch them walk away.

The day had come to a close faster than they realized. The walk to Gretchen's had been sidetracked a lot, as old stories of embarrassing moments of Chris and Lance's past were brought back by Jenn to share with Lexi. Rushing back to the parking lot, they saw their impatient parents awaiting them.

Standing beside his car as his wife talked to the other parents, Mr. Bowman questioned, "Where have you guys been?"

"Sorry, Dad, we lost track of time," Chris apologized without making eye contact. Opening the rear door, he waved goodbye to his friends. "Thank you for hanging out with me today."

"No problem, buddy. See you Monday," Lance called out, as he got in the passenger side of his mother's car.

Chris looked to say goodbye to Jenn and Lexi but the sight of the two girls climbing into the Harrison vehicle with loud music playing made him realize he had missed the chance.

"You really have some great friends there," Mr. Bowman said to his son as he started the car.

"So, Chris, who's the new girl?" his mom asked as his father pulled out of the parking lot onto the one-lane road leading out of the park.

"Oh, that's Lexi. She's new to the school, her family just moved here from Wales. I think her father is some big wig at the new plant in town," Chris told his parents.

Mrs. Bowman raised an eyebrow. "There you go, she's cute, and her family has money," she said.

"MOM! Stop that. She's just a friend, like Jenn," Chris countered. In frustration, he turned his attention to look out the window.

"Hun," Mr. Bowman said to his wife, in response to her playful teasing of her son.

"Ok, ok, ok, I'll stop. But I'm just saying, face it, son, you hit the jackpot with her," she quickly added, then reached over and took her husband's hand in hers.

Mr. Bowman looked at his wife, then smiled "Kind of like when I hit the jackpot with you," he told his wife.

"Yuck, get a room," Chris uttered from the back seat.

His parents smiled at each other. Chris's mom winked at her husband and mouthed "Later," bringing an eyebrow raise from her husband.

Taking a second to find his composure, Mr. Bowman looked at his son in the rear-view mirror, "So what did you kids do this afternoon?" he asked, jarring Chris's attention from the daytime nightmare he was having about his parents' bedroom activities.

"I found an Indian arrowhead," he said as he dug deep into his pocket to find it. A look of shock spread across his face as the location of an unknown hole in his pocket was discovered by his searching fingers. "Oh, no," Chris called out as he frantically searched other pockets.

Mrs. Bowman turned to watch her son search around his pants. "What's wrong, Hunny?" she asked.

"I lost it. I did not know I had a hole in my pocket, it must have fallen out on the hike somewhere," he explained. Frustrated by the loss, Chris couldn't believe he had made such a stupid mistake.

"Don't let it get to you, son," his father comforted. "When I was on my first dig in college, my class was in this area. We unearthed a piece of intact ware from Sprucevale Pottery just downstream from where our present dig is. As I was tagging it I dropped it."

"What! You dropped it? Oh man, that would have sucked. Was the professor mad?" Chris asked. The thought of his father making a mistake like that didn't seem possible in his mind. His father was diligent in every aspect of his life, and he was like a surgeon operating when it came to artifacts. He knew his father would meticulously dig with his small trowel and then gently brush away the dirt from the delicate artifact.

"Well, let's say I got an earful but after that, the professor took me aside and told me something especially important. He placed a hand on my shoulder and explained about how to be sure of yourself and always be patient." His dad stopped, then finished by saying, "But always remember, you can do everything right but in spite of that, sometimes, shit happens." The family broke out in laughter in their surprise at hearing the elder Bowman's colorful vocabulary.

Arriving home, the Bowmans made their way into the house.

"I call dibs on the shower," his mother called out. Chris went to his room. Lying on his bed, waiting for his turn to wash up, he unhooked the bracelet from his belt buckle. Laying it on his nightstand, he laughed to himself, *Today was a day to remember, today was the first day I ever heard Dad curse.*

"Yes, Dad. It does. It does happen."

Chapter 31

A light fog greeted the Bowmans as they pulled into the park
Sunday morning. Chris hoped that his friends would surprise
him again, but deep down inside he knew since it was Sunday,
in this small town in eastern Ohio, all the stores would be
closed, nothing would be open. Unlike the big cities, it was
church day and family day in this corner of Chris's world.

"Your mom and I are going to go lay out some grids for
some future digs, so go have some adventure time for a while
but stay somewhat close by," his father told Chris. Nodding in
agreement, he turned to retrace his steps from the previous day.
Losing the arrowhead bothered him. He had laid in his bed
thinking about everywhere they went yesterday in the park.
Knowing the chances were very small, he still had to try. This
morning Chris decided to start from the beginning, where he
knew he put it in his pants. The arrowhead most likely fell out
later in the day but maybe there was a chance that he had missed
his pocket when he first tucked it into his jeans. It might be
lying beside where he and his friends were sitting. Chris walked
the path to the dirt and rock covered area where not more than
24 hours ago he and his friends first discovered the Indian
treasure. He slowly watched the ground, stopping every few feet
to scan the surface left and right. The fog was burning off as the
morning sun started to shine rays of light through the trees. The
park was void of humans this early in the morning, birds sang,
as the water running over the rocks added just enough sound to

make his soul relax. Chris closed his eyes; the beauty around him didn't need to be seen, all it needed was to be heard and felt. *Mr. Washington, I didn't need to build my Walden, I think I found it,* he thought as a smile crept across his face.

All year long he had heard that saying at the end of every week. He asked his parents what it meant; they would always say the same thing, "You'll understand when you find it." *Should I tell them that I found it, admitting they were right? Nope! I don't want to hear Mom saying things about mother knows best.* Making his way to where they had sat, Chris stood in disbelief. There it was, sitting on top of a rock that he was nowhere near when he put it away. "How did you get there?" he asked the arrowhead, reaching down to pick it up. A movement from behind startled him as he turned in time to see what he thought was the edge of a dress disappearing behind a tree. "Why are we playing these games?" Chris shouted into the woods. He stood there hoping to hear a response that never came.

Chris stood there biting his lower lip trying to figure out this girl. He let out a small chuckle. "Well, not just this girl, but all girls," he said softly. Lately he had not been seeing things the same anymore. The opposite sex was something he never thought about much at all, but for some reason he found himself starting to notice them. *Maybe it was me, or maybe it was the girls who had changed, 'cause Jenn was still one of the boys even though she was a girl.* He had never found himself looking at her that way. This problem would have to be shelved because he knew his parents would be waiting for him. Picking up a stick he would try something different to make contact with this strange female. In the sand he wrote in capital letters,

"THANK YOU."

Chris arrived just as his parents had finished gridding off the sites. "Look what I found!" he said while walking up to his father who was in the middle of rewinding the string he used for the grids. Chris handed it to his dad.

"Whoa! You found it. That's great," he told him, as his father examined the item. "This definitely looks like Mingo and the age and style look about right, too." Mr. Bowman handed the item back to his son, then said, "We are going to make an archeologist out of you yet." Chris smiled at his dad's comment but deep down both son and father knew that digging in dirt was not where his passion was. Physics was the field he would most likely go after, but Chris did once joke with his dad about cryptozoology. His father figured that came around from his love of Sunday afternoon monster movies and comic books.

Chris walked to the car and took out a container he had taken from his mother's kitchen plastic bowl collection, then placed the arrowhead inside and sealed the container.

"Is that one of your mother's irreplaceable party prizes?" his father asked as he approached the boy from behind.

"Yes, I needed something secure so that I won't lose it again," he explained to his dad.

"Don't let your mother see you doing that!" his father warned him. Chris softly chuckled, as he hid the container under the back seat of the family's car.

The morning work went fast with just his parents and himself. His job today was to hammer stakes into the ground to mark out the areas. Pretending he was Abraham Van Helsing and the grid pattern was vampires' hearts, as he drove the wood spike into the ground he thought, *One more blood sucker dusted.* He enjoyed this game, then before he knew it, it was lunch time and to his surprise his parents gave him the rest of the day off.

"Go have fun, but stay close," his mother told him. Chris smiled as he headed to the creek to sit. He enjoyed this spot, plus he could look around to see if there were any more artifacts to be discovered along the waterway. When he arrived, the peaceful quiet he had found in the morning was still there. He figured most of the people were still in church. His family believed in God, but his parents did not go to church that often at all anymore. When he was younger, they would be there every Sunday but now that he was older, it had been a year maybe since they had gone. Many times, Chris, had wondered if they only went when he was younger for him or to up their standing in the community. He walked downstream from where he and his friends sat yesterday to search the ground when he abruptly stopped. The thought shot through his mind like a bolt of lightning, *Oh my God, I've become my parents. I'm searching the dirt.* That made him laugh, but he decided that if they didn't see him doing it, it didn't count. He started to search more when he approached the spot where earlier he had written in the dirt, *THANK YOU.* Looking down he saw there was a single yellow flower with small red and white spots on the petals. Below the flower, it simply said,   ***YOU ARE WELCOME***.

Stunned by this exchange between him and this mysterious girl, he needed to know who she was. She intrigued him. As he stood there, the sound of a twig snapping across the creek on the hillside commanded his attention. He carefully examined the forest looking for the brazen hair that had been spying on him since this summer adventure had begun. Suddenly, a small doe jumped over a fallen tree then hurried up the side of the incline. Chris let out his breath he had been unconsciously holding; a laugh erupted from him as nervous energy found its release. He returned to staring at the message on the ground. He wiped it clean with his hands like using an eraser on a chalkboard, then wrote his return message to his secret friend.

> *HELLO.*
> *MY NAME IS CHRIS BOWMAN.*
> *MAYBE WE COULD MEET AND TALK.*
> *I HOPE YOU SAY YES.*

Satisfied with what he wrote, he headed back to his parents. When he arrived, he found that they were heading home after calling it a day. Chris found himself happy, but sad at the same time. *How long would it take for his new friend to read the message?* He had planned to check it later before they left. But now he could only hope that if she replied today, no rain would come and wash away her response.

Confused, Chris found himself strangely excited about a girl for the first time in his life. *Could there be something wrong with me? A chemical imbalance could be happening in my brain. I need to call and talk to Jenn tonight, maybe she could help me out. If that doesn't work, I will ask Mom to make a doctor appointment for me.*

Once home, Chris sneaked into his room with the arrowhead. He would go to the school library Monday and see if he could identify it. Sitting on his bed, he opened the plastic bowl. Shock and surprise jarred him hard, causing him to drop the container spilling its contents on the floor. His mind raced for an explanation, how could that be possible? Lying on the floor next to the arrowhead was a single yellow flower with small red and white spots on the petals.

Chapter 32

"**J**enn, I think I'm losing it. I know I put the arrowhead in the container by itself. There is no way a flower was in there at that time. How could it have gotten there? Did she break into mom and dad's car? Should I be worried that she is some kind of criminal?" Chris excitedly asked.

"How do you know it was her?" Jenn asked.

"CAUSE IT WAS THE SAME DAMN FLOWER THAT I LEFT LYING BY THE CREEK!" Chris informed her.

"Well then, my handsome lad, sounds like someone is infatuated with you. She must have seen you with the bowl and placed it in the container when you weren't there," she told him. Chris pondered her theory. Her idea made sense, but he now found himself at a crossroads. Should he find her action romantic as Jenn was leaning towards? Or should he now be worried? He had seen too many movies about crazy people showing their affection, only to find out later they were serial killers.

"Hello, Mr. Bowman," a familiar voice was now on the phone. *Lexi must be at Jenn's house and without warning she must have handed off the phone to her*, he quickly thought." Did you have fun today down at the nant?"

Chris stared at the phone in confusion. "Nant?" he asked her.

"Oh! I'm sorry. I forgot you call them streams here in the colonies," she replied with embarrassment in her voice. Chris smiled. He started to find it cute that she would slip and use Welsh words as she talked.

"Yeah, it was fun. I think my secret admirer, possibly stalker, was down there, too, watching me again." Lexi became quiet with that statement. Chris wondered if he had said something wrong.

After a moment of silence, Lexi said, "Well, I guess I'll see you tomorrow for the last week of school." After another pause, Lexi simply said, "*Nos Da*." Chris started to ask, when she laughed and told him, "It means good night."

"Aww, ok. *Nos Da*, to you, too," Chris replied as he heard Jenn tell Lexi good night. The sound of a closing door could be heard over the telephone, then Jenn returned to their conversation.

"So, tell me, do you like Lexi?" Jenn asked, waiting to hear his reply.

"Honestly, she's nice. But there is a big problem. Lance is crushing on her bad," he told Jenn.

She growled into the phone. "Chris, she likes you, plus she's not some psycho stalking you. She's real and will talk to you face to face. Lance is nice but she's attracted to you, not him," she told him. Chris remained silent. He could not do this to Lance, it would maybe kill their friendship if he even made a move to be near Lexi. That was something he couldn't do. Lance and Jenn were his best friends, and he would do anything for both of them. With that thought, the answer was right in front of him. "I can't, Jenn. Please tell Lexi I only want to be friends with her."

Jenn was disappointed in his answer but deep down she understood. That was something that made her respect and love him. "So, since you won't cross that line does that mean the redhead at the park is where you're going to direct your attention?" Jenn asked. Even though she couldn't see him, Jenn could imagine Chris's cheeks were red and his eyes were rolling. She started to speak when she heard the phone being picked up and buttons being pushed. "Hello, I'm on the phone," Jenn said quickly. Chris heard frustration from her line, then the voice of her mom.

"I need to call your father's aunt so let me know when you're done."

"Ok, Mom, I'm hanging up now." Jenn replied as Chris heard the other phone click. "I'd better go. I'll see you tomorrow. Good night, Chris." She abruptly ended their phone call. He told her good night as the dial tone rang in his ear.

* * *

The last week of school had finally arrived, and for the first time in a while, Chris was excited by that fact. He had waited all week. Today was Friday. Tomorrow he would be down at the park, hopefully reading the mysterious girl's message. This strange feeling about talking to a girl was scary but exhilarating at the same time.

"Hey you," a familiar girl's voice interrupted his thoughts of his new pen pal.

"Oh, hey, Jenn, what's up?" Chris replied as his friend came up alongside him wrapping her arm around him as they walked.

"Um, soo, who is your very, very, very bestest friend?" she queried.

"Did you forget your lunch money again, little girl?" Not waiting for an answer, he handed her 50 cents.

"You're the best, that's why I love you so much, Daddy," she responded, giving him a peck on the cheek, then running to the cafeteria. Smiling, Chris made his way down the hall when loud shouting caught his attention.

He looked around the corner that led to the staircase to find Lance crouched down leaning against the wall where three boys had him cornered. Chris recognized them from their matching dirty blue jean jackets. Heavy metal band names written with magic markers covered their backs.

The leader, George Martin, was always causing trouble in and out of school. He once showed up drunk at the skating rink and was promptly thrown out and barred for life. At 16, he was bigger than most of the 14-year-old eighth graders. Bullying the smaller students was his favorite pastime. Today, Lance was his target. Without a second thought, Chris rushed toward the backs of the three boys. With everything he had, he launched himself into George, knocking him forward into the wall above the crouching Lance. Chris jumped up to his feet, hoping he had bought Lance enough time to escape. Clenching his fists, he then readied himself for the impending brawl. He was not good at fighting, but he would defend his friend. The first and only fight he ever had was against Jenn in third grade. She bloodied his lip and beat him up pretty badly before the teachers broke it up.

"Oh, sooo, someone wants to play," George said as he started to get up. His companions tried to assist him, but George knocked their helping hands away from him. "Go watch for teachers," George said as he motioned for the boy to his right to stand guard.

Chris knew he wasn't going to win this fight, but it would be worth it to save his friend. Behind George, Chris could see Lance starting to rise, blood ran from his lips, tears pooled in his eyes. Anger pushed down the fear in Chris's mind as the sight of his friend's pain caused him to lash out with everything he had. Swinging wildly, he punched George in the face, knocking the older boy back a few steps. Chris stood astonished by his success, but all hope disappeared when he saw the boy smile as he squared himself up to him.

"TEACHER!" a voice shouted out. George quickly relaxed, then pointed at Chris, "This isn't over, watch your back."

Chris did cartwheels inside, he was saved. With summer coming up, the chances of running into George were slim to none. *Most likely he would be in juvie,* he thought and next year would be high school where George would be a small fish in a big pond.

Chris walked over to help his friend. "I don't need your help." Lance pushed him back. He felt bad, all he wanted to do was help and protect him, but Chris knew this was pride talking. Lance had always been picked on for being a little chubby. He was a great person, but most only saw him as the awkward fat kid. People could be so cruel.

"One day, no one will push me around," Lance said as he wiped the blood from his lip.

"What were you thinking? You know the rules, never walk alone and run when it comes to George and his fellow delinquents."

"George was saying nasty things about Lexi. I was not going to let him get away with that. Someone needed to defend her." Chris smiled but also shook his head after hearing Lance's vows of chivalry.

"Sir Lancelot," Chris said while pretending to knight his friend with an imaginary sword. Lance grimaced as he tried to smile.

"You think it will make me look tougher and win Lexi's heart?" he asked. Chris smiled while patting his friend on the back.

"Well, I've heard it said that chicks dig scars," Chris replied.

"I'll tell you one thing. I'm done with this." Lance looked at him, then continued, "This summer, I'm going to take some kind of karate. Getting picked on stops this year!"

Chris looked at his friend with appreciation. "You know what, if I have time I might join you." Both boys entered the cafeteria, skipping the lunch line completely. Jenn, Lexi, Bart, and Rick sat at a table by themselves in the back corner of the lunchroom. Jenn jumped up and rushed to Lance upon seeing his busted lip.

"What happened?" she asked angrily as the others joined her in the questioning.

"I tripped on the steps," Lance told her as he waved off the rest of them. Chris looked puzzled. He wasn't sure why his friend made that statement but decided not to say anything at this time.

"What do you mean, you tripped?" Bart asked, knowing Lance's excuse was not the truth.

"Who did it?" Jenn's eyes squinted as she asked. He looked at his friends, knowing they only meant to protect him, as they had done many times before. But after today it was his burden to carry, not his friends'. Lexi pushed her way through Jenn and Bart, with a napkin in her hand to reach up to wipe the blood from his lip.

"No!" Lance said while pushing her hand away. "I'm ok. I don't need help." Lance turned as Jenn reached for him, but he pulled his arm away before she could grab him.

"Let him go," Rick said to Jenn. "Sometimes guys need to be alone to figure things out," he told her.

"So, what is it? Some stupid guy thing?" she asked.

"Yes," all three boys answered in unison.

"Come on, Lex. Let's leave these boys to their measuring competition." Jenn grabbed her friend's arm as they headed out of the lunchroom. Bart turned, then asked Chris what had really happened. After a few seconds of hesitation Chris recounted the story to his friends.

"Beating up George is not going to help Lance out. He is going to have to stand up to his bully because it's going to keep happening 'til he faces his demon," Rick said to them both. It pained Chris, but he knew that Rick was right. Rick and Bart could beat up George but all that would do is make it worse for Lance when they were not around to protect him. With that, they headed for their afternoon classes.

Mr. Washington's was the last class of this school year. Chris and his friends sat and listened to the teacher as he told them stories of his youth. He had tried to talk to Lance but his friend just nodded most of the time and when he did answer, it mostly was one word. Looking up at the clock, he was happy only five minutes of school remained, then the summer of Gretchen's Lock awaited him. His thoughts returned to the excitement of the phantom girl. He hadn't thought about her much since lunchtime. He wondered if there would be a reply waiting for him tomorrow.

"Remember everyone, I will be one of the volunteers down at Gretchen's Lock and everyone is welcome to help Chris and his parents this summer with the dig." Chris cringed when Mr. Washington's voice broke his daydreaming. He wondered if he had told every period the same thing. Having his friends down there was nice, but he really wanted to get to know the new timid girl. But with the extra help showing up, the shy girl may never talk to him with so many of his friends hanging around him.

"Coming?" Lance asked him as they all got up and left the classroom.

"I have to make sure I got everything from my locker," Chris told him as Lance headed to their bus. He rounded the corner of the crowded hall, when a shove in his back knocked him forward, causing him to stumble into other students. Chris regained his footing and turned around to see George Martin. The older bully placed his index finger to his lips to express a quiet gesture, then smiled and slowly turned away to disappear among the rush of students. Confused by the gesture, Chris could only stand and watch, as hastily moving students made their exit to begin their summer vacations.

Chapter 33

Chris awoke early Saturday morning. He was surprised he was able to sleep at all with thoughts of the girl and Lance filling his mind. He had talked to Lance last night on the phone a little, but Chris decided not to mention anything about being pushed by the bully in the hall. Lance sounded better, so telling him of the event would just bring him back down. The statement his friend had made about taking self-defense lessons from the one-handed karate instructor they had met last summer at the youth group surprised him. He knew they had talked about it in the past, but they talked about a lot of things. Maybe he should join Lance in some lessons, too, but he doubted his parents would approve. Many times, throughout Chris's young life, he had thought of his parents as hippies. Violence in any form was one thing his parents did not approve of. Taking self-defense lessons most likely was not an option for him. But Chris felt the need to learn something for his protection as he got older. Maybe Lance could teach him some things without his parents knowing.

Lost in thought he didn't notice the first honk of the car horn, but his mother's voice calling out to him got his attention. Chris quickly finished dressing, grabbed the pendant wristband from his nightstand, and joined his parents in the car. They made it to the park a little before 8 a.m. Other than a few empty cars probably owned by local people fishing, he and his parents were the only ones there. Stepping out of the car, Chris asked,

"Would it be ok if I went over to the creek for a few minutes to check something out?"

Chris's father looked up from the map he was laying out on the ground. "Sure, just make sure you're back before too many people arrive." With a smile, Chris turned and headed down the path to the place he and the mysterious girl had started leaving messages last weekend. With mother nature in full bloom this morning, Chris decided today would be a good time to jog. Not even halfway into his run, a sharp pain in his side started to rear its ugly head. Stopping to place pressure on his side, he stood there panting, as the pain of the side stitch brought a cringe to his face. He was not very athletic, studying took up most of his time, but now he realized that maybe he should start getting into better shape.

"What is wrong with me?" Chris asked softly as he tried to walk the pain away. "First, I'm getting excited about talking to a strange girl, then wanting to learn self-defense, and now I'm thinking about exercising!" He wondered where all this was coming from, maybe it's just part of being a teenager. He did know one thing: He was changing but was not sure if he liked that.

Chris walked the last bit to the clearing by the creek. Looking down, his heart jumped as the message he had left last weekend was now replaced with something new. Leaning down, Chris looked at the message.

"*Tá áthas orm bualadh leat*, Christopher,"

"What the hell is that supposed to mean?" Chris murmured in puzzlement.

"You could have at least left me your name!" he then shouted into the woods. Feeling dejected, Chris made his way back to the main parking lot. *What did that message mean?* He pondered over and over in his head as he walked, looking back and side to side to see if she was watching him. Chris tried his best to hide the disappointment in his heart as he walked up to his parents, who thankfully were too busy talking to one of the volunteers to notice his expression. With a steady voice he announced his return to his father who just said, "ok" to him as he walked by them to sit on the rear bumper of the car. All week he had waited in anticipation for today, now he could only stare off into the distance at the grass and small white and yellow flowers. "Daisies," he said softly, "That will work; I'll leave them for her and hide. Then when she shows up, I'll walk up to her and talk." Excitement filled his soul. Jumping up, he rushed to his parents' side.

"What would you like me to do today?" he asked his mother.

Looking up from her plastic tote, she replied, "I don't think we will need you this morning, so if you want to go do some exploring, I don't see a problem with that."

Smiling, Chris leaned down and kissed his mother's head. "Thanks, Mom. You're the greatest. Oh, can I borrow some of that blue marking ribbon you have in the trunk?" Mrs. Bowman nodded and smiled as she saw the radiant look on her son's face. He quickly went to retrieve it, then made his way across the grass field.

"What was that about?" Mr. Bowman asked as he walked up to his wife while both of them watched Chris leave.

"Well, either your son is on the threshold of the greatest scientific discovery of any century, or," she paused, "our son has officially become a teenage boy."

Mr. Bowman looked at his wife, confusion filling his eyes. "Girls."

"Aww, ok," Mr. Bowman replied with a smile that was soon replaced by a worried look.

"Oh no. That means it's time for the talk," he said as Mrs. Bowman picked up the supplies and as she walked away, said,

"That's all you, Tiger."

Chris examined each delicate flower, looking for the longest stem of each daisy. He carefully broke each one at its lowest point. He meticulously arranged the flowers in his hands, looking at them from each side. After the adjustments were made, he tied the blue ribbon around them. With a new sense of purpose, he made his way down the trail to his personal earth pen pal spot. Chris gently laid the bouquet of flowers on top of the writing the young girl had left him. Looking around to make sure no spying eyes were about; he quickly made his way to a large oak tree he had seen just off the trail. That location would allow him to view the resting flowers while providing a perfect hiding place for him.

The morning sun slowly made its way overhead to take away the shade Chris had enjoyed earlier in the morning. While still hiding behind the tree, he peered at the flowers every few minutes then returned back to the safety side of the trunk which blocked most vision from the creek. *Anytime now,* Chris thought to himself. *Why was she so shy, and what was the message she had left behind?* He looked at the spot only to return to his hidden position. A small squirrel jumping from branch to branch started to win Chris's attention. He was amazed how the grey furry mammal could navigate the limbs so quickly and spring across distances so effortlessly. With his loathing of heights, he would never make a good squirrel. He quietly chuckled at the thought of himself as a squirrel and never leaving the safety of the ground. Chris returned to checking when he saw her standing directly in front of the flowers that lay on the ground. The copper-haired girl stood there as her muslin dress moved slightly with the breeze. She bent at the waist, straight kneed, to examine the gift closely. Curlettes of red hair flowed downwards as her tresses danced slowly with the spring breath of wind. Picking up the flowers, she then gracefully returned upright. Chris watched as she clutched the flowers in both hands, raising the blossoms to her nose to smell them as she stared lovingly into the floral vision of beauty. He slowly crept from around the tree, careful not to make a sound. Then silently he made his way to the path, watching the girl at all times. She brought the petals to her cheek, then closed her eyes as she rested them against the side of her face.

She seemed to light up, Chris thought. *She is radiating with a golden shimmer as the sun smiles down on her in her private moment of bliss.* He had edged closer to the illusive girl when her eyes shot open as she stared directly at him. A look of terror and fear covered her face. Chris brought both of his hands up to try and calm her when a voice came from behind.

"There you are. We have been looking all over for you, should have known you would be back here." Chris turned to see Lance, Jenn, Lexi, and Rick making their way to him from the main trail.

"Your mother said she thought you were up here, but no, Lance decided you would be down creek, 'cause he knows everything!" Jenn said.

Lance shot back, "Shut up, Jenn!"

Chris turned back to the girl to only find that she was gone. The bouquet of flowers with the blue ribbon lay on the ground where she had once stood.

"Where did she go?" Chris remarked as he rushed to the area where she had been only a few seconds ago. Looking left and right, he could find no sign of her.

"Whatcha looking for?" Jenn asked as she and Lexi came to rest next to him.

"That red-haired girl. She was just here," Chris said as he squinted to look.

"Well, I didn't see any girl. Did you, Lexi?" Jenn asked as Lexi just frowned at the thought of Chris being so obsessed with a mysterious rival.

"There was no girl here when we came up. We could see the area just fine. We saw you slowly walking up.to the clearing. Hell, I thought you were trying to catch some mouse or a frog," Rick chimed in, then continued, "Maybe you ate some weird type of mushroom and you're tripping."

241

Laughter broke out among the companions, except for Lexi, who slowly in sadness backed away from the group.

Chapter 34

"**W**hy can't you just give Lexi a chance? Instead, you are wasting all your free time chasing after a girl who is so shy and backwards, that she won't even meet a great person like you." Jenn, in frustration, said to Chris as they sat on a rock out of earshot of the rest of the group.

Chris tried to explain to her about Lance and his crush on Lexi. "I can't do that to him. He's my best friend, just like you. I would never go after a girl you liked." The words escaped Chris's mouth before he realized what he had said.

She started to speak, but her lips failed to move. She looked at him with shock in her eyes as her mind raced in panic at Chris's statement. *How does he know? Oh my God, What should I say? Should I lie?*

Knowing it was too late to go back now, he needed to reassure her that it was ok. "I know, Jenn," he simply said. She sat there, unable to answer, as he leaned over and hugged her. "No one else suspects, so your secret is for you to tell. Who you like doesn't matter to me. You're still my best friend," he comforted her.

"How did you figure it out?" she asked in a shaky voice.

Choosing his words carefully, he responded, "Jenn, I've known you for a while. You never really look at boys. The only boy you have spent a lot of time with is me. I had my suspicions, but honestly, I wasn't sure until Lexi came into our world." She sat there silently listening. "All I had to do was watch your eyes when she was around. You light up," Chris told her. "Does your family know?"

Jenn shook her head, "I think my mom suspects, but I haven't told anyone."

"Your family is awesome, and I know they will love you, no matter what. I think you should tell them," Chris suggested.

"So, you're saying I need to walk into my house and shout to everyone, 'Guess what family, your daughter is gay. Yup, she likes girls.' I'm sorry, Chris. That's not something I can do." Jenn explained as he placed an arm around her shoulder, hugging her again. Jenn melted into his hug, taking a few minutes away from the world.

"I am sure if you talked to the school counselor that they can help you."

"Ha, Oh, yeah! I am sure they have plenty of pamphlets in the racks on the wall! I can see the title of the brochure now, 'Hi Mom, I'm a Dyke,'" she responded sarcastically as she pushed away.

Chris sat there silently. Then said with a devilish grin, "Why would you tell your mom you are a levy?" Jenn stared at him, confused by his response, then started to grin as she pulled Chris into her own hug.

"I am sorry to go off on you like that. It's just really hard on me to have to keep this secret. I am who I am, and I am proud of it, but you know, society says I should be ashamed to be what I am.

"I love who you are. Don't ever change. Just be my Jenn." Chris smiled.

"You know, if I wasn't, I'd be after you, too," Jenn said as she smiled and kissed his cheek then pulled away to see her friend's face start to flush.

"Well, if you were after me, no other girls would stand a chance in my eyes!"

Smiling, she got up, then extended a hand to help her friend up. "Will you at least talk to her and explain yourself?" Jenn asked him, changing the subject as she turned to rejoin the others.

"What about you? Are you going to tell her that you're crushing hard on her?" he asked her.

Jenn turned back to him and said, "Remember, it's my secret to share, and I choose not."

He couldn't help but feel bad about the whole situation, Lance and Jenn both wanting someone, but that person had eyes for someone else. He knew deep down that this was going to end badly for everyone. He was starting to not like growing up. He found himself missing the times of the three friends arguing over who got the better Christmas present or which new sci-fi tv series was better.

The distinct sound of movement, followed by the noise of a twig breaking from behind him, snapped his mind back from those times of innocence. Chris turned to just catch a small glimpse of something red dodging behind a tree, *And to top it all off, there's her, Chris* thought to himself. *This girl who watches me like I am a shoplifter in a store, never approaching, always keeping a safe distance from me. I would probably have a better chance of talking to Bigfoot or the Mothman than this sentinel of the woods.* He picked up his pace to join his friends as he walked up a slight grade to close the distance between them. They were now standing in a small clearing in the woods. A large rusty shape lay on the ground, with smaller shaped pieces of steel resting nearby, and rotting slabs of wood outlining the clearing. Chris approached the larger piece of metal. Many times, he had been to this site, but every time his mind would start pondering on one question, *Why did they just leave this all here?* Through the years he had heard several stories about the abandoned lumber mill. They ranged from people hearing a young girl scream to poachers stealing lumber. None of them seemed correct in his mind.

"What is this doing out here?" Lexi asked, breaking the silence of the group.

"This is the old sawmill that was abandoned here a long time ago," Lance told her.

"Why is it just laying here like this?" she asked him.

Before Lance could answer, Rick replied, "Well, Lexi, the story goes something like this. They say back in the '30's or maybe it was in the 40's, there was a small group of men logging this area. At first, everything was normal, just cut down trees, bring them up to the mill's blade, and make lumber. But then strange things started to happen. Sometimes the equipment would mysteriously quit running. They would take it to get repaired but as soon as they took it out of this area it ran again." Rick paused for dramatic effect, looked around at each member of the group and then continued. "The mill operators sometimes claimed to hear the sound of a young girl screaming or crying as the wood passed through the saw blade. Many of the loggers blamed it on being tired, or their ears playing tricks on them. This happened for months until the one evening, as lumberjacks were discussing taking out a huge oak tree on the hillside downstream, the mill operator heard the shrieking sound again, louder than before. Freaking out, he shut down the engine which you see here laying in front of us. The screaming continued to come from everywhere and nowhere at the same time. It was so bad, all the workers near the mill heard the unholy sound of the girl's screams causing them to abandon the mill and refusing to return to this area."

"Most likely it was carbon monoxide poisoning from poor ventilation, C-O not C-O-2," Chris said with a grin remembering the student's question in class.

"Aw, plant food," Lexi spoke up with a smile "So, this is what you Yanks were talking about on my first day in class. Why didn't they just add windows if they needed better ventilation?"

"It was an outdoor mill, Lexi," Rick informed her.

Walking around, Chris studied the scattered parts of the old mill that now was nothing but slowly deteriorating pieces of rusting metal. *That's right. It was out in the open. So, the effects of the carbon monoxide would have been minimal,* Chris thought.

"Outdoors, hmmm, seems like that poor ventilation theory just went out the invisible windows," Lexi said with a cocky smile.

Chris stood silent as he realized the holes in his assessment of what might have happened here those many years ago.

"It's still weird that no one ever came back to remove the equipment. You know this most likely cost a lot of money back then," Lance told the group trying to help his friend out in this embarrassing moment.

Chris tried to hide his wounded pride as Rick came to his side, "It's ok, buddy, at least now we know you're not a robot."

Laughing, the group of friends came up to hug Chris as a show of compassion.

"Makes you wonder what might have really happened down here," Lexi said as she slowly helped move the conversation forward.

"Something happened," he said to her. Smiles were exchanged as they both looked at each other.

"You think sometime today, we could take a few minutes and talk in private?" Lexi softly asked with what Chris could see in her eyes was a huge "please." Looking at Lance, Chris wondered how they could manage that without hurting his friend's feelings. Jenn was right. He needed to have a talk with Lexi and explain everything to her. She was a good person. Hearing the words from him would be better for everyone involved.

"Let's head back. I need to check with my parents to see if they have anything for us to do today," Chris told his companions.

Looking at his watch. "Yeah, I need to be heading back soon. Mom is picking me up to go shopping with her today," Lance said as they all made their way back to the main parking lot. With Lance leading the way, Rick and Lexi following behind, Chris and Jenn laid back some from the group.

"If we don't have to help my parents this afternoon, with Lance leaving, I will have a talk with Lexi," he informed her as they walked. Jenn smiled, then gave Chris a quick sideways hug.

"I'm glad, but I still think you should give her a chance. I know you're being a good friend to Lance, but honestly, she really doesn't see Lance like that," Jenn whispered while walking beside Chris.

Jenn felt a little sad about playing matchmaker for her friends, but if she couldn't have the one she wanted, even though it would be painful to see Lexi with someone else, Chris was the clear choice. Reaching down, she took Chris's hand to hold while they made their way along the trail.

Mrs. Jones waved at Lance as he emerged from the woods. Turning to the group, he said his goodbyes, "See you guys later." he called out as he headed to his mother's car.

"Yep. See you later. I'll call you tonight," came Chris's reply, which was answered with a raised hand acknowledgement from Lance. The group of friends waved to him as the car left their view.

Wonder where Mom and Dad are hiding, Chris thought while looking around. His question was soon answered by the Bowmans hailing him from the tree line behind the group.

"You guys having fun?" Chris's mom asked as she walked up to the youths.

She was answered with, "We sure are, Mrs. Bowman."

"Well, looks like we had a large number of people today to help, sooo ...", dragging out the "o" with a theatrical pause, she then took a deep breath and looked back and forth between the teens. "Go have more fun but stay out of trouble!" she said in a quick sped up reply.

Four smiling faces rewarded Mrs. Bowman's statement.

Chapter 35

"Let's go to Frogman's Rock," Rick prompted upon hearing the group's new marching orders from Mrs. Bowman to go have fun.

"Frogman's Rock?" Lexi queried, looking to the group for an answer.

"It's a big rock in the middle of the creek. Some of the local horseback riders called it that because of a log laying against it. It looked like a big frogman from downstream," Chris told her. He started to tell her more when Jenn cut him off.

"The rock is kind of a local legend, no one knows how long it's been there or exactly how it got there," Jenn said as she reached down and took Lexi's hand, as she led the way.

"This is going to be exciting to see something like that around here," Lexi told Jenn as they walked the trail with Rick and Chris behind them.

"Don't forget to tell Lexi your theory, Jenn," Rick spouted from behind. Jenn turned and gave him a stern glare as both young men laughed.

"Theory? About what?" Lexi asked while looking at Jenn.

"Well, the boys are talking about an idea that came to me about this place. I'm sure you have heard about how the creek didn't follow the same streambed as it does today." Lexi nodded. "Well, I had a neat thought that perhaps Frogman's Rock might have been closer to the shore, and if it was, then people a long time ago could have come here. Who's to say

Gretchen or Esther might have sat or hung out there when they were alive?"

"Who knows, Jenn? Maybe their ghosts have tea parties there," Chris added as both boys started laughing again.

"Come on Lex," Jenn said in an irritated voice. As the girls picked up speed to put distance between themselves and the teasing boys, Rick turned and looked at Chris, who just shrugged his shoulders.

"I thought it was funny," Rick said as he answered Chris's unasked question.

Chris simply added, "Yeah, me, too!"

Following the trail past Gretchen's Lock, Lexi took in the beauty gracing the sides of the man-made trail that swayed back and forth from the creekside to deep-wooded areas. Majestic hardwoods, as well as groupings of evergreens, greeted them around each new bend. Coming to the end of the three-mile hike, Jenn pointed to the water and simply said. "Ta, da!"

"That's lush that!" Lexi said in excitement. Jenn turned and looked at her in confusion, "Oops, sorry, it's lovely, but it is strange," Lexi said, as she and the three friends stared down a steep hillside into the creek to see a huge rock just sitting in the water about 10 feet from the stream bank.

"I know! Right? It's like someone just picked up this huge rock and placed it in the creek!" Jenn replied.

Chris had heard her use that same statement so many times in the past, to the point where he had climbed the hillside when no one was with him, to find where the stone had actually come from. He found its original resting place, but never told anyone.

He secretly loved seeing the excitement in her eyes when she gave her theory of how this small monolith, which was bigger than a full-size pickup truck, got to its present location.

"Can we go sit on it?" Lexi asked as she studied it.

"The water is too swift and deep to try and wade to it," Rick replied, looking at Lexi as her face showed some disappointment.

"Let's go ahead and start back, Rick," Jenn proclaimed as she gave Chris a meaningful nod.

"Already? I wanted to head…" Rick's comment was stifled by Jenn's dagger glare. "Yeah, you're right. We should start heading back." Taking Rick by the hand, Jenn pulled him away from the other two.

Walking back, Chris slowed his pace to create space between the two pairs. He watched as Jenn and Rick disappeared from his view. They followed the trail as it elevated to a small clearing. Large rocks dotted the area, with long needled pine trees providing a canopy from the sun. A lonely, heavy wooden picnic table sat just under the drooping pine tree branches. Chris wondered, *How many people had it taken to carry it from the park's picnic ground?* Walking over to the table, he brushed the fallen pine needles from the seat for him and Lexi to sit.

"Would you like to sit down and take a short break?" Chris asked. Lexi walked over as he took her hand and guided her. He lowered himself to sit next to her. He could feel her gaze, but he found himself unable to look her in the eyes.

"I hope you enjoyed the hike today," he said while still keeping his eyes averted.

"It was fun. I was wondering if we could take a boat and then we could climb up Frogman's Rock. Maybe even have a picnic there," Lexi replied while she joined Chris in staring at the ground.

"You know that I really think we could become really good friends," he said in a very low, almost mumble of a voice as he scuffed the ground with his feet.

"I know. Jenn told me, you are not interested in dating girls, you just want to be friends. A lot of relationships start out as friends. You know that, don't you?" she said with a hint of disappointment in her voice.

"I know, but we could never be more than just friends," Chris countered while turning to look at her. *Why do I have to be the one to do this?* Some anger flickered deep down inside of him. *I didn't ask for any of this,* Chris thought to himself.

"May I ask why?" the visibly hurting female asked him. Chris bit his lip, trying to decide if he should tell her about Lance's desire for her. He couldn't betray his friend like that, let alone tell her of someone else's unrequited love.

"I can't. I'm so sorry. I want to be your friend and I want to be honest with you. My interest lies with another person." Chris found the words of admittance came from his mouth before he realized he even said them.

"What do you mean, that *cochen geneth*?" Lexi asked as he turned to look at her in confusion. Lexi wondered why he had the questioning look on his face, not realizing she had spoken in her Welsh. "The redhead girl," she clarified, as she waited for his response. Chris stood up to face her and placed his hands on the outside of her arms.

"Please understand, you're a great girl. I want to be your friend, just as of right now, I can't date you." She fought but failed to hide her sorrow. Verklempt, she tried to smile her best but inside she was crying.

"Don't hate me, Lexi. I will still be here for you," Chris told her. He hoped these words would help. This was all new to him. *Wonder if I should start reading romance novels and cut back on comics,* he made a mental note.

"I'll be ok. Like they say, who knows what the future holds, plus it will never work with a redhead," she smirked.

Chris stood there puzzled again, then asked, "Why?"

"Gingers don't have souls," Lexi said as she started to smile.

CRASH! Lexi let out a scream as she jumped into Chris's arms. Holding her, he could feel both of their hearts racing from the unexpected interruption.

"Where did that come from?" Chris asked, as both looked to see the large pine branch resting on the ground just a few feet away. Nervous laughter broke out between the two. Lexi turned to look Chris in the eyes and smiled as their laughter subsided, as both realized the closeness of their unintended embrace.

"Hey," she softly whispered with a smile.

"Hey," he responded with his own smile.

Without another word spoken, they both moved closer. Their eyes slowly closed as their lips prepared to meet. Lexi could feel his warm breath as she slightly tilted her head preparing for their intimate moment of discovery.

Suddenly, Lexi and Chris recoiled back, both crying out in distress as they clutched their chests.

"What the hell!" Chris yelled, as he started to rub his chest. Lexi joined in the chorus of pain.

"I think something bit me!" she cried out. "I feel like my skin's on fire!"

"Mine, too," Chris answered. "Could be stinging nettles or it could be that poisonous caterpillar that causes a burning sensation," he explained to her, while in obvious agony.

"Well, bloody hell! If that is what your caterpillars do over here, you Yanks can keep them," Lexi admonished. Pushing past the pain, he started to break out in laughter from her comment.

"What happened? We heard a scream. Are you ok, baby?" Jenn asked as she ran up to the pair with Rick close behind. *Oh shit, I just slipped. I sure hope Lexi didn't catch it.* Jenn frantically thought, as she feared that her secret was being revealed, washed over her.

"First we were almost hit by a falling branch and then something bit us," Chris explained as the realization hit him that Jenn and Rick must have been eavesdropping.

"It's ok," Lexi told Jenn as her friend took her hand to pull her aside to comfort her, as Rick walked up to Chris who was in the middle of taking off his shirt.

Noticing the tree limb lying on the ground, Rick said, "That would have given you a headache! Looks like the bug got you both." He examined the red welt on Chris's chest.

"I think Mom's got a first aid kit in the trunk, let's head back," Chris said.

"You think she has something in the kit for this?" Jenn asked as she pointed to the red area just below Lexi's collarbone.

"We can check when we get back," Chris stated, as he started the trek.

Jenn started to ask about what happened between her and Chris before the bug bite, but Lexi simply mouthed "Later," to Jenn's query, as they finally made their way back to the parking lot.

"Are you still staying over tonight?" she asked Jenn, who replied with a nod, as Lexi waited on Chris's mom and the first aid treatment.

Later that evening, Jenn listened to her friend recant the conversation that had happened with Chris. She stared in disbelief when Lexi told of the almost kiss, after he had just turned down her invitation to go steady with her.

"Chris is a real jerk, you know that?" Jenn said as she lay on her stomach across Lexi's bed.

"No, he's not," Lexi countered. "He's a sweetheart and you know it."

"Yeah, you're right. He is, but we can both hate him for tonight, right?" Jenn asked as she watched Lexi come out of her personal bathroom.

"This bug bite still burns a little," Lexi said while she prepared to rub more antibiotic cream on the area. Jenn jumped up and turned Lexi to face her, pulling down the front of Lexi's tank top to examine the inflammation. Raising her hand to cover her mouth, she stepped back in shock.

"Oh my God! Lexi, that's a handprint!"

Chapter 36

Chris stared out the window of his parents' car as they drove to Gretchen's Lock that Sunday morning. He mulled over the strange phone call he had with Jenn and Lexi last night.

"Really Chris! Trying to cop a feel? After you just told her you had no interest in dating her?" Jenn's voice yelled at him through the phone. "You had no right to touch Lexi's chest, you pervert!" He stood there in shock with the phone in his hand trying to comprehend what Jenn meant. He remembered hearing Lexi's voice in the background telling her that he never did anything like that.

"Come on, Lexi, you have a handprint on your chest. You couldn't have done it. The thumb points down!" Jenn told her as she returned to accusing Chris. "Well, I'm waiting," Jenn said as Chris fumbled for an explanation.

"It must have been on her shirt when we hugged and maybe," he stopped, trying to think. "When we pulled back and started to wipe our shirts the venom moved to our hands," Chris stammered again with the only thing he could think of. He had thought of stinging nettles but that didn't last and would have been all over their legs as well.

Thumb pointing down, that thought had haunted Chris most of the night. Now, on the ride to the park, the same question was there in his head again.

"You ok?" Chris's mom asked, pulling him back to reality. He looked around to notice that they were now sitting in the parking lot of Gretchen's.

"Uh, Yeah, I'm ok. Sorry, I was thinking about something," Chris replied as he opened his door to exit the car.

"Something or someone? Maybe a teenage girl from Wales?" Chris's mom smiled as she asked the question. She enjoyed the friendly teasing that their family had routinely taken part in throughout his young life.

"Mommm!" Chris fired back at her, with a look of disgust on his face, even though he knew her comment was all in fun. He realized this banter was something he would have to suffer through when it came to girls. Deep down, he was smiling because he wanted to tell her, "Yes, but it was three girls." Chris turned his head quickly to hide from his mother, just in case the smile crept to his face without him knowing. "So, what's the plan today?" he asked his parents, as they all stepped out of the car.

"Well, your mom and I have to work on a dig site, so there won't be much for you to do today. Go have fun, son," his dad informed him. Chris smiled, turned to the path, then looked back at his parents.

"You sure?" Chris asked. His parents smiled, then nodded. In a slow jog as the bracelet bounced against his hip, he headed for the spot where all the messages he and the unknown girl had shared. He wondered if she had left one, but a thought hit him hard, *Shoot! I forgot to leave one yesterday. She's going to think I don't want to talk anymore. How could I forget to leave one?*

He remembered his friends unexpectedly arrived to spend the day with him. He had been side-tracked when they showed up. Chris jogged down the path to the creek, picking up his pace a little. His excitement rose inside as he got closer. Chris strained his vision looking for a message before he was even close to the spot of their earth writing. The message from yesterday was gone, only a few letters were still visible from her response from the previous day. Footprints from hikers or fishermen now replaced the girl's handwriting.

Feeling despondent, Chris sat down on the shoreline. *How could I have forgotten, even though I wasn't sure what the message meant, I could have at least left her a question mark.* Closing his eyes Chris took in the peacefulness of the park in the morning. Although it had only been a few weeks now since his parents had kidnapped him for their own pleasure and what he thought would be his personal torture, he found this area blissful, especially on Sundays. He only had to share the morning with a few fishermen.

"My Walden," Chris said with a smile. Should he tell his parents, or would it be better if he kept that secret to himself, he pondered again. He heard footsteps quickly approaching. *Cool, wonder who was able to come down today?* he considered as he started to turn and look.

"Look who I found," a stranger's voice announced. Chris's vision was blurred as a fist hit him in the face. Falling to his side, he struggled to grasp the actions that had just happened. As he looked toward the person who had hit him, another punch landed on his jaw. The salty bitter taste of iron flooded his mouth as he fell back to the ground again.

"Did you really think you could get away with what you did in school?" George Martin asked as he towered over his victim lying on the ground. "Wasn't it a pleasant surprise on the last day of class to have Mr. Washington announce about your family being down here and looking for help?" Chris started to get up from the ground when the points of boots found the side of his stomach. He curled up, fighting to catch his breath. Tears filled his eyes from the pain as his assailant dropped to one knee to inspect his damage.

"Aww, poor little cry baby," the bully mocked. "Should I go get your mommy for you?" He strained to get to his hands and knees as George returned to standing, "Well, I guess you have almost learned your lesson, a few more kicks should do it."

Without thinking, Chris balled his fist and punched up as hard as he could, landing his punch between his attacker's legs. George grasped for his crotch and staggered back while bending over at the waist. Chris fought to get his balance to take the fight to his attacker, while the opening was there. Blood ran from his mouth as he threw a wild punch, hitting George's shoulder. Ducking below Chris's punches, George wrapped his arms around the young boy and drove him backward into the creek. Splashing on his back, Chris fought to regain control as George held him down. Chris rolled to his belly to push up with his hands to help get the bully off him.

"You little bastard!" George yelled as he stood up and kicked Chris hard in the chest again. He felt the air leave his lungs.

Falling face down in the stream, he felt George's weight bear down on his back. Chris suddenly felt the pressure of a hand submerging his head as his panicking screams for help became nothing but air bubbles.

"You dare to touch me, you little bitch!" George proclaimed as he pushed Chris's head deeper into the shallow ripples. Liquid filled Chris's lungs as he tried to breathe but the older boy held the downward force on the back of his head.

Suddenly, Chris felt the hand on his head disappear followed by loud splashing around him.

Raising his head up, he quickly inhaled, only to cough gore out of his lungs. Pushing his arms down to raise most of his body out of the stream, Chris coughed again, spitting out more blood and water. Sounds of a person thrashing in the streambed close by caught his attention.

George stared in horror, then quickly rose to his feet. He ran downstream away from Chris to a clearing, clambered onto the bank and then disappeared into the woods.

"DON'T YOU EVER LAY A HAND ON HIM AGAIN, YOU NO GOOD BLOODY PIECE OF SHITE!" a screaming voice of a girl, with a strange accent, rang out through the hollow. Chris turned to the shore to see his brazen-haired heroine standing there in a plain earth-tone dress flowing around her ankles in the breeze.

"Are you alright?" the young girl asked as he gingerly crawled his way to the shore.

"I think so, thanks," Wincing from the pain of his injuries, Chris coughed as he wiped the blood from his lips. He watched as the girl bent at her waist, cocking her head to the side while looking directly into his eyes.

"Well then, I guess, 'You are welcome,' is in order, Mr. Christopher Bowman," she responded with a grin.

Chapter 37

Chris stared at the smiling face of the young girl he had been desperately trying to meet, and there she was only a few feet from him with a hand extended to help him up. Chris started to reach, but pride, the ugly sin inherited from his parents, kicked in. Shaking his head "No," he pulled back. Pushing up with his arms, the young male stood up to stand face-to-face with the girl he had been obsessing over.

Returning her smile, Chris was taken aback by her beauty. Naturally laying red hair, in long soft spiral curls hung just below her shoulders. Slate-colored eyes, with a tint of green, shone with her smile. Complementing her hair, freckles adorned the soft features of her thin face, adding to her beauty. Chris observed she had full, almost pouting lips when her smile faded.

"Did getting hit render you unable to speak, now?" the young girl said to Chris in a strange accent, breaking the endless gaze he was caught in.

"Oh, I'm sorry. I didn't mean to stare," Chris apologized to her, "Your accent, are you Welsh?"

"What?" the young girl quickly responded to his question, "I am no bloody Taffy. *Tá mé*
Irish!" she added.

"Oh, I'm sorry. I meant no offense. It's just I have a friend who is from Wales and I thought your accent sounded like hers," Chris said, trying to calm her down by slowly raising both hands as he flinched a little from the sharp pain in his ribs. *Why did she get so upset? Did I say something wrong?* Chris wondered, also making a mental note to ask Lexi later what "Taffy" meant.

"You're from Ireland?" Chris asked the young girl, who was calmer than she had been a few moments ago.

"Yes, I am from Ireland. I came to the Americas with my father. He was hired to be an engineer on a big project."

"Really?" Chris asked the girl as she nodded her head in reply. "My friend Lexi's dad is working on a project, too. They probably know each other."

She looked at him in silence. Chris wondered if he said something wrong again to her, *I really suck at this girl stuff,* he told himself. He found his mind racing back to all the times he and Jenn had talked. Maybe it was because they had known each other for a long time, because he never had trouble talking to her. But lately with this girl and Lexi, he never seemed to find the right words.

"Why was that *buachaill* fighting you?" the girl asked. Chris laughed to himself as he thought *She and Lexi have a lot in common. They both slip into another language when they talk.* It was a trait Chris was starting to find endearing with these strange new girls in his life.

"Well, he was picking on a friend of mine at school, so I guess you could say he was giving payback for me interfering," he told her as she looked a little bit lost at his statement.

"He's nothing but a *meater*. Young men like that will never amount to anything. You shouldn't waste time worrying about him." Chris was shocked how this shy young girl seemed to shift from a fiery temper to being timid in such a short time. Maybe the old sayings and warnings about redheads were true.

"Well, Christopher Bowman, I have to be going. I've been here too long" she said as she turned to start down the path.

"Wait, can I have your number?" Chris asked. The girl stopped, turned around with a confused look on her face, then cocked her head to the side.

"Can I call you?" he asked, half afraid he had overstepped his boundaries.

"If you want to yell for me down here, feel free to," the girl laughed as she sashayed away.

"What's your name?" Chris shouted at the girl.

She tilted her head. "Gretchen," is all he heard and disappeared around the corner of the path.

He stood there dumbfounded, as thoughts rushed around inside his mind. *Would he ever get a real answer out of this girl?* Shaking his head, he headed back to the parking lot. Still spitting out some blood, Chris struggled to walk casually but the pain in his ribs made the effort difficult. He knew he would have to tell his family something to explain his lip and wet clothes. At least he had some time to come up with an alibi for their probable inquisition.

"I knew it! You were playing around the creek and fell in, didn't you?" Chris's mother's question made it much easier than he thought. With a simple nod he made his way to the car with her as she dug in the trunk for a towel and the first aid kit.

"Did you hurt your ribs when you fell?" she asked upon seeing him holding pressure against his side.

"I fell on a rock in the creek," he told her as she cleaned his lip off to examine the area.

"Well, I don't think you will need stitches, but it's going to be sore for a few days. Let me check your ribs." Chris moved his arms to allow his mother to feel around his sides. "Well, I don't feel anything broken, so most likely you just bruised them."

He nodded to his mother as she put away the med kit.

"Why don't you stay around the car? There isn't too much to do today, so we will be leaving soon," she advised as she walked away to find his dad. Looking at the time on his watch, Chris was happy to see that it was past noon, and everyone would be home from church.

I have to call Jenn first and tell her about everything, he thought to himself. Leaning down slowly he moved the side mirrors on the car to look at his badge of honor. Yes, it hurt, but for some strange reason, he found pride in standing up for himself. Even though a crazy red viper helped some and he did get beat up, this was his first real fight. He knew, in some cultures, the first fight was a rite of passage for becoming a man.

Chris hobbled into the house as soon as he and his parents arrived home. His mom told him to go on ahead to get out of the wet clothes, but Chris decided to make a call first. "Jenn, you will never guess what happened today," Chris said while waiting for her to reply. Excitement had built in his mind all the way home from the park. He had replayed the fight over and over to the point where the story had become how he stood toe-to-toe with George. Jenn listened to him tell her about the clash.

"Are you ok?" she asked in a worried voice.

268

"I'm fine, just a little sore. But you will never believe who I met today." Before she could ask who, Chris answered, "I met the redhead. You won't believe it. Her name is Gretchen. Isn't that too funny?"

Jenn listened to him go on and on about the girl. She felt conflicted about everything. *I'm happy that Chris is excited about a girl but it is the wrong girl. Lexi is the one for him, not some stranger that has appeared in his life. I don't know this Gretchen girl, but I already know that I don't like her, nor do I have plans on getting to know her first before formulating an opinion of her. As of this moment, the redhead Gretchen girl is my enemy.* she thought as he rambled on.

"She had a strange accent and I asked if she was from Wales like Lexi," Chris told her. "She got really upset and said she was Irish and wasn't a Taffy. Jenn, what does that mean?"

"Taffy?" Jenn asked. "I don't know. I've never heard that expression before. Hard to say, maybe it's some Irish saying. That would be my guess."

"Maybe I should call Lexi and ask if she knows what that meant," Chris said.

"NO, DON'T! I'll call her," Jenn's heart raced upon hearing his idea. She really needed to talk to Lexi about this before Chris did something stupid like boys do and call to tell Lexi about this girl. Chris was the smartest kid Jenn knew but when it came to common sense, he was the dumbest. She would have to make sure to explain to Chris about telling Lexi about this girl, but that would have to wait until she could talk and explain in person.

"You sure? I wanted to tell her about everything since we straightened everything up. She's cool and understands now about us just being friends."

"Let me talk to her, Chris. I was going to call her just before you called."

"Oh! Ok," Chris told her, then asked "About what?"

"Well, if you want to know, I was going to ask her about my heavy flow day," Jenn told him as she started to grin. She knew that was a subject that would shut Chris up immediately. She could still remember the look of shock on his face when she explained a woman's cycle to him. His eyes were wide with horror as she told him about pads.

"Ohh, ok, bye," Jenn heard Chris hang up the phone. Jenn picked up her princess phone and made her way to her bed, picked up the receiver and dialed her friend's seven-digit number.

"Hello?" came the reply on the other end of the call.

"Hello, Mrs. Plant. This is Jenn. Is Lexi there?

"Yes, dear. But she is in the bathroom. I will have her call you back."

Jenn flopped back on to her bed as she thought of the song she was writing for Lexi. Her latest project was a love song about secretly loving someone but never being able to tell them. She wrote it as her personal confession to her friend, but this confession was something she had decided she would not act on weeks before she had confided in Chris. Her thoughts were disturbed as the sound of her phone rang.

"Lexi, we need to talk."

Chapter 38

"**W**HAT THE BLOODY HELL? THAT GINGER PADDY CALLED ME A TAFFY!" Lexi yelled into the phone. She never liked to get angry but upon hearing what Jenn told her, she was seeing red.

"It's ok," Jenn said calmly to her friend, "Chris is our friend and if she thinks she can just waltz right in and take him from his friends and people who really love him, well..." Jenn paused to rethink about saying people who loved him. She knew how Lexi felt about Chris, she hoped dearly that she didn't catch that.

"That's right, Chris is ours! And she's gotta another thing coming if she thinks that," Lexi finished Jenn's statement.

"What do you have in mind?" Lexi asked her friend.

"Let me check with my mom first. Would you care to join me tomorrow down at Gretchen's Lock? I think you and I need to have a little talk with little miss carrot-top," Jenn told her with such an intense voice that Lexi could almost see her grinning through the phone.

"Let me ask my dad, but I see no reason I won't be able to. That ginger mick and I need to have a little talk!"

Chris slowly made his way to the car Monday morning. He was still sleepy from a restless night. The pain of his ribs had made it almost impossible to find a comfortable way to lay on his bed. If it weren't for the chance to spend time with Gretchen, he might have asked his parents if he could stay home.

He knew what his mom would say, "Just put some vapor rub on it and you'll be fine." His mom's words echoed in his mind. That was his mother's answer to all his aches and pains, and it just wasn't her; his friends' parents all said the same. "When we were sick or hurting, your grandmother would rub that on us and we would be better." Chris could hear her voice in his head.

What kind of medicines did they use back then? Chris had thought many times growing up.

I guess sometimes home remedies win out over medical science.

He was surprised to see Lexi and Jenn waiting for him as they pulled into the parking lot. The two smiling girls quickly approached the car as his dad pulled into the parking spot and turned off the engine. Greedy hands opened his door.

"Guess who's spending the day with their favorite future Nobel Prize winner!" Jenn said, with Lexi standing next to her.

"Hi girls, did you come down to help out?" Mrs. Bowman asked, even though she knew that the kids would just hang out for a bit then head off to explore. Jenn had a good head on her shoulders, and Chris's mom was happy about her being his friend. And she knew that Jenn came from a good family since she had gone to school with her mom. Whenever Jenn was around, she felt more at ease.

"Yes, Mrs. Bowman. Someone's got to crack the whip on Chris," Jenn said as Mrs. Bowman smiled but then chuckled to herself as she thought, *Not even 15 and already whipped.*

As Jenn reached in to give Chris a hug, she saw the grimace on his face. "OH, your ribs, I'm sorry. Do they still hurt?" He nodded. Lexi looked at Chris and Jenn, then she extended her arms to ask for her hug. The two smiled and pulled Lexi in for a group embrace.

"I'll make a deal with you three. If you help carry the equipment up to the dig site, you can have the rest of the day to be kids," Mr. Bowman said, looking to see the excitement in their eyes as he finished his statement.

They nodded in agreement. Chris and Jenn eagerly headed to the trunk of the car to grab totes. He turned to see Lexi staring off to the tree line to the north.

"Lexi, are you going to help?" Chris asked her.

"I'll do it now, in a minute," she replied without moving her eyes from the spot of interest. Jenn noticed Lexi's strange behavior as she moved next to her. She peered in the direction of Lexi's line of sight.

"See that big oak over there?" Lexi nodded in the direction. "Look about a meter up."

Jenn stared at the tree then she caught the sight of the hem of a muslin dress flickering from behind the base, then red hair sneaked from around the trunk.

"What does she think she's doing?" Jenn asked Lexi as they both carefully watched. Jenn found herself wondering if this girl was crazy.

"Let's go, forget that *gwirion merch*," Lexi said as she turned to join in carrying equipment. Walking up to Chris, she purposely reached out to place her hand on his shoulder. "Do you need me to help you with that?" Jenn smiled upon seeing and hearing Lexi's actions.

"No, I'm good, but thank you," Chris told her as pride pushed down the pain in his ribs.

"You are so bad! I love it!" Jenn said as she passed Lexi with an ornery grin on her face. Lexi, still smiling at her pissing contest with the other girl, returned to the trunk of the car to pick up a small box, then followed Jenn up the path to the dig site.

After unloading the car was done, the trio found a picnic table. Jenn had pulled Chris aside earlier and told him not to talk about the girl in front of Lexi, so he spent most of the time asking her about music and Wales. While talking to Chris, she would gaze past him to watch the woods. Smiles would grace her face every time she noticed the redhead voyeur spying on them. *How could a girl be that shy and backwards?* she thought. Lexi had lots of female friends back in Wales. None of them ever acted like this. Even the most shy wouldn't take to spying. Lexi decided this girl either had something mentally wrong with her or maybe something traumatic had happened in her past.

"Do you see her?" Jenn asked Lexi in a whisper.

"Yes, she's been following us all day," Lexi told her as she noticed Chris periodically looking side to side.

"Chris, why don't we go to the mill and look around?" Jenn asked as she tried to get his attention to her and Lexi.

"Sure, let's go." Chris and the two girls walked across the park passing the old, abandoned farmhouse that sat in the clearing along the way to Hambleton's Mill. The old mill, a large three-story stone building, stood across the main road into the park. Chris had speculated in his head that the people who cut the stone for the lock system had also cut the stones for the walls of the mill. Now it sat, only an empty shell of its former self, like a sleeping giant in the park. All signs of a working mill were gone with time. Eight boarded up windows and a padlocked door greeted them as they approached the front of the building. Chris felt sadness in his heart as he thought about how much time and intensive labor had gone into the construction of this building just to have it stand here, abandoned.

"We can go into the basement and look around but most of it has been gutted," Chris told Lexi.

"Gutted?" Lexi looked at her friends, confused by their words.

"Gutted. They took out everything inside, so all the working parts of the mill are gone," Chris explained as he led the way to the back cellar.

The three explorers squeezed through a half-opened door to enter the basement of the mill. Sadness again filled Chris's heart to see this amazing structure was nothing but a skeleton of lumber making its way back and forth from wall to wall. The building actually felt dead. Old rotting lumber was scattered across the dirt floor with a damp musty odor permeating the air.

"So, what do you think?" Chris asked Lexi as he was stepping over a broken board.

"In a strange way it reminds me a little of the Wolf Hall back home." Before Chris could ask, Lexi continued, "It's an abandoned castle in Wales that my parents and I visited last year. Dad has a love for the history of the UK, so we travel a lot.

Every year some historic place is on his agenda when we are on holiday."

"Well, I have to use the bathroom. I'll be right back," Chris told the two girls as he walked to the half-opened door.

"You're not walking all the way back, are you?" Jenn asked.

"No, I'm going to go outside around the back, so no comments or coming out to bug me," he told her as he disappeared out the door. Lexi looked at Jenn with a questioning expression on her face.

"He is pee shy," Jenn told her. As soon as the words left her mouth she started to giggle, which was soon joined by Lexi. "Go look through the cracks in the boards to see where he is," Jenn said while pointing to the boarded-up areas. Lexi quickly made her way to the one closest to her with a mischievous grin on her face. Looking through the vertical gap, she only saw the road they crossed. Moving to the left side of the building to get a different view, Lexi could hear movement from outside. *Found you!* she thought, and grinned as she looked through the panels expecting to see Chris. In disbelief, Lexi shirked back from what she saw. A girl was standing outside about eight feet from the building wall. Looking at the woods, her light scarlet hair waving in the wind brushed along her cheeks. The girls wanted to confront her, but with Chris here, this would be the wrong time. Lexi moved back to look through the slit in the wood. She jumped away from the narrow opening as the sight of a lifeless, cataract-covered eye looked in directly at her.

Chapter 39

Jenn rushed over to Lexi as soon as she heard the gasp. "What's wrong?" she asked, but Lexi just stood pale-looking, her right hand covering her mouth as she pointed to the window.

"She's... she's outside."

Anger raged in Jenn's eyes as rushed to the door with the intent of giving this girl a piece of her mind. She started through the opening, but it was now blocked by Chris, who was trying to re-enter the door.

"MOVE YOUR ASS!" she shouted at him as she pushed her way past him. She rounded the corner of the mill, only to find nothing. No girl stood outside the boarded-up window. She heard Chris and Lexi coming up behind her.

"What's going on?" Chris curiously asked.

"Oh, nothing. Lexi thought she saw someone," Jenn said as her anger subsided. She looked at Lexi who looked very shaken, and very unnerved from the whole experience. She walked over to hug her friend.

"Those eyes," Lexi whispered to Jenn as she fell into her friend's hug.

"What do you mean?" Jenn asked as she lifted Lexi's chin to look at her.

"Is she ok?" Chris asked, walking up to the girls. Many times he had seen his friends scared, from a movie, or from a friendly prank. Chris could tell by the concern in Jenn's face, this was what true fear looked like.

"They were dead, there was no life in them," Lexi told them in a shaky voice, "Can we just please leave this place! Something is not right here!"

As they walked back through the park. Jenn walked next to Lexi, peering over to look at her every few feet to check on her. Lexi just walked, eyes averted, not saying a word. Deep inside, Jenn found herself getting upset again. Lexi being scared was something she could not bear. This girl Chris was obsessed with had crossed the line, and Jenn planned on righting this wrong. No one messed with her friends, not even some bloody ginger, as Lexi called her. Chris motioned to Jenn, then nodded towards Lexi, silently asking if she was ok, and Jenn just shrugged her shoulders.

Once back at the parking lot, they found a picnic table to sit on. Propping their feet on the bench seats, the two girls watched as Chris went to check in with his parents once he was sure Lexi was ok.

"Lexi, why were you so upset? What really happened?" Jenn questioned. Lexi sat there trying to find the right words to explain to her friend what she had seen.

"Jenn, I know you're not going to believe me, but when I looked out of the peep hole and saw her there, she was just looking around, and then the next thing I knew she was looking through the hole at me." Lexi said in a clearly shaken low tone. "You know how when you look at a person's eyes you can see the twinkle of life there? Well, this girl's eyes didn't have that light, Jenn, her eyes were dead," she paused, "I think that girl is a cyhyraeth."

Jenn looked at her completely confused. She knew that Lexi had problems flipping back and forth from her own language and English, so she tried not to make an already upsetting ordeal worse.

"A wraith, I think that's what you Yanks call it," Lexi clarified.

"You mean a ghost?" Jenn asked.

"No, not a ghost, a wraith!"

"You lost me," Jenn said as she leaned back on her hands.

"A ghost is a disembodied spirit; a wraith is a spirit that takes form for vengeance." Lexi folded her hands then leaned to rest her elbows on her legs. "There are many stories and legends about cyhyraeth in Wales, and one thing about them is, you don't piss them off!" A cold chill went up Jenn's spine at the sound of that, but she was a realist. She didn't believe in ghosts or fairy tales, but she would never make fun of someone else's beliefs. She did know that Lexi believed in this wraith so she would stick by her side and comfort her.

Chris wasn't sure what had happened to Lexi at the mill. He didn't want to ask too many questions. He didn't have much experience with girls, but he had learned when two girls are talking in hushed tones, it's best for boys to stay out of it. Even though the day had ended strangely, hanging with Jenn and getting to know Lexi better was fun. He was glad that she was fine with just being friends. He was a little sad that Gretchen didn't come to the park today. He knew deep down inside that she, Jenn and Lexi would really hit it off. Lexi and she could talk about things in the UK. Chris figured it would be a win-win all the way around.

Climbing the small slope, Chris followed the trail as it turned left around a large walnut tree. A voice jumped out from behind him as he rounded the turn.

"Where are you off to, Mr. Christopher Bowman?" Chris turned to see Gretchen walking next to him, her arms held behind her back, leaning slightly forward, her shoulders swaying, with her head cocked and a grin on her face.

"Hi, Gretchen, where have you been? I've looked for you all day."

Skipping along next to him she smiled and stopped in front of Chris. "I've been around. I saw you earlier, with those two wagtails."

"You mean my friends, Jenn and Lexi?" Chris asked her in confusion. Gretchen nodded in response. "They are the best, especially Jenn, I would love for you to meet them."

"No! I don't like them," she answered quickly to his request.

Chris felt hurt by her reply. The pain must have shown in his face before he could mask it. He didn't know why she wouldn't want to meet his friends, but she must have had her reasons. He knew she was shy so he decided to try another way around it.

"I'd like to meet your friends one day," Chris told her. But her smile was gone, and loneliness took its place.

"I don't really have any friends. I had one long ago. But... she's gone." Chris watched as the girl looked down at the ground. He found himself so badly wanting to comfort her but touching her was something he couldn't do. They had only just met and that would be crossing the line.

"Don't you have anyone to at least talk to?" Chris questioned.

"Yes, I do. I talk to you. So, I guess I do have a friend." She quickly perked up.

"No, not me. I'm sure you have someone else you talk to in your life," Chris said while pushing forward to help explain his point.

"Oh, you mean like Charles?"

"Charles?" Chris asked.

"Yes. Charles. He camped one night in the woods a long time ago. We spent all night sitting around a small fire. Very handsome gentleman, but something bad happened the next day to him up over the hill. Well, maybe Lisa, but she's mean and never talks to me." Gretchen told him. Chris studied her in complete confusion.

"My parents are just up this trail. I would like for you to meet them, then maybe...." his voice trailed off as he thought hard about how he could get Gretchen to meet his friends.

"I'm sorry, I can't meet your parents today. I have somewhere I need to be."

"But, they are just up ..." Chris was cut off by Gretchen.

"*Slán leat*, Mr. Christopher Bowman," she said, with a wink as she quickly headed back down the path.

Chris watched her round the large tree and disappear among the growth of the woods. Unsure what to think about this strange girl named Gretchen, he was sure about one thing when it came to her, and that was his feelings towards her. She fascinated him. Her odd and quirky ways made him even more attracted to her.

Chapter 40

Lexi stepped out of the shower, wrapping a towel around herself. She walked over to stand in front of her bedroom mirror. Today's events had taken a lot out of her. Taking a shower had always helped wash away the worries of the day as if they were dirt. Reaching down to brush her wet hair, she leaned in close to look at her eyes, *I look like I haven't slept in days,* she thought. She decided no alarm clock tonight, sleep would be more important than walking in the morning.

Since moving to the Americas, walking around the large circular paved path at the park near the high school made her feel like this area was becoming more her home. Stepping back from her reflection, Lexi started dragging the brush through her wet auburn hair. She always cringed at the ripping sound it made as she forced the boar bristles through her tangled locks. *Maybe I need to try some of the hair conditioners they sell here in the States,* she thought. After what felt like forever, the brush passed through her hair with no snags. She whipped her mane forward to brush the underside. Stroking from the back forward, Lexi thought about how lucky those girls in the UK were with their pixie cuts or shaved heads. Maybe she would talk to Jenn. They could have a sleepover again, with a haircutting party. Grinning at the thought, Lexi stood up straight while flipping her head back. Looking into the mirror she saw blazing scarlet tresses adorning lifeless grey eyes. A ghostly apparition with pale skin that stretched back on her face as she made an evil grin stood behind her. Lexi started to gasp as a bony hand grabbed the back of her head. She heard the glass of the mirror shatter before she felt the impact of her face.

Lexi's eyes shot open as she sat up in her bed. Without thinking, her hands covered her face.

"It was just a dream," Lexi told herself as she reached over to turn on the lamp on her nightstand. As the light flooded the room, her eyes were drawn to the touch of crimson smeared on her hand. "Oh no. It can't be, I just finished two weeks ago." Lexi threw the blankets aside as she looked down to examine the bed. She felt the wet warm feeling trickling on her upper lip. Rushing to the mirror she could see red streaming with intensity over her lips to splash down on her nightgown. She cried out in horror for her parents then rushed out of her room, stepping over an unnoticed single wilted yellow flower laying on the floor next to her bed.

The next morning, Jenn was still upset and angry with the redhead thing, as her mom dropped her off next to the Bowman's car at the park. Knowing that they would all be at the dig site, Jenn decided showing up late would be the best idea if she wanted to confront this slut named Gretchen. She had talked this morning to Lexi who told her about the nightmare and the nosebleed. Jenn tried to explain she probably hit her nose during the dream, but Lexi was sure it was the wraith that attacked her.

"Ghosts!" Jenn said, exhaling in complete disgust. She knew people believed this area was haunted. Chris called them fairytales and she didn't fall for the old wives' tales either. *Ghosts don't talk to boys and hide behind trees,* she thought to herself. No, this was a little brat who had scared the girl of her dreams and was playing a twisted game with her best friends.

Her plan was easy: find a place somewhere to hide, wait for this bitch to show up, then give her a piece of her mind. Maybe something else, too, if she wanted to act all tough. Walking down the path, Jenn found a perfect tree to hide behind. The sycamore reached up high into the sky, the large base was surrounded by brush and other foliage. She made her way behind the tree, squatted down, and arranged the brush around her to camouflage herself. Jenn found it hard to believe how many people actually walked the paths. She had only been there for about ten minutes when a slight blonde-haired boy with a red cap came jogging by. She recognized him as a cross country star from another school district. *Cross country running for a sport,* she shook her head at the thought, *not something I would ever do.* About every ten minutes or so, people passed her, including a loud-talking man and his daughter riding mountain bikes. She smiled knowing that this was a good spot, well-traveled, and not being seen was a plus.

After what seemed like hours, needing to stretch her legs, Jenn looked down at her watch, deciding it would be a good time to take a break. She came out of her spying place and walked down the path. A movement off to the right caught her eye. *What was that?* she wondered. Standing still, Jenn watched a female deer slowly walk, nose down to the ground, foraging along the forest floor. She had seen many deer in her life in Ohio. She couldn't count how many times her parents had almost hit one while driving at night, but this was different. Jenn stood, mesmerized with the graceful slow movements of the deer's legs, her ears twitching, then stopping and looking alert, searching for any danger. Jenn slowly moved forward to see how close she could get. To Jenn's surprise, the doe must have decided she was not a threat and continued to graze. The whitetail had walked a little forward to nose about the base of a tree when Jenn noticed her raise her head. She was astonished to see the deer's tail wagging like a dog happy to see its master.

Jenn stopped to observe when a shape appeared from behind the tree. She froze in amazement at the sight of a girl with light copper hair walking up to the deer and bending at the waist to touch its head. The doe lovingly nuzzled against her hand as she bent down to rest her forehead against the top of the beautiful creature's brow. The girl closed her eyes and rested her cheek upon the animal. *Is she really speaking to it?* she thought as she viewed the girl's lips moving and the doe's ears twitching as if they were communicating. Jenn's fascination with the moment was soon replaced with shock as the girl's eyes flew open and locked on Jenn. A strange grin graced the red-head's face, as she kissed the forehead of the doe. Backing away from it, the copper-haired vixen turned towards Jenn and winked at her with a smirk.

Fear replaced the feeling of amazement as the air suddenly felt cold. The doe snorted and sprang into a full run straight at her. The terrified girl turned to break into a sprint. The wild animal closed the distance so fast that Jenn had only covered a few feet when she felt the deer's head ram into her back, knocking her forward onto the ground. Sharp hooves crashed down unmercifully upon Jenn as wetness flowed along the young girl's back. Screaming for help, she tried to stand but the deer slammed its front legs down onto her again. Cries of pain now replaced the cries of help.

She barely was able to make out the yelling of men who came running up the trail. Jenn knew there were people around her, but she couldn't make out who they were.

"Damn! That deer got her good. Just keep pressure on the wounds," advised someone among the group of people carrying her out of the woods. Time seemed to blur to Jenn. One minute she was in the woods, the next she realized she was lying in the back bed of a truck as several men rode with her.

"Don't worry, miss. We are on our way to the hospital. You're going to be ok," a strange but comforting voice told her. She stared up toward the sky, as one man held a shirt against her shoulder, while another stroked her hair. *What is going on? Who are these people?* she puzzled as she looked at the group of strangers riding with her in the truck bed. Looking up, Jenn found a strange fascination for the tree branches that streaked by overheard as they drove.

"Get that damn blanket back on her," Jenn heard as the truck turned to the right. More confusion was setting in. She could feel herself getting cold, which she found strange because it was a sunny summer day. *Why am I so cold and why is my back all wet?* she thought.

Chapter 41

Chris sat on a large stone along the banks of the creek, reading through a biology book. He had brought it to help pass the day as he waited for Gretchen's arrival. To make the best use of the time he figured reading and learning seemed like a smart idea this afternoon. *Where is she?* he impatiently thought while looking around. These feelings he had for this girl were something new and scary, but exciting at the same time. Chris started to worry that Gretchen wouldn't be able to find him, and he almost went to his usual spot. However, if his friends showed up, they would have found him there. He really liked the friendships he had with everyone and hiding like this did make him feel a little guilty, but he had decided today was for him and his new obsession.

Chris studied the diagram of human anatomy, calling out each body part by name without looking to the line that highlighted the proper identification. He felt something near his ear, but figured it was a bug of some kind.

"Are you studying to be a Victor Frankenstein?" a voice from over his shoulder whispered in his ear. He jumped and turned quickly to see Gretchen standing behind him, arms folded behind her back as she was bent over, an ornery grin flashed across her face. Chris's heart raced from the jump scare she had given him. If it had been anyone else, he would have been upset at them, but one look at her radiating beauty brought a smile to gift the girl in return.

"Frankenstein?" Chris asked. He was a little taken aback that this sweet girl would know something about Frankenstein. "Do you mean being made from dead pieces of humans, walking around with my arms straight out while people are chasing me with fire?"

"No, you *óinmit*," Gretchen laughed. "That was the creature. His creator was Victor Frankenstein."

Chris felt his embarrassment creep up into his cheeks as he realized she was right. *How did this girl know that?* "You've watched Frankenstein?"

"Watched? I've read the book. Mary Shelley is such a true artist. Her writing pulled me so much into the story, some nights I felt like I was living there."

"You read the book?" Chris had known it was a book, but who read those books when you can watch the movie.

"Yes, I love reading, but it's not something I've been able to do for a while now."
Chris was about to ask her why, but the answer was right there, *of course she hasn't been able to read much, just moving here, dummy!* he thought.

"I looked for you this morning, I was hoping you could have hung out with me as I helped my parents."

"I was busy this morning, I was spending time with Mother Nature. I had a problem, but she helped me out." Chris studied the girl as she finished with her statement. He wasn't sure, but he swore he saw a touch of mischievousness in her smile.

"A problem?" Chris asked. He wondered why these foreign women were so hard to understand.

"I had a problem with too many hens in the henhouse," she smiled at him. "It's all taken care of now."

"Oh, you have chickens?" Chris asked with excitement. Even though he was all about science, something about farms and a simple life appealed to him ever since his parents took him to his uncle's farm when he was younger. Feeding the cows, riding horses, and the danger of getting hurt in the barn were so much fun.

"No, no chickens," she said to him. Confusion reached a new level for Chris upon hearing her reply.

Taking a seat on the ground next to where his book lay, she looked up at Chris and asked, "Can you explain this book to me? It looks very interesting."

Chris looked at her, then nodded. He found it curious how she lifted her light brown dress to sit upon her knees. For some reason he found her very lady-like action only added to his fascination with the girl.

Returning to his seat next to her, he picked up the book and fanned through the pages until she asked about one.

"Well, this is what a nervous system looks like and how it runs through the human body," he told her. While explaining it to her he would look up from the book to see how she, with excitement and wonder, took in every word he spoke about the subject.

"You're so intelligent, Christopher. Can you teach me more?" she said with elation in each word she spoke.

"Like?" he asked.

"Everything! Teach me about everything!" Chris looked at her and smiled. She was like a child who just discovered how to change the channel on the TV with the tuner knob. Chris couldn't help but notice how she almost seemed to glow; her red hair lightened almost to a soft light copper with a golden aura around her. *So, this is what love makes everything feel like.* The thought almost knocked him over inside. *How could I fall in love so quickly with this girl, this Irish beauty that I barely know?* He battled with that thought in his head, but he knew that love was the only way to understand what he was feeling.

"What else does this book have in it?" she asked. Happily, Chris flipped a few more pages stopping on each page to see if she was going to ask for an explanation. Chris turned the page, fear and embarrassment hit him all at once. He forgot all about the human reproduction section in this book. He quickly slammed the book closed, then turned his face from Gretchen's view to hide his red cheeks.

Laughing, Gretchen raised her hands to her mouth to muffle her outburst, "Christopher, it's alright, don't be embarrassed. I know what a tallywag is."

Chris turned to her with a smile of amusement after her use of the word, tallywag. Gretchen looked deep into his eyes. Lost in the moment he started to move closer to her face as the thoughts of feeling the touch of her lips against his became something he needed at this moment.

"Your eyes are so beautiful. Your blue eyes remind me so much of a person I once knew. His last name was Bowman, too, but his name was Johnny," Gretchen told him, breaking the moment they both shared.

"Well, I had a great, great, great uncle named Johnny Bowman. He was kind of the black sheep of the family that we didn't talk about much," Chris told her.

"Why?" Gretchen asked with a strange curiosity in her voice.

"Well, if I remember right, he got caught stealing and was imprisoned and hanged back in the 1830's, I think. At least that is what my grandpa said," Chris answered. Suddenly he saw what he was sure were tears springing up into her eyes.

"Ohhh, nooo, Johnny!" Gretchen cried out, while covering her mouth with one hand. Chris started to reach for her, but she rose to her feet, backing away, "I'm sorry, I have to go." Gretchen wheeled around and started to run down the path disappearing from Chris's sight.

He sat there dumbfounded. "What just happened?" he asked himself. Chris slowly replayed everything in his mind. He must have said something wrong, but the answer was beyond his reach or understanding. *I'll have to call Jenn when I get home. She will know,* he thought as he rose and headed back to the dig site. Walking back through the woods he heard his name being called out.

"Chris, where have you been?" his dad asked him. "We have been looking for you everywhere." Chris noticed his father's face had a strange paleness to it.

"What's wrong?" he asked, choosing not to reply to his father's query about his whereabouts.

"We have to go!" his dad said.

"Why? What's wrong, Dad?"

"It's Jennifer. They had to rush her to the emergency room. She was attacked by a deer earlier," his father informed him.

Chapter 42

Jenn lay in her bed, waiting for her pain medicine to kick in. It had been almost 24 hours since the attack had happened. She had slept through most of the night, but this morning the pain was unbearable at times. Well over 100 stitches now adorned her back along with the multi-colored bruising. The worst part was that she would forget about the cracked ribs until she breathed deeply or moved the wrong way.

She had told what happened several times but chose to leave out the part about Chris's temptress to Lexi, or Chris when they both showed up at the hospital yesterday. She was going to wait till it was just him and her, then he was going to hear it. Jenn closed her eyes and tried to get some rest. Again, her mind was pulled back to the redhead, not the deer attack, but the sight of that evil witch looking at her and smiling and that unnerving wink. *Maybe Lexi was right*, she speculated. Shaking her head, Jenn knew ghosts and wraiths were nothing but fairytales.

"Hey, you," a male voice broke her train of thought. Jenn looked up to see Chris walking into her room carrying a bouquet of blue and white flowers highlighted by small red ones in a white vase.

"Hey," she said while trying to sit up to greet her friend. Sharp stabs of pain made her flinch and grimace a little while she struggled up to a sitting position.

"Whoa, whoa, whoa, let me help," Chris said, setting the flowers down on her dresser. He helped her upright, then quickly adjusted her pillows for her to lean back on.

"How are you feeling?"

"Well, how do you think I feel? I still have a cracked rib that hasn't healed since you saw me yesterday, lots of bruising and pain, headaches that come and go, and oh, God only knows how many stitches I have in my back and every breath I take or move I make; it hurts like hell. On the bright side, Dad's taking me deer hunting this fall and I am definitely getting a doe tag!" Struggling to hold back the grin from her final comment, Chris reached down to hold her hand.

"Thank you for the flowers," she told him.

"Where would you like them?"

"Right there is fine," Jenn told him as she looked into his concerned face. "I'll be alright. The doctor said I was lucky. There is a good chance that I won't even have a scar."

"I'm glad," he looked at Jenn but thought, *Yeah, doctors always say that.*

She knew her best friend too well and one thing she had learned was to know when he wanted to ask a question but resisted asking.

"Go ahead and spit it out," she directed him.

Chris hesitated, then asked, "What were you doing down at the creek by yourself?"

Jenn pressed her lips tightly together as she decided how much to tell him. *Should I tell him the truth or would lying be better at this time?* she thought, but threw caution to the wind. "I went down to confront your vixen that you're all googly-eyed over." The words were out before she realized she had said it in anger.

"What? You went down to cause trouble? Jenn, are you jealous of Gretchen?"

She felt the anger start to grow, "No, I'm not jealous, or of your puppy love you have for her, so don't even go there!"

Chris could feel himself getting upset. He knew that Jenn wanted him to date Lexi, but he never thought she would resort to bullying Gretchen away from him.

"I can't believe you, Jenn. You are honestly jealous. You're supposed to be my friend and support my decisions. I just can't believe you would sink that low," Chris admonished her, "Well, looks like karma ended up biting you in the end."

"And what do you mean by that?" Jenn fired back at him.

"Well, you went down to scare a sweet innocent girl away from me, but karma sent a deer your way."

Jenn could feel her anger boil over. "Well, karma had nothing to do with it. Your little miss innocent bitch sicced that deer on me, and now I'm hurt because of her. I could have died, Chris!"

"What? Come on, Jenn, really? Gretchen sent the deer after you? Think about it. It's not a dog you can train to attack, it's a plant-eating deer!"

Jenn started to speak then rethought his last statements. He was right. *Am I losing my mind, maybe the deer hit me in the head.* "I hate you!" Jenn told him, while crossing her arms across her chest and looking away from Chris's direction.

"I still love you," Chris said to her with a small grin. He and Jenn had had words before, he hated fighting with her, but he knew their friendship could survive this. He reached over and rested his hand on her shoulder, being careful not to place too much pressure.

"Well, I'm still pissed, but I'll support you and this soulless ginger, but if she hurts you, her ass is mine. Understand?" she told him while still facing away from him.

Chris reached up to her chin and turned her head towards him, "Yes Ma'am," he said to her with a sparkle in his eye. Jenn extended her arms to invite him into a hug.

"I'm sorry," Jenn told him as they carefully embraced. She could not take this out on Chris. He was her best best friend. She meant what she said about supporting him but she would keep an eye on the girl. Somewhere in the back of her mind she could hear that little voice of warning, *"Don't trust the girl named Gretchen."*

Chris spent a few hours with her until his mom showed up for his ride home. Jenn loved the flowers he had brought her. She had received others, but these really showed her how special she was to him. She had her mom bring them over to her nightstand next to her. She wanted them to be the first thing she saw when she woke up. Jenn turned the vase to find just the perfect angle but stopped when one single wilted yellow flower caught her eye. Plucking it from the vase, she held it up close for inspection. Since Chris had been gone, she had looked over at the arrangement in admiration many times. "This was not here before!" she said out loud.

Chris saw him as soon as his mom's car turned into their driveway. George Martin stood there in his denim jacket and blue jeans, next to his three-speed bike.

"Looks like one of your friends stopped by," Chris's mother said as she put the car in park. Chris stepped out of the car, not sure why, of all people, George would be at his house.

"Evening, Mrs. Bowman. Is it ok if I talk to Chris?" he asked her, then looked at Chris with a pleading look in his eye. Chris had known him from school for a while now, but this was a George Martin he had never seen. George's face was pale with a look of defeat in his tired looking eyes. Then Chris saw it. There was fear in the bully's face.

"Sure," Mrs. Bowman told the boy, then turned to look at Chris and smiled. "I like him, very nice manners," she added, then walked to the house.

Chris met the boy halfway from where he was standing, "I'm not going to fight you here in front of my parents' house."

"I'm sorry," was all he said. George kept his eyes lowered, never looking up, "For what I have done to you and your friends, I truly regret how I treated everyone."

Chris stood there completely bewildered after hearing the words from the bully, "Well, I think you need to talk to Lance more than me. You have really made his life hell."

"I already have. We have talked and I'm going to be a better person towards him. We are going to start taking self-defense classes together," he told Chris. "Again, please accept my apology and I ask for your forgiveness." This time George looked up and extended a hand while meeting his gaze. Chris gasped then took a step back. He had seen George's face when they pulled in the drive, but this was the first time since they started talking that he could see him clearly. He looked to have lost a few pounds in his face, dark circles now underlined his eyes.

"Are you ok?" Chris asked.

"Yeah, I'm ok, just haven't been sleeping well at night," George replied while still extending his hand. Chris studied his face for a few more seconds then reached out to shake his hand. George smiled, then turned away, climbing back onto his bike. He took off his jacket to tie it around his waist, then waved goodbye. With his jacket off, Chris saw two welted red marks around his neck. He studied them as the boy rode off. A thought popped into his mind, then he said it out loud.

"Those looked like handprints."

Chapter 43

"**W**e're leaving in a few minutes, with or without you," Mrs. Bowman yelled to Chris from the doorway that led to his room. He quickly tried on another shirt. *Trying to look good for girls is so much work*, he thought. Unhappy with his latest choice in tee shirts, Chris pulled the shirt off and tossed it onto a pile of clean shirts that he was displeased with. Finally settling on a simple short- sleeved tan button-down shirt he grabbed his pendant wrist band, then rushed to the car.

"And who is the lucky girl?" Chris's mom asked as he climbed into the backseat.

"I heard she's some cute little redhead," his dad said teasingly at him. Chris didn't reply but smiled at the thought of the vision of beauty.

"Oh my God, did you even comb your hair?" Mrs. Bowman licked her hand then began combing Chris's hair down with her wet saliva-covered hand.

"Mom, stop please," Chris protested at her action.

"We just want you to make a good impression," Mr. Bowman explained to his son, then turned to share a proud parent's smile to his wife.

"Listen, we will make a deal with you today." Chris leaned forward in his seat to hear what his parents had started to say, "If you help us with the car today, and promise to stay away from wildlife, well… you can have the rest of the day to yourself and this girl," his mom told him. His dad nodded while looking at his son in the rear-view mirror.

"Ok, deal," Chris replied with a bright smile.

Chris quickly helped his parents with unpacking the car, then helped carry the equipment to the dig site. His mind drifted to the conversations he had with Jenn and George yesterday. Their words had stuck with him, causing him to start questioning everything in his mind. But now was not the time to hinder his mind with nonsensical things. He needed to find his little red-haired woodnymph. Spending time with her both calmed and excited his spirit. He wasn't sure what it meant but he knew he liked it and wanted more. Before yesterday, kissing a girl was never high on his list of priorities, but, after the almost-kiss yesterday, feeling her lips against his was something that now haunted his mind. *What is wrong with me?* This thought had hounded him more and more this summer.

After carrying the last piece of his parents' equipment, Chris told his parents goodbye with the promise to avoid all wildlife. He rushed to the usual meeting place for him and Gretchen. The trail was blessed with the morning sun. Soft euphoric beams of sunlight kissed the path on his quest to the creek bank. He arrived to an empty area with no signs of Gretchen anywhere. Dejected, he sat on the ground watching the water flow by. Slowly his mind drifted again to the argument with Jenn. *Why would she make a crazy statement about Gretchen telling a wild animal to attack her? Something must be going on with Jenn. Maybe struggling with her identity might be the cause of some of these problems or maybe it's her time of the month.*

Chris stood up, then looked around for signs of Gretchen. "Maybe she's not coming down today," he sadly murmured. Walking up the path he realized maybe she couldn't get away, then felt a little guilty from expecting this girl to be waiting for him every time he was down here. He knew that her father worked, and she must live near here, maybe on one of the nearby farms, with cows, horses, but no chickens.

Taking a detour of the path, Chris decided to go hang out at Lock 41. As he came closer to the canal he noticed someone sitting on the west side of the cut stone rocks that made up the walls of the lock. Climbing the small hill he recognized Gretchen with her feet dangling over the edge. As he approached she made no acknowledgement of him. Chris sat next to her and joined her in staring down at the ground, "Are you alright?" he asked in a low caring voice.

"I think I will be," she sadly uttered.

"If you want to talk, I'm here for you."

"Your unexpected information of Johnny's demise really made me start thinking about what he must have gone through."

Chris sat there, then replied, "I'm sure it was quick. They say it's almost instant when someone goes that way. I'm sure he is in heaven. I guess, most likely he is with his loved ones."
Gretchen kicked her feet a little, "No, not really. When you die alone you get lost. Like when you're walking down a crowded street on a foggy night, you can make out the forms of people, but no faces. You must have a connection to someone as you die or something precious to find your way. If not, you find yourself hopelessly wandering around alone."

Chris thought about what she said. The thought of being like that would be awful. Sadness crept into his heart.

"Would you like to see something special to me? It's my secret place?" she said as she turned to him. Chris turned to look at her face, sorrow filled her eyes, but he could tell she was fighting back the tears with a smile.

"I would love to," Chris told her. Gretchen stood up, walked a few feet then turned to him and smiled. Chris jumped up and followed her lead.

They had walked almost all the way to the parking lot in silence, when she turned left. The slope of the hillside wasn't too bad, but Chris found himself becoming short of breath from the incline.

"Do you need me to find a beast of burden to assist you up the hill, Christopher?" Gretchen asked in a laugh as her temperament started to change.

"Oh, you're so funny," Chris told her as she quickly ran up the hill. He was clearly winded as he came to a patch of pines dotting a plateau.

Chris stopped to catch his breath. Looking around he wondered why he never was up this way. He turned to his left to see Gretchen leaning with her back against a huge oak tree. Her hands extended down to her sides with her palms caressing the bark.

"This is an old friend of mine," she said as Chris looked up to admire the size of the tree.

"Must be very old, funny how it stands alone among these evergreens," he told her.

"He's the valley's protector," she proudly told Chris, smiling at him. "Come here and introduce yourself."

Chris smiled as he walked to her. Gretchen lowered her chin and started to blush as he neared.   Chris reached and placed his outstretched arms outside of each of her shoulders.

"Hi," Gretchen bashfully greeted him in a soft voice. An innocent smile grew on her face as he moved closer to her.

"Hi," Chris softly said, tilting his head a little as he moved to her lips. He could feel her spirit radiate as he neared her. Chris could see the red flush more in her cheeks as he closed his eyes.

He pushed forward to meet her lips but found nothing but air. Gretchen stood about ten feet from him farther up the hill. Giggling at him, she motioned him in invitation for him to keep following her. *She must have ducked under my arms, that cute little brat,* Chris told himself. Smiling, he took to his pursuit, racing up the hill. A small descending path cut to the left to drop under the cliff face. Chris walked slowly down the trail.

"I never knew this was here."

Gretchen laughed as she sat on a large stone in front of him. Carefully navigating the loose rocks, Chris climbed up to join her, his wrist bracelet dangling from his belt loop. Gretchen eyed it as he sat next to her.

"This view is incredible, you can see the trail and the lock, no one would ever know that you're up here." Then it all made sense to Chris, as he said it. Gretchen most likely sat up here and watched, so she would always know how to find him. Laughing to himself, his doubts about the girl disappeared. All the questions, after listening to Jenn, just faded.

"Don't know if you heard, but my friend, Jenn, got attacked by a deer the other day. The funny thing is she said you ordered the deer to assault her. Isn't that crazy?" Chris said to her as he continued surveying the valley from this new vantage point.

"Yes, I asked the hind to do me a favor. She was more than willing to help."

Chris laughed out loud at her comment, "You are so funny, I love your sarcasm."

Gretchen smiled at his outburst, "Sometimes people need to be punished. Someone must help deal out vengeance and wrath."

"Deer justice," he said as their eyes met. Chris decided this would be the best time to try again, but this time he would ask to make sure. "Gretchen, would it be alright if I kissed you?" Chris nervously asked. His query was met with an eager nod from the young girl. Leaning in, he felt the strange warm feeling of a soft electrical charge. Her tender lips greeted him with passion and longing. Closing his eyes, he struggled with the urge to reach out and touch her. He could feel the warmth of her body even without the personal contact he desired to have.

Chris slowly ended the kiss as he pulled away, then opened his eyes to find Gretchen sitting in front of him beaming with fervor. A golden brilliant light shone as her skin took on a translucent glow. The young teen shielded his eyes from the effulgent pulsing aura growing around Gretchen. Chris gasped at the sight of her breathtaking radiance.

"Wh... Wh... What are you?" Chris stuttered in shock.

Smiling, she looked at him, "I told you. I'm Gretchen, and I believe you have something that belongs to me, Christopher Bowman," she said while pointing to the bracelet.

Chapter 44
Europe
2008

Ralph Russo had worked for the local newspaper in East
Liverpool going on 20 years now. He had accepted his fate a
long time ago that he would be nothing more than a small-town
reporter. Getting to travel to France, and doing a local piece on a
hometown native, who now was a celebrity, was something he
couldn't believe happened to him. This was a long way from
reporting on high school sports or arranging the local police log
report. But here he sat, in France, waiting for the interview of
his life.

When he was first informed, he was requested for the story,
he thought it would have been an over-the-phone interview.
Who would've thought that the world-famous Christopher
Bowman, Ph. D would still get the local paper, know who he
was, and pay for his flight and his stay? Ralph's editor told him
that Dr. Bowman really liked his style and face-to-face was how
he preferred to be interviewed.

Sitting in the hotel conference room, Ralph laid out his
digital and cassette recorders on the table in front of him,
double-checking that both had full charges. He opened his
reporter's notebook and pulled out the index cards on which he
had written his questions before the flight here. He looked
through his notes to try and memorize the information he had
researched on Christopher Bowman. "Born December 13, 1966,

in East Liverpool, Ohio, Graduated valedictorian in 1985, attended Harvard from '85 to '90, where, on the honors accelerated program, he earned a doctorate in physics. Received a degree in engineering at M.I.T. in '94."

"Overachieve much?" Ralph said while shaking his head.

"Yes, I do, but you left out yoga instructor." The voice jolted Ralph from his reading. Looking up he watched as a well-dressed man with blonde hair entered the room. Another man and a woman followed behind him but stood at the door. Ralph could feel their watchful eyes fall upon him as he rose, extending a hand to greet the hometown celebrity.

"Dr. Bowman, it's a pleasure to finally meet you." Ralph watched as the man extended his own hand to shake his. *Pictures did not do this man justice.* The reporter thought, as he noticed that Christopher Bowman had an unnerving presence about him. He was tall, athletically built with a model's handsome looks. Add in those alluring blue eyes which demanded you to look into them and this man commanded your attention and respect.

"Please, Mr. Russo, call me Chris," he told the reporter with a friendly smile.

"Thank you, Doctor... I'm sorry. Chris," he said a few times in his mind to help find comfort in calling him by his first name. Still standing out of respect, he waited for Dr. Bowman to sit first.

"Have a seat, get comfortable, Mr. Russo."

"Oh, It's Ralph."

He smiled in acknowledgement, "Ralph it is," then turned to nod dismissal to the man and woman at the door.

Ralph turned to watch the man leave as the woman stayed but made her way to a chair in the far corner of the room. Turning back, he watched as Chris adjusted in his seat, then rolled up the sleeves on his button-down shirt, exposing a strange looking item that didn't match his well-dressed casual look. On his right wrist he wore a weathered leather bracelet with an old piece of jewelry adorning the center of it.

Following the reporter's gaze, Chris smiled. "I found it a long time ago at a dig site, the first one I was ever at with my parents. It's kind of a good luck charm."

The reporter noticed a little flash of sorrow when he mentioned his parents. Ralph quickly recalled reading somewhere that his parents had both passed away a few years ago in the Christmas Day tsunami in Indonesia back in 2004. *Don't mention his parents, just let him go there if he wants to,* the reporter told himself. Watching the doctor regain his composure, the reporter continued.

"Shall we begin, Doctor., umm, Chris?"

"Anytime you're ready," Chris said as he watched the reporter with great attention.

"Yes, um... let's see, where to start?" The reporter flipped through his index cards, "Ok, yes, Doctor.. oops, sorry, Chris. First let me say that it's an honor to meet East Liverpool's most famous resident."

"Second," Chris said as the reporter looked up to him. "The second most famous."

Ralph quickly searched his memory, then it hit him. "Yes, your two friends from school that formed a band," he replied, feeling a little embarrassed.

"Boulton's Crossing," Chris stated.

Ralph nodded. "Yes, the second most famous, um let me see," he said while trying to regain his composure.

"It's ok, Ralph, we can start over. Take a breath. Find your center," he told the shaken interviewer, then turned to the woman sitting in the chair, "Liz, can you get Ralph here a bottle of water? Thank you."

Ralph watched as the tall woman vexed at him, then shook her head in defiance. Chris rolled his eyes, then chuckled, as he stood up to walk over to the table which held beverages. Returning with a bottle in each hand he gave one to the reporter and sat down again. Ralph drank from the bottle, then turned to spy on the woman. She was slender built and tall, almost the same height as Dr. Bowman. Long wavy strawberry blonde hair hung down over her shoulders as she sat with her arms crossed showing signs of irritation, one leg kicking up the hem of her earth-tone dress. She was very attractive. Ralph decided, even with this attitude, she was a looker.

"Ok, let's try this again if you're ready, and may I make a suggestion, Ralph?"

"Yes," Ralph answered, raising an eyebrow.

"Let's try it with your recorders on this time," Chris said, smiling.

Ralph stared wide-eyed at them, then quickly reached down to press record on both. "Calm down, you got this," he said in a hushed voice. Clearing his throat, he began again, "Doctor."

"Chris."

"Yes, Chris, ok, I got this," he said to himself. "Ok, what first got you interested in the paranormal? I mean you have a doctorate from Harvard, a degree from M.I.T."

"And, I'm a certified yoga instructor," Chris added with a smirk.

"Yes, and the yoga," the reporter smiled back, "With all that, why the paranormal? Why a ghost hunting show that, as of last month, is the most popular reality show in the world?" he asked, then watched the adult male's eyes as he gathered information for his answer.

"Being born in East Liverpool, we all have heard the local ghost stories occurring in the Sprucevale area. When I was younger, I had something very wonderful happen to me while working with my parents at Gretchen's Lock. That event changed my life and opened up my mind to all kinds of possibilities. In the history of man, one unsolved mystery has plagued humanity, even when he was using stone tools as he sat around a fire at night in a cave." Chris paused and asked the reporter, "Do you know what that is? Proof of an afterlife has been a continuous quest. But do you know what the one constant is that makes man want to believe?" Chris stopped to look at Ralph to make sure he still had his attention. "Ghosts, ghosts are the one constant. Even in all major religions, spirits fill the pages of their doctrines," Chris said as he took a drink.

"So, back in college, a few frat brothers of mine used to go to a local cemetery to ghost hunt. They would take small hand-held recorders to try to capture voices on them. Every weekend they would be out there with the little recorders trying to catch a disembodied voice. Then somehow through word of mouth, the broadcasting department on campus found out about them and started filming them for fun, at first. It started to take off with other students wanting to see the footage that was shot. I was approached by a friend of a friend, to give my opinion, kind of a scientific voice for the show. At first, I had no interest in doing it, but a friend," Chris looked to the woman sitting in the chair, "talked me into it. You could imagine my surprise when I found out that the little boy from small town Ohio had a knack for TV."

"When did this start?" Ralph asked while shuffling his question cards.

"That would have been my junior year, so I think it was '88," Chris stated, then looked over to his female companion for her to confirm his answer.

"Yes, it was '88," she replied. Ralph was shocked to hear the woman's soft tender voice with a slight accent that Ralph couldn't identify. If he had the chance, he would ask her about it. Turning his attention back to his subject, he readied his next question.

"So, how was it that this little frat brother show made it to become, as of last month, the number one watched reality show on cable?"

"Well, that part came as a surprise. A couple of my frat brothers decided to send out copies of the videos we made, to try and sell their idea of a reality ghost search. Let's just say they found a cable network that had an interest in it. They bought the show, but on one condition. The network wanted me, which was a complete shock. They said something like, how they wanted the scientist, a skeptic, to take lead on the investigations. So several years later, here we sit," Chris apprised him.

Ralph flipped to another card, "Can you tell me, um, us some of your fondest memories of growing up in East Liverpool?"

Smiling, Chris looked at the reporter, "The safety of growing up back then, we never had to lock the house doors, we could run around the neighborhood and not have to worry about some stranger in a van. Sundays with the families. Kids today will never know the joy of having no place to go shopping on Sundays because all the stores were closed. It was just me and my parents spending time together. Then, I thought it was hell, but looking back now, I miss those days." Chris looked away as thoughts of his parents came rushing back into his mind.

"The park," Chris's female friend said, bringing his attention back to the interview.

"Aw, yes, the famous Gretchen's Lock, home of a snot-nosed, ten-year old girl walking the creek at night calling out for her mother," Chris said smiling while looking back at his female friend. Ralph turned in time to catch sight of her rolling her eyes and turning her head away. Chris let out a small laugh, then returned to the question. "The skating rink still to this day, has a special place in my heart, when I think of meeting my friends on Friday and Saturday nights. Mostly though, I miss the friendships I had back then. We still keep in touch, but it's not the same."

"Have you ever thought of doing an investigation of Gretchen's Lock?"

"Well, we talked about it, but I feel sometimes some things are better left unsaid," Chris answered with a grin.

"Would you care to elaborate on that statement?" Ralph asked, at which Chris smiled and shook his head "no".

"One question that's been weighing on my mind is your degree in engineering and doctorate in physics. After all that, you're a reality TV star now. Some people may question who the real Dr. Christopher Bowman is."

"Well, honestly, I like having hobbies," Chris answered, then looked back at the woman, who was tapping her wrist. Chris looked down at his watch and frowned a little.

"Hobbies? Which one is a hobby?"

"Well, when I figure that one out, you'll be the first one to know," Chris replied while standing up. "I'd like to continue, but I've a few things that need my attention." Chris extended his hand to the reporter.

"Chris, I only have a few more questions."

"Sorry, they will have to wait," Chris said as he finished shaking the reporter's hand.

"Can I ask one thing? Why me? And why fly me here?"

Chris turned and looked at Ralph, "Well, Mr. Russo, I like you. That's why I'm going to give you a one week, behind-the-scenes look, full story just for you. We will have plenty of time for the rest of your questions. My assistant will handle all your accommodations. Are you ready to go, Liz?" Chris led as the woman followed.

Ralph fell back into his chair, completely amazed at this turn of events, he couldn't wait to call and share this with his wife.

Chapter 45

"**I** don't like this, or him," Liz said to Chris as they walked into his room. "You don't know him. You're giving that man way too much access to yourself."

"It will be alright, trust me. I know what I'm doing," Chris said as he sat on the bed while reaching down to remove his shoes. "You know you worry way too much."

"Well, I'm sorry if I care about you and your well-being. Why didn't you talk more about your experience at the park?" Liz queried, while standing next to him, watching as he leaned back, stretching on the bed.

"Cause that is mine. When you share something, it will lose its value."

Liz shook her head, "I'll never understand you, Christopher."

Taking off his shirt, Chris turned on his side to prop his head on his hand while lying on the bed. "Care to join me?" he asked with an innocent smile.

"REALLY!" came the reply from Liz, placing her hands on her hips in frustration. Rolling her eyes, she turned away from his view to hide the trace of an ornery smile.

Chris started to make another comment but was interrupted as his cell phone rang. "Hello."

Liz stood there watching Chris as his eyes widened and his face turned pale. "What's wrong?" she asked him.

Chris held up a finger. "Ok, thank you for letting me know." He turned to Liz. "That was my friend, Rick, from East

Liverpool with some bad news. One of my childhood friends was in a car accident. He passed away."

"Oh God, I'm so sorry, Christopher," she said while raising her hand to her mouth. Chris sat up then moved to sit on the edge of the bed. Thoughts of Bart Miller flooded his mind. He knew that Bart had married and just had a baby, that was… a girl….a boy? His mind raced trying to remember the details of the last time they had talked. *I should have taken time just to call and say hi*, he thought to himself. Guilt, a feeling that he had not felt since his parents' death, crept into his heart.

"Is there anything I can do?" Liz asked, when seeing Chris's eyes verklempt.

"No, it's alright. The funeral is in a couple days. I need to be there."

"I understand and completely agree. What do you need of me?"

Chris looked at her. "We need to let everyone know there is a change of plans." Liz nodded towards him as he searched through his phone for a number. "Please, give me a minute. I need to make a call to Jenn, and it's not something I'm looking forward to." Chris had stayed friends with Jenn, but their friendship had taken a bad hit over a questioning encounter. They found themselves talking less and less. Both had tried to fix it, but that summer had brought up some things which at that time in their lives seemed trivial. But over time, as they thought about the words that were exchanged in anger because of extremely high expectations, ugly scars had been left on their relationship. After the first two rings, Chris started to feel at ease, with the hope that it would go to voicemail.

"Hello," a female voice answered on the other end of the call.

"Jenn, it's Chris. I got... some bad news. There was a car accident back home. Rick called to inform me that Bart has passed away." Chris listened to the gasp followed by silence from the other end of the call.

Later that evening, Ralph finished talking to his wife, excitedly telling her the news of this huge opportunity of spending a week with a celebrity. After the call, he decided to go out into the city. The chances of visiting a foreign place most likely would never happen again. At the best, vacations and a possible retirement to Florida was all he ever imagined for his future. This was a once-in-a-lifetime chance to see Paris. As he decided that a jacket was not needed, he opened the door to leave, only to be greeted by the same tall woman he had met earlier that day during the first interview with Dr. Bowman.

"Mr. Russo, I hate to inform you but due to the death of a close friend, Dr. Bowman will be heading back to Ohio for the funeral. You will be an invited guest to accompany him on the journey back," Liz told him in a very monotone voice.

Upon hearing the dire news Ralph nodded his head, "When should I be prepared for the flight?"

"It should be sometime tomorrow. When all the arrangements have been finalized, someone will notify you," she advised him, then turned and walked away.

Ralph walked back into his room, looked at his watch and the reporter in him took over. "It's just after six o'clock in France, so it should be afternoon at the paper," he said out loud to himself. Reaching for his phone, he called his newspaper to find out the details of the story.

"Hello, this is Ralph Russo. Can you tell me of any deaths that have recently taken place?" he asked a female worker whose voice he recognized, though her name slipped him at the moment.

"Yes, Mr. Russo, there have been a few, but we just had a bad accident happen on the Sprucevale Road."

"Can you tell me the details on that one?' he asked her.

"Well, the report was that a car driven by... Bart Miller, was traveling down the Sprucevale hill at a high rate of speed. Looks like he missed the bend to cross the bridge down at Gretchen's Lock and crashed into the creek. It was really bad. Someone said he died instantly upon impact."

"Is there any other information at this time?" he asked her.

"No, not at this time" came her reply.

Ralph thanked her. After ending the call, he went to his reporter's notebook and jotted the information down before it faded or became blurred in his mind.

Being from the area himself, he knew that name. Ralph thought he remembered him from wrestling, if his memory served him right, or maybe it was baseball. Rubbing his head, he wondered how he had gotten to be 60 so quickly. Looking in the mirror his once sandy brown hair now was mostly grey. "Where did the years go?" he wondered out loud, while sitting down in his room. A knock at the door snapped him back to the moment. A young man stood at the doorway and handed him the schedule for tomorrow's departure. Taking the information, he went back into his room and repacked the suitcases he had unpacked only a few hours earlier.

* * *

The afternoon flight out of France was met with perfect weather. Looking out the window the journalist stared at the vastness of the Atlantic Ocean. Ralph turned to see a silent Chris Bowman paging through some kind of science magazine he had never heard of.

"Is Miss Liz not joining us on this flight?" Ralph asked him.

"No. Liz had a few things to take care of before joining us," Chris told him while not once looking up from the magazine.

"Can I ask a personal question?"

Chris nodded as he kept his eyes on the story he was reading.

"Liz, is she your manager, or is she your personal assistant?"

"Yes," is all he said, offering nothing else.

Shocked by his cold response about Liz, Ralph knew he was close to crossing a line he shouldn't tread when getting personal.

Being cautious, Ralph queried, "May I ask, who passed away?" Knowing that it was a friend of Chris, one thing he had learned in his years of reporting was never let them know you know more than you do. Playing dumb would get you more information if they thought you didn't know the details. Subconsciously, people would usually tell their saga and sometimes more than just the story.

"My friend from high school, Bart Miller, died in a car crash," Chris said with sadness in his voice. Ralph watched as he could tell that Chris wanted to say more about his friend.

Trying not to push too hard, Ralph gently nudged a little more, "How close were you to him?"

Chris closed the magazine. "Well, not as close as a few other of my friends, but he was a good guy, a true daredevil in school. The last time I talked to him all he could talk about was how much he loved being a husband and a father. Back in school, he was known to change girlfriends like shirts, but you know one thing, I think everyone liked him even though he lived his life like most people only wished. When he got married, he completely changed and settled down. My heart just keeps aching with the thought of his family having to carry on without him."

Ralph sat there listening, making mental notes in his head as the doctor's voice trailed off. Reopening his magazine, Chris returned to reading. Ralph wondered if the thought of Chris's parents had made their way into his head as he was telling him about Bart's family. "Loss creates voids, no matter what the size, they can haunt your life forever," Ralph said softly while thoughts returned of losing a parent a few years ago.

Chapter 46

Arriving early at the airport in Pittsburgh allowed Chris time to rent a car and get settled in at the motel room in East Liverpool before his meeting at a local tavern. He and Ralph parted ways after exchanging cell numbers. Chris had invited him to ride along tomorrow after the funeral, promising him complete access to his life growing up. This was something he knew she would be very much against, but she wasn't here right now, which allowed him to live on the edge a little. The drive to the town of his childhood took him past Aliquippa, which brought a smile to his face as he remembered the time he found the arrowhead. Shortly, he drove through the steel mill town of Midland. The skeleton building remains of the mill which had at one time been the beating heart to the area lay dormant next to the road he traveled. The sign reading, "Welcome to East Liverpool" jumped out at him, making his heart spring with happiness. But that emotion was soon replaced with sorrow, as thoughts of Bart's loved ones returned.

Parking in the lot of the motel, Chris stepped out and stretched his arms. "Calcutta sure has grown a lot," he said. Even though the area was part of East Liverpool, everyone called it Calcutta, something he always wondered about. However, of all the things he wanted to know, that mystery was something he liked to leave alone. Chris decided after he checked into his room, that a small nap would be just what he needed to mentally prepare himself for this evening's meeting.

The ringing of his cell phone woke him from his stupor.

"Hey bud, you make it into town yet?" came the voice of Rick Golden over the speaker.

"Hey, Rick. Yes, I got in a few hours ago."

"How long are you staying?"

"I'm not sure what my schedule looks like the rest of the week, but I'm hoping for a few days," Chris replied. Spending some time with his friends would be nice. The thought of not keeping in touch with Bart rose in his mind again. *Why didn't I at least call Bart just to say hi?*

"Well, if you find any free time, I would love to have you over. My kids are huge fans. They still think I'm lying to them about us being friends," Rick laughed.

"Is that so?" Chris replied and joined in with the laughter, "I will see what I can do. Are you going to be able to make it to the funeral?"

"Yea, I'll be there, so I will see you then."

"Ok, I'll see you then. Take care, buddy," Chris said as he ended the call.

He still had a few hours before he had to be at the meeting at the bar. Chris decided to use this chance to do a little sightseeing, maybe even sneaking down to get a cheddar chili dog from his favorite eating establishment in the city. But he knew where he would go first.

His family house still looked the same, but the unknown owner of the cars that now sat in his childhood home driveway unnerved him some. He likened the feeling to that of seeing an ex with her new boyfriend for the first time. No matter how he tried to make his house in Virginia feel like home, this place would always be home in his mind. Fighting the urge to stop and ask if he could see it, he continued on. He retraced the route he and his parents had traveled that magical summer a long, long time ago, the summer that changed his life forever.

The roller arena had long ago closed. Just a part of the facade of the building was all that remained because of a fire a few years ago. He tried to recall if he had read it in the local paper, he had a subscription to or if someone called and told him. Stopping at the side of the road, he stared at the location of one of his fondest memories growing up with his friends. Pulling the car back on the road he drove on. The hill to the park would have excited him in the days of his youth, but he knew the signs of Bart's wreck would still be present as he approached the bridge.

Tire marks were still visible on the blacktop, leading to torn up grass which showed where the car left the road. Red paint and broken concrete now decorated the corner of the old bridge. Small strips of police tape, connected to the railing of the overpass, waved in the light breeze. Pulling off the road, Chris shut the car off and stepped out of it. Walking to the edge of the creek, Chris looked down into the low clear water. A large sunken area of the creek bed showed how far the car had traveled in the air before coming to rest. "What the hell was going on with you, Bart?" Chris asked no one. Walking back to his car knowing that no answers would be found here, Chris turned the car around. He still had one more stop to make.

The hill cemetery was busy this time of day, but it was one of the biggest in the area. Chris watched as people planted flowers in front of gravestones, while trying to avoid the caretakers as they cut the grass. He pulled off to the side of the one-way road and placed the car in park. Stepping out of the vehicle, he walked to the large black granite headstone. Gold leaf letters spelling out the name Bowman greeted him. "Hi Mom, Hi Dad," Chris said as he knelt down to pull out a few weeds that had grown close to the base. "I'm home." He closed his eyes, wishing he could hear their voices one more time.

"I thought I'd find you here," a female voice broke his moment of silence. "Hello, Mr. and Mrs. Bowman," Liz said while laying a hand on Chris's shoulder.

"Did you just arrive?"

"Yes," came her reply.

"I have to meet someone soon. Did you want to tag along?"

"No, I'll just meet you later. I need to visit an old friend while we are here."

Nodding, Chris stood up to look at her, "Something just doesn't feel right. I just came back from the crash site. Why would someone drive his car that fast in an area that he knew all his life?"

"Maybe he had too many ales. You know how men can get if they drink too much," she replied.

Chris looked at her face and caught a glimpse of sadness in it. He nodded to her as he made his way back to his car. "I'll see you tonight."

"Yes, tonight," Liz said as she turned back to the Bowman's plot. "You would be so proud of the man Christopher has become," she said while placing a buttercup blossom on top of the gravestone. She then turned and walked away.

The drive to the bar in downtown East Liverpool was met with one detour. Chris wanted a cheddar chili dog. That guilty pleasure would not be denied. With Chris's schedule, visiting here again would not happen any time soon. After enjoying his hotdog, he finally arrived at the meeting place. Scotty's Bar had been a mainstay in the area for a long time. Chris's first time in the bar was his freshman year in college when he came home for Christmas break. The bar was small, giving it a relaxing atmosphere. Patrons, both young and old, made Scotty's a stop after work to have a few before heading home, or just gathering for a friendly game of pool.

Pulling the door open, Chris was met with the smell of beer and chicken wings. Music played softly from the jukebox as he walked in. A few people sat at the far end of the bar. Three older gentlemen sat together talking to the young black-haired girl who was bartending. Finding an empty barstool near the entrance, Chris sat down and rested his arms on the counter. He found himself looking around the interior of the place. Awards for the pool team hung on the wall along with football memorabilia from nearby pro teams.

"What can I get for you?" the young bartender asked him.

"Just get me what's on draft and a shot of tequila."

Nodding, the young female turned to work on his order. Chris had decided on the trip here that if he had to do this, he might as well be ready for what might come. Liquid courage seemed like a good idea. Handing the bartender a twenty, Chris waved off the offer of lime and salt. Picking up the shot glass, he raised it up, then he said, "Here's to you, Bart. I'm going to miss you, buddy." Bringing the shot glass to his lips, he downed it quickly, when a voice startled him.

"You're drinking without me. Shame, shame, shame," Jenn said, standing in the doorway of the bar.

Chapter 47

Chris smiled as a vision of loveliness walked to him. Jenn truly looked like the rock star dressed in all black, her blonde hair with purple streaks cut in a shag style. She was almost as tall as he, with her high heel hip boots that Chris could see as she removed the trench coat to reveal a black leather sheath, with a silver chain belt.

"Two beers and two more tequila shots," Jenn called out to the bartender as she sat next to Chris.

"I always knew you were meant to be a star," Chris told her as she laid her purse on top of the bar in front of her.

"Lexi's the star. I'm just the keyboard player," Jenn said, smiling at him. She took a $100 bill out of her purse and handed it to the bartender. "Keep them coming till it's gone," she told the young lady behind the bar.

"You look great. How are Lance and Lexi?"

Taking her shot and handing one to Chris, she raised her glass. "To Bart," Jenn toasted as she drank the shot. "Well, Lexi is Lexi. She still is the same girl we knew from school, but now everyone thinks she is such a deep, dark, and mysterious woman. But, she's just the same nerd from Wales we all know and love."

"And Lance?"

"Well, being the head of the security for the band and personal assistant to Lexi, what do you think?"

"So, he is still carrying that torch for her after all these years?" Chris said, then drank some of his beer. Jenn nodded. Chris looked at her, "And what about you and your torch?"

Jenn turned away as she spoke, "Mine to tell."
Looking at her, he wondered if he should pursue this subject farther when Jenn turned quickly to him with a smile on her face, "Well, what about you? Is Liz still stuck up your ass?"

Jenn had met her at the end of his second year of college when he brought her back for the All-Class Reunion. There was no love lost between the two vixens. "Liz is still Liz, but lately she has been a bit of a ghost of her former self," Chris chuckled, then drank again from his beer. "I still can't believe that Lance became a Navy Seal, and with George Martin, of all people."

"Yea, who would have thought that Lance's bully would turn out to be his best friend?" Jenn said, as she did another shot. "They both wanted to be here, but that press tour for the new album is crazy."

"Bart would have understood." Drinking again from his beer, Chris softly spoke, "It's just good to see you again."

Reaching over, Jenn wrapped an arm around Chris and pulled him in close for a side hug, then kissed his cheek. "You know, you're the only man I've ever..."

"Kissed," Chris said with a smile. Laughter broke out between the two friends.

"Yes. Exactly, kissed. How long are you in town?" Jenn asked when their laughter subsided.

"Maybe a week, I have a shooting schedule to keep up with," Chris told her with a smile on his face, as the feeling of their old friendship crept its way up between them. Old scars were still there, but there was still a place in his heart for his dearest Jenn.

"I saw a few episodes. Your show is interesting," Jenn told him, while fighting the urge to let him know that she had never missed it. She even bought all the DVD's when they came out.

"Thank you. Boulton's Crossing's last album had some great songs on it. I tried to catch your Wembley show but the flight out of Greenland got delayed," he told her as he drank from his mug.

Jenn watched as he drank. "So, you still have that old thing?" she commented while nodding towards his wristband. "Nice to see that you finally grew up enough for it to fit."

Smirking, Chris looked at her chest, "Kind of like you finally grew into bras."

She smiled and friendly-punched him in the arm, then motioned to the bartender for more shots.

* * *

The next morning Chris lay in the motel bed trying his best to open up his eyes, but the pain of his headache was winning that battle. Rolling over to his side he pulled the blankets over his head.

"So, was it worth it?" came a female voice from inside his room.

"I'll let you know once my heart returns to my chest and gets out of my brain."

"Well, it's almost 11. Don't you think it's time to get up?"

"I know, I know," Chris said while throwing the covers off to reveal the same clothes that he had been wearing since yesterday.

"You do understand that you're not in college anymore, don't you?"

"Yes. I am an adult. I think I'm allowed to cause some liver damage every once in a while," he said as he staggered to the bathroom then closed the door. Liz walked over to listen as the shower was turned on.

"Remember the funeral is at one o'clock, so you have a few hours before you have to go. Sober up and get ready. I have something to do. I'll see you tonight."

Chris had barely heard her voice but knew most likely what she had said through the door. The shower felt good as he let the hot water run over his head as he stood there with his arms outstretched against the wall for balance. At the time, not removing his clothes to stand under the shower, seemed like a good idea, but he now wished he had at least taken off his shoes before getting in.

Chris stepped out of the car at the funeral home. Dark sunglasses combined with a little more than daily allowances of aspirin had helped make the drive possible. A black sports car pulled in beside his. Chris watched Jenn step out of the car, large dark sunglasses covered her eyes. Using her hand as a sunshield she made a half-hearted smile at him.

"Are you doing better than me?" she asked.

Painfully smiling, Chris walked over to her and held out his hand, "This should make a great photo." Chris motioned across the street to see a reporter taking a picture from a car.

"Ughh," replied Jenn as she saw where he had looked. The two made their way hand in hand into the funeral home.

The large viewing room was adorned with many arrangements of flowers on each of the tables placed along the walls. People filled the rows of chairs lined up in the center of the room. All faced a closed casket with a very large spray made up of blue and white carnations. Jenn excused herself from his side as he made his way to the front of the room. A large picture board with photos of Bart at different times throughout his life greeted him as he walked up. Chris stood there remembering some of the times and places of the memories that were captured. Images of Bart and his child stood out to him. *I should have at least called to say hi.*

"Chris?" a fragile sounding female voice announced as he turned to watch a petite mournful woman walk toward him. Sky Miller had been a few years behind him in school but she was a very nice girl. No one thought ill of her, but she was almost a wallflower. When he had heard that Sky and Bart got married, Chris thought it was a joke. Looking back now, it's exactly what Bart needed to settle him down.

"Sky, I'm so sorry," Chris told her as he grasped her hands.

"Thank you. Bart would have been glad to have you here, you know he really missed you. We would watch your show, and he always bragged about you to me," Sky said with tears in her eyes.

"Sky, I don't know what to say."

"Well, as long as it's not, 'I'm here for you' or 'Anything you need, just ask,' you will be good," she said to him with a small smile.

Chris nodded, remembering his own parents' funeral with everyone saying the same thing, but not really meaning it. Some would call a few times, but after a few weeks the phone would stop ringing. "Well, I wanted to tell you that I talked to the network. They are going to help with donations from this upcoming season's merchandise sales. We want to make sure that you and your daughter will be comfortable and I'm going to make sure college for her will be paid in full."

"Oh, Chris. Thank you so much," she said as she hugged him. Pulling back from him, she looked him in the eyes. "Chris, I have something I want to give you. Can you walk with me?"

Chris nodded, then followed her to a small room across the hall, then closed the door. He watched as she reached for her jacket hanging on the coat rack. Searching through the pockets, she pulled out a small rusty piece of metal.

"Bart found this metal detecting down by the bridge at Gretchen's Lock. He was so excited that he found it, going on for hours telling the story about how you found a locket down there back in school." Chris reached to touch the wrist band, remembering how he showed it off to everyone. "It's a knife. But that's when everything started, after he found it."

"What started?" Chris asked.

"First it was nightmares. He would wake up at night screaming about someone taking her away. I would ask what he meant. But he just said it was a bad dream."

Chris nodded, "Did anything else happen?"

"Well, the nightmares didn't let up even with the help of sleep aids, but then things started happening in the daytime. Strange red marks would appear on his skin, right in front of me."

Chris's eyes grew a bit wider with worry and interest.

"Then the day he had the accident, everything was fine, till I suggested maybe going to a psychiatrist. He went crazy, screaming 'I'm not going back to that place.' That's when he ran out the door and took the car." Tears started flowing down her cheeks. "I don't understand why he said that, Chris. I checked and he had never been to a psychiatrist in his life."

Chris stood there holding the knife in his hands. Trying to hide the fear on his face, Chris hugged her. "Can I keep this to do some checking on it?" he asked.

"Yes, keep it. I don't want it in my house. I don't ever want to see that damn thing again."

Chapter 48

The next morning, Chris sat at the desk in his motel room putting the finishing touches to the letter he had just written. After sealing it in an envelope, he simply wrote, "Ralph Russo" on it, then attached it to a box and placed it aside. Reaching for his cell phone, Chris dialed the reporter's number.

"Hello," came the voice from the other end of the phone.

"Hello, Ralph, it's Chris Bowman. I'm going to investigate Gretchen's Lock tonight. I wanted to know if you would like to tag along?"

"Yes, I'm free this evening."

"Great, I'll meet you there, say around seven in the parking lot," Chris told him as he hung up the cell.

"I don't like this," Liz said, standing in the corner of his room.

"Doesn't matter what you don't like, this is my call," Chris told her, not once meeting her eyes as he walked around the room gathering different items.

"At least rethink this before you do this. I'm just worried about your well-being."

Chris stopped, moved close to her, and started to reach up to touch her cheek, when she suddenly pulled back from his hand. "It's going to be alright, remember there is an afterlife," Chris said, smiling at her. Rolling her eyes, she turned to leave. He told her, "No, no, no, you don't. I want you here tonight," She started to protest as he brought his finger to her lips. "Please, don't."

Chris felt the trip to Gretchen's Lock was different to him. Maybe because he wasn't traveling the same route his parents had always taken or was he feeling this way because he was going there this late in the evening? The fall sun hung low in the sky creating beautiful shadows that moved as he drove past large trees, whose branches hung over the road as he started the descent into the park. Slowing down on the last bend before crossing the bridge of Bart's demise, Chris tried to push the pain of losing a friend to the back of his mind. Through his years of investigating, one thing was a constant, to keep your mind open and free of emotions.

Chris turned into the parking lot at Gretchen's Lock. A flash of memory of pulling in with his parents all those years ago popped up in his mind. How those times were so innocent to him, when all the legends were fairy tales, before he knew the truth. Times had certainly changed. Chris parked his car as Ralph Russo walked up to greet him.

"Evening, Ralph. Surprised you beat me here," Chris said as he stepped out of his rental then made his way to its trunk that he had opened before shutting off the car.

"A good reporter always arrives early." Looking at Chris, he said, "Reporting 101, never let an interview wait on you."

Nodding to him, Chris started to unload equipment from his car. "Times like this I know why my parents had me," Chris said with a chuckle.

"Excuse me?"

"Well, when I was younger, I couldn't tell you how many times I had to unload my parents' car at this same park," Chris told Ralph as they both shared a smile.

"So, what's with all this stuff?"

"Well, you're going to get a crash course in ghost searching 101." Chris said with a smirk.

"Really?"

"Yup," Chris replied, "You mind giving me a hand?"

Reaching down, Ralph grabbed a couple of camera cases as Chris threw a large duffle bag over his shoulder, then headed to the path that led to Lock 41.

Funny how it seems different but still the same, Chris thought to himself. He had spent so much time down here in the summer of his awakening. The journey he knew so well had changed. Trees now stood where once small saplings had outlined the route.

"Shouldn't we be doing this with your film crew?" Ralph asked Chris, as they made their way down the trail.

"Not everything I do gets filmed. Most of my investigations never see the camera lens. I scout out a location, then decide if it makes good TV."

"But isn't this supposed to be reality?"

"Reality is in the eye of the beholder."

Ralph thought about that comment, then nodded. After a few minutes of silence, Ralph told Chris, "I love this area. My wife and I spend most of our free time hiking down here."

"Is that why you started the volunteer program down here?" Chris questioned.

"You know about the F.O.G. project?" he asked in surprise.

"Fog?" Chris asked with a raised eyebrow.

"Friends of Gretchen," Ralph answered.

"Hmm, F.O.G. I like that, very clever," Chris smiled. "I heard what you're trying to do, and I am very interested in helping you. I wanted to meet the man who discovered Walden in the same place I did, so many years ago. I was pleasantly surprised when I found out you were a reporter. Sooo, I made some calls and now you know the rest."

Shocked, Ralph stopped walking, and stood there looking at Chris, his mind trying to wrap itself in the realization that all his work had not been for nothing. Someone noticed and appreciated his selfless contribution. He and his wife spent so much of their free time cleaning up the hiking area to what he thought was no fanfare. The idea started when he and his wife decided to get in shape. Walking the trails would be good for their health and souls. But to his astonishment, the beautiful locks and trails of his youth were gone. When he came down here to the park as a teen, the local boys' clubs would donate their time to help with the upkeep of the locks and trails, but now with no one to help, nature was taking back its possession.

"Thank you, for everything you have done and all your hard work," Chris said with a smile as he continued to walk. "We really appreciate it."

"We?" Ralph said to Chris, waiting to see who he meant by that.

Turning left at the Y in the trail, the two men approached Gretchen's Lock. Small trees rose from the top of the lock with small briar bushes adding a strange crown to the base. Long gone was the grass that carpeted the brim of the lock, where he and Gretchen had spent many a day learning about each other that wonderful summer. He felt his heart sink as he looked upon the area, "Welcome to Gretchen's Lock," Chris sadly said as he reached to his wrist to touch the wristband on his arm, "You're home," he said in a soft voice.

He laid the bag on the ground then instructed his companion where to place the instruments he had carried. Taking cameras from the cases and using tripods, Chris positioned the equipment around the area that he called home base.

"Are we going to try to contact Gretchen?" Ralph asked as he unwound cables to connect to a small monitor Chris had placed on a makeshift table.

"We are going to try to help give someone the peace they have long deserved."

Chapter 49

The evening sun had set as the last of the equipment was finally in place. Chris walked over to the monitor to double check all the camera angles, then instructed Ralph to lock them down to keep them from moving if they happened to get bumped during the night. Making his way over to the last tripod, Ralph asked, "Do you think Gretchen will show up?"

"Not Gretchen," Chris replied while he removed a funny colored yellow camera from its case.

"Not Gretchen? Then who, or what are we looking for?"

"A long time ago, there were two teen girls, with their whole lives ahead of them. A very evil person ripped their innocence away from them, causing a deep scar of sadness that lingers to this day in Gretchen's Lock. Tonight I'm going to try and right a wrong," Chris said. Then he reached down into his pocket to produce an old rusty knife. He laid it on one of the fallen stones from the lock. Curious about the object, Ralph moved over to examine it.

"What is this?" he questioned while reaching for the knife.

"DON'T TOUCH THAT!" Chris warned, causing the reporter to back away. Chris explained "It's a conduit, a connection to Esther's spirit."

"Whaaaat? Esther? You mean as in 'Crazy Ass Esther Hale,' the one who haunts the bridge?"

"The one in the same, but I don't think she's as crazy as they say," Chris said. "Remember what I told you earlier about reality? Think of her as a misunderstood, heartbreak of a story,"

Chris told him as he looked down into the screen on the yellow camera.

"Great, misunderstood crazy, not fun crazy, but misunderstood," Ralph said as he walked back over to Chris, "So what do we do now? Just sit and wait?"

"Kind of, but we need to get some base readings," Chris explained as he held out a small handheld meter. Looking at the digital screen, Chris wrote down numbers in a notebook which he had produced. "Entities have a habit of playing around with electromagnetic fields in the air, so we will keep track of them. Right now it's a baseline reading of zero. Any spike in the readings will let us know something is going on," Chris said to help answer Ralph's questioning look.

Handing a meter to him, Chris explained how to read it and what to watch for. "What's that yellow camera for?" he asked while pointing to the object.

"Well, that's a FLIR camera. It measures the temperature of an object on the screen. It helps detect hot and cold spots in the surroundings that we could never notice with our naked eye."

Ralph looked as Chris switched it on. The screen came alive with colors of reds and yellows.

"What is that?" he asked while pointing at a blue spot on the screen. Chris looked down at the monitor then followed it up to match the location with his eyes.

"Hmm, that's strange. It's coming from the knife," Chris said as he walked over to it. Touching it, he quickly recoiled his hand. "It's cold."

"What does that mean?" Ralph asked in an almost panicked voice.

"Well, it could be a chemical reaction to something the knife is made of, combined with some minerals in this stone. That, in theory, could cause the change in temperature, but most likely we have caught someone's attention."

"What?" Ralph asked wide-eyed.

"It will be fine. The worst-case scenario would be that you might get a burning sensation," Chris said in an unconcerned voice.

"Ummm, Excuse me! Exactly, what does that mean, burning sensation? Care to elaborate?" Ralph asked.

"When a spirit touches you, if they draw enough energy they can leave red marks on your skin, but you'll be ok. It's nothing. If it helps, think of Esther as being just a little confused. She's harmless, like a little kitten," Chris told him, then turned around to let out a worried breath. *This isn't going to be good. Maybe I should send him away.* Chris thought to himself.

Quickly pulling out the meter that Chris had given him, Ralph sporadically waved it around in the air, "It's reading zero. So, we are ok, right?" he asked.

Chris nodded as he returned to checking the FLIR camera again. "We should break out the digital recorders and try for some EVP's. It might be too early, but since she seems to be active it may be worth a shot."

"EVP's? I'm almost too afraid to ask."

"Electronic Voice Phenomena. If you use a recorder, sometimes you can capture disembodied voices that you can't hear with the human ear at the time you recorded it. When you play them back, you will hear them," Chris informed him.

"That's crazy, but why is it too early?"

"I have found that EVPs seem to be more active at night. Having already picked up a hit on the FLIR, maybe we can give it a shot," Chris said as he walked over to the resting knife to set a digital recorder. "Chris Bowman, EVP session, east side wall at Gretchen's Lock, near knife."

Chris stepped back a few feet from the knife, then he began asking a series of questions. "Who are you? Do you know where you are?" After each query Chris would pause for about ten seconds. "Do you know who this knife belongs to?"

After the last question, Chris walked over and picked up the recorder and returned to the laptop next to the monitor. Ralph watched as Chris downloaded the recording onto the computer.

"Ok, now we just need to filter out some of the noise to find the sweet spot." Chris listened through his earphones intently, clicked a few times on the laptop, then nodded his head, "Ok, I think we got something. Let me play it through the speakers."

Chris connected a wire into the small speakers he laid on the table, then tapped on the play button on the laptop. Ralph stood next to Chris, cocking his head to the side to listen closely. The sound of Chris starting the recorder came from the speakers, followed by his footsteps walking away. Soon Chris's voice on the recording could be heard. Each question was greeted with the sounds of nature. Then the last question was asked, "Do you know who this knife belongs to?"

"MINE!" a female voice thundered through the speakers. Chris and Ralph looked at each other in shock. Quickly Chris reached down to play it again, when suddenly the laptop flew from the table, landing about 20 feet from the men.

"What the fu…" Ralph's voice rang out but was cut off from the sight of smoke rising from the broken laptop. Without thinking, Ralph ran and tried to rescue the smoking electronics, but found his motion was abruptly stopped when an unseen force pushed him backwards off his feet to land hard on the ground. "Damn, what was that?" he asked while rubbing his chest. "Felt like someone hit my chest with a baseball bat."

Reaching down to help the reporter up, Chris tried to help him laugh it off, but Ralph could see the worry in the other man's eyes. "You should feel a burning sensation soon," Chris told him.

"Oh, we are way past that, but I think we have another problem. I landed wrong on my ankle," he told Chris as he hobbled trying to keep the weight off his left leg. "But seriously, what was that?" Ralph asked.

"Well, my friend, you just had contact with a spirit."

"What? You mean this shit is real?" Ralph asked wide-eyed.

Chris could see how the man was terribly shaken. "Yes, but you will be fine. She won't have any more energy to do anything like that again, trust me," Chris said, trying to reassure him.

"Trust you? I'm sorry, but this is a lot to take in, so I'm not sure about this trust thing after what just happened," Ralph informed him, as a small amount of anger started to replace the other emotions he had been experiencing just a few moments ago.

Walking over to a dead standing tree, Chris broke off a branch to make a crutch for the injured reporter. "Here, this should help. I think we should maybe call this off," he said after seeing how shaken Ralph was.

"Why? You're saying she can't do anything like that again!"

"It takes a long time to store up that amount of energy for a spirit to do that. We will be fine. The most she might be able to do is barely a mosquito bite. Promise, no more big surprises. But we should call it a night and get your ankle looked at," Chris said with a friendly smile gracing his face.

"No way, that bitch done pissed me off!" Ralph said, causing laughter to break out between the two men.

After helping him to a resting spot near the monitoring station, Chris checked Ralph's ankle. "Looks like a sprain," he said. "Bet we are going to have a fun time getting you back to the car."

"Chris, what just happened? How is a ghost able to do that?" he asked while pointing to the broken laptop, then to his chest.

"Well, it's hard to explain. It would be best if I give you a crash course. Spirits live in this dimension but are out of focus in ours, so that is the reason we can't see them. To them, our world is like walking on a crowded street at night with a thick fog. They can see silhouettes of people, but trying to make anyone out is almost impossible, so they bump into them to get their attention. That causes us to notice them. But to us, it's more like a fleeting glance that we just ignore. If you have something that's personal to them, say their knife, well then, it's like a spotlight in the dark, that will guide them right to it," Chris told him.

"Ok, well, that kind of makes some sense. But what about hitting me or what just happened to your equipment?"

"Well, spirits feed off energy. They need to build it up to punch through the haze between worlds. The battery in the laptop was a good power source for electrical energy in the atmosphere. But the biggest one is emotions. They can build a lot of energy off their emotions or other people's, ergo, the stronger the emotion, the better the connection."

"Are they self-aware?" Ralph asked, still a little confused.

"Some are, but most are what we call 'Residual Hauntings.'"

"Residual Hauntings?" Ralph questioned.

Chris thought for a second, then explained, "Imagine an action played over and over, kind of like a song on repeat. Those spirits don't notice us, nor do they interact with us. So that's a 'Residual Haunting'. But then there is an 'Intelligent Haunt'. That's what we have going on here. They can interact, move things and touch you. They are completely self-aware and aware of us, but both can manifest," Chris finished and looked back towards the knife resting on the stone.

"Manifest, like in, you can see them as they used to be?" the reporter asked.

"Kind of, see it's more like a two-way street on their part with the 'Intelligent Haunt'. They can appear in this realm how they looked in life, but a lot of that also depends on our perception. You may look at an entity and see a young girl, but another will see someone older," Chris informed him.

"How does that work?"

"Still working on that one," Chris said with a smile

"Have you seen one, I mean really seen a ghost?"

Chris just smiled as he walked to look at the monitors again.

Ralph sat there, trying to get a handle on all this information that Chris had just told him. For years, he had always thought that everything about Gretchen's was just campfire fabrications for the kids to tell, but now, he didn't know.

"How in this world do you know all this stuff?" Ralph asked.

"Well, let's just say that in the summer of '81, I met someone who changed my life forever."

Chapter 50

"**H**ow's your chest feeling?" Chris asked.

Ralph opened up his button-down shirt to examine his chest, "Well the redness is gone, but still a little sore. If I didn't know better, I'd think that our Ms. Esther found a *got moxie* in the afterlife," he said with a laugh, with Chris soon joining in. "Though she still doesn't hit as hard as my wife."

Sitting up a little straighter, Chris looked at him with a child's curiosity in his eyes, "Oh, please, do tell. I have to hear this."

Ralph chuckled a little to himself then began his story, "Well, it was back in my junior year of high school. A few friends and I went to this Halloween party. Looking back now, it's kind of funny,"

"Why was it funny?" Chris questioned with a raised eyebrow.

"I wore a sheet over my head with sunglasses on. Thinking about it now, it's kind of ironic sitting here telling you about me pretending to be a ghost. And now, much to my surprise, here we are, looking for them."

"Yes, it is, I have found life seems to be a circle," Chris responded, then waited for the man to continue his tale.

"I agree, but at that time I was just trying to be cool and hoping to attract some girls. So, there I was, trying to walk around in the dark with only a blacklight lighting my way into the corridors of the house, with my hands extended so I didn't walk into a wall. Then suddenly my hands came to rest upon something soft, so of course I had to squeeze and feel what my hands had found. All I kept thinking as I touched the object was, 'These are some firm pillows,'" Ralph said with a half-smile on his face.

Chris grinned, "Let me guess, they weren't pillows?"

"Well, I figured that out, when I got hit on the side of my face. My sunglasses got knocked off and I almost fell down. I took the sheet off to find the most beautiful girl I had ever seen holding her forearm across her breast with the other balled in a fist and anger in her eyes," Ralph stated.

"How much apologizing did you have to do?"

"None, she apologized to me the next day," Ralph said with a grin.

"What?" Chris asked. Astonished, he moved closer so as not to miss a word.

"Well, remember the balled fist?"

Chris nodded. Then Ralph reached up and pulled out the dental plate that contained two top front teeth. "She knocked them both out with one punch," Ralph said with a smile that showed Chris the empty space from the missing teeth.

"I found out the reason they say you don't mess with farm girls. After she hit me, she realized it was an honest mistake. She felt so bad about knocking my teeth out, that I got a date out of it," Ralph laughed.

Chris joined in the moment of bliss when both men's moments were cut short with the sound of the knife falling to the ground. Chris jumped up and grabbed the FLIR camera. A deep blue spot appeared on the screen that moved back from the knife then slowly faded away.

"Looks like someone really wants it badly," Chris surmised as he walked over to place the knife back on the stone again.

"Are you really sure it's wise to taunt her like that?" Ralph asked while holding the meter gauge in his hand.

"It's ok. She used most of her energy the first time, she's just gasping air right now. A battle of wills, shall we say?" Chris smirked as he walked back to stand next to Ralph. "Damn! What was that?" Suddenly he raised his hand to the back of his head after feeling the unknown impact. Turning quickly, he looked around for the source of the pain. Looking down, he was surprised to find the knife lying next to his feet.

"Looks like someone is being a little brat or maybe playful," Chris said as he rubbed the back of his head.

"Playful? I thought you said she was done?" Ralph replied in a frantic voice. "Looks like she is showing you who is the alpha here tonight."

Chris once again picked up the knife and placed it back on the rock. "You're funny," Chris said in a soft voice to the tormented soul. This time he backed away, keeping an eye on the knife as he moved. "Yes, I'd say playful," Chris said to help ease the tension surrounding the men.

"If you say so, after all, you are the expert." Ralph laid the meter back on the table. "So, out of curiosity, what are we trying to accomplish here tonight? Besides picking up the knife after a ghost knocks it off the rock."

Chris picked up the FLIR camera once again, "Well, my friend, it's simple. Esther is tormented and I'm going to try and bring peace to her soul," Chris replied as he focused the camera on the spot of the ghost activity. A small blue dot grew then faded away on the screen just as fast as it appeared, "Come on girl. You can do it. Just punch through," Chris spoke in almost a whisper.

The next few hours were filled with the ghost continuously knocking the knife off the stone and Chris repeatedly picking it up and placing it back in the same spot.

"You know, watching you two kind of reminds me of a man trying to train a dog," Ralph told him with a look of amusement on his face.

"What?" Chris asked.

"It's like a movie I saw a while ago. The guy was throwing a ball for the dog to fetch, but the dog would just watch as the ball rolled by. I know it's not the same, but it feels like that scene," Ralph said, when, what seemed to be on cue, the knife fell from the stone coming to rest on the ground.

"Esther, give up. You're not going to get your way," Chris spoke in a loud voice.

"Again, are you sure this is wise on your part?" Ralph asked with a hint of concern back in his voice.

Frustrated, Chris leaned against a tree, raising his hands to his face and said through his hands, "I don't think this is going to work. She must have a very strong hold on this knife."

"Wonder what her tie is to it?"

"Not sure, maybe it belonged to someone she knew, maybe it has a connection to Jake," Chris replied.

"What?"

"It was found near Jake's Lock," Chris said as he walked to pick it up again, deciding in his mind this would be the last time he would do that.

"Maybe Jake was special to her. Maybe he was the one who stood her up on her wedding day. Esther, was Jake your beloved?" Ralph called out loud into the night.

Chris reached for the knife as it moved, flying in the air towards the reporter's head. Ralph barely moved in time to avoid the flying projectile. "What the hell?" Ralph called out from the ground. "I told you she was crazy!"

"You shouldn't have said that," Chris said as he shook his head. "I'm going to have to end this, now." Walking over to Ralph, Chris found the location of the knife. "No matter what happens, do not move or say anything," Chris told him as he walked back to stand in a small clearing near the lock. "Esther, look!" Chris shouted, holding up his arm in the air to expose the locket on his wrist band. "You see this? She's mine! Not yours!" Taking the knife in his hand he pushed it behind the wristband, "And now, so are you!"

Chapter 51

Chris stood there, with his forearm extended up in a stance of defiance to an unseen presence.

"Come on! Where are you?" Chris murmured under his breath, looking around the area, then to the bracelet, with the knife tucked in behind the leather band. He watched as his breath became visible through the dim lighting from the camera. He could feel the temperature dropping by the second. Bracing himself, Chris felt the burning feeling before the grip of unseen hands tugged his extended arm. "No!" Chris shouted, "This is mine!" Pulling back hard he felt the slipping of unseen hands on his arm. *She is losing energy,* Chris thought to himself as the rush of adrenaline moved in his body. "It's working!" he shouted to Ralph.

"What the hell's working? What are you talking about?" Ralph yelled back, wide-eyed at the strange dance being performed in front of his eyes. He had seen Chris standing there struggling with something that he, himself, couldn't see. If this had been somewhere else, the reporter would have thought Chris was acting like a mime. Without asking, the reporter reached for the FLIR camera. Looking through the screen, he saw the reddish-yellow figure of Chris's body on the monitor. But in front of Chris stood a blue green image, almost human shape, that pulsated slowly on the camera. "There is something on the screen," Ralph yelled.

Chris pulled and stood fast as he felt the final release of his arm. Staggering backwards, Chris fell to the ground. "She's a tough one," Chris called out as he stood up, then brushed himself off. "That would have made some great TV," he said with a laugh to Ralph.

"Would you care to explain to me what just happened?" Ralph asked in a confused voice.

"Well let's just say I showed someone who's boss." Chris spoke as he stood next to the reporter. Ralph started to speak but watched as Chris was knocked violently hard backwards onto the ground. The reporter recoiled unconsciously in shock by the sight of greyish looking smoke, in the shape of a person grasping at Chris's arms. Without thinking, Ralph swung his nature-made crutch at the form only to see it break in two by some force that came from the smoke. It wasn't solid, but soft and dense. The reporter looked down at the broken branch in his hand while the other piece stuck in the ground a few feet away. Chris fought hard holding onto the wristband with his other hand. Then just as quickly as the grey fog showed up, it dissipated. Both men remained silent, then looked at each other.

"Um, I hate to say this, but I think someone just showed you who's boss." Ralph said.

Chris smiled at the other man, "I think you're right," he told him. "If I didn't know better, I think I might have pissed someone off."

Both men laughed a little in relief, as Ralph helped Chris to his feet. "What are you trying to do?" Ralph asked.

Chris started to answer but walked away a few feet, then, with his back to the reporter he explained, "I'm trying to get a response from Esther. If I can get her to wear herself out some, she may listen to reason. She is just confused and lost."

"So, kicking a hornet's nest will make her listen?" Ralph asked with a touch of sarcasm in his voice. "Listen, I'm no expert, you are. But this doesn't seem like a particularly good idea."

"Well, it's not a proven science, there are a lot of unknown factors, and maybe a few holes in my theories," Chris told the man while trying to offer a smile of comfort towards him.

Ralph took a deep breath then blew out his checks, "So, what kind of holes are we talking about here? Annnd... Here's a thought, how about we rethink these unproven things for tonight," Ralph said with a large amount of worry in his voice.

"Well, I'm sorry the science of the paranormal isn't as perfect as you wish," Chris yelled at the man, with a brief break in his patience. Realizing his mistake, Chris took a second to gather his composure, then explained in a calm voice to Ralph, "I'm sorry for yelling. I apologize. The science of the paranormal is still in its infant stages. We do know some things, but honestly, we are like a third grader trying to understand the workings of the atom. Every year we learn more and more. But it does take time."

"Umm, who's we?" Ralph asked with a raised eyebrow.

Chris smiled and started to speak when he suddenly flew back, coming to rest against a large maple tree. Ralph stood there aghast, as a grey smokey shape held Chris against the trunk. Fighting, Chris held fast to his wristband, as the form moving like smoke rolling from a large fire embraced him. Chris kicked frantically with his feet, searching to find a target in his panic of the assault. Green and grey colors with streaks of black moved through the form as he struggled to no avail. As Ralph moved to help, Chris's voice broke the air with a simple warning, "Don't."

Against the man's command, Ralph started to move toward the assault when an unsettling feeling pulled at his soul, beckoning him to hold back.

"Christopher," the panicked female voice rang out next to Ralph.

Turning, Ralph's eyes came to rest upon Liz standing next to him. "We have to help him," he told her in a distressed voice as the form swirled around Chris's body. Looking up to Chris's face Ralph could see small traces of blood flowing from his mouth as the smoke constricted around him. Ralph turned to see Liz walking forward. Reaching for her, he tried to stop her but the injured leg hampered his movement as she passed beyond his reach.

"KittyKat, no, please stop!" Ralph heard her call out as she stood only a few feet from the form. Violently throwing Chris aside upon hearing the pleading female voice, the smoke turned its attention away from the men. Ralph watched as Chris landed where the broken piece of the crutch once lay, but now was no longer visible.

Illumination flowed over the forest floor as Ralph crawled his way to an unmoving Chris who now lay face down. "You ok, buddy?" Ralph asked, but only a muffled sound replied to his query. Rolling Chris over, the reporter wrenched back in shock at the sight of the pumping crimson fluid coming from the fallen man. Ralph quickly pulled off his shirt to cover the blood-soaked area on Chris's neck, where a piece of the broken crutch now protruded. "Liz! Chris is hurt badly. We need to get help. Now!"

Ralph looked up, then shook his head at the sight of a golden aura floating around Liz, who now stood a few feet from the smoke form. "It's alright, KittyKat. I'm here," Ralph heard her say as Liz extended her arms to the spirit. Slowly the grey form moved into the woman's embrace. Ralph watched as Liz wrapped her arms around the smokey figure. A brilliant light radiated into the night, momentarily blinding his view of her. As the light slowly dimmed, Ralph found his vision returning to the sight of a small young redhead girl standing where Liz just stood. Emerging from the light, she quickly rushed to the two men, then knelt next to Chris's side to look deep into his eyes. Holding pressure against the wound, Ralph struggled to grasp what had just happened.

"Who...who...who are you?" he asked the young girl whose skin still pulsed with a hint of golden light but paid no attention to the reporter.

Leaning down to Chris, Ralph listened as the girl spoke to him, "It's alright. Esther's finally home now, Christopher. *Mo grá.*"

Ralph looked down to Chris, whose eyes were focused on the young girl. A small smile broke across Chris's blood-stained lips as the two exchanged an unspoken message between them. Ralph cried out for help as the blood filtered through the cloth to paint his hands. Fighting to add more pressure, tears streamed down the reporter's eyes as he screamed for help. Finding no reply to his begging, he looked down to see Chris take a deep breath, then exhale.

The girl leaned down and kissed Chris's forehead then rose as the last breath escaped his lips. Rising up to meet Ralph's eyes, the young girl spoke directly to him, "Don't cry, Mr. Russo, we are all home now." Ralph felt Chris's fallen body relax and go limp. He looked down at his friend then to the girl who smiled at him with kind grey eyes that pulled his attention into them. Ralph watched speechless as she slowly faded into darkness, as the forest grew quiet.

Chapter 52

Ralph stood at the bathroom sink in his house washing his
hands again, but no matter how many times, or how hard he
scrubbed them, the feeling of the crimson coating remained. He
had done this action over and over the last few days since that
night at Gretchen's Lock. "A hiking accident" is what the news
reports called it. *Accident my ass, if they only knew the truth,* he
had told himself every time he heard or saw them use that tag
line. It had been almost daylight by the time he was able to
hobble back to his car to drive where he had cell service to call
911. Cops and emergency workers had rushed to the scene of
the night's tragedy.

Looking up into the mirror at his tired reflection, he knew no
answers would be found in his stressed face that stared back at
him. All he kept finding were more questions. *How did the
mysterious package with an envelope with only my name arrive
on my doorstep? Who was responsible for placing the small
leather satchel containing Chris's wristband, the knife, and for
some strange reason, a flower resting on the driver's seat of my
locked car?* They had taken him to the hospital and released him
that evening. Between that time someone had to have retrieved
Chris's wristband and placed it in his car. He knew it wouldn't
have been the police.

But, there it was, along with this mysterious box staring him
in the face. He knew he needed to open the package. But the
thought of Chris lying there dying and not being able to help

him, now haunted every moment of peace he tried to find. Ralph had cut the tape on the box the day he found it. However, opening it was something that he couldn't find the strength to do.

"I'll help you look in the package," a loving female voice broke him away from his thoughts. Ralph looked at his wife in the mirror. She had always been his rock in time of need, and this time he may have to lean on her more than she can handle. She tried to understand, even when he went on and on about the woman's voice not being on the recording from the first interview in France. He knew she couldn't comprehend the events he had just experienced. How could she? He barely did but being strong for the two of them was something she could do for him now. He nodded a "yes" to her in the mirror's reflection as she reached to take his hand and led him to the room with the package.

Sitting on the couch, Ralph set the box in front of him. Unfolding the flaps, his wife opened it. Then she handed him the envelope and he pulled out a folded letter with a simple, "To Ralph" written on it. Unfolding the letter, he started to read,

Ralph,
Enclosed is all my research I have done over the years. I know this isn't how you wanted your exclusive interview to end, but don't worry, buddy, I'm giving you something even better, my secret.

Gretchen

The notebooks are dated, you will find the first one is dated 1981. That was the year I met Gretchen Elizabeth Gill, my immortal beloved. That summer my life changed for the better. She showed me so many things, along with helping me to understand what she saw, and her history. I recorded everything in these pages.

I've left part of my estate and assets to the Friends of Gretchen organization. You should be financed for a very, very long time.

I will end this letter now, because I must hurry and meet you down at the park here shortly. I wish we would have had more time together. We would have made great friends.

Now you know my secret, I leave it to you to share, if you wish.

Your friend,
Chris Ph.D./yoga instructor

Ralph laid the note down beside him on the couch, closing his eyes, "That S.O.B. knew he wasn't coming back, he had this all planned when he invited me to join him!" he said to his wife as she reached over to hold him as he broke down again.

* * *

Lexi and Lance stood in the parking lot at Gretchen's Lock. It had been a month since Chris had passed away, and the shock still hung over them as they watched limos being directed down the road by the local sheriffs' departments. The main road that led to the park was littered with TV crews' vans and abandoned cars, which Lance knew belonged to the paparazzi trying to get a photo of the wake. Rubbing his shaved head, Lance said, "Who would have thought all of us would end up here again?" He put his sunglasses back on, as they strode over to the newest addition of limos that had arrived. Lexi watched as Jenn stepped out of the back door of the limo, held open by the driver.

"Jenn, we need to have a little talk," she told her in a serious tone. Jenn, dressed in all black, lowered her sunglasses and looked at Lexi, whose black gothic dress took Jenn's breath away. Lance stood behind Lexi in his three-piece security suit, sporting the same serious look he always wore. Even after all these years together, his change from the chubby shy little boy to this shorter muscular man with tattoos, goatee and shaved head, still had Jenn in awe sometimes.

"What did I do now? I've been behaving, seriously Mommy! I've been a good girl," Jenn whined in a little girl's voice, while batting her eyes at her and biting on the tip of her index finger.

Lexi tried to hide that smile that Jenn could always bring out of her. "Jenn, stop. I'm being serious."

"Ok, ok, ok, I'm listening. What did I do this time that I didn't mean to?" Jenn countered.

Lexi loved Jenn. She had always been her best friend, but Jenn worked for her, and this was her band, and bad P.R. was something Lexi took very seriously. "Jenn, you can't offer the limo driver money to hit any deer along the road that he might see with the limo on the drive here," Lexi told her while still trying to hide the smile.

"Chris loved this area, but I hate this place. Hell, I know even you despise it. Even before the incident I only came here for Chris!" she said with a touch of anger in her voice. Taking off her sunglasses, Jenn inched closer to her, "The scar I was left with. Well, thank God, they were able to cover it with a tattoo."

"I know Jenn. I was there after it happened. Or, did you forget?" Lexi fired back at her, looking her up and down. Then Lexi added, "So, out of curiosity, what scars were you trying to cover with all those other tattoos?"

Jenn stood there for a second as a smile started to form on her face, "If I give you a hug will you forgive me?"

Lexi, unable to fight the smile back any longer, reached for her and pulled her in for a big hug. Tears streamed down both friends' cheeks as they held each other tight. "Everyone misses him," Lexi told her in a soft voice.

"I can't believe it; we were drinking a few days before the accident. Now, he's gone," Jenn said sobbing to Lexi. "What was he doing out here at night with that reporter? And where was that "thing," Liz, at?"

"We don't know. No one has seen her since the night Chris passed away. Someone said that she left, heartbroken, unable to handle what happened to him," Lance answered.

"That's bullshit. We loved him more than she could ever know. All his friends are heartbroken but still we are here for him," she said as she pulled back from Lance. "Is Rick here yet?"

Lexi nodded as Jenn took her hand as she led the way, "He's over with his family."

"Out of curiosity, how did you find out about me trying to pay the driver for my deer hunting expedition?" Jenn asked in a coy way.

"Well, Jenn, seems like you have a way with men, also," Lexi said to her as they walked.

Jenn looked at her. "What do you mean?" she asked.

"Well, the driver called the dispatch to check if it was ok to do that. Then the owner called Lance to inform me of your little plan," Lexi said with a smile.

Turning back to look at Lance, Jenn said to Lexi, "Well I learned from the best."

Standing across the park from the wake, Ralph watched the guests arrive. He knew that he was welcome at the event, but he had decided to honor Chris in his own way. The reporter watched as Chris's friends all took turns standing in front of the group, most likely telling stories of their fond memories of their fallen friend. Turning away from the gathering, Ralph made his way up the trail to the lock. He had been back a few times, the first time was with his wife, to help with his personal ghosts. This time it was for respect. Ralph could hear the sound of people moving from the folding chairs. *They must be preparing to spread Chris's ashes now*, Ralph thought to himself as he continued to walk forward. His ankle had healed, but thoughts of the pain he had experienced that night still played in the back of his mind. Before Ralph realized it, the fork in the path to Gretchen's Lock appeared in front of him. Taking the left trail, he walked up to the stone feature sitting quietly on the forest floor.

He ran his hands along the cold stone, trying to imagine a picture of the way it looked a long time ago. The notes that Chris left him gave him new respect for the Sandy and Beaver Canal system. He now needed to find the perfect place. Next year, with the money Chris's estate had left his organization, the plans for the restoration would begin, so he needed the perfect place.

Ralph walked along the base of the lock wall. A small opening in the stones near the ground came into view. He reached down to examine the opening. "Perfect," he said as he reached into his pocket to pull out a piece of rolled up leather. Ralph unrolled the satchel to expose the wristband and rusty knife. Arranging them in a snug tightly rolled package, he pushed it deep into the opening, then filled it in with dirt and a few stones that lay about. "Goodbye my friend. Rest in peace," Ralph said, then knelt down and closed his eyes for a short prayer.

He stood up and headed away from the lock hoping the wake for Chris had finished, when the sound of laughter caught his attention. Ralph turned his head, trying to find the direction of the noise. He walked back to the lock as he heard the sound of splashing water coming from further upstream.

"I'm going to get you," a young voice called out. Ralph could make out shapes through the foliage that obscured his view. Moving through the curtain of vegetation, he could see them, a young boy and girl playing in the water. *Aww, to be carefree, what a wonderful feeling that is,* Ralph thought as he approached them closer. The reporter watched as the girl splashed the boy and then ran from him. Both of them were unaware of his intrusion. The boy looked to be a young teen, skinny with blonde hair. The girl might have been younger, but her strawberry blonde curly hair flowed around her head with her movement, almost looking magical. The feeling of being a voyeur washed over Ralph, making him start to turn, when a third person broke through the tall grass just up from the two playmates.

"Are you two coming or not?" a raven-haired girl called out to them. Ralph could see that this new girl was older, but the distance made him strain to see details of her.

"Coming KittyKat," the red-haired girl called out.

Ralph watched as the two in the water started to head towards the girl. The boy stopped, turned to Ralph's location, and smiled. Blue eyes cut deep into Ralph, with a hint of recognition. Holding his breath in shock, Ralph watched as the boy smiled at him then waved, with a friendly boyish charm.

"Come, my love," the young girl said as she kissed the young blue-eyed boy on the cheek. The reporter watched as the girl took the boy's hand and led him to the stream bank before they disappeared into the woods.

Ralph finally released the air he didn't know he was holding. Taking a breath, he said,

"It's not mine, Chris, it truly is your secret to tell, it will never be mine."

* * *

Gretchen

* * *

ABOUT THE AUTHOR

Owner of a small engine repair shop, Ohio-born, Brian K. Little met his writing muses during his walks at Beaver Creek State Park with his Shiba Inu. He also sculpts and draws as well as writing and performing music in his spare time. When he is not working on lawn equipment he enjoys reading, discovering a variety of music, and researching local history. Brian has several more books in various stages of progress.

FOR MORE INFORMATION

Beaver Creek State Park (East Liverpool, Ohio): This 2700 - acre wooded park has a website and Facebook page on the internet.

Gaston's Mill (Conkle's Mill): restored to operational status by Friends of Beaver Creek State Park. Follow them on the internet (Facebook and website) for dates when the mill is open with demonstrations of grinding of grain as it was ground in the 1830's.

Sandy and Beaver Canal (Ohio): Several websites, as well as books are available, including: *The Sandy and Beaver Canal* by R. Max Gard and William H. Vodrey, Jr. (copyright, 1952.)

Brian K. Little

Made in the USA
Coppell, TX
01 November 2022

85588602R00203